Miss Bizzy Belle

by

Larry G. Johnson

Vabella Publishing
P.O. Box 1052
Carrollton, Georgia 30112
www.vabella.com

©Copyright 2016 by Larry G. Johnson

All rights reserved. No part of the book may be reproduced or utilized in any form or by any means without permission in writing from the author. All requests should be addressed to the publisher.

This book is fiction. Similitude of its characters to any actual persons, whether alive or now deceased, is coincidental.

Cover art by Nan Perry
http://nanperryart.blogspot.com/
Email:jperry009@centurytel.net

Manufactured in the United States of America

ISBN 978-1-942766-27-8

Library of Congress Control Number 2016919130

10 9 8 7 6 5 4 3 2 1

Dedication

To my granddaughters, Julia, Jenna, and Abby

Spread your wings!

Episodes

Part I: The Redheaded "Scarlet Woman"

I'm what?
You what?
Now what?
What did we do wrong?
So what!
Say what?
Granny to the rescue
Baby blues
The X-factor
The "F" List
Watt
Cornfield
Suburbia
The Very Hungry Caterpillar
Cork-screwed
The little black dress
How sweet is that!
Mrs. T's and Miss Bizzy B's
The pachyderm in the parlor
The gall of that woman
Rough spots
Pre-K
K-9
90 K
TKO
K-7
K-1

Part II: It's *Tone-yuh*

Okay
KO
Hairy situations
The snoop

The bottom fell out
The live wire
M.A. Bell
The Villa Bell
Partners in crime
Ebb and Flo
Code T
The Holy Grail
George King
Everybody's a winner
Stars fell on North Carolina
Under his wings
A brush with the law
Grace not always greater
On angel wings
Whatchu looking at, boy?
The Naturalist
A pain in the patootie
Look what I've done to my daddy
A grave insight
In the nick of time
Messing around
Brad
Monumental fun
A night to remember
When the Bell tolls
The meltdown
Up the hill
The quickie
WOWs
Driving him crazy
Self-esteem
Sealed instructions
Transitioning
Giving her the Dickens
Across the pond
Dilemmas

Part III: The Metamorphosis

Brandi
The fugitive
The showdown
A little guidance from a counselor
Mrs. Hattie
The Manila Villa
Bashville
Ranger Rick
The proposal
Her doctor "friend"
The Englishwoman
The potlatch
Holding patterns
Dancing close to the edge
Lost and found
Homer-sapiens
The bequest
The eagle has landed
Christmas lights
The Cornfield Legacy
The Bell tolls again
I'm what?
You what?
A what?
Say what?
It's what?
What?
Walt made his flight

Part I: The Redheaded "Scarlet Woman"

I'm what?

Thumbing through a magazine in the waiting room at her doctor's office, Nurse Michelle Bell saw a cartoon with a smiling newborn. Fresh from the womb, the baby was clutching an IUD. The caption underneath grabbed her attention. *Hey, Ma. Look what I found.*

Turning the page, she grimaced. "That's not funny." At that very moment, Michelle was waiting to have an intrauterine device removed.

"The pill" had been on the market for a few years, but the nurse was not convinced of its safety. When she and Walt Williamson moved in together in June of 1968, she opted for a more judicious form of birth control. Michelle was a nurse at Walter Reed Hospital in Washington, D.C., and he was an army counselor. She had no way of knowing that she would need the device for such a short duration. Yet, nothing was certain during those turbulent times.

When it came to medical procedures, being a nurse did not necessarily guarantee preferential treatment. Neither did it relieve the anxieties surrounding them, and it possibly even amplified them. A half-hour after the customary lab tests, Michelle was growing impatient. By the time her name was called, she just wanted to get the deed done and get on with her life.

The matronly office RN was old school. Her starched dress was pure white, and her traditional cap was neatly situated. Insisting on more relaxed attire, Michelle's generation of nurses was making waves. One of her colleagues irked the supervisor when she showed up at work wearing sneakers.

The wait was still not over. Michelle sat in the examining room for another fifteen minutes. It startled her when the door opened abruptly.

The physician's nurse declared gently. "Dr. Orlando will see you now."

After making eye contact and nodding, he gestured for his staff nurse to stay. The middle-aged OB/GYN did not speak immediately but continued perusing the lab reports. Peering at his patient over his reading spectacles, he then addressed her impassively.

"Ms. Bell . . . The procedure is going to be a little more complicated than we initially anticipated. You're pregnant."

"I'm what?"

Michelle tried to stand, but she collapsed back in the chair. Her face flushed as indiscernible emotions flooded every corner of her being. The doctor was droning on about something, but his voice seemed distant.

The brain does strange things in response to shock. The young woman's thoughts went not to what was implanted inside her womb, or to the embryo's father, but to the magical moments when she made love with the love of her life. How could she ever forgive herself for betraying her one and only?

When Michelle's consciousness rejoined the others, the nurse was standing beside her holding her hand. They were waiting for her to say something, but no words came. The RN handed her a tissue to corral the tears. The doctor started going over the options, but all she wanted to do was get out of there. Without a word, she bolted from the room, rushed past the perplexed receptionist, and raced to her American Motors X Model.

Michelle's emotions were engaged in an all-out tug of war. Instead of rejoicing over a new life growing inside her, she was rather languishing at the thought that her own life might as well be over. The preliminary skirmish ended almost as soon as it began. Nevertheless, her insides were still not ready to declare a truce. The battle was far from over.

Getting the IUD removed was supposed to be a breakthrough. She had held on long enough to what might have been. The simple procedure was to be the milestone, the marker indicating that both she and Walt had moved on. He might have, but Michelle Bell's being was now and forevermore entwined inextricably with Walt Williamson's.

Panic took precedence over everything else. She had to get out of that parking lot. Her keys? Where were her keys? The angst-driven woman thrashed about in her purse. She dumped the entire contents of her bag in the passenger seat. No keys.

Michelle took a deep breath. Her swollen eyes focused for the first time. Her key was in the ignition where she had carelessly left it in her earlier haste. With a quick turn, the powerful engine sprang to life.

The RN was scheduled to work the second shift. She had presumed that her doctor's appointment would not hamper her. Instead of looking forward to going to work, Walter Reed was unexpectedly the last place that she wanted to be. It was from her workstation that Michelle first laid eyes on Walt. Just down the hall, they had their initial conversation. Little did she know that she would come to rue the day.

The distraught woman fought traffic as she drove through the streets of Washington. When she got back to her apartment, she discovered that she had left it unlocked. Typically, she was careful and meticulous. What was going on?

Michelle had taken precautions not to get pregnant. Yet, the contraption failed. She knew an IUD was not foolproof, and now it had proven her foolhardy. The distressed woman recoiled when she went into her bedroom. She felt immediate disdain for the bed where it happened.

Miss Bizzy Belle

Lonely nights, with trouble admitting that she genuinely missed Walt, were over. For now, she was just a woman in trouble.

She let out a shriek when the phone invaded her space. What now? Michelle did not want to answer it, but the nurse in her instinctively reached for it. She was surprised by how shaky her voice was and tried to compose herself as she waited for a response.

The doctor's office was calling to check on her. Once Michelle gave assurances that she was okay, the receptionist asked her to come back. To prevent further complications, the physician wanted to go ahead and remove the device as quickly as possible. There was that "C" word again. Schooled to follow doctors' orders, Michelle said that she would be there as soon as possible.

Slowed by lunch hour traffic, she began trying to process the mess that she was in. Growing up, Michelle knew she was unlike the other girls. Her classmates all seemed to be living for the day when they might become mothers. She wondered why nothing about pregnancy and the ordeal of giving birth appealed to her. Even more repugnant, was the thought of being responsible for the well-being of a child. Her own mother had reassured her that she would feel differently when she met the right man.

Michelle grew up in northeastern Alabama in the area known as Sand Mountain. The only surviving child of career educators, she saw nothing remarkable about her raising. Her father, Tolbert, was a high school math teacher. Her mother, Connie, taught in the elementary grades. The fourth was her favorite, but she dutifully accepted whatever assignment that she was given.

Religion played a big role in the lives of those in Michelle's hometown. Her family was usually at church whenever the doors were open. The preachers took a dim view of a modern world straying far from the mooring of the simple Gospel. They vigorously proclaimed the old time religion.

> *Be sure. Your sins will find you out.*
> *The wages of sin are death.*

One bright spot in the girl's life was her paternal grandfather, "Pa Bell." The robust man with gleaming white hair told her many stories about his days as a mule trader. She loved spending time with him and never passed up an opportunity to ride along in his old truck. As a child, she also got to sit in his lap when he plowed. Sometimes, he even let her "drive" the tractor.

As incredible as it seemed, when Michelle and Walt started comparing notes, they discovered that they already had a connection. Their grandfathers were friends of the same trade.

When Michelle was four-years-old, a little brother was added to the family. The infant was frail when brought home from the hospital. She was allowed to touch his tiny hand but not to hold him. Since her parents did not discuss things with her, the situation was more than a bit overwhelming for the little girl.

When no one else was in the room, the big sister put her hands under her baby brother's sickly body. She gently lifted him as she had seen her mother do and tenderly put his cheek against hers. He whimpered, and she put him back down.

The baby died the next day. Michelle did not tell anyone about her breach of conduct, but she was never able to pry the episode from her mind.

Not many career opportunities were available for females as she came of age. One thing the girl knew early on was that she was not going to become her mother. Since the incident with her brother, she yearned for a chance to redeem herself and always presumed that she would become a nurse.

When her high school had a career day, Michelle gathered up all the information available on nursing schools. She was accepted into a three-year residential program in Birmingham and began her studies after graduation in 1962. Students were enrolled jointly with a college for the academic courses.

Always a bit shy, she never understood why boys found anything attractive about her red hair and freckled face. While still in junior high, one brazen classmate asked if the carpet matched the drapes. She had no idea what he meant, but her face flushed to match the color of her drapes when she figured it out.

Michelle was caught a little off guard when a young musician asked her out. Grover was a college student, and he played drums at a coffee house near the nursing school dorm. He was kind and sensitive, and for the first time in her life, she felt like a male was interested in who she was.

The student nurse had never been in love, and if Grover had, he did not let on. The program that she was in was rigorous and demanding, and his schedule was full. Nonetheless, the two always found some time to spend together. As Michelle entered her third year in 1965, they announced their engagement.

An elephant was in the room, however. The United States was at war, and the country felt no compunction about disrupting young people's plans. Like so many of his contemporaries, Grover received his draft notice.

Miss Bizzy Belle

Seeing him off to enter basic training, was bad enough. Saying goodbye when he left for Vietnam, was heart-wrenching.

Grover promised to come back to Michelle, and she vowed to wait for him. The last time he held her tight, he whispered in her ear that staying focused on coming home to her would give him something to live for.

The man Michelle loved was in no way suited to be a soldier. The music he played was about bringing people together, not ripping them apart. He was an advocate of the "Make Love—Not War" mindset. Nothing in his young life had prepared him for what fate had thrust upon him.

The nursing student interrupted her studies each evening to watch the news in the lounge of her dorm. The savagery of the war dominated every broadcast as casualties continued to mount. A letter from Grover showed up in her mailbox about once a week. Hers eventually caught up with him.

Michelle prayed every day for the fighting to end so that her man could come home. According to the reports, the hostilities were only escalating. Whose name might appear next on the casualty list was the new elephant in the room.

If something happened to her future husband, Michelle wondered how long it might take for her to find out. She did not have to wait long. The somber officers showed up at his parents' house the day after he was killed. She got the call within an hour.

After taking time off for the funeral and then another day to catch her breath, Michelle was behind in her studies. The instructors worked with her to help her get back on track. Still, she felt like she was floundering. Her life had no purpose.

Grover made good on his promise to come back to Michelle, but neither of them had counted on it being in a body bag. The one and only time they made love was the night before he deployed. Unexpectedly, she was now with child by a man she cared for but did not love.

An unlikely turn of events had brought Michelle to this precarious point in her life. Always a good student, she kept her grades up in spite of everything. When she went to the Placement Office as graduation was approaching, she saw a notice about a nursing shortage at Walter Reed Hospital in Washington, D.C. Waves of warmth washed over her. As a tribute to her lover, the newly capped and pinned RN dedicated herself to the care of wounded veterans.

In June 1965, Michelle Bell packed her meager belongings in Grover's old Ford Falcon wagon, told her parents and grandparents goodbye, and headed to the nation's capital. The shifts seemed endless and the work was tiring, but the young nurse poured herself into her duties. She was ever mindful of whom it was that she was honoring. Over time, she began adjusting to the culture shock of living in an area so vastly different from anything that she had ever known.

The young nurse felt somewhat insulted the first few times fellas asked her for dates. How could she betray the memory of the love of her life? After three years of perpetual grieving, she thought she might finally be ready.

Simultaneously, a new professional military counselor was assigned to her floor. While she was focused on soothing physical pains, Walt Williamson worked to help bind up the emotional wounds of the downed warriors.

Walt had never given Michelle a second look, but it was not just she. The lieutenant seemed indifferent toward all the females at the hospital. The counselor then gained some unintended notoriety when word got around that he had brought President Lyndon Johnson down a notch or two as the politician was making rounds during his reelection campaign. Regardless of whether or not he paid attention to them, women certainly started noticing him.

Michelle was one of them. When nothing else seemed to get Walt's attention, she decided to get in his face. After some verbal sparring, she boldly proposed that he ask her out. The nurse could hardly believe her ears when the handsome young army officer and southern gentleman agreed.

They decided on a dinner date and then a movie. Walt suggested the academy award winning box office hit, *Dr. Zhivago*. Michelle was antsy as the evening approached. She had a real date, the first since her late fiancé's death. Her uneasiness spilled over into hollow chatter. Walt, on the other hand, seemed so laid back. The nervous nurse presumed that she got through dinner without embarrassing herself.

Michelle was mesmerized by the movie. The young woman was caught up in the tragic tale acted out on the big screen and hardly noticed when her date planted his hand into hers.

Walt did not hang around long when he dropped her off at her apartment. She felt certain that he had no further interest in her. As she soon learned, Walt Williamson was always full of surprises. He was fascinated with her spiritedness, and they started spending some of their off hours together.

In June 1968 when Robert Kennedy was assassinated, the country found itself once again brokenhearted and on bended knees. The wheels were coming off the nation's wobbly wagon. The times were out of joint, and the future was riddled with uncertainty. Michelle's lease was up, and with neither giving it much thought, she moved in with Walt. It mattered little that this was very much out of character for both of them.

Walt's apartment was a duplex in a quiet neighborhood. This setting was a big change from the noisy apartment building where she had lived. Michelle did not mention to Walt that she was not a virgin. He did not tell her that he was.

Michelle was not ready to call it love, but her feelings for Walt were undeniably growing stronger. He treated her with genuine respect. More than anything, they were having fun—a commodity in very short supply as the nation braced itself for the next upheaval.

The two awakened with the single purpose of getting through each day so they could get home to relax, rest, and unwind. What Uncle Sam had in mind for Walt became another lingering elephant, one that also refused to be ignored. After less than three months of living together, he was transferred to Ft. Benning in Columbus, Georgia, to serve out the remainder of his military obligation.

Since Michelle had been agreeable to going with him when he first asked for the transfer, Walt had mixed feelings about leaving her behind when she backed out. The woman that she was, she also left the door open to change her mind again. They both knew that she could always get a job.

On the Friday of Labor Day weekend, Walt said goodbye to his patients and the several friends that he had made at Walter Reed. He was barely out of sight the next morning when Michelle regressed into an already familiar pattern. She started second-guessing herself, a tendency that would plague her throughout her life.

Adjusting to being alone again, she thought about the IUD occasionally. She certainly had no intention of being intimate with another man. For some reason, she kept putting off making a doctor's appointment. When the first touch of fall reached out and embraced her, she made the call. Perhaps, the changing of the seasons was the symbolic signal that she had been waiting for.

The day before her appointment was Halloween. Working the second shift, she did not have to worry about trick-or-treaters. When she got home, wearied from an unusually difficult day, Michelle remembered that it was Walt's birthday. After a momentary self-rebuke for not sending him a card, she reminded herself that he was gone from her life. There really was no reason to stay in touch. The next day, their last common thread would be plucked.

When Michelle reentered the doctor's office, she apologized to the receptionist for her earlier rashness. With other patients scheduled ahead of her, she was not ushered back immediately. More waiting only compounded her growing apprehension. It was unnerving to see another expectant mother in the waiting room contentedly knitting some booties. Even after the physician's nurse came to get her, it was a replay of earlier. The sudden intrusion of the door startled her again.

The kindly doctor took a seat in his rolling chair, and he reached for her hands. "Have you decided what you're going to do?" When Michelle shook her head no, he went on. "For the best chance of removing the IUD without harming the fetus, we need to act soon."

Michelle winced when she heard the "F" word.

"When did you have your last period?"

In all of the stress, she had kind of lost track of her monthly schedule. She had never been as regular as clockwork, to begin with. Upon reflection, Michelle said that she had missed one for sure, and thought maybe the previous one had been very light.

Without softening the impact of the blow, Dr. Orlando then went straight to the "A" word. "You know abortions are illegal. If the embryo is still small and undeveloped, we can do a D&C, and that will take care of it. Nothing about your pregnancy will go on your record. As a nurse, you must surely know that we do that all the time if the patient gets to us early enough."

"But what if I'm too far along?"

"There are other ways around it."

Michelle shuddered visibly and then grew very still.

The OB/GYN then declared frankly. "We must take care of the most urgent matter immediately."

The doctor asked her to lie back. With his hands, he gently palpated her abdomen, prodding a little in a couple of places. He said nothing during the examination, but his face betrayed his growing concern.

"Today is Friday. Are you off on weekends?"

Michelle nodded.

"This is a big decision. Go home and think about this tonight. Meet me here in the morning at nine. We're normally closed on Saturdays, but I will ask my nurse to assist. I will remove the IUD. You can tell me then if there's anything else that you'd like me to do."

Michelle nodded again. The physician left the room just as curtly as he had entered it. She had no idea how bothered he already was about her situation.

Unable to turn the ignition key, Michelle gripped the steering wheel. As she sank deep into the bucket seat, the inner tussle started up again. If

Miss Bizzy Belle

growing inside her was something to live for, then why did it feel like she was dying?

Michelle was scheduled to report to work in only two hours. Everywhere she turned, she was faced with still another distressing dilemma. Should she call in sick? She never called in sick. Could she do her job with everything weighing on her mind? Would she be better off at work than at home? Should she call Walt?

The silence was shattered. Her head was leaning on the horn. "Get a grip, girl." Then she burned rubber leaving the parking lot.

Driving aimlessly, Michelle's mind took a brief mental vacation. Diverting itself from dwelling on her predicament, she revisited the day that she bought the American Motors X model. The little station wagon, handy for carrying Grover's bulky drums, was about worn out when it was handed over to her. His parents gave it to her after he was killed.

Walt kept nudging her to walk a little on the wild side. Michelle suspected he thought that getting rid of her old boyfriend's vehicle would be a good way to snip that tie with the past. With the money that she was saving on rent, she could afford the payments. After visiting several dealerships and still unable to decide, she spotted the bright red sports car front and center in a showroom.

"No." "No." "No." She kept repeating, shaking her head.

Walt laughed at her. "Why shouldn't a redhead have a red car?"

Michelle still had trouble imagining that she actually did it. Programmed to take care of others, it just did not seem right to indulge herself. She even accused Walt of encouraging her so that he would have a new toy to play with. Saying goodbye to another part of Grover was not easy as she drove away, leaving his wagon on the lot. Walt started calling her sporty car simply the X.

The sound of another horn ended the digression. The light had turned green while her mind was a million miles away. Once again, the X responded, and the car almost spun out of control. Her foot found the brakes, and she came to a screeching halt. Steering into a parking space, her tear ducts started dribbling their almost depleted reserves.

Michelle's customary lilt had begun to wilt. The clock was ticking, but time stood still.

The X was reined in, but Michelle's mind was going off in all directions. She winced at a sudden incursion and turned her head to see a policeman tapping gently. Jarred into the moment, she rolled the window down.

"Ma'am, are you all right?"

Sniffling, she mumbled something about needing a few moments to get herself together.

"Do you realize that you're parked in front of a fire hydrant?"

Instinctively, Michelle swiveled her head toward the sidewalk to see for herself.

"Just move along. And whatever it is that's troubling you, I hope you get it resolved."

Muttering to herself, she shifted the X into drive. "Get it resolved. That'll be the day."

Michelle had a few acquaintances, but no close friends. Walt was the only person that she could talk to about this implausible situation. Should she contact him? Why shouldn't she call him?

Back at her apartment, the nurse was finally able to make one decision. She called her supervisor and told her that she was not well but gave no further details. After receiving a brief reprimand for waiting so late to call in sick, the dutiful professional promised to be back on Monday.

Michelle looked at the clock. In only seventeen hours, she would again be in the doctor's office. Every fiber of her being was hanging in the balance. What a short time she had to figure out what to do.

When the expectant mother's tummy growled, she realized that she had not eaten anything all day. She had intended to stop for a bite on the way home, but those plans went entirely awry.

Half-heartedly slathering mayo on two slices of bread to make a sandwich, Michelle remembered something else. When she was shopping for new wheels, Walt chided her for being so conservative.

"Look, woman. You're twenty-four-years-old. Live a little before you have more mouths to feed."

The fiery redhead shot back. "Huh! I won't ever have any more mouths to feed. And buddy . . . You'd better make sure that you know how to keep feeding yourself."

After the first couple of bites, something suddenly made sense. It was not just a case of nerves that had been causing her recent nausea.

Walt had checked on Michelle a couple of times after he got settled. She realized that she had not been very cordial, and the calls stopped. She had his number somewhere, but where? If she could not locate it, that would be her sign not to get in contact with him.

"There it is." It was clipped to the inside back cover of the phone book. Keeping notes there was a habit that she had picked up from her mother. Staring at the number for several seconds, Michelle rehearsed in her mind what she was going to say. With fingers trembling, she began to dial. If he did not answer, might it be her second sign?

After the third ring, a click was followed by a recorded message. "Hello. This is Walt Williamson. I am not available to take your call right now. Please leave your name and number." Michelle was not prepared for that. She had never gotten a recording before except the phone company's. Caught off guard, she complied, and then wished immediately that she had just hung up.

With no one else to talk to, she tried to console herself. "He does not want to talk to me again. Perhaps, he will just ignore my call." In her heart, she knew better, but that assurance was about to be sorely tested over the next few hours.

Why did she keep looking at the clock? Walt was probably still at the base. After she felt certain that he was off duty, she tried again hoping that he might answer. Maybe he had not found her message. Once more, she got the machine.

Convinced now that it had been a mistake to try to get in touch with him, Michelle started crying. What was she going to do? Walt would know. He always knew, but he was gone. Why did he apply for that transfer? Where was that man now that she needed him so much? Why did she not move with him?

"Why?" "Why?" "Why?"

"I'll go take a hot bath. It's better that he never knows anything about this. He still has his life ahead of him, and I would never do anything to entrap him."

Michelle's mind kept searching for an off ramp. "I'll go ahead and have the baby and then call him when it's born. Walt could then take the child and raise it. I know he would. And he would make such a great father."

The hot soapy water began soothing her nerves. Then, something hit her right between the running lights. "How can I ever face my folks?" Because of her religious upbringing, neither abortion, nor a baby born out of wedlock, was tolerable.

Her thinking flip-flopped yet again. "There's really nothing to worry about. The D&C will take care of everything, and nobody will ever have to know."

Michelle just about jumped out of her skin when her namesake, Ma Bell announced rather rudely that somebody was trying to get through. The phone was on a stand outside the bathroom. Was it Walt? Should she just let it ring? Wrapping herself in a towel, she went to answer it. Not sure that she would even recognize her own voice, she let out a feeble, "Hello."

It was not Walt, but rather a co-worker at Walter Reed. Someone could not find a file that had been misplaced. Why does the phone always ring at the most inopportune times?

As she was settling back down, Michelle ran more hot water. Refusing to let her eyes even wander toward her belly, her mind just skipped right over the pregnancy part. Instead, it went straight to bringing a baby home from the hospital. Her face contorted, and she let out a painful "Ugh!" She was just not the mothering type.

Could she go through with getting rid of what was implanted inside her? The nurse was well aware of the debates going on all over the country about abortion. Women were demanding control of their bodies. Why should a bunch of crotchety old men make those decisions? Would it be very different if they were the ones who had babies? This was not an open forum, however. This was *her* body.

Where was Walt? Why had he not returned her call? How Michelle needed to hear his voice. Would he want her to move to Columbus as quickly as possible? Might they get married and live happily ever after? At least she could turn the majority of the parental duties over to him and continue with her career. That would be it, though. No more children. She knew how to fix that.

When Michelle realized that the water was cold, she got out of the tub and began drying herself. The clock said it was a little after eight. It was beginning to look like Walt was not going to call.

Thirteen more hours.

Nurse Bell was never without pharmaceuticals. Free samples were scattered around at the hospital. Her body ached for a tranquilizer. Should she take a couple of sleeping pills, try to get some rest, and wait until morning to make a final decision? Why not take the entire bottle? If she did not wake up, there would be no decision to make. She had sinned and her sins had found her out. Was not death her due? Maybe it was time for her to take her medicine.

"No." "No." "No." God might forgive her if she took her own life, but not that of her unborn child. Had she just made up her mind about what she was going to do?

Michelle switched on the TV. It was 1968, a rowdy election year, and it was the first week in November. The news turned her stomach and nothing else was on. At some point, the heaviness of the day caught up with her. Stretched out on the sofa, she drifted off into a fitful sleep.

Just before midnight, the expectant mother's shrinking bladder got her attention. She looked at the clock.

Nine more hours.

In her drowsiness, Michelle decided to try one more time to reach Walt. Perhaps, he went straight from work to meet friends, or maybe even had a date. Surely, he was home by now. When he still did not answer, she varied her message. She simply asked him to call her as soon as possible, day or night.

Immediately, she burst into tears. Why did she just do that? He obviously did not care about her, or she would have heard from him. At the same time, she kept rehearsing what she might say if he did call.

As she crawled into what had been their bed, Michelle confirmed what she had decided earlier. The doctor could do the D&C. If it was too late for that procedure, he would go ahead and take care of it. Her mind was made up. Yes. That's what she was going to do.

You what?

As he entered his apartment, the first thing that Walt noticed was the light blinking on his answering machine. He had just gotten in from an emotionally draining trip. He left on the full week-long pass with his spirits soaring, but things had not gone well with some family visits.

At least, he was able to see his new nephew, Ben. Walt had intended to stay the night at his sister, Emma Lou's house, in Etowah, Georgia. After some off the wall accusations were hurled at him, he felt unwelcome.

Trying to wrap his mind around the things that his sister had said, he embraced the solitude of the night driving. He wondered if he would ever be a father. Like everything else that had always seemed to come so naturally for her, Emma Lou had taken to motherhood. He was just not sure that he was the marrying type.

His first love was a married woman. Hannah was making the most of her situation taking care of a husband who had been wounded in Vietnam. During his leave time, Walt had a very meaningful discussion with her at the food court of a mall in Asheville.

Combining the insights that he had gained watching the movie, *Dr. Zhivago*, with perceptions from that conversation, he gained new understanding about people coming to terms with who they were. He regretted not having that discernment when he had written his master's thesis. There were still things that he had not figured out regarding his parentage, but nothing could stop him from being who he was.

Coming down the road, his mind went to Michelle, the only woman that he had been intimate with. It seemed apparent that she was not going to join him in Columbus. He let his mind meander to what the outcome might have been if she had moved with him. When she changed her mind, Walt suspected that it had to do with her family background. She might have kept from her parents that she was living with a man in D.C., but it would be hard to explain a move to Georgia.

Intrusively, his intuitions gave him a jolt. He had an urge to check on Michelle after he got settled back in. It had been about a month since their last phone conversation. Glad to be back to his apartment, the inadvertent soldier was a little beyond exhaustion.

Answering machine technology was new to Walt. In an effort to keep communications on the cutting edge, the military had purchased several of the still primitive devices. The lieutenant had been selected as a guinea pig because his commanding officer wanted him at his beck and call, so to speak.

Since he had not planned on being back that night, Walt's inclination was to let the messages wait until morning. Yet, he could just imagine the chewing out that he would get if something was urgent, and his boss found out that he was home and just did not check the machine. He decided to at least listen to them before falling into bed. Two were work related. No reason for alarm. Both were informing him of upcoming meetings.

The buzz around the base had to do with the impending election. Some of the brass was concerned that if the Quaker, Richard Nixon, were to win, big cuts in the military might follow. The consensus was that the hawks so outnumbered the doves that there was nothing to worry about. It mattered little to him one way or the other. He planned to complete his tour, sign up for VA benefits, and then get on with his civilian life.

As Walt listened to the messages in order, the next three were from Michelle. The first two just said to call her as soon as possible. He sensed some anxiety in her voice. "What could that be about?" He remembered his concerns about her coming down the road.

The third was more specific. Michelle said to call her, day or night, no matter what the hour. He looked at the clock. It was a little past midnight.

Having just drifted back into a deep sleep, the exceedingly troubled young woman thought she was dreaming. The sound of the phone seemed so far away. Shaking her head to penetrate the fog, she raced to pick up the receiver.

From the shakiness in her voice when she answered, Walt could not tell if Michelle was asleep, or if she was just distraught about something. He apologized for not calling earlier and told her where he had been. He then asked if anything was wrong.

"Walt . . . I am so sorry."

He could tell that she was crying.

She said between gasps. "I shouldn't have called you."

She paused.

With growing concern, he waited for her to go on.

"I took care of it, and I shouldn't have bothered you."

"Michelle? Would you please tell me what's going on?"

She was sobbing uncontrollably.

"I am so ashamed."

"What are you talking about, Michelle?"

"The baby, Walt . . . Our baby."

Michelle was so lightheaded that she almost fainted. She could not believe the words that slipped out of her mouth. Of all the things that she had rehearsed, none of it sounded anything like what she had just said. That settled it. In her mind, she had already taken care of it. Now, she could get some rest. It was just a matter of following through with the procedure.

An arrow shot right through Walt's heart, and it was not from Cupid's quiver. Of all the reasons he might have imagined for the phone messages, nothing like that would have ever occurred to him. Before he had a chance to even gather himself, much less to respond, Michelle hung up on him. After the blood was circulating back in his brain, he redialed her number. She had left the receiver off the hook.

Michelle was glad that Walt had just gotten home from an extended leave. It would be a while before he had any additional time off. She was so ashamed of herself. How could she ever face him again?

Walt kept dialing and getting a busy signal. What possessed her to get an abortion? That was his baby, too.

Michelle was sure now that Walt hated her. He would never be able to forgive her for what she was about to do, and what he thought that she had already done.

The ache in his heart was mounting. More than anything in the world, Walt yearned to take Michelle in his arms and try to console her. She should not be going through this alone.

Meanwhile, Michelle Bell settled something in her mind once and for all. She never wanted Walt Williamson to lay his eyes on her ever again for the rest of her life.

Now that the decision had been made, Michelle's internal coping mechanisms gradually took over. The next time that she looked at the clock it was just past four in the morning. Had she passed out? Had she gone into shock?

Five more hours.

The family problems that Walt had encountered on his trip paled in comparison to what he was facing now. He had always been an oddity, and he was struggling with the sting of being disowned by some members of his family. Now this. He might have been a father, but that had been ripped away from him as well.

Michelle could not go back to sleep. She wanted a cup of coffee, but it was not allowed in the pre-op instructions. She started thinking about the procedure ahead. The nurse was not all that familiar with dilation and curettage, but she knew women who had been through it. The D&C would take care of everything. She could rest up for the remainder of the weekend and be back to work on Monday. Things would quickly return to normal. Everything was going to be fine.

Walt eventually gave up on getting through to Michelle. He would try again the next day. He collapsed in a heap without even unpacking.

Her decision firm and then reaffirmed, she had herself another good cry. She was in the hands of a very good doctor. What could possibly go wrong?

Once the dreaded enemy, now the clock could not tick fast enough. At the crack of dawn, Michelle put on a sweater and took a spirited walk. The nip in the air was a reminder that winter was gearing up. With crime on the rise, she wondered how much longer she would feel safe in that neighborhood. When she came back inside, it was already seven.

Two more hours.

Driving to the doctor's office did not take as long on Saturday, but the apprehensive woman did not want to be late. Even though she had soaked in the tub the night before, the shower was calling her. She wanted to feel clean. The warm water flowing over her body was in stark contrast to the brisk air outside.

The pregnant woman let her hands rub gently across her stomach. She had put on a couple of pounds since Walt had been gone but could not detect any additional swelling. Or, was that a little protrusion? Refusing to wrap her mind around anything else, she kept telling herself. "It's just a medical procedure. Women go through this all the time."

As she was getting dressed, the clock passed eight.

Miss Bizzy Belle

One more hour.

Only one vehicle was in the parking lot at the doctor's office. Michelle tried the main door, but it was locked. Another car turned in, and the physician entered through the back. Still five minutes before the hour, she went to the front again, and it was open.

The staff nurse heard the door and came out to greet her. All business, she escorted Michelle to the office where the doctor was sitting behind his desk. As before, he gestured for his assistant to stay.

Some additional business needed tending before things went any further. Dr. Orlando would not proceed without a signed consent form. He asked the patient if she only wanted the IUD removed. He reminded her that under the best of circumstances, this intrusion could still cause the fetus to abort spontaneously, especially if they were in any way entwined. The sound of both the "F" word and the "A" word was a bit unsettling.

Michelle did not respond immediately. The physician was patient. A spontaneous abortion was a possibility that she had not considered. That would solve everything. Her conscience could be clear. The device had to be removed, and what might result, could not be helped.

"What are the odds of that happening?"

"Maybe one in five."

"Not very good." She muttered under her breath, wondering if anyone heard her. The physician frowned.

Dr. Orlando continued the verbal prep. "I know this is not easy. Since you are not sure when conception took place, an embryo might still be scraped off with a simple D&C. If it's too late for that, then the fetus would have to be extracted. Are you sure that's what you want? As I mentioned yesterday, no record would be made of that part of the procedure."

Again, Michelle hesitated, but not for long. Her mind was made up. She had told Walt that it had already been taken care of. Without saying a word, she just nodded.

The OB/GYN said calmly and professionally. "Then go with my assistant."

Michelle was given a hospital gown and told to empty her bladder. She kept reassuring herself. "This will soon be over—over and done with." The nurse helped her onto the table and into the stirrups.

The doctor scrubbed, donned a mask and gloves, and entered the procedure room. The patient's emotions were all over the place, and her mind was having trouble keeping pace. She closed her eyes and tried to shut down.

Slowly and meticulously, the physician went to work. Modesty and dignity had been checked at the door. He worked quietly, which was just fine with Michelle.

Finally, he spoke. "There it is."

Michelle held her breath when she heard "it."

"Right where I put it a few months ago." She realized that he was referring to the string attached to the IUD.

She exhaled.

"You didn't do your job, though, little fellow." He addressed those comments to the flimsy rubber object still inside her.

"This might hurt a little."

Michelle grimaced with the probing.

"Got it."

The diminutive device was bloody as the doctor held it up for her to see. Nobody said a word.

Michelle felt some spasms. Was that it? Was her body ridding itself?

"Sorry for the discomfort. It's perfectly normal." The physician was watching his patient's every move. Her eyes were fixed, and she said nothing.

Dr. Orlando broke the silence. "If you are positive that you want to go ahead with the procedure, I need to conduct a more thorough examination."

She gave a quick nod and closed her eyes again.

The OB/GYN was aware of a new technology called ultrasound. Unfortunately, he had only seen it demonstrated at a medical convention, and all he had to rely on was a physical exam.

As he had done the day before, the doctor began pressing and prodding on Michelle's belly, but this time with more purpose. She let out a couple of yelps. He made no apologies.

Somberly he spoke. "It seems to me that you're near the end of your first trimester." Michelle winced. How could that be? She felt like she had just been sucker punched right in the gut.

He paused to let the diagnosis sink in.

"This is going to be more complicated than I had anticipated."

Michelle breathed in and held it. He kept using the "C" word. How much more *complicated* could this get?

"Are you sure that is what you want? There will be some risk to your own health. We are not in a hospital, but I might have to rush you to one if things don't go well."

She muttered. "Maybe . . . I will just die, too."

With that, Dr. Orlando stood up straight and faced his patient.

"Ms. Bell . . . If you want your baby aborted, you will have to go elsewhere. I am stopping the procedure right now."

Without another word, the doctor turned and hurriedly left the room.

One dutiful nurse then reached out and took both hands of the other.

Miss Bizzy Belle

Now what?

The physician's vehicle was gone as the office nurse walked Michelle to her car. Trying to make small talk, the RN made some comments about the AMX. The owner offered to take her for a ride sometime.

The nurse advised Michelle that she might have a little bleeding. "If you have pain, take a couple of acetaminophens. Do not hesitate to call the answering service if you need us. And by all means, go to the ER if you start hemorrhaging."

Her next words went beyond the call of duty. "Michelle . . . I know that you're a nurse. But I also know that nurses don't always take good care of themselves." They shared a knowing smile.

The X fired up and the powerful engine started purring. As she pulled into the street, Michelle started getting it out.

"Walt Williamson. I hate you. You said that I could afford this car because I didn't have any other mouths to feed. What am I going to do now? How am I ever going to make ends meet if I'm forced to keep this baby?"

She then reached down and turned up the volume. It stopped her in her tracks. The car radio was playing the theme music from *Dr. Zhivago*.

As her eyes welled, Michelle steered the X into the parking lot of a mini-mall. The traffic cop might not be so understanding if he found her in another no parking zone. As the sounds of "Lara's Theme" filled her spaces, the stroll down memory lane exacted a heavy toll.

Somewhere my love . . .

Michelle's mind was transported to Vietnam. Just as nurse Lara worked alongside Dr. Yuri Zhivago in the movie, she imagined herself kneeling over Grover, and holding him in her arms as he lay dying. From the time she got the news, she always imagined that his last thoughts were of her.

Somewhere . . . a hill blossoms in green and gold . . .
And there are dreams all that your heart can hold . . .

Michelle sobbed.

Someday . . . we'll meet again, my love . . .
You'll come to me out of the long ago . . .

Time stood still.

Larry G. Johnson

Godspeed my love . . . till you are mine again . . .

But wait. That was not their song. It was supposed to be hers and Walt's. Why did her thoughts always go to Grover?

Someday . . . there will be songs to sing . . .

But not today.

Michelle did not remember the melody ending. She did not even know how long she had been sitting there until something else was vying for her attention. That other mouth to feed was hungry. Looking around, she saw the neon light of a little diner.

The place was packed on a Saturday morning, but she saw a couple gathering their things to leave. Michelle took a seat to the scorn of the waitress who was perturbed that the customer could not even wait for the table to be cleaned.

"Great. Now I've pissed off my waitress."

Eating out was not common in the rural area where Michelle grew up. She hated dining alone. She knew it was not just her imagination that single women did not get the same prompt service that men did.

The peeved server walked past her several times before finally giving her a menu. It was a few more minutes before she came back to take her order. Maybe that was just as well. Michelle needed some time to think. The din of the diner was not a distraction at all.

What if she had gone with Walt? He would be holding her hand. That yearning was first soothing, but then the thought of him touching her again made her skin crawl.

How could she have been so sloppy? Why was she so unmindful of her own body? How many signals did it send that she did not even notice? Why was she oblivious when she missed at least one period? She had never had indigestion after breakfast. If she had just been paying attention, a simple, timely D&C would have taken care of everything. What was she going to do now?

Over the next few days, Walt kept trying to get in touch with Michelle. He even called the desk at the hospital, but she was not at work.

About a week later, he got a recording that her number was no longer in service. It made no sense. Why did she first reach out and then cut him off?

The baby's father was ever in the back of the expectant mother's mind. She had no reason to think that he did not believe her when she told him that she "took care of it." She also knew the compassionate counselor would presume that she was distraught about the abortion. Because the baby was his, she feared that he would keep trying to contact her.

Michelle began feeling like a prisoner in her own apartment. Every time the phone rang, she jumped. She stopped answering for fear it was Walt. A turning point was the day she arrived at work and was given the message that he had tried to reach her. She called the phone company and got an unlisted number.

After agonizing for an entire week over what to do, Michelle made the determination to carry the baby to term. She had been okay with scraping out a tiny bit of embryonic tissue. As she kept turning it over in her head, she decided that she could not live with herself if she aborted a fetus with a heart already beating.

Putting the baby up for adoption was one possibility that the pregnant woman contemplated. It was unlikely, though, that she could keep everything from her family. Her plans were already made to go home for Christmas, and her parents had already told her that they wanted to visit the nation's capital during their spring holidays.

Over the next couple of weeks, Michelle heard nothing more from Walt. Uncle Sam largely controlled his schedule. Thank goodness. As Thanksgiving approached, she did not know what to expect. He could have some leave time, and she worried that he might show up unannounced. She had already agreed to work through the weekend to have Christmas off.

When at the duplex, the anxious woman kept expecting a knock at the door. There was no way to hide the X. When she came home from work, she was always apprehensive, afraid his car might be in the drive.

Just as she breathed a sigh of relief that Walt did not show up during Thanksgiving, she recalled how the military works. If he was on duty through the weekend, he might be granted a pass and already be on his way. If he was planning to do something, why did he not just go ahead and get it over with?

Christmas was only a few weeks away. Before Michelle was aware of her condition, she had enough seniority at the hospital to be off for a week during the holidays. Her folks seemed enthusiastic about her plans to come home. Michelle was, at least for the time being, unable to find joy in anything.

Her first inclination was to say that nurses at Walter Reed were in short supply, and with some unexpected resignations, her leave time had been revoked. Michelle was good at some things, but lying was not one of them. Nonetheless, from the time Walt came into her life, she had gotten some good practice in the art of deception.

Without appreciating the significance of it at the time, Michelle had covered her tracks well. When she and Walt moved in together, she told no one at work. For obvious reasons, neither did she mention it to her family. Her parents were aware that their daughter had moved to a different apartment and had a new phone number, but they knew nothing about a roommate. She had not said anything about the X, either. That would also take some explaining.

Fear gradually gave way to resignation. Michelle dreaded going home, but at least she did not have to face each day during Christmas Week wondering if Walt might show up.

So many things about the future were uncertain. At the same time, the mom-to-be was sure of one thing beyond the shadow of any doubt. Walt Williamson was out of the loop. Michelle—and Michelle alone—would know the identity of her baby's father. She would take that with her to her grave.

Bellville, Alabama had changed little since Michelle's ancestors settled there. The Sand Mountain area was situated in the northeast corner, and it was sort of like the state's appendage. Geographically and demographically, the elongated elevated sandstone plateau was unlike anywhere else in the region. It was not really a mountain in the customary use of that term. At almost a thousand feet higher in elevation than the surrounding area, it was the coolest part of the state.

Chattanooga was the closest city of any size, and it was in Tennessee. Huntsville was not too far away, and it was growing in leaps and bounds thanks to the space program.

Four things came to mind when outsiders thought of Sand Mountain, and they all started with the letter "S." One was that it was home to several "sundowner towns." Well into the twentieth century, "niggers" were told never to let the sun go down on them within their city limits.

The region was put on the map when one of the most important civil rights trials in American history took place in the sundowner town of Scottsboro. Twice, it went before the U.S. Supreme Court. In landmark decisions, the justices determined that all criminal defendants have the right to an attorney and that jurors may not be excluded on the basis of race.

Snake-handling churches were also scattered throughout the area. Folks in those congregations took seriously the Scriptures admonishing the devout to prove their faithfulness by passing around rattlesnakes.

Sand Mountain was, furthermore, famous for sacred harp singing. Many rural churches still used shaped note *fa-so-la* music in their worship services. The area was home to some of the oldest and continuously held sacred harp singings in the country.

The fourth distinguishing feature was the sandy soil on that elevated plateau at the tail end of the Appalachians. Unlike the rocky iron-rich red clay throughout other parts of northern Alabama and Georgia, the dirt was more like that of a coastal area. Farmers made a living growing a variety of vegetables and produce. Many also raised livestock.

The soil and climate were ideal for growing sweet potatoes. After harvesting and curing, the yams were shipped all over the country. Pa Bell supplemented his income by operating a sweet potato curing house when his redheaded granddaughter was a little girl.

For Michelle Bell, Sand Mountain was just where she was from. A number of her peers saw nothing "cool" about the place, left, and never looked back. Although Michelle never had any desire to push them in deeper, she enjoyed reconnecting periodically with her roots. For the first time since leaving home, she was not looking forward to her next visit, fearful that it might also be her last.

Growing up the kid of not just one, but two teachers, was burdensome. The best part, and ironically also the worst, was that her parents' hours were roughly the same as hers. All twelve grades were housed in adjoining buildings.

Michelle's father, Tolbert, was stern and serious. As a mathematician, he was concrete and saw things as black or white. If a person arrived at the correct answer to a problem, it was right. Otherwise, it was wrong. Doing things his way was a given, and for those subject to him, he often seemed impossible to please. Michelle was never assured of gaining his approval, but that only motivated her to try even harder.

Tolbert Bell was the first from his family to get a college education. With the encouragement of his teachers and the support of his family, he was able to work his way through Ephesus A&M School in North Carolina. The agricultural part did not interest him in the least. He had enough of that growing up on a hardscrabble farm. Following the mechanical curriculum, young Bell found that he had an aptitude for math.

During his second year, he met a quiet, unassuming coed who lived about halfway between Ephesus and Asheville. She commuted from a little community called Ferndale. The two were little more than casual acquaintances until their senior year.

Constance Baker took a fast track and finished in three years. She always knew that she wanted to be a teacher. Connie was also the first of her family to go to college. The A&M School, situated in the beautiful mountains of North Carolina, would later be called Ephesus State University.

Teaching jobs were scarce, and Tolbert was delighted when openings were available at his old alma mater. This allowed him to stay close to his parents. Michelle knew little about her folks' courtship, or even if there was one. They were married during the summer of 1942, and she came along two years later.

Neither did she know the reason why they had no other children after her brother died. Matters like that were just not discussed. She and her mom did the usual mother-daughter things, but they were not particularly close.

Both parents were devoted to their careers. Tolbert had always worn thick glasses, so when his draft number came up, it was no surprise that he failed the physical. Because he was such a lookalike, behind his back, the students called him Wally Cox.

Mr. Bell was the unofficial school disciplinarian. In the course of a year, he paddled about as many pupils as the rest of the faculty combined. Michelle's mother was well liked by the students who affectionately called her, Ms. Connie.

The teachers' kid felt that her parents were especially hard on her to be exemplary. Her father had made one thing clear when she was in nursing school. The pragmatist was not happy when his daughter started dating a shiftless musician. The perfectionist would have no doubt been mortified if he had discovered that his offspring actually lived with a man outside the bonds of matrimony. Tolbert's daughter did not want to even think about his reaction if he found out that he was going be the grandfather of a bastard child.

After quibbling, Michelle decided to go home for the holidays as planned. She decided to spend Sunday and Monday nights with her mother's parents in Ferndale before going on to Bellville on Christmas Eve. She would stop for another night with Granny Addie and Papa Doc on the way back. With the X, she hoped to shave some time off the long drive.

The solitude gave the distraught young woman time to think. Chief among her concerns was how to break the baby news. She had already told her folks to expect a surprise. They would certainly not anticipate her driving up in a red sports car.

Michelle had a particular fondness for her maternal granny, Adeline Baker. Friends and neighbors referred to her as Ms. Addie. It was from

Granny Addie that she got her red hair. The highlight of every summer was spending time with her grandparents in the mountains.

Ferndale got its name from the lush growth of ferns along a stretch of "No Bidness Creek." The botany department at the university in Ephesus often took students on field trips to Ferndale. Routinely, they identified more than a dozen different varieties of common ferns, and a few very rare species.

Michelle asked Papa Doc once how the stream got its name. He said legend had it that back during Prohibition, some lads were walking up the creek one day looking for a fishing hole. They noticed fresh tracks on a seldom used logging road and presumed that they were made by hunters.

A rickety old truck came lumbering toward them, and an old mountaineer shooed them off. He told them they had no "bidness" up that creek. The name stuck. Her grandpa also said that nobody ever knew for sure who the moonshiner was, and none of the boys ever owned up to being in the bunch.

Doc Baker was a decade older than his wife and was in declining health. He was a widower when they met. Mr. Baker's name was actually Madison, but somewhere back, folks took to calling him Doc. Michelle's mother had a half-brother about five years older than she was, and a full brother, Charles, about that same span younger.

Granny Addie had taken Michelle under her wings. She had taught her granddaughter how to apply makeup, although, with her freckles and ruddy complexion, the girl never wore much. Coordinating clothes and matching them with jewelry was especially challenging for a redhead. Fortunately, Michelle had a natural ally. Her granny also worked with her on such things as poise, style, and grace. The Ferndale stop required some finesse, but she did not dread it nearly as much as the one in Bellville, a couple hours farther down the road.

While not the most fashionable vehicle, the old Falcon wagon had room for stuff. Not so with the new sporty AMX. It barely had a trunk, and the backseat area was tiny. Cramming her things in, along with a couple of Christmas gifts, Michelle left D.C. early on Sunday morning headed for North Carolina. Her doctor was not happy that she was going to drive straight through. He was not sure that his nurse-patient was taking good care of herself.

The leaves were all gone when she came through the Shenandoah Valley. Traffic was heavy on the two-lane highway as others were also on their way home for the holidays. It was Michelle's first time to have the X out on the open road.

After being stuck behind an old West Virginia mountaineer for about five miles, she found a small window before the next curve. The horses under the hood leaped forward throwing her head back. The vehicle darted out, and then back in. "That felt good."

What she saw in her rearview mirror was not so good, though. The X had attracted the attention of a Smokey, and he had a blue light special in mind. The County-Mountie looked surprised to see a female at the wheel of the muscle car. Void of any semblance of originality, he wanted to know where the fire was.

Michelle explained the frustration of being stuck behind the old pickup truck. She tried to convince him that she really was a careful driver and pleaded with him.

"Please don't give me a ticket. I've never gotten one before. I'm just trying to get home for Christmas. I promise I will be more careful."

Acting as though he had the authority to decree or revoke an act of congress, the deputy lectured her about the dangers of speed. He described in gruesome detail accidents that he had worked. Michelle grimaced. Making sure she understood that he had done her a huge favor, he let her go with just a warning.

Holiday music played almost nonstop. The X was Michelle's first vehicle with an FM radio. If the carols were supposed to put her in the Christmas spirit, they were failing miserably. No joy was in her world. Several places on the way, the reception was weak and she switched it off. Nothing about the silent night felt holy.

Elvis was at the top of the charts. Not allowed to listen to popular music while growing up, Michelle was not sure about the king of rock and roll. When "Blue Christmas" began playing, she took her foot off the accelerator and let the vehicle coast almost to a stop.

Michelle had made love to only two men. Every Christmas would be blue without her first love. She let her mind wander to Walt, the other one. She supposed that his Christmas was merry and bright.

Getting through Asheville was difficult for the weary traveler. Her grandparents lived about twenty-five miles out toward Ephesus. She felt sure that Papa Doc would already be in bed, but she was equally certain that Granny Addie was waiting up for her. The weary driver was worn to a frazzle when she finally pulled into the yard.

The porch light came on and the front door opened. Michelle's body was beat, but her spirits got a shot of rejuvenation. She unbuckled her seatbelt and bolted toward the house. The granny and granddaughter had a greeting ritual about to be manifested in another rendition.

Granny reached out and put a hand on each shoulder. Doing her best impression of the Beatles, the lyrics sprang from her lips. "Michelle my belle . . ."

Michelle's middle name was Anne, and growing up, her friends often called her Ma Bell. The Beatles put a new spin on it with one of their hit tunes.

The granddaughter chimed in. "Sweet Adeline . . ." Michelle twirled the syllables trying to mimic a barbershop style.

After the ritual, Granny put her hands down. "Well . . . Let me get a good look at you . . ." Michelle froze.

"But first . . . Let me get a look at what you came driving up in . . . Hmm."

Her granddaughter blurted out. "It's all your fault, you know. Remember at Myrtle Beach what you told me when we saw the sea turtle? It's Michelle, not Me-Shell. Granny Addie . . . I stuck my neck out."

They laughed.

"For one time in my life, I decided to walk a little on the wild side."

Her granny teased her. "If you call this walking, I shudder to think what running is."

The older woman then moved on to more practical matters. "Let's get your things inside. I know you must be spent. We have all day tomorrow to get caught up on things."

Michelle was not sure whether she fell asleep or just passed out. Her next awareness was of her bladder trying to get her attention. The smell of coffee was wafting through the house commingled with the aroma of country ham. When she walked in the kitchen, her granny was taking a pan of biscuits out of the oven. Red eye gravy was simmering in the skillet, and the sorghum syrup was already on the table.

Simultaneously, Papa Doc came in the back door in search of some breakfast. The old mountaineer dispensed with the preliminaries and looked censoriously at his granddaughter.

"What in tarnation is that contraption doing sitting in my yard? It doesn't have anything to do with you, does it? What the heck are my neighbors going to think?"

"Now." "Now." "Doc." Sweet Adeline soothed him. "You told me yourself the last time she drove out of this yard that you were afraid the old Ford wouldn't get her home. Michelle went out and got herself something fun to drive."

Doc Baker did what he always did when chastened by his wife. He just clammed up.

Michelle thought she caught her granny looking at her tummy a couple of times. If the best estimate was right, the baby was due sometime during the first half of May. The sweat pants and bulky Christmas sweater were doing a rather good job concealing what was growing inside. Thank God for Christmas sweaters. She had quite a collection and had brought along enough to wear a different one every day.

As they were clearing the table, Michelle knew the time had come. "Granny . . . I have something to tell you . . . But you must promise that you're not going to hate me."

"Child . . . There ain't nothing you could say that would ever cause me to turn my back on you. How dare you even entertain such a thought!"

"I can't tell you everything, so please don't ask me to."

The matronly woman stood facing her granddaughter with a serious look on her face. With a simple nod, Michelle got the answer she wanted.

After she got it out, she could not even remember how she said it. What she would never forget were the outstretched arms that enveloped her. For a moment, it actually felt good to have the slightly bulging belly snuggled between the two of them.

Michelle stayed through lunch on Christmas Eve. She spent the morning helping her granny get ready for the horde about to descend the next day. Exchanging gifts had never been a part of their traditions. In that, Papa Doc prevailed.

Granny Addie, in her own peculiar manner, reminded her favorite granddaughter that she could always come to her with anything—no matter what. Before Michelle left for Sand Mountain, her sweet little granny told her that she hoped things went as well as possible with her folks. She did not have to explain that "as well as possible" was not likely to be very well at all.

What did we do wrong?

The drive from Ferndale to Bellville was about two hours. Even though it was only a couple of days past the winter solstice, Michelle still hoped to get in well before dark. Needing gas, she pulled into a station in Ephesus. A credit card surely was a convenience. After settling up, she buckled up and gunned the X to merge into the traffic.

Walt Williamson was coming from the opposite direction with his old landlady, Mrs. Neumann. They had been grocery shopping for Christmas dinner. He almost got whiplash when he spotted the distinctive red AMX. It looked exactly like Michelle's, but he could not get a good look at the driver.

His first impulse was to turn around, but with that head start, he had no chance of catching up. Why would Michelle have any reason to be in that part of the country? In the short time that they were together, it was amazing how little they actually knew about each other.

The roads were much more familiar, but Michelle was still on strange new turf. She tried to remember how she had told her granny about the baby so that she might adapt it. It hardly mattered, though. The situations were radically different.

One possibility was still intriguing. If she went ahead and put the baby up for adoption, maybe she could get through the next couple of days without arousing suspicion. Maybe she could find a reason to dissuade her parents from making the trip to Washington during their spring break, and they would never have to know anything. She knew that she could count on Granny Addie not to breathe a word to anybody.

The first thing that she had to deal with was the X. Purchasing such an automobile was totally out of character for the daughter that Tolbert and Connie Bell had raised. How could she ever explain it without mentioning the one who talked her into it?

If she did actually drop the baby bomb, perhaps she might use the old good news/bad news routine. The good news is that you are going to be grandparents. The bad news is that you are going to be grandparents. That would go over about as well as a flying pig.

As she got closer to where she had grown up, Michelle decided just to table everything until after Christmas Day. Her blue Christmas need not put a dark cloud over everybody else.

When she pulled into the yard, the first thing she noticed was that her dad's truck was not under the shelter. Maybe that was a good omen. Her mother did not hear the rumble of the X, so Michelle grabbed a handful of cargo and went in the back door.

"Anyone home?"

"Is that you? I've been watching for you all day. How did you manage to sneak in on me?"

Without giving her the once over that Michelle feared, her mom reached for a handful and headed to her daughter's old room. The conversation turned quickly to her trip down and how her grandparents were getting along. The mother never noticed her daughter's jazzy little coupe.

"Where's daddy?"

"Oh . . . He's over at the church getting some things set up for the Christmas Eve service. I do hope you're going with us tonight. Everybody will be so glad to see you."

"Sure." That was the last thing Michelle wished to do. Why did she automatically become so compliant when back under her parents' roof?

"Did mother feed you well? The cupboard is bare around here. We'll be bringing home leftovers from your grandma's tomorrow, so I've just not done much cooking lately."

Christmas dinner was always at Michelle's paternal grandparents' house, and Mama Myra insisted on doing all of the cooking. Tolbert had an older widowed sister and a younger brother. Their families came each year.

Michelle had several cousins, but she was not especially close to any of them. She was attached to her Grandpa Buford Bell, however. Somewhere back, the grand part got dropped, and the grandkids just called him Pa Bell. She never really connected with her grandma, Elmyra. The grandchildren called her Mama Myra.

Michelle was nervous, but her mother seemed not to notice. She thought she heard another vehicle come into the yard. Sure enough. Her daddy came walking into the kitchen with a bewildered look on his face.

"Oh . . . That's you. When I saw that strange vehicle in the drive, I thought we had company."

Her mother mumbled. "What strange vehicle?"

The three of them went to the front porch. Four eyes turned to Michelle.

"Santa Claus came early." Michelle had not thought about saying anything like that until it just tumbled out.

"Let me get the key, and you can take it for a spin." Nothing like that had crossed her mind, either.

Two pairs of eyes were now facing each other.

"Maybe later." Her dad walked away scratching his head. To the mathematician, this equation did not compute.

Redirecting the attention, Michelle mentioned that if she was going to church, she needed to go take a bath. Soaking in the tub, Michelle wished that she could be a fly on the kitchen wall and hear what was being said. She imagined the expressions on her parents' faces as they went out to take a second look at the X. She could just see them circling it like an alien spacecraft had landed in their yard.

After she got dressed, they were at the kitchen table nibbling impassively on some cake and sipping coffee. Her mom jumped up, retrieved a salad plate, and handed her a knife. Connie made her fruitcakes days in advance and let them soak in grape juice. No alcohol was ever a part of their cuisine.

Michelle took control of the conversation. "What kind of program are we having tonight?"

Her mom was typically the initial spokesperson. "The usual . . . You know . . . A traditional kind of pageant. One thing that we will not have, though, is kids carrying lighted candles during the processional. Everybody still talks about the year the boy behind you caught your hair on fire. Folks around here say it turned redder after that."

Miss Bizzy Belle

Ah . . . Just the kind of levity that Michelle needed.

Her dad customarily followed up with what was on his mind. "Some of us are a little concerned about the program running too long. The young people are going caroling afterward, and they don't need to be out late. Our new preacher thinks that anytime anybody shows up, he's supposed to deliver a sermon."

As they were going out the door, Michelle's father was still trying to process things. "I guess we could ride with you, but I don't think all three of us would fit in your . . . What kind of a car is that anyway?"

"It's an American Motors X model. I'll tell you more about it later."

Never one to claim the spotlight, Michelle wanted to make herself as inconspicuous as possible. That was virtually impossible when the teachers' kid came back to the church where she grew up. The preacher mostly took the advice of his advisors and kept his remarks rather brief.

Michelle was exhausted by the time they got home. As she headed for bed, her daddy joked. "No need for you to get up early in the morning since Santa has already come."

Michelle thought to herself. "If he thinks he's a comedian, he'd best keep his day job."

As the noon hour was approaching on Christmas Day, the clan started gathering at the home of Buford and Elmyra Bell. The old home place was aging about as gracefully as its residents were. Elmyra complained that the barn was in better shape than the house. Buford told her that she could go live in it anytime she wanted to.

While Michelle was in nursing school, her family had decided to start drawing names, which made gift-giving much simpler. Her mother had written and told her that she had gotten her Cousin Jerry's name. She bought the high school junior a Washington Redskins sweatshirt. Aunt Naomi, her daddy's sister, drew her name and gave her another Christmas sweater.

Michelle also got her mother some cologne and her dad two new neckties. Her father always wore a dress shirt and tie to work. She would wait until they got back home to give them their gifts.

Sitting around the dinner table after another one of Mama Myra's feasts, no one was in a hurry to move. Elmyra had already gone through the list of everybody who had died during the year. Since Michelle lived so far away, her grandma was especially concerned about keeping her updated.

The granddaughter could not always remember who she was talking about. That sparked a lengthy discussion about all the ways that the dearly departed were connected to the larger community in general, if not directly related to the extended family.

With that important item of business out of the way, the conversation was going nowhere in particular when Aunt Naomi started speaking. She said she had been rereading the letters that her late husband sent when he was in the war. She then turned to her father.

"Wasn't that man, George King, who came through here a time or two from Mason, Georgia?"

"I do believe that was the name of the little town he was from. Why do you ask?"

"In one of Pete's letters not long before he was killed, he mentioned a fellow soldier who was from Mason. I had forgotten about it, but he said the private got his name in the Paris newspapers. It had something to do with some valuables the GI found along with a frog. He said the man's name was 'Toad' Williamson. Did you ever hear Mr. King mention any Williamsons?"

Michelle sat in stunned disbelief. Once, she had looked forward to telling Pa Bell that Mr. King's grandson was a special friend. Now, she just wanted the name Williamson to be forgotten.

Pa Bell scratched his head. "Seems like in the back of my mind George said that his daughter married a Williamson, but I can't say that for sure."

With that, the giant of a man shifted in his chair. "You know . . . I haven't heard a word out of old George since we stopped handling mules. I'm a good mind to load up one day and go looking for him."

Michelle grew fidgety, trying hard not to squirm.

Her grandpa was not through, yet. "I do remember that George was mighty proud of his grandson. I don't recollect his name at the moment, but I wonder whatever happened to that boy."

At that very moment, Buford Bell's granddaughter was sitting with her feet under his table carrying that boy's baby.

Michelle just needed to get through Thursday. One morning, she lost her breakfast but found sanctuary in her bathroom. Her parents had been surprisingly conciliatory. They had not pressed her for more details about the X, and nothing had been said about her appearance. Her mom had planned to take in the after Christmas sales in Huntsville and invited her daughter to go along.

Michelle needed new clothes, but she did not dare try anything on with her mom around. She told her mother that she did not want to offend

Miss Bizzy Belle

her, but that she needed to rest. She reminded her of just how grueling her life was as a nurse at the military hospital.

Michelle's father had school work to do. He was behind grading papers and stayed in his study most of the day. When it came to his job, Mr. Bell was intensely serious. The country was in the midst of a space race with the Russians, and rumor had it that the Americans were going to put a man on the moon sometime during the next year. He struggled with getting poor country boys and girls to see the importance of science and math.

Michelle got out and walked around. She revisited spots where she had spent many hours playing as a child, brooding that she might never see them again. Afterward, she took the X for a little jaunt down some familiar roads. She wondered if her own kid would ever have a place to call home.

As Michelle was putting her things in the car Friday morning, nothing had been said about her condition. She was still not sure what she was going to do when both parents came out to see her off. The moment of truth had come—at least a part of the truth.

"I can't talk about it, and please don't ask me any questions. I'm pregnant."

Her mother stammered. "You're *what?*" Tolbert stood mute, as though shell-shocked.

Michelle avoided eye contact and went on. "I'm thinking about putting the baby up for adoption."

With that, her mother said emphatically. "Then consider it adopted. If you don't want your baby, I am not going to stand idly by and have my own flesh and blood handed off to total strangers."

Without another word, Michelle jumped in the X and sped away.

With his countenance deflated, Tolbert Bell looked at his wife. "Where did we go wrong?"

As soon as Michelle was on the highway, she patted her stomach. "Well, kiddo, looks like we're stuck with each other. There's no way that I'm going to dump my mess back on my folks. If I've heard my daddy say it once, I've heard him say it a hundred times. 'When you make your bed, you have to lie in it'."

The redheaded Bell girl was indisputably a "scarlet woman."

Snow had fallen in the mountains while Michelle was gone. How pure and white the world appeared. What a stark contrast that was to the way she felt inside.

Disguised under their powdery coating, the landmarks in Ephesus were a bit confusing, and the driver missed a turn. At the edge of town, she saw a "snow woman" in a yard with some exaggerated distinguishing features. "How original. I wonder who would have thought of that."

Michelle soon realized her mistake and turned around. When she went back by, an older woman and a younger man were admiring Frosty's girlfriend. They were all bundled up, but something about the man reminded her of Walt.

Concurrently, Walt took his place beside his creation for Mrs. Neumann to take his picture just in time to get a glimpse of the X. "There it goes again. I wonder if someone at the university has a car like Michelle's."

The granddaughter called out to her granny standing on the porch. "I see you had a white Christmas. It didn't reach far enough south for us to get any at home."

Granny Addie was concerned. "I sure hope you don't have any problems with the roads tomorrow. The temperature's already above freezing, and the snow is melting fast, but it will refreeze overnight. Get inside before you catch your death of cold."

A fire was burning in the fireplace. Living in Washington, Michelle missed things like that. She had no idea how much longer she might stay in the D.C. area. For the time being, she had nowhere else to go.

The afternoon passed quickly. Michelle gave a bare minimum report to her granny about the Bellville visit. Then again, there was really not that much to tell. Sitting around the table enjoying leftovers, she told her grandparents that she wanted to get an early start the next morning.

"Doc will get you up and going, but I sure do hate to see you leave." There were no parting rituals, just tearful goodbyes. Papa Doc disappeared after breakfast. His nurse granddaughter was growing more concerned about his health. He refused to go to a doctor and put it in his own characteristic manner. "When it's my time to go, it'll be my time to go."

The roads were clear, but Michelle knew that she had to be cautious because of black ice on the north side of the slopes. While the X was fun to drive, it had very little weight on the rear. Even on dry roads, it had fishtailed a couple of times when she goosed it.

Michelle had to admit that she was becoming more attached to her wheels. When she said "Giddy up," the horses under the hood, neighed. All of her life, she had stood out like a sore thumb. When sporting around in her car, she turned heads in a different way. She had actually gotten a few wolf whistles. Never mind that the narrow-minded folks on Sand Mountain did not appreciate it.

Christmas was over and the airwaves were again filled with the latest tunes from the pop charts. On up the road, Michelle cranked the heat up, rolled the windows down, and blasted the volume to an all-time high. It did not take long for the frigid air to overpower the car's heater, but it felt good as long as it lasted.

As she got closer to D.C., Michelle's thoughts started trying to reconnect with her life there. Many of the patients at Walter Reed were struggling to maintain their equilibrium. Even the ones with messed up minds saw her as an angel of mercy. She might act as though she did not like their sometimes inappropriate overtures, but deep down she loved the attention. The nurse lost count of how many wounded soldiers told her that they were in love with her and wanted to take her home with them. Not one of them would want her now.

As she parked and headed toward the door after the taxing drive, Michelle was relieved to find no evidence that Walt had been. Dr. Orlando wanted to see her as soon as possible. He determined that she was no worse for wear. The baby's heartbeat was strong. Michelle's heart hardly mattered.

A baby elephant was now in the room. No matter which way Michelle's mind turned, it always circled back to the inevitable. Within a few months, she was going to be a mother. Working the second shift, she was home alone to deal with bouts of morning sickness. The dreaded evening hours also went by faster on the job.

Already, her clothes were getting tighter. With the Christmas sweaters put away, it was time to get some maternity clothes. Nursing uniforms for expectant mothers did not come cheap.

Winters in Washington were nothing to write home about. The postman, nevertheless, made his appointed rounds. Walt did not have her phone number, but he knew her address. Once upon a time, it had been his. Why had he not written? That was it—the clue Michelle had been missing. As every week passed with no letter from him, she became more confident that she would never hear from him again.

So what!

A letter arrived in mid-February from Michelle's mother. That was the first contact she'd had with her parents since Christmas. Without giving any explanation, her mom said that they were not going to be able to make the trip to D.C. She also wrote that she hoped things were going well.

After reading it, Michelle went and lay down on the bed. She could not help but think what a huge disappointment she had been to her own parents. She presumed they had told no one that they were going to be grandparents.

Connie Bell never got to plan a big church wedding with her daughter. Tolbert Bell would not walk his little girl down the aisle. They could not show off their grandchild or compete with others for the grandparent of the year award. A baby shower on Sand Mountain was simply out of the question.

Michelle did not respond to her mother's note.

So what!

The baby's clock was ticking, and there was no way to shut off the alarm. This expectant mother was carrying a live one for sure.

Michelle started getting comments at the hospital regarding her more and more obvious condition. The nurses often chitchatted about their personal lives, but the redheaded nurse with the southern accent was mostly an enigma to them. She did not wear a wedding band, but no one questioned her marital status or mentioned anything about the baby's father.

As the due date was getting closer, the nursing supervisor sat down with her. She asked the usual questions about when she planned to stop working and whether or not she was coming back. Michelle had to work. She was going to have another mouth to feed.

The mother-to-be kept expecting her maternal drive to kick in. Still, nothing about the prospect of giving birth, and then bringing home a baby excited her. Her breasts were getting bigger, but the idea of nursing an infant did not get her juices flowing. Dr. Orlando encouraged her to breastfeed, but that was not feasible since she had to put the kid in daycare. Michelle was struck by the irony that she was a nurse with no nursing instincts.

The gender of the baby came up one day in the doctor's office. Michelle had thought it might be nice to know, but she did not dwell on it. Dr. Orlando acknowledged that his track record was not something to make book on, but based on the size of the fetus and its hyperactivity, he suspected that she was carrying a boy.

There was also the matter of names. Michelle had already chosen one for a girl, but she was unable to come up with anything for a boy. Nothing could give any hint as to the identity of the father. Under the circumstances, using family names was not a good idea.

Little by little, Michelle made some progress getting ready for the big event. She finally went out and purchased a couple of gender neutral infant outfits. She also picked up a bassinet and a changing board at a secondhand store. Praise the Lord, for disposable diapers!

It was looking more and more like the OB/GYN had hit the nail right on the head regarding the due date. In mid-April, he told her he did not think that she would make it another month. He was concerned about no backup plan in the event that she was unable to drive herself to the hospital. She reminded him that she worked at Walter Reed.

The doctor replied rather sardonically. "That's no place to deliver a baby."

During her next exam, Dr. Orlando told the mother-to-be that the baby was getting very large for a normal delivery. "I prefer an induction to a Caesarean if it comes to that. If you've not gone into labor within the next two weeks, I'm going to check you in and get things started."

The countdown was nearing its final stages. Michelle went grocery shopping and came home with about all the X had room for. These victuals would have to last for a while.

On Friday, May 9, Michelle started dilating. The doctor sent her home with instructions to get to the hospital quickly if she felt labor pains. She was in such discomfort that she was afraid she might not be able to distinguish every day, run-of-the-mill, garden-variety pain from genuine labor.

Dr. Orlando called her at home on Saturday afternoon, but she had nothing new to report. If she did not go into labor during the night, he gave her instructions to check into the hospital the next morning around eight.

Michelle was up and down the first part of the night, but managed to get some sleep on over toward morning. When she roused, the clock read seven-thirty. She felt no need to be in any hurry. Then her water broke.

"Okay, kiddo, it's show time."

Say what?

The nurse meticulously cleaned up the mess and then got dressed. Her bag had been packed for several days. While in considerable discomfort, she still did not feel anything that she recognized as labor. Michelle called the hospital to alert them that she was on her way. As a precaution, she placed a layer of towels in the driver's seat. Although some of the pressure had been relieved, sitting was far from comfortable.

Breathing deeply, she set out on the adventure. The next time she walked in that door, nothing would ever be the same again. For once, she wished that she might attract the attention of a cop. The streets were mostly deserted on the beautiful Sunday morning in May.

When she arrived at the hospital, an attendant was waiting with a wheelchair. Michelle asked if he would go back and park her car once he got her inside. She felt miserable all over, but especially all under.

When Dr. Orlando arrived, he asked how she was feeling. The patient found the question aggravating. Wasn't it obvious that she was not about to run a marathon? He felt her belly, and then took a look. The time for nonchalance had passed.

"Quick! Get this woman to delivery!"

Michelle protested. "But I haven't even started labor yet."

"From the looks of things, I would say that you've been in labor for hours. It's a wonder that you did not have to deliver your own baby."

Everything was a blur for the next several minutes. Even as an experienced nurse, Michelle had never heard so many orders being barked at the same time.

"Push! Pull! Don't push! Don't pull. Get out of the way!"

Was she delirious? Whatever was in the shot started taking effect. Things seemed to grind into slow motion. Then everything went dark . . .

Somebody was talking to her in the fog. What was she saying?

"It's all over. Congratulations, Ms. Bell! You are the mother of a beautiful baby girl."

"Say what?"

Michelle soon started coming around. What did she say? "All over? What a joke."

The nursery nurse told her everything went fine, and that the doctor would be with her in a few minutes. She would soon get to hold her little girl.

Tonya Willa Bell weighed in at eight pounds, one ounce, and she was twenty inches long. When the nurse brought the baby from the nursery, the newborn was wrapped snugly in a blanket. The initial bonding session was, in a word, awkward.

Michelle was twenty-five-years-old. It probably would not have taken the fingers of more than one hand, but certainly, not more than two, to count the number of times that she had ever held a baby. When her girlfriends back home started having kids, she was already in nursing school.

Miss Bizzy Belle

The anxious new mother took the bundle clumsily. She did not dare release either hand, so the nurse pulled the blanket away to uncover the little girl's face.

Michelle let out a gasp. The attendant thought the baby might have turned blue. She leaned in but saw no reason for the alarm.

When the new mom looked in at her daughter for the first time, she saw nothing that reminded her of herself. There was no chance that they had brought her the wrong baby, though. With that full head of black hair, she was the spitting image of Walt Williamson.

As the sun was setting outside her hospital room window, Michelle winced yet again. What day was it? Then, it hit her. Her baby was born on Mother's Day. For the first time ever, she had forgotten to send her own mother a card.

About an hour later, her baby was brought to her again. This time around, she did the obligatory counting of fingers and toes. As Tonya was sleeping soundly in her arms, the infant stirred a bit when her mother let out a little shriek. Michelle had just calculated something else. May 11 was the anniversary of her first date with the baby's father.

On Mother's Day weekend 1969, Walt Williamson was miles away in Columbus, Georgia. About mid-afternoon, he had a weird sensation. Strange as it might seem, it had nothing to do with his own mother. His thoughts went, rather, to Michelle. The connection he felt was with his child that she had conceived. Walt had no strong feelings about reincarnation. He had never given much thought to when a life actually becomes a being. Strangely, he could feel the presence of his baby.

From somewhere deep inside, he always knew that she was a girl. He tried to imagine holding his little daughter. Then, it hit him. He counted the months on his fingers. It was just about the time that his baby would have been born.

When she crawled into bed the night after her first date with Walt, Michelle replayed a number of the scenes from the movie in her mind. She was enamored with the young woman who might have been the famous Dr. Yuri Zhivago's daughter. Tonya was her name, and she was only forward looking, refusing to be trapped in the tragedies of her beginnings. Realizing that she was mired in her own past, Michelle found inspiration.

One day the next week, she went out and purchased the soundtrack from *Dr. Zhivago*. The theme music captivated her, and she often put the record on when she wanted to relax. She could just imagine how Grover would have loved it, too.

After she became pregnant and decided to keep the baby, Michelle knew if her newborn was a girl, that she would name her Tonya. On the other hand, a number of times she chuckled at the prospect of calling her son, Yuri.

Tonya's middle name, Willa, did not come as easily. Not wanting to tip her hand regarding the child's father, she went ahead and selected one with the same first four letters in his last name. She did not think anybody would pick up on that. Besides . . . Tonya Willa Bell had a nice ring to it.

Michelle was given shots to dry up her milk, and the baby was put on formula. The nurses did most of the feeding, but they encouraged the new mother to hold her infant a few times each day.

Baby Bell might have been the only newborn in the nursery who received no visitors. Even so, every time Michelle walked down the hall to look through the window, she imagined Walt standing and admiring his new daughter. Why couldn't she just let that go?

"I need to submit Tonya's birth certificate so it can be recorded." Dr. Orlando reminded Michelle that one thing was still incomplete. "You have yet to tell me what to enter for the baby's father."

"Just say 'unknown'."

"I don't recommend that. It implies multiple possibilities, and that you are not sure which one it is. Should you ever seek child support from the baby's father, you have already more or less granted him impunity."

"I will never ask for any kind of support. The father of my child will never, ever know anything about her."

"I will do as you instruct. But let me remind you again of the legal ramifications."

"Then enter 'name withheld'."

"What about your daughter? What if she needs to contact her biological father because of medical issues or such?"

"This is just the way it has to be."

The doctor sighed. "I hope you know what you're doing."

Since Michelle would be driving herself home, Dr. Orlando kept her an extra day. About mid-morning on Thursday, Tonya was put in an infant seat and placed on the floorboard. With a complementary supply of products including a small case of formula in the trunk, mother and daughter set out to begin their new life together. What was not provided by the doctor, the hospital, or the staff was any kind of instruction manual.

"Okay kiddo, here we go."

Miss Bizzy Belle

Granny to the rescue

One of the few things Michelle knew about parenting was that offspring often mirror the anxieties of the mother. She braced herself for her baby to be a basket case.

After placing the infant carefully in the secondhand bassinet, the unlikely mother unloaded the supplies. Tonya had not so much as let out a whimper. The peacefulness would not last very long. Feeding time was not far away. The diaper changing ritual would begin soon afterward.

While she had a few moments, Michelle needed to make some phone calls. No long distance calls could be placed from her bedside phone at the hospital, and she had no change for the payphone down the hall. She could have called collect, but she also knew the real reason she had remained mute was that she did not know what to say.

Proper protocol was to call her parents first. Since they were still at school, she went ahead and called her sweet Granny Addie. Twice, she started dialing the number. Both times, she hung up before completing it. The third try was successful.

Her granny answered on the third ring. Michelle tried to speak, but no words came. After the third "Hello," the caller was able to utter a faint, "Granny . . ."

"Michelle? Is that you? I've been worried sick. Please tell me that everything's all right."

Through sniffs and sobs, she told her favorite grandmother about her new great-granddaughter.

"Why didn't you let me know? I've been calling every day. I could have caught the train and been there. Why do you have to be so dern independent?"

"Oh, Granny . . . I don't want to be any trouble."

"Well, then . . . I would have come for Baby Tonya's sake."

A little smile appeared on Michelle's face.

"Now, you listen to me. You can't do this all by yourself. I'll get Doc to take me to Asheville in the morning, and I'll be on the train leaving the station around seven. I've already checked the schedule. I won't get to Washington tomorrow night until after nine. But don't you fret yourself. Your granny might live out here in the sticks, but she knows how to catch a cab."

"Oh, Granny . . ."

"Oh Granny, nothing. You just hold on tight 'til I get there."

She hung up before Michelle could offer any further resistance.

What had she ever done to deserve a granny like that?

According to the clock, it was time to feed Tonya, but the baby had hardly moved since being put down. Should she wake her, or just let her sleep? When Michelle walked over and peered into the bassinet, she let out a gasp. Panic-stricken, she could not tell if the infant was breathing. Had she killed her baby, too?

Holding her own breath, she extended her hand slowly toward the little girl's face. It was surely just a reflex, but Michelle thought Tonya smiled.

"Get a grip, Nurse Bell. If she had stopped breathing, she would have been blue. If you don't stop holding your breath, you're the one that's going to be blue in the face."

The new mother went to the kitchen and started warming the bottle. How would she know if it was too hot or not warm enough? She was a nurse, for Christ's sake. She was supposed to know those things.

The new mom must have gotten it within a tolerable range because Tonya took the artificial nipple and went to work. Michelle was so afraid that she was going to drop her, or not support her head properly. Did the baby need to burp? The blundering mom breathed a big sigh of relief when she put her baby back in the bassinet without breaking her.

"I can do this . . . I can do this . . . I know I can."

The call to Bellville was much different from the one to Ferndale. Michelle's father answered.

"Daddy . . . I have some news." He interrupted. "Let me go get your mother."

After a silence that seemed to go on forever, her mom finally said, "Hello." Unemotionally, Michelle told her about Tonya's birth. No words of congratulations or anything like that came from the other end of the line.

Her mother did ask if she and the baby were okay, and Michelle assured her they were, and that both were in the hands of good doctors. No mention was made of Granny Addie's plans. Neither was anything else said about adoption.

Michelle was depleted. Her body was still serving notice that it had been through quite an ordeal. Fortunately, there had been no complications. She did not know why she ever thought she could get through it alone, but she did not think that she had any other choice. If she could just hold on for twenty-four more hours, help was on the way.

Each time the new mother took care of little Tonya's needs, she became a tad more confident. Yet, nothing seemed to come naturally. Was her daughter already feeling it? Would she grow up to disregard her?

Miss Bizzy Belle

During the short time that Michelle spent with Walt, he had shown her how liberating it was to really enjoy just *being* in the moment. That all changed the day she went to get the IUD removed. Since then, she had been unable to ignore the incessant intrusions of a life controlled by the clock. The ticking timepiece vacillated between being her ally and her enemy. At the moment, whether it was a.m. or p.m. hardly mattered.

When was Tonya's next feeding? Should she set the alarm to make sure that she did not oversleep? How many more hours before Granny would get there? The night finally passed and a new day wore on. How much longer before that cab would show up?

The anxious mother looked up at the clock when the phone startled her. Granny Addie had found a pay phone at the train station and called to let her know that she had arrived. Michelle began calculating how long it might take for a taxi to get to her apartment. She could not keep her eyes off the clock.

Michelle was wondering if anything had changed. Would her granny treat her differently now that her granddaughter was certifiably a scarlet woman?

Waiting impatiently at the door of the duplex, lights finally appeared in the drive. Mrs. Baker did not hail a cab every day. It took a bit of effort to get her luggage out of the trunk and extra time to sort out the fare situation. The cabbie grumbled at the size of the tip and did not even offer to put her things on the little stoop. Appalled by his rudeness, the woman wished for the opportunity to teach him some manners and to educate him about southern hospitality.

Whatever qualms Michelle might have had earlier dissolved quickly. Sweet Adeline took her belle's hands and the ritual began.

Afterward, Michelle reached reflexively for one of the bags. Granny intervened.

"You're in no shape to go toting things around. When I had your mother, they wouldn't let me out of bed for a week. Now . . . Where's that baby?"

When they got the luggage situated, Michelle moved between her granny and the bassinet. "I have to tell you something. I hope you're not going to be too disappointed, but I broke a tradition."

Granny brushed past her. "What are you talking about?"

As she got her first glimpse of her great-grandchild, still not sure what her granddaughter was worried about, Michelle clarified. "Tonya doesn't have our red hair."

Standing in awe of the little person with beautiful black hair, Granny

Addie said what was on her mind. "I think that baby must have a mighty fine daddy." The room grew restive and then silent for a moment.

After some "oohing and aahing," Michelle told her granny she knew that she must be plum tuckered. She said that she was going to sleep on the sofa and let her have the bed. Granny Addie would have nothing of it. She said that she was going to take the cushions and make herself a pallet on the floor where she could keep an eye on the baby in her charge.

"Child . . . I'm here to take care of you. I'll be just fine. You are the one who needs to get some rest. Show me where everything is. I see bottles. I presume that you're one of those modern women not breastfeeding. When did Tonya eat last? I'll take care of the next feeding."

Michelle thought to herself that her granny was a better nurse than she was. Content that her little girl was in good hands, she collapsed on the bed and got her best night's sleep in a while. Not once during the night did she wake up and look at the clock.

As Michelle came crawling out the next morning, Granny greeted her. "Tonya's such a good baby. I want to hear her cry, but all I can get out of her is a whimper."

The anxious mother mouthed with her forehead furrowed. "Do you think something's wrong with her? Is she retarded or anything?"

Granny Addie chided her. "Oh, don't be silly. What were you expecting, a little monster?"

Actually, that was pretty much what Michelle had anticipated. Dr. Orlando thought it was going to be a boy to boot. She was afraid that she had already ruined her own flesh and blood before she was even born.

While carrying her child to term, there was apparently something that Michelle Anne Bell still had not fully come to terms with. Tonya Willa Bell was Walter Othell Williamson's daughter, too. There was not one single solitary thing on God's green earth that could ever change that.

The new mother did not know what she would have done if Granny Addie had not come to the rescue. Even though they had not discussed how long her grandmother might stay, Michelle knew that it would soon be just she and her little stranger.

Out of the blue, Granny Addie made a proposal. "Why don't you come back home and move in with me for a while? I can take care of you until you get back on your feet. You can get a job around there when you're ready."

Reflexively, Michelle responded. "Oh, Granny . . . I love you for offering. But I could never do that to Papa Doc. That's his home, too, and

Miss Bizzy Belle

you know how he keeps to himself. Having us under his feet would drive him crazy." As much as she hated to admit it, the woman knew that her granddaughter was right.

Michelle added the punctuation mark. "Besides . . . This is my little red wagon, and I'm the one who's going to have to pull it."

Granny's assessment of Tonya after only the first night tending her did not change. She was a good baby. Michelle could not get over her amazement. She had birthed a happy, healthy child.

When Michelle went for her doctor's appointment, Granny kept the baby. They both went for Tonya's first checkup. By all accounts, mother and child were doing as well as could be expected.

Adeline called Doc every day or so to check on him. He did not say much, but she knew that he was ready for her to come home. After she had been gone three weeks, he admitted that he was ailing a bit.

Granny Addie did not have to deal with a crabby cabbie on her way out of town because mother and daughter could drive her. On the way, she told Michelle she wished so much that she would consider moving closer to her.

Her granddaughter knew she was not ready for that, but she told her granny that she would give it some thought. What she didn't convey was how much easier it was to live in an impersonal environment where few knew her, and where judgments didn't sting quite as severely. Since the women had no idea when they might see each other again, their parting was mostly sorrowful.

With Tonya tucked in her infant seat on the floorboard, Michelle was compelled to handle the X more cautiously than ever before. It was not far out of the way to go by Walter Reed. Why not stop by and show off her baby? Michelle needed to speak with her supervisor about coming back to work, anyway. The new mother had to be assigned to the first shift because her child would be in daycare.

Even though the hospital had told Michelle that she could take up to two months off, the unrelenting bills gave her no such reprieve. After making a satisfying fuss over the beautiful baby, the supervisor agreed to let her start back to work the following Monday. Michelle had the next five days alone with her little girl.

After they got home, the mother looked over at her baby sleeping so peacefully in the bassinet. "I have no idea what to do with you, but I'm so glad that I did not do away with you."

Baby blues

Michelle was just not feeling well. She kept telling herself that it was because her body had been so traumatized. She discussed it with Dr. Orlando, and he mentioned something about the "baby blues." He said that it might take a little time for her hormones to get back in balance. She didn't feel like going back to work, but she had no choice. She had another mouth to feed.

About three weeks before Tonya was born, Michelle picked out a neighborhood daycare center, Mrs. T's. The owner, Mrs. Thornhill, was pleasant and the place seemed adequate enough. She kept only about a half dozen or so infants and toddlers to avoid regulation issues. The new mother felt certain that her baby would get the individual attention she needed.

On the first morning, Michelle placed Tonya in her familiar spot in the X. When they drove up to the daycare center, the mother said to her little girl.

"Well, kiddo, go in there and strut your stuff."

Mrs. Thornhill met them at the door. It took a couple of minutes to go over everything, and then mom was off to work. It was okay that she shed a tear or two. Maybe Tonya was better off with the more experienced Mrs. T than she was with her own mother.

At the hospital, Nurse Bell was welcomed back with open arms. The other nurses kept telling her how adorable Tonya was. They were patient with her when she needed extra time off her feet. The supervisor knew that Michelle was anxious about her baby and let her off an hour early.

Still not used to the routine, she missed the street to Mrs. T's. The X recovered with a quick U-turn. Mrs. Thornhill's assurance that they'd had no trouble at all went a long way toward making Michelle feel better about the arrangement. She just wished that she could start feeling better.

After struggling for a week, her supervisor scheduled an appointment with one of the hospital counselors. Throughout the session, Michelle had trouble listening to what he was saying. She kept looking across the desk and seeing Walt sitting in the chair that once belonged to him. The therapist believed that she was indeed suffering from postpartum depression and sent her back to her OB/GYN.

When Walt Williamson was transferred from Walter Reed to Ft. Benning, he had no expectations regarding his job. He left a harried schedule of counseling veterans at the rundown hospital to become a flunky for the base psychiatrist. One of his main duties was to see family members of military officers.

Many wives from traditional homes were unaccustomed to moving abruptly when orders changed. They were also ill-equipped to deal with the circumstances when husbands were gone for such long stretches, especially those away in combat. Additionally, there was never a shortage of army brats living up to their name.

Confidentiality was ever an issue for Walt. While he had the assurance from his boss that his files were secure, he was never certain that he was the only one with a key. More and more, he relied on his memory, placing fewer and fewer things of a sensitive nature in a client's file.

When a colonel's wife came for her first appointment, Walt had a hard time getting her to open up. He knew that she had issues or she would not be there. He sensed that she was tiptoeing around something, but she held back. Maybe she needed time to adjust to the therapeutic setting.

The woman was back a week later. Only after Walt gave his solemn promise that nothing she said would go into her file, did she start to confide in him. The colonel's wife first confessed to having a one-night stand. With her husband overseas, she had succumbed to the advances of a brash younger soldier that she met in a bar. Even though she had an IUD, she still got pregnant. A military doctor performed an abortion and then recommended that she see a therapist.

For years, the military wife had been conditioned to suppress her emotions. Walt tried to help her get in touch with her bottled up feelings. Little by little, she began letting it all out. The client did not realize it, but the counselor was struggling almost as much as she was. He kept imagining Michelle sitting in the chair before him.

The X-factor

Eventually, Michelle settled back into some routines. The pills that Dr. Orlando gave her seemed to be helping. Being on her feet much of the day, while tiring, did have one notable benefit. She was getting rid of some baby fat, and her figure was returning.

Tonya was soon waking up only once during the night. The little girl was growing and changing before her mother's eyes. At two months, the pediatrician was delighted with her development.

Meanwhile, crime was encroaching on her neighborhood. Maybe it was time to start looking elsewhere for a place to live. Granny Addie's proposal certainly had its merits. While she did not want to impose, it was impossible to ignore the benefits of being closer to her.

Michelle just could not stomach the ridicule she was sure to get. Since she was in neither the physical nor financial shape to make a move anytime soon, she decided to set Tonya's first birthday as a target date. Maybe by then, she would know what to do.

On the way home from work a few days after the country's birthday, Michelle had the radio blasting. That was a little ritual she had gotten into, hardly paying attention to what song was playing. Just the noise provided a few minutes of diversion.

Suddenly, sounds did not blend. Recognizing the blaring of a siren, her senses went on high alert. As she caught a blur in her peripheral vision, she hit her brakes hard. A speeding car went flying through the intersection just feet from her front bumper. A police car was hot in pursuit.

The X came within a gnat's whisker of having its front bumper ripped off. The one on the rear of the vehicle didn't fare as well. Michelle's neck was thrown back from the force of the impact. Something did not feel right. From her medical training, she knew not to move. Her first thought was relief that she had not yet picked up her daughter from daycare.

People started gathering. The teenage driver of the car that hit her was apparently uninjured but was in tears. She kept apologizing to Michelle. The man who lived in the corner house came out and said that he had called the police. She asked him to go back inside and call an ambulance.

After being stabilized, Michelle was taken to the same hospital where Tonya was born. While filling out the paperwork, she gave Mrs. Thornhill's number to the attendant and asked that the daycare center be notified. Mrs. T said if no one picked Tonya up, that she would gladly keep her overnight. What a relief that was. The working mom was growing more appreciative of just how fortunate she was to have Mrs. Thornhill.

The ER doctor ordered X-rays. He said it could have been a lot worse, but cautioned that it was too early to determine the full extent of the damage. He felt optimistic that once the swelling resolved, the pain might go away with no lasting effect. Only time and proper care would tell.

Michelle's neck was put in a brace, and she was released. The doctor told her to go home, but to be extremely careful not to make any sudden moves. She was not to lift anything weighing more than five pounds for at least a week. He prescribed medication for her discomfort, and it was brought from the hospital pharmacy.

She thought as she downed one. "No telling what the insurance company was billed for those pills." While waiting to be released, the pain began to subside.

Meanwhile, a police officer found her to finish his report. He told

Michelle that her car had been towed to a precinct parking lot. He thought it was drivable, but he was not sure. Then, he added with a little smile. "I bet it's fun to drive."

Without batting an eye, she said to the cop. "I'll let you drive it sometime if you'll give me a lift to where it is." He mumbled something about regulations but then agreed. Michelle was aware that he had her address and phone number in the paperwork. He was not bad looking, either.

Officer Spearman steadied her as they walked outside. When they got to the cruiser, she asked if she should sit in the backseat. He loved it. His laugh proved it.

The policeman went inside the precinct building with her to get the key and sign a release form. The handsome young man in uniform stayed with her until they determined that the wounded X could get her home. He gave her his badge number and said that if she got stopped for a taillight violation, he would vouch for her.

Michelle suspected that he might have given her a personal escort if she had asked. All in the line of duty, of course. He would likely lose a bit of his enthusiasm, though, if she had to stop on the way home and pick up a two-month-old.

She doubted that she would ever see him again, but she made a note of his badge number just in case. You never know. It might come in handy somewhere down the road.

On the way to collect her daughter, Michelle already knew that she had no choice but to ignore some of the doctor's orders. She just had to be extra careful handling the infant. What else could she do? She just hoped that between insurance and sick leave, she would not lose more wages. Mrs. T agreed to keep Tonya during the day while the little girl's mother was recuperating.

As Michelle turned the corner to enter the street her duplex was on, her resolve slipped a cog. What a welcome sight Walt's car would be sitting in the drive. How nice he would be to come home to. Why was she being so foolish by shutting him out? Speedily, she reversed herself and got it back in gear.

The insurance company provided a rental vehicle while the X was being patched up. Since Michelle was not at fault, the other driver's insurance was picking up the tab.

During the second day of her unscheduled furlough, the phone rang. Her first thought was that somebody from the hospital was calling to check on her. Or, it might be Mrs. Thornhill.

The person on the other end identified himself. "This is Rodney Spearman. I was just calling to check on you." Was this a wrong number?

Michelle made a quick recovery when she recognized the voice of Officer Spearman. She responded politely. "Oh! How nice of you to call. So far. So good." He then wanted to know if he could help her with anything.

As a matter of fact, there was something that he could do. She had not quite figured out how to pick up her rental car, and drop off the X at the body shop all by herself. The young cop was delighted to be of service. He was free the next day.

Michelle felt a twinge of guilt for just using the officer. Yet, she did not have to beg. He called and offered.

The off-duty cop pulled into the driveway in a sleek cream-colored Camaro. How 'bout that, sports fans? He followed her to the body shop and then delivered her to the rental car place. As they were about to go their separate ways, he asked if she would like to go out sometime. She said that she would have to think about it.

The outing along with the pills helped pull Michelle out of the doldrums. She had no interest in dating a cop. Of course, she didn't. Why didn't she just say no? She would probably never hear from him again, anyway.

During the week at home, Michelle had no unexpected complications other than some soreness. Then again, medications might well be masking the pain. She'd certainly had her share of pharmaceuticals during the past couple of months, and the nurse was not a glutton for punishment. She got the prescription refilled.

Indeed, she heard nothing from Officer Spearman throughout the next week, although she thought about him a couple of times. After her second day back at work, the phone was ringing when she and Tonya came through the door.

Rodney asked Michelle out for a real date. Redheads do indeed blush.

Michelle had never needed a babysitter, and she asked Mrs. T to recommend one. The woman, now spending more waking hours with Tonya than the child's own mother, was a widow. After losing her husband following a lengthy battle with multiple sclerosis, she had converted her basement and fenced-in backyard into a daycare center. Mrs. Thornhill said that she could use the extra cash and would be happy to keep Tonya anytime.

Wow! A real date. It would be Michelle's first since Walt. Still a little wobbly on her feet since the accident, she was, nonetheless, plunging headlong into a new adventure. She hoped the officer was a gentleman. On the other hand, a bad boy might be more fun. Fun had been in short supply for most of her life. Maybe she had some catching up to do. The antidepressant was working.

Miss Bizzy Belle

The next day on the way home, she stopped at a department store and purchased a summer A-line dress in a floral pattern. It had somewhat of a plunging neckline. A little tight in the tummy, she would wear her girdle. Latex had come a long way since the corset that Granny Addie stuffed herself into when she spiffed up.

The arrangement with Mrs. Thornhill was working out nicely. Since Michelle was paying her by the hour, it did not matter if she ran a little late. If all of the other kids had been picked up, the woman took Tonya upstairs with her.

The date helped Michelle resolve another problem. The X was ready. Mr. Knight-in-Shining-Armor was waiting when she dropped off the rental. He told her how nice she looked on the way to pick up the X. When they brought it around, he personally inspected it to make sure they had done a good job.

Then, he turned to Michelle.

"Race you home."

"But, what if I get a speeding ticket?"

"You're on your own."

"What if you get pulled over?"

The cop did not skip a beat. "The law recognizes the law."

He grinned with self-assurance. "I'll give you a full minute head start."

"Okay. But turn your lights on so I can see you if you get within sight."

They started their engines. Michelle could not believe that she was doing this. She braced her neck tightly against the headrest. Two green lights in a row. After a red, full throttle. No cops anywhere. Her confidence soared.

Michelle kept checking her review mirror and no headlights were coming up from behind. She bet old Hot Rod wished he had never given her that head start.

There was one thing that she had not counted on. The policeman knew the streets better than she did, and he took shortcuts that she knew nothing about. A vehicle was sitting in front of her apartment when she came to a screeching halt. Hot Rod was standing beside his Camaro, twiddling his thumbs.

Michelle muttered to herself. "He got lucky. He'd better not think he'll get used to that."

It was still four hours before time for her next pill. Michelle decided to go ahead and take another one when she went into the bathroom to powder her nose. Maybe it would help her relax. When she looked in the mirror, she liked what she saw. "If Granny Addie could just see me now."

It was nice to sit on the passenger side for a change. Rod obviously enjoyed driving his Chevrolet muscle car. Because it cornered so sharply, the Camaro brand had acquired the handle, "The Hugger." For now, the driver kept both hands on the wheel.

When the wine steward came around, Michelle asked for a glass of "Sin Infidel." Of course, everybody was thrown off course. Feeling coy, she smirked and changed her order to white zinfandel. Why not have some fun? Maybe it was time for the redhead to let her hair down.

There had to be a story behind that, and Michelle's date egged her on. She explained that in her strict upbringing, her folks were teetotalers. She had gone all the way through high school and nursing school with nary a drop of alcohol touching her lips.

Michelle could not believe that she was telling on herself without even blushing. She described being at a convention, shortly after moving to D.C., where wine was served. Like a child who hears something strange and then converts it into familiar vernacular, she heard something other than zinfandel.

Rod was enjoying this. She then told him about another first date a few years earlier when a young army officer took her out to dinner, and then to a movie. Just like moments before, the waiter asked if they wanted a glass of wine. She confessed her ignorance and said the only wine that she knew anything about was Sin Infidel.

Michelle said the night ended with her very much unaware of her faux pas. Her date did not mention it for a few days, but to him, it was so hysterical that he found it impossible to keep it to himself. At first, she saw nothing funny about it.

Just as two glasses of wine were set on the table, Michelle said that she'd always had problems laughing at herself. Maybe it was about time.

"Hear!" "Hear!" Her escort said as he raised his glass.

So far as she knew, Michelle did not stick her foot in her mouth on this date. She let Rodney do most of the talking, and the brash young police officer never lacked for anything to say. Neither of them made much eye contact. Hot Rod's kept finding their way to just below her chin. The sexy sun dress was worth every penny that she paid for it.

Michelle wondered if she should mention that she was a mother. It would certainly be easier to pick up Tonya on the way home. She was a little lightheaded from the wine and had already made up her mind that she was not going to ask him in. Would he try to kiss her? Was that all he might want?

Miss Bizzy Belle

Even though having her little girl in her arms might prevent anything from getting out of hand, so to speak, Michelle decided not to say anything. Her handsome date was nothing but mannerly when he got her home. He had been paying careful attention when she described her conservative background. He did not want to risk doing anything that might offend her.

Michelle made coffee before trekking to Mrs. T's. The last thing she needed was a DUI. Then again, she did have the badge number of a D.C. cop.

Michelle was not all that surprised when Rod called again. After dinner, he asked if she would like to go to a club. Alcohol was not the only vice lacking from her growing up days. Her daddy considered dancing the work of the devil. When she declined, he was obviously disappointed.

"I don't even know how to do the Teaberry Shuffle." She confessed and they laughed.

On the way back to her apartment, she told him about Tonya. He said that he was divorced and had a two-year-old little girl. He kissed her on the forehead when he walked her to the door, and she never heard from him again.

If Hot Rod Spearman lived up to his name, she would never know.

The "F" List

When Walt Williamson walked into his apartment from work one evening, his answering machine was blinking. The office manager asked him to return at once. He had no idea what the emergency could be so soon after he had just left. At least, he had not gotten out of uniform.

As he approached the desk, his co-worker apologized for the inconvenience. She told him that the situation had to be handled with extreme caution. Just the two of them, and the person waiting in his office, would ever know anything about it.

"Who is it?" Walt wanted to know.

"It's the boss's wife. She's suicidal."

"Will you please stick around?"

"I wouldn't think of leaving you alone with this."

Walt had met the woman a couple of times at social gatherings, so they needed no introduction. Getting it all out in the open took a while, and he took no notes. It was not easy being any kind of military spouse, especially during wartime. This wife of an officer, who had both doctor and major in front of his name, had found it particularly daunting. It had now become overwhelming.

One thing was for certain. The major was not going to change. He had rank on her no matter which direction she turned. The besieged wife had endured about all of the disparagement that she could stand. The frazzled woman was at the end of her rope.

Walt quizzed her. "What about divorce?"

"Out of the question. He would feel so dishonored and disgraced that nothing would be left after he chewed me up and spit me out."

The beleaguered woman saw only one way out. She had unlimited access to his firearms. Because they had grown children, one side of her wanted to make it look like an accident. The other wished to humiliate her abusive husband. At the moment, the latter was winning.

Walt called for a little time out. He had to get some bearings. The efficient office manager had made fresh coffee, and she handed him a mug as he headed to the break room.

The counselor let his mind explore some imagery. The woman said that she was at the end of her rope. "Kicking the bucket" was one of the synonymous expressions for suicide. A person might theoretically tie a rope around his neck, step up on a bucket, pull the noose tight, and then kick it away, thus hanging himself.

Part of the lore also included the "bucket list." This jargon came to represent the things that a person wanted to accomplish before dying.

Walt returned to his office and tried a novel approach. Presuming that he could not dissuade her from taking her own life if that was what she was determined to do, he asked her if there were things left undone. Did she have her business in order?

As the woman was pondering what he had said, the counselor then became more specific. "Are there places that you would like to go, and things you want to do before you finish your life on this earth? Do you have friends that you want to visit one more time? Are there people that you have never told how much they have meant to you?"

The woman took the bait.

"You mean . . . Like a bucket list?"

"Maybe so."

Walt picked up a legal pad and wrote the heading across the top of the page. His penmanship had always left a lot to be desired, and in his haste, the tail of the "b" dropped below the line. He then handed the pen to the woman and slid the pad to her.

She looked down at what he had written, then up at him with a strange look.

"Fucket list?"

Some things cannot be orchestrated. Walt seized the opportunity just like he had planned it that way all along.

"Actually . . . We're going to make two lists. On one side of the page, you are going to write what's on your 'bucket list,' and on the other, what's on your 'fucket list'."

The psychiatrist's wife got down to business. She was hardly concerned about the column that began with a "B." Punctuated with a passion, she kept adding to the one that started with "F." She did not just write, either. With each entry, she vented years and years of rage and pent up peeves.

Walt Williamson had inadvertently stumbled upon a counseling technique that would subsequently become a part of his own lore. He was not at all sure what the outcome of that marriage was going to be, but he was certain of one thing. The major was about to be dressed down like he was a minor.

As he finally got to bed, his thoughts turned to Michelle. It was now rather apparent that she was not going to get back in touch with him. "I guess I'm on her 'fucket list'." As he reached over and turned out the light, he came to another conclusion. "Maybe it's about time for me to start my own."

Watt

Michelle had to keep pinching herself. It did not seem possible that she was the mother of an infant, soon to be a toddler. The pediatrician said after every visit that the little girl was about as normal and healthy as a child could be. The baby spent hours alone in her bassinet. Her eyes followed the butterflies of her crib mobile.

Alas, Tonya was pulling herself up, and the cradle was no longer able to contain her. At the same second-hand store where it was purchased, Michelle found a crib.

When they walked through the door each evening, Tonya started squirming to be put down. Then, she went scampering. For such a small apartment, the tot had found several good places to hide, and she stayed out of sight when she did not want to be found. Tonya was delighted when her mom came upon her unexpectedly and wished that she might play with her more.

Larry G. Johnson

When Michelle was looking for something in the closet one evening, she came across an old sweatshirt that Walt had left behind. If he missed it, he never mentioned it. She remembered him wearing it the night before he left. A cool front had spilled over from Canada, and the early September evening was breezy. They had gone to a nearby park just trying to fill the void of sadness settling in. He must have forgotten it the next morning when he put on a cooler shirt for traveling.

She pitched the sweatshirt out of the closet and continued searching. When she came out, Tonya had wrapped herself in it. No amount of persuasion coaxed the little girl to surrender it. Michelle decided just to let her be for the moment and toss the old shirt later.

The tot dragged it around with her the rest of the evening. She refused to relinquish it at bedtime. The next morning when Michelle tried to separate the two, Tonya defiantly took her stand. She made it very plain that she was not going anywhere without her new possession.

As Michelle was putting her daughter to bed that night, Tonya pointed to the picture on the front of the old sweatshirt. Her mother told her that it was a waterfall.

"Watt." The little girl learning to say syllables had just given her new best friend a name.

Watt and Tonya were already inseparable.

Mrs. T offered to keep Tonya for all of Thanksgiving Week. Whatever Michelle needed to do, she said the little girl was no problem. The mother was delighted that her daughter had bonded so well with the daycare owner. Mrs. T said that Tonya felt like her own granddaughter.

The woman's only child was drafted while in college. He became a helicopter pilot and was killed in Vietnam. He met his wife in Texas while in basic training. His widow and Mrs. Thornhill's grandson, Brad, lived in Dallas. She rarely got to see them. Not wanting to raise any questions about her past, Michelle never mentioned their war casualty connection.

Granny Addie put Michelle and Tonya on her Christmas wish list, but Michelle was not ready to make that long of a haul with her little busybody. She considered flying but then checked holiday fares. They were good excuses, but not the real reasons that she was not going. Michelle had heard nothing about drawing names. She presumed her parents framed it in such a way to make it appear that their daughter no longer wanted to be included in the family.

Miss Bizzy Belle

Since the nurse was not going out of town, she was asked to work throughout Christmas Week. Mrs. Thornhill again came through for her.

As soon as Tonya started crawling, the nimble little girl was always right in the middle of everything. Mrs. T started calling her, "Miss Bizzy Belle." When Michelle came to pick up her daughter about a week before Christmas, Mrs. T invited her in to see how Tonya had assisted with decorations. On Christmas Eve, she invited them to stay for dinner.

Walt could hardly wait to get on the road for a holiday break. He was headed to the Outer Banks of North Carolina to visit a former professor and to interview for a job. His discharge was only about six months away.

On the long drive, he realized that it was not much farther to D.C. He considered driving up to check on Michelle, but three things dissuaded him. One was that she was likely home with her family. Furthermore, he had some pressing business in Ephesus. The third reason was that he did not want to intrude where he was not welcome. That did not stop him from thinking about the daughter that he never had. This would be her first Christmas. He could just imagine her all decked out in a pretty red dress.

A parcel was on the porch when Michelle turned into the drive after the surprise Christmas Eve dinner at Mrs. T's. Seven-month-old Miss Bizzy Belle put Watt down for a moment to help open it. Out she pulled a bright red dress from her Great-Granny Addie.

The first snow did not arrive in D.C. until the second week in January. Tonya was fascinated by it. She smiled as her eyes followed the falling flakes. She had to feel that strange white stuff. Tonya had to touch everything that she explored. Did all kids have so much curiosity?

Mrs. Thornhill read to the infants and toddlers in her care every day. She wondered if their parents gave them the attention they needed. Tonya always seemed to find her way into Mrs. T's lap. The little girl was mesmerized by the words and the pictures on the pages. She was getting good at repeating some sounds. Now that she was on the floor except for naps, Miss Bizzy Belle played well with the other kids.

About the time of the spring equinox, the cherry blossoms were at their peak. Mother and daughter went on an outing. Tonya remembered to bring Watt, but Michelle forgot her camera. The mother did recall the time when she and the girl's father held hands when they once went to the National Mall. For a fleeting moment, she imagined the three of them going together as a family.

Michelle was a little disappointed in herself because of how few pictures she had taken, but Granny Addie was the only one that she ever sent snapshots to. She also neglected to make entries in Tonya's baby book. It just did not seem that important when so few things could be shared.

She wondered if her granny ever showed any of Tonya's pictures to the girl's grandparents, or if they ever even thought about their granddaughter. She could not blame them. Their daughter was the very personification of so many things that they abhorred.

One day near the end of April when Michelle stopped to pick up her daughter, Mrs. Thornhill said that Miss Bizzy Belle had something new to show her. The mother started looking around for that something, but it was not a thing at all. With a bit of sweet-talking, the little girl took wobbly steps to the daycare owner's outstretched arms.

Exuding pride, Mrs. T elaborated. "She's been working on this for about a week, and today she took her first steps. Now hold out your arms and let her come to you."

Tonya's birthday was fast approaching. What a tumultuous couple of years it had been since Michelle's first date with Walt. Maybe when the girl was older, she would give her a party. It seemed silly while she was still too young to remember anything.

Michelle reminded herself this was the marker that she had set to reexamine her housing situation. So far, she had not been the victim of any maliciousness, but the neighborhood was definitely in a state of transition. She was afraid that the X might be targeted.

When the big day rolled around, the mother decided that they should celebrate in some small way. Before picking up Tonya, she stopped to get a pizza. The toddler wanted to carry it, but it was just too cumbersome. Mom let her little helper tote her purse instead.

Once everything was dumped inside, Michelle went back to the street to check the mail. She was on a ton of lists, which usually meant there was plenty of junk to sort through. On this day, only one item was in the box, and it was obviously the size of a greeting card. Granny Addie must have remembered that it was Tonya's birthday.

When Michelle reached in and retrieved it, she had to steady herself. The envelope was postmarked in Columbus, Georgia.

How did he know?

What did he know?

She wanted to just rip the card to shreds, but she had to see what was inside. With fingers trembling, she lifted the flap. Slowly, she removed the card. The back came out turned up. Precious seconds passed with her unable to flip the card over. Then she did it!

"Happy Anniversary" was emblazoned across the front. With Tonya

tugging at her leg signaling that she was ready to eat, Michelle ignored her long enough to open the card.

> *Thinking of you on the second anniversary of the BIG date. I hope you celebrate with a glass or two of Sin Infidel.*
>
> *I plan to,*
> *Walt*

Michelle did not know whether to laugh or cry. Maybe both. The good news was that Walt knew nothing about Tonya. The bad news was that he was still looking over her shoulder.

With the leftover pizza in the fridge and Tonya put to bed, Michelle picked up the card again. Walt had just punched her one-way ticket out of town. It was time to move and leave no forwarding address.

The mailbox was full of tabloids and glossy fliers again the next day. Michelle tossed them on the table to sort through later. Her mind was on her next move.

A letter from Granny Addie was near the bottom of the stack. That put a smile on the weary woman's face. It began with birthday wishes for Tonya. Michelle's granny remarked how it hardly seemed possible that a year had passed since she made the long trip to see her new great-granddaughter. But alas, the years seemed to be slipping away faster than ever.

"Don't you think it's about time for you to come home for a few days? I think that baby is ready to travel. And I miss both of you so much."

Michelle's first reaction was predictable. "That's not going to happen." She could never go back. Nevertheless, the notion did not just vanish like the light in the bedroom when she switched off the lamp. Unable to fall asleep, the idea kept playing in her head. A nice little break started beckoning her. She needed some time to start figuring out what she was going to do. Her parents didn't have to know. She had no wish to embarrass them further.

The other mouth to feed had certainly kept Michelle's nose to the proverbial grindstone, but she was making some headway. She had two credit cards now, and neither was maxed out. She only had twelve more months to pay on the X, and then her money might stretch a little farther. She also had some vacation days that would expire if she did not use them.

Figuring that it might be easier to travel at night, Michelle fixed a place for Tonya to sleep in the backseat. Both floorboards and the little trunk were crammed. With a thermos of coffee to sip on, she could always pull in for the night somewhere if necessary.

Ahead of the Memorial Day weekend, and of school letting out for the summer, traffic was surprisingly light. Miss Bizzy Belle crawled from the front seat to the back several times with Watt in tow before falling asleep in the front.

"That girl. How could she possibly be comfortable all scrunched up like that when she could be stretched out in the back?"

Mom knew that she had to be more cautious with her precious cargo. When she made a pit stop, Michelle carefully relocated Tonya to the back. The one-year-old hardly roused. Not five miles down the road, and the child was back beside her in the front seat.

The AMX was one of the first vehicles equipped with reclining bucket seats. After it was well past midnight, Michelle was afraid that she might fall asleep at the wheel. She pulled into a motel parking lot, locked the doors, and let the seat back to rest her eyes. Five minutes later, a little girl was nestled on top of her.

It was past Papa Doc's breakfast time when the X finally rolled into the yard. The driver could have been mistaken for a sleepwalker, but the passenger was rested and raring to go. The little girl looked on curiously as her mother and great-grandmother went through their greeting routine. Lugging Watt along, she then went to check things out.

Granny Addie went to work fixing her second breakfast of the day. Papa Doc saw them drive up and came in from working in the garden. He took a seat at the kitchen table, and his wife poured him another cup of coffee. Michelle busied herself unloading the car.

Granny Addie called to her granddaughter as she came from the bedroom. "Come here. I want to show you something." Tonya had crawled up in Papa Doc's lap. He tried to make like he couldn't have cared less, but he was lapping it up.

He held the little girl at arms' length so that his nearsighted eyes could get a better look. "So . . . You're Miss Bizzy Belle."

After breakfast, Michelle went to bed. Tonya took her Great-Granny Addie's hand, and they went for a walk. The woman picked up the little girl as they neared the garden where Papa Doc was hoeing the beans.

She said to her aging husband as he looked up. "I was so afraid that Tonya might be frightened of us old folks. But I think she knows we're family."

After about five hours of shuteye, Michelle yawned her way back into the kitchen. She had slept right through lunch, and Granny Addie had already put Tonya down for her nap.

"I just can't believe what a good baby she is . . . Well . . . She's not much of a baby anymore."

The little girl's mother agreed. "She's no trouble at all."

"No trouble? She's an absolute joy!"

While Michelle was munching on lunch leftovers, Granny Addie asked her granddaughter if she was planning to see her parents. Michelle reacted, shaking her head.

"No . . . I just can't. I've hurt them so much. Anyway . . . They don't care a thing about us. I heard not one word from them during Christmas, or on Tonya's birthday."

Granny countered gently. "Just be patient with them. Give them some more time. I'm working on them, and I think they'll come around eventually."

"Did you tell them that Tonya and I were coming?"

"Nary a word. I thought about inviting them for supper on Saturday without letting on, but I don't think they're ready yet. Maybe next trip."

"Will Papa Doc say anything to them?"

"No. He understands his daughter better than any of us. And from the looks of things, he's getting to know his great-granddaughter pretty well, too." About then, that same great-granddaughter sauntered into the room clutching Watt.

Her great-granny reached out her hand. "Let me see that thing." Tonya obligingly handed it to her, knowing it was safe. Unfolding the shirt, the woman commented. "That looks a lot like Canyon Creek Falls. It's not far from here."

Cornfield

Sitting on the front porch, Michelle started thinking ahead. "It's going to be culture shock when I get back to D.C." She had to get back on the road the next morning, leaving the peaceful mountains behind. "No need for night driving. Tonya made a mockery out of that."

Without telling her granny what precipitated it, Michelle mentioned that she might be moving soon. She told her that her neighborhood was just not the right place to raise a child. She added that she was thinking seriously about getting a job somewhere else, maybe in a smaller town near Washington.

"Why don't you move back here? You wouldn't have any problem finding work, and I could help you with Tonya."

Michelle was a little more specific. "I just don't think I can move back to the south."

Granny caught her off guard once again. "I know nurses don't make much money, and the cost of living is so high where you live. How are you getting along?"

"I made out a budget after the baby was born, but so many unexpected things have come up that it's almost impossible to stick to it. I manage to get by, though." Michelle did not mention that she might have to take out a loan to make a move.

Without saying anything, her granny got up and went inside. When she returned, she handed her a check for $1000.

"Here. Tuck this away somewhere. The only thing not filled in is the date. Use it if you get in a bind."

"Oh, Granny, I could never . . ."

"Oh, Granny, nothing. Consider it a loan if you have to cash it. You can pay me back whenever you're able. The only carrying charges will be keeping Tonya when you will let me."

The X was loaded soon after breakfast the following morning. With bellies full, the mother and daughter were about to pull out.

"Watt!" "Watt!" Tonya shrieked and Granny Addie went scrambling. There were times Michelle swore that her daughter was saying "Walt."

Before she got to Asheville, Michelle thought to herself. "Granny thinks I can't even take care of myself or my child. I've disappointed her, too."

At the same time, that check in her purse was seed money. Her finances would not hold her back from what she knew she must do before it was too late.

Tonya mostly amused herself. She might have slept more going home than she did on the way down. That gave Michelle time to think. She confirmed the decision to stay in the greater D.C. area, but to relocate farther out.

The RN had two main concerns. One was her career. Working as a nurse in a hospital had its drawbacks. She would go into a new situation as low man on the totem pole and might not even be assigned to the first shift. Another possibility was working in a doctor's office.

The other issue was childcare. How could she ever get along without Mrs. Thornhill? Perhaps, she could find something within commuting distance.

Tonya had gotten off her schedule and was a bit cranky the first morning. When they arrived at daycare, the girl perked right back up and ran to outstretched arms.

"Cornfield . . ."

Michelle wanted to know what she meant by that.

"Didn't you know that's what she calls me? She must have picked it up from one of the stories that I read to her. As you know, children often hear words that they don't always understand, and then relate them to others they already know."

Michelle smiled and responded without giving any personal references. "Adults do that, too, sometimes."

Suburbia

Michelle started putting her feelers out. She was not interested in going north toward the Baltimore area because of the congestion. West of Washington, or perhaps southwest appealed more to her. After a couple of weeks, she got a good lead about a position at a Fairfax, Virginia doctors' office. On her next day off, she went to check it out, but only after she made sure that it was not for an OB/GYN practice.

The pay scale was surprisingly more than what she was making. The nurse was also assured that there was room for advancement. The office manager did most of the interviewing. She had been working for the three general practitioners for almost ten years. That meant something. The nurse Michelle might be replacing left only because her husband was transferred. That meant something, too.

The position was for Dr. I. R. Payne's personal nurse. When called back for another interview, Michelle was ushered into an office where the physician soon joined her.

She sized him up and decided that he was very professional. That he was lacking any detectable sense of humor did not bother her. She supposed that a doctor with a name like his must surely be immune to wisecracks.

Michelle's credentials and experience matched what the doctor was looking for. After almost four years of working at Walter Reed, she turned in a two-week notice effective Sunday, June 15, 1970. She told no one at the hospital where she was going. While typing her letter, she winced and thought of Walt when she realized that her last day was Father's Day.

The commute was not nearly as bad as she feared. The distance was almost twice as far, but the traffic moved about twice as fast. Mrs. Thornhill was thrilled that she could continue taking care of Miss Bizzy Belle.

One perk of Michelle's new job was that she could wear pants. The supervisor also encouraged her to purchase some conservative, but comfortable shoes. The physician's staff nurse also found herself working with different kinds of patients than the ones to which she was accustomed. These were just ordinary folks with common health issues. The facilities were modern, and the equipment was state-of-the-art. For the first time since Tonya was born, the nurse actually looked forward to going to work.

Michelle kept reminding herself that the career move was not her main objective. A couple of times, she took the office copy of the local newspaper home with her to check the classifieds. Housing was not quite as expensive as in Washington, but it was far from cheap. Fairfax was a fashionable suburb experiencing rapid growth generated by white flight.

The new employee went apartment hunting several afternoons after work and did not pick up Tonya until after Mrs. T had fed her supper. Michelle insisted on paying extra, not just for the hours, but also for the food.

Tonya's ersatz grandmother eased her mind. "That little girl is not going to eat me out of house and home. I just hope you're not going to move so far away that I won't be able to take care of her."

Michelle eventually found another duplex that she could barely afford. What the moving company charged was highway robbery, considering how few things she had, and for such a short distance. Then again, these folks were just trying to make a living, too.

The mother found a cute little girl's bedroom suite at a discount furniture store, and it was delivered the same day that they moved in. She was so grateful for Granny Addie's check.

Little Miss Bizzy Belle was right in the middle of everything. Michelle never actually sat her down to explain what was going on, but somehow the little girl seemed to understand. The new apartment had two small bedrooms. Even though Tonya was unable to articulate it, the girl was delighted that she and Watt had their own room.

For the time being, Michelle decided to make the trek back and forth to Mrs. T's. The woman only kept kids under the age of two. Other arrangements would have to be made after Tonya's second birthday.

When the new resident went to fill out a change of address form, the post office assured her that they never gave out personal information. After three months, her mail would no longer be forwarded.

When she had her telephone put in, Michelle did what was becoming commonplace for single women. She used her initials instead of her name. M. A. Bell might well be a man's name. She was not sure Walt would even remember that her middle name was Anne. Besides . . . He had no reason to think that she was living in Fairfax.

As Michelle Bell's head hit the pillow, she breathed a big sigh of relief. For the first time since their first date, Walt Williamson had no idea where she lived, or where she was employed.

Miss Bizzy Belle

Father's Day was just a Sunday off from work for Lieutenant Williamson. It was warm and muggy. The old mountain boy never liked the Columbus, Georgia climate. He would be packing up soon and leaving for his new job as a counselor for veterans at the Outer Banks State University. Tired of eating his own cooking, he decided to take himself out to lunch. The restaurant was packed as dads were being treated.

He wondered who was benefitting the most, fathers who might have preferred a home cooked meal, or the ones taking a kitchen break. He suspected that most of the dads were picking up the tabs as they were accustomed to doing.

His thoughts went to the man his mother, Maude, said might have been his father. Walt tried to imagine what it would be like to have a real dad. He hurt for Maude's husband, Todd, somehow trapped into raising a son that was not his.

When he sent Michelle the anniversary card, he was fully aware that it would have been about the time of their child's first birthday. He deliberately avoided any mention of the corresponding nearness of it to Mother's Day. He heard nothing back from her. Did she ever even think about him? Would anyone ever wish him a Happy Father's Day?

Once settled into his new job, Walt made regular jaunts from the coast to the mountains of North Carolina. His graduate school landlady never rented the basement where he had lived, and she was always so glad to see him.

While he varied his routes, he usually went through Asheville on the last leg to Ephesus. He had never paid much attention to the little Ferndale settlement about halfway in between. On one of his voyages, he stopped at the family-owned general store to get gas.

While waiting to pay, Walt asked the woman ahead of him if there was any significance to the community's name. She told him about the beautiful ferns growing on the creek bank and then suggested that he go by and see for himself.

As he got back in Mary Lou, his top of the line Toyota, he thought to himself that even though the woman was much older, something about her reminded him of Michelle. Maybe it was her hair. She was graying, but the original red still showing through was the same color. When he saw the name of the creek, he mused that there must be a story behind that, too.

Larry G. Johnson

The Very Hungry Caterpillar

While the kids in her care never seemed to tire of her reading the same stories over and over, Mrs. Thornhill visited her local bookstore occasionally looking for something different. One Saturday in July, she spotted a book that she had not noticed before. After a quick perusal, she purchased a copy of the beautifully illustrated, *The Very Hungry Caterpillar*, by Eric Carle.

When she read it to the toddlers, Mrs. T had never seen Tonya so attentive. She wondered how much the fourteen-month-old actually understood. When the little girl saw the picture of the butterfly, she started waving her arms and fluttering her fingers. As Cornfield was about to put the book away, Tonya kept repeating. "Gin." "Gin." She couldn't get enough.

Once Tonya started walking, it was not long until she was talking. You could always count on her to put her own spin on things, too. Deadpan when fracturing a word or expression, neither Michelle nor Mrs. T could tell if the child really knew the difference, or was just being cute.

On the way home one day, Tonya pointed her finger in the direction of an orange and white truck. She then declared it a "Me-Haul." It took her mother a moment to get it. The little girl's favorite place to eat was "Turkey Fried Chicken." Michelle often heard her muttering, and when she investigated, Tonya was jabbering to Watt. The mother had no idea what those conversations were about.

Thank goodness for Mrs. T. Not many parents could drop their kids off at daycare and never worry about them. Michelle was aware that her daughter had a special bond with Cornfield. At times she was a bit jealous, but mostly she was just relieved. She kept putting out of her mind the fact that Mrs. T only kept toddlers up to age two.

From a distance, Mrs. T observed Tonya's latest routine. When the mother came to pick her up, the daughter went into hiding. Michelle was not quite as amused. At the end of the day, she was not interested in playing games. The little girl just wanted to have fun with her mommy.

One of the best things about working at the doctors' office was having regular hours. The nurse did not have to worry about shift changes, or being called back while off duty. For the first time in her career, she could count on having holidays off.

Mrs. Thornhill invited mother and daughter for a Thanksgiving feast. She claimed it was no trouble at all since she could get things done during the kids' nap times. Michelle asked what she could bring, but the woman just waved her off.

Tonya already had her regular place at the table. Since Mrs. T did not mind the extra money, Michelle sometimes left her daughter at the daycare center until almost bedtime. After a strenuous day at work, it was nice to have a little time to herself.

The young mother admired the way that Mrs. Thornhill talked to Tonya. As they gathered around the table, Cornfield held Miss Bizzy Belle's hand and told her the Thanksgiving Story. She then asked her to bow her head while they offered thanks. Michelle was surprised when her daughter put her hands together and placed them under her chin.

About two weeks before Christmas, Michelle was invited to the office dinner party. She looked forward to meeting the spouses of her coworkers for the first time. The three physicians, Doctors Payne, Aiken, and McFeely, took turns hosting it. That year, it was Dr. Aiken's turn.

When Michelle told Mrs. Thornhill about it, she said not to worry. Since the party might run late, Tonya could just spend the night. The little girl not only had her place at the table, but she also now had her own bed.

The invitation said casual dress. Michelle learned as soon as she entered the front door that casual in upper-middle-class suburbia was a horse of a different color from what it was in Bellville. In her newest Christmas sweater and black pants, she was the only female in attendance, including the maids, not flashing sequins.

At least she was comfortable. Some of the others were having a hard time keeping their bra straps out of sight, and their tummies tucked in. The hostess was nice to her, but Michelle detected an air of condescension. Using Tonya as an excuse, she left early.

Cork-screwed

Mrs. T announced that she was closing from Christmas Eve through New Year's weekend. She said she hoped that it would not be an imposition to any of the families, but she was going to Texas to visit her daughter-in-law and grandson, now five. Her son's widow was getting remarried, and Mrs. Thornhill had received a special invitation to be part of the festivities.

It was, in fact, very much of a hassle for Michelle. She was looking forward to some downtime during the holidays, away from work, and without a child under her feet. The physicians were running only a skeleton crew between the red-letter days. Because of her babysitting situation, the supervisor gave Tonya's mother the entire time off.

Michelle was very familiar with depression and did not need an official diagnosis. She had the holiday blues again, and she was having a hard time snapping out of it. Since the doctors did not normally treat their personal RNs, she discussed it with Dr. Aiken. He prescribed a different drug from the one that Dr. Orlando had given her.

Granny Addie was hoping to see that shiny red sports car in her yard for Christmas. It was one thing to make that trek with a seven-month-old. It was something altogether different to be cooped up with a nineteen-month-old for thirteen straight hours each way. Michelle's modest Christmas bonus, along with daycare savings, was offset with missing a week's paycheck. Thus, she did not have any extra money lying around for travel.

On December 23, Cornfield gave Miss Bizzy Belle an extra-long and very tight hug. Then, she gave her a little Christmas present—her very own copy of *The Very Hungry Caterpillar*.

Michelle did not sleep well. It was the first time since Tonya was born that she had her daughter all to herself for a whole week. What could they do? It was the dead of winter. How might she amuse a toddler?

On Christmas Eve, Michelle took Tonya grocery shopping with her. Since the mother normally took care of errands while the daughter was at daycare, the two had not done this together in months.

The little girl flirted with every man that looked her way. Michelle could not get any man to take a second look at her. On the way to check out, the woman did something that she had never done before in her life. She put a bottle of wine in her buggy.

After Tonya was asleep, Michelle decided to pour herself a glass of Sin Infidel. When she finally got the foil off the top of the bottle, she had no idea how to remove the cork. She almost butchered her hand using a knife. Disgusted, she put the wine back in the refrigerator.

"I'm such a loser. I can't even get drunk on Christmas Eve."

Santa Claus was not nearly as popular when she was a little girl growing up on Sand Mountain as he had become. Tonya was too young to understand, anyway. On Christmas morning, Michelle made them breakfast. The toddler ate and then went to her room dragging Watt behind.

As the day got warmer, the mother bundled up Miss Bizzy Belle to take her for a walk. She barely knew the people next door, but they were leaving about the same time. After exchanging Christmas greetings, Michelle had a request. "I know this is going to sound crazy, but may I borrow a cork screw?"

Tonya did not seem to care what day of the week, month, or year it was. Putting her down for a nap, Michelle puzzled at how nothing seemed to perturb the child. After muddling through Christmas Day, the harried mom was exhausted.

Soon after her daughter was sleeping peacefully in the Christmas pajamas Granny Addie sent, Michelle decided to try her skills with the corkscrew. It was not a pretty picture since the cork was already mutilated. Finally, it popped, spraying some of the contents all over her.

"I was planning on drinking it, not wearing it." Trying to get herself in the right mood, she then added. "Oh well. No need to whine over spilled fruit of the vine."

Michelle was anything but a wine snob and had by no means perfected the art of sipping Sin. She did not even have any wine glasses. Drinking from a tea glass, she snorted, and some went through her nose. Why did it burn so much? This did not stop her, though. Before she turned the bottom up, she had a buzz. That did not stop her, either.

After she had downed the second glass and poured herself another, something suddenly made perfect sense to her. It was as clear as a Bellville bell. She should call the girl's father. She had his number somewhere.

Feeling no pain, the woman was on a mission. She'd done the hard part. It was now time for the man to step up to the plate. She started throwing books out of a box that had not yet been unpacked. The old phonebook with his number gem-clipped to the back cover . . . Where was it? Ah, there it is. She started rehearsing what she was going to say.

Michelle's eyes were having a little trouble focusing on the numerals. Just to make sure that she got it right, she said each digit aloud, and then she spun the dial with a little attitude.

Ah, the last number. "Ring, ring."

"I'm sorry, but the number you have reached is no longer in service."

That should have sobered her up, but it didn't.

Watt . . . thish ish M'shell.
Ish your turn.
Come git your presh-ish daughter.

In her zeal to relocate so that Walt could no longer find her, Michelle had lost track of his calendar. He was discharged back in the late summer and had left Columbus, Georgia. She no longer knew where he lived, or where he was employed, either.

Walt now hung his hat just a few hours straight down the road from her. She still would not have reached him at his residence that night even if she'd had his new number. He was spending Christmas with his "Cornfield" that he did not find until after he was grown.

Tonya's father was also only about thirty minutes away from Michelle's Granny Addie and Papa Doc. If she had accepted the invitation to spend the holidays with her grandparents, she might have run into him.

As Michelle tried to rouse herself the next morning, she became excruciatingly aware of three things. One was her head. It was pounding, unlike anything that she had ever experienced. Also, when she opened her eyes, she could not see a thing. The other was her right arm. She could not move it.

Her left arm was still mobile, so she lifted it slowly toward her face. Gradually, she slid Watt off to the side. Good. She was not blind. She looked over and saw Tonya sound asleep on her right arm, clutching the book that Cornfield had given her.

Walt had not gotten there yet.

That was the first time the little girl had crawled in bed with her mother since she had her very own room. What time was it? Eyes now beginning to focus, Michelle could see that it was a couple of minutes past ten.

Tonya must be drenched, or worse. What had the child done while her mother was sleeping it off?

As Michelle endeavored to right herself, the throbbing in her head intensified.

"Coffee!" "Coffee!" "Coffee!"

The night before was mostly a blur, but one thing was imprinted indelibly in her inebriated brain. Michelle remembered trying to call Walt. Did she get through? What did she say to him? Did she tell him where she was? Did she give him her phone number?

Suddenly, the silence was shattered. "Who turned the ringer volume up so high?" The hands of the woman with an enormous hangover went to her ears. "Was it Walt?"

She wanted to let the phone ring, but she had to stop the noise. She thought about lifting the receiver, and then quickly putting it back down. Yes . . . That is what she would do. As she took the phone off the hook, she heard a familiar voice. Granny Addie was saying something to Papa Doc while waiting for her granddaughter to answer.

Not trusting her voice, Michelle said a feeble, "Hello."

"Hello back to you. And a belated Merry Christmas. I tried to get you yesterday morning, but you must have been out. By the time I finally had a chance to call back last night, I guess you were already in bed. I hope the phone did not wake you."

"I didn't hear it. I must have been out like a light."

"Did Santa Claus come to see you and Tonya?"

"He dropped a couple of things off for her, but nothing for me. I guess I've been a bad girl."

"Oh, Michelle . . . You're always so hard on yourself."

Tonya's mother was understandably jumpy the rest of her Christmas vacation. Walt did not call back, and he never showed up. She made just one New Year's resolution that year—never again to get plastered.

Bright and early the first Monday morning in January 1971, Tonya ran to Cornfield. Other boys and girls were also arriving, so they had to wait a while to talk. Both had much to share.

The little black dress

Not long after Christmas, Joyce, one of Michelle's co-workers tried to fix her up with her twin brother, Royce. "He's divorced like you." Michelle had never indicated that she was divorced. Apparently, that was the presumption, and she did not correct it.

After quibbling for a few weeks, she agreed to go out with him on the Saturday night before Valentine's Day. Joyce was excited about getting to play Cupid.

Since Michelle wore uniforms to work, lounged around the house in sweats, and squeezed into jeans for grocery shopping, the selection of dress clothes in her closet was slim pickings at best. She still had the sun dress that she bought when she cavorted with the cop, but it was February. How she wished Granny Addie was with her to help pick out a new dress. Redheads and Valentine red do not go together very well.

Ultimately, Michelle settled on a "little black dress." Regardless of how the date played out, it would be nice to have it if she needed it again. Playing it safe, she asked if Royce could pick her up at Joyce's house. The sister of her date was excited, and she invited Michelle to come over early so she could help her get made up.

Mrs. Thornhill was delighted to have her own little valentine for a sleepover. Tonya ran to Cornfield waving her arms and fluttering her fingers. The little girl's mother had butterflies in her stomach.

Michelle felt better when Joyce told her that Royce was just as nervous as she was. He arrived about five minutes early, and his sister went downstairs to let him in. She hoped that his date would take his breath away when she slowly descended the steps. Michelle just wanted to get down safely without tripping in her heels.

Royce was not exactly tall, dark, and handsome, but she was no Miss America, either. At his sister's insistence, Royce brought a corsage and pinned it on his date. That was awkward. Both felt like seniors on the way to the prom.

When Royce saw the AMX, he asked Michelle if she preferred to go in her car. He was not sure she would be all that thrilled riding in a Ford Pinto, but she reassured him. "Oh, no. I want you to drive. I had a Falcon wagon before I got the X."

Even with a reservation, they waited almost a half hour before being seated. Small talk was teeny.

The nervous woman had trouble deciding what to order, but one thing she knew for sure. She was not going to ask for a glass of Sin Infidel.

Michelle was not looking forward to a report come Monday morning. Joyce surprised her. "I think Royce was smitten with you."

Royce might have been infatuated, but Michelle was not. She relented for a couple more dinner dates. Each time, he picked out the place and used a discount coupon. She turned him down when he wanted to go to D.C. while the cherry trees were in full blossom. The thought of things flowering made her depressed.

Winter was a little slow to loosen its grip. Around the first of March, big coats finally gave way to lighter jackets. It was not quite as much of a bother dressing Tonya each morning. It was about to get a little easier.

When Michelle went to pick her up one afternoon, Mrs. T announced that the little girl had a big surprise. Her mother did not notice at first until her daughter strutted a bit, and then bent over. Tonya was wearing training pants.

Mrs. T took pride in explaining how it came about. "She just about trained herself. She had been watching the older boys and girls, and then took matters into her own hands, so to speak. She has not had an accident all day. She might still need a diaper at night for a while, though."

Caught off guard, Michelle did not respond immediately, but Mrs. Thornhill had more to say. "When that girl sets her mind to something, she doesn't let anything get in her way. I know you must be very proud of her."

Seemingly unaffected by it all, Miss Bizzy Belle went fluttering off to find Watt. The three of them had to stop on the way home to pick up a pack of big girl panties.

Miss Bizzy Belle

On Good Friday, Mrs. Thornhill invited Michelle to bring Tonya to the Easter egg hunt at her church the next afternoon. Frowning, the girl's mother said that she felt a migraine coming on.

"If you can get her here, I'll take her. Better still . . . Let her spend the night, and she can go with me to church on Sunday."

Michelle complained that her daughter didn't have anything to wear.

"If you'll drop her off sometime in the morning, I'll find her an Easter bonnet. Don't worry about a basket, either, or boiling any eggs. We'll have time to get them colored before the egg hunt."

Tonya had been standing by taking it all in. Her puckered lips were no longer pouty once she heard her mother say, "Okay."

In 1971, Tonya's second birthday was two days after Mother's Day. It had been a year since Michelle had gotten the anniversary card from Walt. She thought less about Grover as time went by. On the other hand, it was hard not to think about the father of her child. How could she not? Little Waltene lived with her.

Mrs. Thornhill wished Michelle a Happy Mother's Day on Friday afternoon. She then asked if she could have a little birthday party on Tuesday. Mrs. T said that she always did something special for her children on their birthdays. Michelle had made no particular plans, so she agreed.

"Let me help with the expenses." Mrs. T said not a word in reply. She just shook her head and went to help Tonya gather up her things.

When the mother came to pick up her daughter on Tuesday, Tonya took her inside to see the birthday decorations. Butterflies were dangling from the ceiling.

Michelle told Mrs. T how nice the place looked and then asked her a question. "How did you know that she likes butterflies so much?" The woman had no idea how to answer. How could she not know?

Michelle decided that she could wait no longer to have "the" conversation with the daycare owner regarding Tonya's terminal age limit. She had asked around at work for recommendations and had even visited a couple of centers around Fairfax where she might enroll her daughter. While she would hate to be disconnected from Mrs. Thornhill, she was looking forward to less commute time. The response to her question was not what Michelle expected. Mrs. T said that she was going to make an exception for Tonya.

"If those folks at the licensing board say anything, I'll just tell them that she's my granddaughter. She might as well be, you know."

Tonya had seen several new babies come in, and a number of other kids leave during her two years. After she started talking, she learned most of their names. Regardless of where she fit in the pecking order, she always had rank. Little Miss Bizzy Belle knew she was Cornfield's favorite, and there was nothing that any of them could do about it.

How sweet is that!

After a year on her new job, Michelle had earned a week's vacation with pay. This time, she could not turn down Granny Addie's invitation. Combining her time off with both Memorial Day weekend and the next, she had ten days for the trip.

She took the X to get an oil transfusion and a new set of tires. The vehicle was paid for, but the young mother still had trouble bringing her finances under control. Her credit cards were not over the limit, but barely a dent had been made in the principal.

Tonya said goodbye to Cornfield, but she was unable to grasp how long it would be before she would see her again. While her mother did most of the packing, Miss Bizzy Belle took care of the only two things that really mattered—Watt and the buh-fly book.

Michelle put several other things in the car for Tonya to play with, but what the little girl enjoyed most was looking out the window. If she got sleepy, she put herself down for a nap in the backseat.

Tonya could not remember the earlier visit. Her mother prepared her for the greeting ritual, and the girl stood patiently by until it was over. Then, her great-grandmother took her in her arms.

"Oh, me. How you have grown." That was certainly not the last time Tonya would ever hear those words.

Papa Doc seemed a little feebler than he had on the previous visit. Just as before, it did not take long for Tonya to grab the old man's attention.

The subject of Michelle's parents was sure to come up soon. She preempted and asked how they were doing.

"Are you going to try to see them this time?" Granny Addie wanted to know. "I told them you were going to be here."

"I can't do that. They don't care a thing about me or their granddaughter. All they're interested in is protecting their precious image."

Granny hesitated a moment to let Michelle settle back down.

"That's not the way they tell it. They say you've turned your back on them and that you never call or send pictures. They say you're keeping their granddaughter from them."

Miss Bizzy Belle

The younger of the two redheads was about to show her true colors.

"How dare they try to turn this all back on me! They weighed me in their self-righteous balances, and they found me wanting. If they are waiting for me to crawl back to Sand Mountain, then . . ."

Michelle stalked off in a huff and a puff. Granny knew to let her be.

The women were sitting on the front porch late the next afternoon, chewing the fat, as her Pa Bell might say. Little Miss Bizzy Belle was flitting in and out.

The older redhead picked up where she had left off before. "I wish you would consider moving closer by. I could use some help with your grandpa. I know you have a good life where you are, but I think about all that your daughter is missing. She has no father in her life, and . . ."

Michelle flashed a stern look, signaling for her granny to go no further.

The woman just went off in another direction. Michelle did not want to go there, either.

"You know . . . It could make a difference with your folks if you were closer by. It might be easier for everyone to come around."

Michelle shot her granny another perturbed look. She did not like the inference that both sides shared equally in the responsibility.

Granny ignored the body language and went right on. "I guess what concerns me most is that my great-granddaughter is not getting to grow up here in the mountains."

Interrupting herself, and with a measure of reverence in her tone, Granny Addie pointed and exclaimed. "Would you just look at that?"

Tonya was standing out in the yard with her arm extended. A beautiful blue butterfly was sitting on her hand. The little girl then raised her arm and it fluttered away.

After almost a week of R & R, Michelle was getting antsy. She invited her granny to go shopping with her in Asheville.

"Why don't you go on alone? I really don't need anything, and I will take care of Tonya. Go off and enjoy yourself."

Michelle was not much of a shopper, but she coveted the chance to do some serious looking. Wearing uniforms to work, she had no style consciousness.

Walt Williamson had just closed out his first academic year at the Outer Banks State University. With some time off before the summer semester, he wanted to go see his Grandpa and Grandma King in Mason, Georgia. He packed up and headed to Ephesus, North Carolina first and would catch them on the way home.

Not too far out of Asheville, he topped a hill just in time to meet a red fastback as it whizzed by. "Somebody's sure in a hurry." It looked like an AMX, but it all happened so fast that he was not certain. It could have been a Camaro, but it was definitely not a Mustang because it did not have a pony in the grill. It might have been the same vehicle that he had seen a year or so back.

Whenever he came through during the summer months, Walt always stopped and took in the ferns along No Bidness Creek. It was not only an opportunity to stretch his legs, but also a chance to get recharged. There was just something about taking in the luscious green foliage that gave him grounding. As soon as he detected the musky smell of the cinnamon ferns, his spirits started reviving.

As he buckled up, he thought to himself. "You know . . . People pay good money to see things not nearly so beautiful as this." About a quarter of a mile down the highway, Walt saw an old man and a young girl holding hands coming down the drive of a little bungalow on the way to check the mail.

"How sweet is that!"

Mrs. T's and Miss Bizzy B's

Now the oldest kid at daycare, Tonya was Mrs. T's little helper. It delighted the child to bring Cornfield things when asked and to anticipate needs before being prompted. When a baby was crying, Tonya was often first on the scene.

Mrs. T beamed with pride when Miss Bizzy Belle gathered a group around her and "read" to them. One of her self-appointed tasks was to round up a toddler and inform him that a parent had come to pick him up. Tonya showed up one morning without Watt.

Mrs. Thornhill thought it was so cute when the girl referred to her as Mrs. T with the others. Only when addressing her directly did she call her Cornfield. Even then, she made sure no other children were in earshot. That was sacred terrain, and she did not want anyone else trampling on it.

The daycare owner wondered if she was guilty of breaking the child labor laws. The girl knew all the routines, and she never seemed to tire.

When she reprimanded kids, she always pointed her finger and reminded them. "Mrs. T says . . ." Or, "Mrs. T wants you to . . ."

Mrs. Thornhill supposed that maybe she should be paying Michelle, and not the other way around. She let out a big smile when she thought about changing the name of her business to "Mrs. T's and Miss Bizzy B's."

During Tonya's third year, Michelle still did not have much of a social life. She could never tell if men were flirting with her when she was taking their vitals, or if they were just being men. Did every guy think he was being original when he said that his blood pressure might be a little high because she was taking it? Did a man really think that he was being clever when he dipped the thermometer in his coffee thermos just to get a little extra attention?

About one afternoon a week, Michelle started meeting some friends for drinks after work. She usually went with Joyce. Tonya always had a change of clothes at Mrs. T's house in the event that happy hour ran a little late.

Mrs. Thornhill was worried about the girl's mother. She seemed to be losing a little pride in her appearance. The woman did not want to be nosy, but she asked Tonya some questions now and then. When asked if they ever had company, Tonya said that "Uncle Vinnie" came over to see her mom sometimes, and that she and Watt didn't like him much.

The pachyderm in the parlor

The Memorial Day weekend vacation was becoming a tradition. The little girl never ran out of questions about things along the way. Her mother often had a hard time coming up with the answers. Trying to deflect her was a useless maneuver.

The X had little regard for limits, so Michelle had to be cautious about speed traps. Having the badge number of a D.C. cop was of no use if she got snared out on the byways.

During the summer of 1972, Granny Addie cautioned Michelle that Papa Doc's memory was not what it once was. "He seems to be getting a little more senile every year."

The granddaughter nurse asked her granny if she knew anything about

Alzheimer's disease. She said that she had heard a little about it, but it didn't matter. Her husband was not going to see no doctor.

Would there ever be a time when no elephant was in the room? Michelle preferred not to have any further discussion about her family situation, but she knew that it was only a matter of time until the subject was certain to come up again. She was correct. Granny Addie was still trying to mediate a peaceful resolution. Her granny said she thought she might be making a little progress with Connie, but that Tolbert was a tough nut to crack.

The arbitrator was a little surprised by a comment Michelle made. She said that if her parents were going to be so disapproving, then it was better that her daughter never be subjected to them. She then became even more emphatic.

"I made some mistakes, but Tonya Willa Bell is not a mistake. I took precautions and still got pregnant. God don't make no junk. I could have made the most horrible mistake of my life by getting rid of her, but I didn't. God has forgiven me and has blessed me with a darling little girl. I can live with myself, whether or not my parents are ever in our lives."

Her granny paused a moment before giving her granddaughter something else to think about. "What about your other grandparents? They would love to see you." Michelle presumed that they stood with their son, but she really missed her Pa Bell.

"You might be surprised if you just showed up unannounced. You know . . . They're not getting any younger, either."

Michelle was torn. She decided to just ride out that way and see how she felt after she was in the area. Granny was invited to go along, but Sweet Adeline declined.

All the mother told her daughter was that they were going for a ride. Otherwise, the child would worry her half to death. Approaching Bellville, the three-year-old had fallen asleep in the backseat. Michelle was not ready to go back down the road where she once lived.

Something kept pulling her toward Pa Bell. As the old farmhouse came into sight, she could see the man sitting out under the shade tree where she had sat at his feet many hours. The driver was not sure if she turned the steering wheel, or if it turned itself. The X was going up the drive.

The change in the road sounds roused Tonya. She sprang up to make sure that she was not missing anything. Michelle switched off the engine.

"Well, kiddo, let's go face the music."

Miss Bizzy Belle

Buford Bell had no idea who had come into his yard. He made no move, knowing that whoever it was would soon make their business known. He squinted a bit when he saw the figure of a young woman with a child. That brought him up out of his chair. Michelle braced herself for Pa Bell to order them off his place.

The spry seventy-two-year-old man rather hopped, skipped, and jumped his way toward them with a big smile on his face. Michelle wished now that she had given Tonya some warning. Pa Bell lifted his granddaughter off the ground with a big bear hug.

He then turned his attention to the little girl who was taking it all in. He picked her up and held her out. "So this is my little Peanut."

Tonya looked at her mother and grinned. Michelle was amazed that no unfinished business needed tending, and no fences needed mending.

The white-haired man suggested that they go inside. "I know your Mama Myra wonders what the heck is going on out here."

Reconnecting with her Grandpa went far better than anything that Michelle could have imagined. The reunion with her father's mother did not go as well. A gigantic elephant was soon to raise its huge leg, and then put its foot down with a vengeance.

Mama Myra was busying herself in the kitchen as though unaware of the visitors, but she knew who they were. She feigned surprise when the trio entered the house. Pa Bell did not help the situation when he announced that the prodigal granddaughter had returned from the far country, and that she had brought a little Peanut back with her.

The stooping woman, who now looked older than her husband, gave Michelle a polite hug. She then turned her back on her great-granddaughter.

Pa Bell was exuberant. "I'll bet that child's hungry. This fine woman of mine baked a cake just this morning. I don't guess she can sing, 'If I'd known you were a'coming, I'd've baked you a cake.' She didn't know and baked it anyway."

That fine woman was not amused. She methodically put plates on the table. For the first time, she acknowledged the little girl. "Will she want a glass of milk?"

"Her name is Tonya. And yes, milk would be fine. I think I'll have some, too."

It was not just a cake, but one of Mama Myra's famous chocolate cakes. Michelle bragged on it. Her grandpa said he thought that he might have married the best cook in the world. All eyes went to Tonya with chocolate all over her face and milk tracing the outline of her lips. She smiled like a circus clown.

After no crumb went to waste, Michelle looked for a way to gracefully get out from under the gaze of her grandma. She asked Tonya if she wanted to go see her Pa Bell's tractor. Her daughter's eyes lit up and so did his. She crawled down out of her chair and scampered to him. He was a little slower getting out of his.

Michelle arose to join them, but her path was blocked. As the other two were going out the door, Mama Myra had her say.

"Where's that child's daddy? Was he not man enough to marry you?"

Michelle raised both hands to shoulder level, palms out. "Thank you for your concern, Mama Myra, but that is a subject we don't talk about."

"Huh. Your father needs to . . ."

Michelle bolted past her to join the others before she heard the end of the sentence. She caught up with them going down the back porch steps. The tractor started up with her daughter sitting in her great-grandpa's lap and both hands gripping the steering wheel. Michelle was not sure which of them was wearing the biggest smile. So much had changed since she was the one who used to sit in that seat.

Pa Bell was a whistler. Tonya was fascinated. She had never heard anybody make sounds like that before. On the way back to the house, she asked the man who had taken such an interest in her to teach her how. After several attempts, she just couldn't get the hang of it.

"Peanut. Keep practicing. The next time you come, I want to hear you whistle."

The grand man knew the visit must be kept short. He sensed that his granddaughter was getting antsy. "Let's go tell your grandma goodbye."

The old woman came out on the porch and handed Michelle about a quarter of the cake wrapped in foil. If anyone had wanted another piece right then, no knife would have been needed to cut it.

When Tonya rode in the front, she had to buckle up. Sometimes she needed a little help, and it was easier to get her situated from the door on the passenger side. As Michelle was walking around the vehicle after getting her fixed, she was thinking to herself. "I still have one connection with Walt if I ever really need to get in touch with him. I can always do what Pa Bell mentioned the last time I was here. I could go pay a visit to Walt's Grandpa King."

Once the driver was buckled in, she fired up the X.

Tonya looked over at her. "Mommy? Who is my daddy?"

Walt Williamson did not get to Ephesus between the spring and summer semesters. Instead, the university sent him to a conference at the Veterans Administration in Washington. He was no longer a part of the military, but he was not separated from it, either. As a counselor working with the irregular students on the GI Bill, the VA paid half his salary.

He could have flown, but he had never had his feet off the ground. This trip did not seem like a good time to be the first since it was not that long of a drive. He also preferred having his own car.

Walt found his work challenging, but not very rewarding. His own bent was that people needed to know who they were before embarking on a career. The students seemed more interested in securing their place in the rat race.

Exploring the Outer Banks area nourished his soul. So did the off-times when he could get back to the mountains. Still. Empty spaces were unfilled. When he stopped in Ferndale, he felt a connection with Mother Nature. He looked forward to the times when he could visit waterfalls, especially Canyon Creek Falls. More than ever, he knew that his being would not find its destiny while trying to stay afloat in a sea of human doers.

Walt was booked in a room not far from Walter Reed. He sat through the first boring session wondering why he was there. When he got back to the hotel, he decided to get Mary Lou out and introduce her to D.C. The Toyota was soon headed to his old duplex apartment. He had not made up his mind about what he was going to do if the X was in the drive.

When no vehicle was parked out front, Walt decided to go by the hospital. He was not sure if anyone would even remember him. Sure enough. His old commanding officer was long gone. So were his other close associates.

The former staff member took the elevator to the floor that Michelle had worked on. He paused at the spot where they had their first conversation. Gradually, he turned his head toward the nursing station. He still did not know what he was going to do if she was standing there. He did not see her. She might be in a patient's room, or even working elsewhere in the hospital.

Walt started toward the elevator but then turned back. At the station, he introduced himself. One career nurse about his age perked up. She remembered him immediately. "You're the one who took on President Johnson." She wanted to know what he had been up to. He had the feeling that he could have had a date while in town if he had wanted one.

Walt looked at his watch and made an excuse about needing to get back to the convention. Before he walked away, he asked about Michelle.

"She just up and quit a year or so ago and didn't tell anybody around here where she was going. I was a little miffed with her for not even saying goodbye. I heard later that she stayed somewhere in the area, and was working at a doctor's office. You two went out a few times, didn't you?"

A patient's light came on. As the nurse was trying to ascertain the need, Walt nodded and mouthed. "Thank you." As he was getting on the crowded elevator, she waved to get his attention. Trying to find a spot to stand, he did not see her. The nurse was going to ask him if he knew that Michelle had a little girl.

The gall of that woman

Michelle knew that Tonya might one day be curious about her father. Her mother just had no idea that she would have to start dealing with it when the child was barely three. So far, the girl did not seem to think anything about some of the other children being carted around by their daddies.

When she dropped Tonya off at daycare the first morning back from vacation, she told Mrs. Thornhill that she needed to talk to her about something. Not sure what Tonya might say, Mrs. T had to be on board. Miss Bizzy Belle was given an assignment on the other side of the basement so they could talk.

"How did you answer her?" Mrs. Thornhill wanted to know.

"I lied, of course, and told her that she didn't have a daddy."

Michelle said she was expecting a question about what the girl had obviously overheard that prompted her own. It didn't come. Would she ever get used to her daughter being so predictably unpredictable?

"Did the subject come back up?"

"I decided that I had better go ahead and preempt. I sat on the bedside with her that night, and I gave my baby her first lesson in the facts of life. I told her that I became a hungry caterpillar—a very hungry caterpillar. I ate and ate and ate. My tummy grew and grew and grew. And then one day, my little butterfly came out."

"What was her reaction?"

"She smiled, gave me a hug, and turned over to go to sleep."

Michelle summed it up. "That will be our strategy for now. I'm sure we'll have several more discussions about this in the future."

This conversation was not over. Mrs. Thornhill had something else to say.

"Michelle . . . I hope you know what you're doing. You asked me not to pry regarding Tonya's biological father, and until now I've done my best to respect your wishes. Since I don't know any details, I can't understand why you insist on carrying that burden alone. I have one very important question to ask you. Are you absolutely positive that this is the best thing for Tonya?"

Michelle raised her hands to waist level, palms out. "That's just the way it has to be."

"If she comes to me, I'll go along with that plan for now. But let me assure you of something." Mrs. T then punctuated what she was saying with her right index finger pointing upward and pulsating with each word. "I will not be party to anything that I feel is not in our child's best interest. Do you understand me?"

Not much was unpredictable about Mrs. Thornhill.

"Did she say 'our child'?" Michelle was fuming on the way home. "She's not 'our child.' She's 'my child'."

Those two little words were all it took to unleash the growing resentment that had been building inside for quite a while. Mrs. Thornhill had been overstepping her bounds for some time. Sure. She helped take a load off. But she was hired help. She was not family. The gall of that woman.

Michelle decided that maybe she should start looking around for somewhere else to leave Tonya. Several good possibilities were so much more convenient to where she lived and worked.

"No outsider is going to decide what is best for 'my child'." From the tone of Mrs. T's voice, Michelle feared that she might well go over her head.

She fumed. "'My child' is not going to go running to another woman with her questions. 'My child' is not going to love somebody else more than she loves me."

Michelle went as far as calling three other daycare centers. They all charged more than Mrs. T did. Each also maintained strict hours with harsh penalties for overages. All of them required monthly prepayments regardless of how many days the child was present. None provided after hours babysitting, and keeping a child overnight was simply out of the question.

Michelle might not have remembered the exact words that Papa Doc once said to her, but the gist of them stuck. "People don't change much until the aggravations start outweighing the benefits."

This mother still could not comprehend that Tonya was not just "her" child, and that had nothing to do with Mrs. Thornhill. The girl was her own little person. Predictably unpredictable was just for starters.

Michelle began having bouts of nausea, but they subsided after a few minutes. At least she had one assurance. She was definitely not pregnant. Working in health care sometimes gives an individual a head's up in personal diagnoses. Other times, it becomes a disadvantage.

After her little snit about Mrs. Thornhill's presumptive role in Tonya's life, the mother decided to do more things with her daughter. On Saturday afternoon, she took her to an amusement park. When Tonya was having difficulty climbing on the merry-go-round, Michelle hoisted her. Later that weekend when she started feeling pain in her upper right abdomen radiating into her shoulder blade, she naturally assumed that she had strained a muscle.

About mid-afternoon on Monday, Michelle mentioned how uncomfortable she was to the nursing supervisor. The chief nurse suggested that perhaps she should discuss it with Dr. Aiken. Because Michelle presumed that she already knew what was causing the problem, she decided to tough it out.

While shutting the office down for the evening, she was beginning to double over. Dr. Payne came to her side. When she described her other symptoms, he suspected that his nurse was having a gallbladder attack. If so, she needed to get to the hospital immediately.

Things are expedited when your boss is a physician. Dr. Payne called the hospital, told them to prepare for surgery just in case, and then drove her to the Emergency Room. While waiting for the surgeon to arrive, Michelle asked for a phone. She had to let Mrs. Thornhill know what was going on. Dialing the number, she was glad that she could still depend on the daycare owner even if the woman did get on her nerves.

Mrs. T said not to worry and that she would take care of Tonya. The little girl was standing beside her hearing one side of the conversation. "Do you want to talk to her and tell her what's going on?"

Michelle explained to her daughter that she was sick and in the hospital, and that she might be there for a couple of days. She was not expecting her daughter's response.

"Mommy? Please get well. I love you."

Michelle winced, but it was not from the pain in her right side. It was because of the ache in her heart. Her eyes welled up. She was ashamed of herself for how few times that she had ever said those words to Tonya. That she herself had grown up in a home where affection was not openly displayed was no excuse.

Her daughter loved her. She was not afraid to say those words out loud.

"I love you, too, baby."

Michelle did indeed require surgery. The ducts in her gallbladder were blocked. It was sobering when the doctor told her that she could have died if she had waited much longer to get to the hospital. She spoke with Tonya on the phone each of the three days before she was discharged. Every conversation ended the same way.

The unexpected retreat at Club Med gave Michelle some time to think. She had always presumed that love had to be earned. No matter what she did, she never truly believed that she measured up.

Michelle entered the hospital because of gallstones, but three little words had rocked her world. Tonya was the embodiment of everything that had been so elusive. She did not have to prove herself, or do anything to gain her daughter's acceptance and approval. Her little unwanted daughter loved her purely and unconditionally.

It was also the first time that Michelle had come face to face with her own mortality. What would happen to Tonya if something happened to her? The child's grandparents had nothing to do with her, and the great-grandparents were in no position to raise her.

A nurse entered the room and it interrupted Michelle's contemplation. As the shot started relieving the pain, the medication also began easing her mind.

After her mother's surgery, Tonya was especially helpful. Michelle started taking up more time with her daughter. She actually began feeling a bit like a mother, and not just the girl's guardian.

The next thing she did was run off Vinnie. Michelle knew that he was a low life when he wormed his way into hers. He always knew just the right things to say to get what he wanted. Then, he became a drain on her already stretched finances. The mother also knew that he was not a good influence on her child.

Still, she was mired, stuck. No pharmaceutical could cure that, but that did not stop Dr. Aiken from experimenting with different prescriptions. He was, after all, very good at practicing medicine.

Michelle kept telling herself that Walt would be so ashamed of her, and that he would think her unworthy of being the mother of his child. At the same time, she must be doing something right. Just look at how her little girl was turning out.

Rough spots

Michelle's co-worker, Joyce, was going through a rough spot. She said that her husband would be playing golf on Saturday and wondered if

Michelle could come over.

"I'll have to bring my little girl."

"No problem. My Melissa can pretend that she's babysitting. Would you believe she is already talking about doing that? And she's just ten. Girls grow up so fast these days."

Tonya disappeared with Melissa while the mothers were having tea. The only kind of tea Michelle knew anything about until she moved to the D.C. area came sweet and iced. She learned to drink it hot to be sociable but could just as easily do without it.

Before the conversation went elsewhere, she asked about Royce.

His twin sister replied, in a manner that Pa Bell might have called dripping with molasses. "He's in love. He finally found a woman just as 'nerdy' as he is." Michelle had never heard that term before, but she did not want to show her ignorance.

Joyce's countenance changed. "I'm so glad you came over. I really do need somebody to talk to. You're not from around here, and you know how to keep your mouth shut."

Michelle was flattered. She had never been anybody's confidant. "Your secrets are safe with me." Immediately, she thought how lame that sounded.

Joyce's husband, Marco La Russo, was a prominent banker. His friends called him Marc. The third generation Italian was as charming as he was handsome. Michelle had met him at the Christmas party. While Joyce did not have any solid evidence, she had suspected for some time that he was running around on her.

The old rumor mill had fired up again. It seemed that an attractive young teller lacking seniority had been promoted to branch manager. The bank was buzzing about a possible mutiny among some who had been passed over.

Conversation like that was new to Michelle. After feebly making a few suggestions, she soon figured out that the woman just wanted somebody to listen.

Joyce was through venting. "What about you? You've never talked much about yourself."

"Oh . . . There's not much to tell."

"Tonya is such a precious child. I know it must not be easy being a single mom."

"She's a handful sometimes, but I don't know what I'd do without her."

The next Saturday, Joyce got a babysitter for the younger girls, and the older gals went into Arlington on a shopping spree. Michelle was still playing it coy, but she was kind of enjoying having a chum.

Updates on the marital situation were not as juicy as the tabloids that she read, but she still looked forward to each new installment. Joyce said that she was thinking about having an affair just to get even. Michelle was not sure if she should take that comment seriously, or if her friend was simply gaining some satisfaction by just thinking about it.

Over a glass of wine one afternoon, Joyce did a little probing again. "I've never heard you mention Tonya's father. He does pay child support, doesn't he? When does he see her? She always seems to be with you on weekends."

Michelle tried to make sure that her body language was in sync with her words when she informed Joyce politely that this was something she would not talk about.

"You mean . . . You don't trust me after all the things I have confided in you?"

Michelle tried to reassure Joyce. "It's not just you, and it's not about trust. I don't even discuss this subject with my own family."

Pre-K

When Mrs. T first started reading to her, Tonya thought that she was just making up stories to go with the pictures. The gibberish underneath the illustrations meant nothing to her. One day, she asked Cornfield why they were there. The girl got her first lesson in the printed word.

Mrs. T purchased some alphabet cards and introduced a few at a time. Once Tonya was familiar with the sound of each letter, she began putting some of them together. They practiced sounding them out. Tonya took it from there.

A few days after her fourth birthday, Mrs. Thornhill put Michelle on the spot. "Would you consider letting Tonya go to the four-year-old kindergarten at my church next year? I'm afraid she is spending too much time with younger kids. I think it would do her good to be around children her own age."

"I don't know. With my schedule, I cannot get her there and back." Michelle should have known Mrs. Thornhill well enough by then to realize that the woman would have already thought about that.

"The church has a small bus that makes its rounds, and it will pick her up and drop her off right here." Seeing that Michelle was mulling it over, she tossed her another morsel.

"The kindergarten director is one of the most vivacious women that I've ever known. There's a waiting list every year because the school is so popular. That's why I'm bringing it up now. We need to get Tonya on the list if she has any chance of being accepted." Mrs. T did not mention that she was on the committee, which approved each new class.

"I'll think about it. Have you said anything to Tonya about this?"

"Of course not. I would not think of going over your head."

"Let me discuss it with her, then."

Mrs. Thornhill advised, with a straight face. "Don't wait too long."

Tonya was all for it, but Michelle had a few other questions. When she picked up her little girl the next day, she wanted to know more about the nature of the religious instruction. Michelle had some regrets that her daughter was not enrolled in Sunday School, but she did not want her child subjected to any kind of indoctrination.

Mrs. Thornhill suggested that they go together to visit the facilities. Because of their schedules, it had to be after-hours. Conveniently, the woman had a key to the Methodist Church.

As they did a walkthrough, Tonya checked things out in her own way. Mrs. Thornhill explained how the pupils were taught manners, respect, and character-building, but that nothing was crammed down their throats. She showed Michelle educational items posted on the walls and let her examine reading materials.

"They have a blessing before lunch, but Tonya is already used to that."

When Michelle inquired about the cost, Mrs. T made her an offer. She told her what the tuition was, but said that she would not charge anything for the time Tonya stayed with her before and after kindergarten.

Michelle objected. "I can't let you do that."

"But Tonya is so much help to me that I would consider it a fair trade."

Miss Bizzy Belle was standing by. The next words spoken gave her reason to smile.

Michelle started calling their annual trip to Ferndale, "the retreat." It was a time of renewal for sure. She was astounded by how much Tonya remembered from one year to the next. The girl recognized many things along the way, often reminding her mother of places they had stopped.

After the ritual greeting that the four-year-old always found fascinating, she had a very important announcement to make. She was starting kindergarten soon.

Michelle learned that her parents were taking courses for

recertification during the summer. "Did you tell them we were coming?" Granny just nodded in the affirmative. Apparently, nothing else needed putting into words.

Tonya kept bugging her mother about riding the tractor again. After a couple of days of rain, they made the two-hour drive to Bellville. Michelle regretted that she could not even show her daughter where she lived when she was a little girl.

Pa Bell said he wished they had come a week earlier. He had finally gone to Georgia to see old George King. "I'd a taken Peanut along with me."

Michelle wanted to ask some questions, but she did not want to mention anything that might raise suspicion. Her grandpa was really sharp. So was her daughter who was seemingly preoccupied with a coloring book and a box of crayons.

"How was Mr. King doing?"

"George is still at the top of his game. We sure did have fun shootin' the breeze. His missus was a bit poorly, though."

"Did he say anything about his daughter? Hadn't she been sick?"

Oops. How was she supposed to know that?

"I got to see her and her husband. They came over that afternoon. She seems to be recovered from her cancer. I almost got to see their son, too. He had been by the day before I got there."

Whew. Pa Bell didn't raise an eyebrow.

"What about Mr. King's grandson? What's his name?"

"I believe George called him Walt. Said he was working for some college up on the North Carolina coast. He sure does think a lot of that boy."

Glued to the television watching her programs, Mama Myra was polite but not over solicitous. Michelle thought to herself how much her own life was like a soap opera.

As they were leaving the yard, Tonya had a question of her own.

"Mommy? Do you know Walt?"

After a few days in Mason, Walt went back through Ephesus. On the way back to his post on the Carolina coast, he made his customary stop to view the ferns along No Bidness Creek. Two days earlier, after an outing to Canyon Creek Falls, he had stopped there with his former landlady, Mrs. Neumann.

While standing at the falls, he revisited the day when Hannah first took him there. He went back on his own again a couple of other times while working on his degree.

Walt's mind drifted in another direction. He recalled purchasing a sweatshirt with a picture of the falls on it. It soon became his favorite. He remembered wearing it the last night in D.C. before he told Michelle goodbye. As far as he knew, the shirt was the only thing that he left behind. Walt stood with spray from the falls tickling his face wondering whatever happened to it.

"Michelle probably just tossed it. Why would she hang onto anything that reminded her of me?"

During the summer, Cornfield taught Tonya how to tell time and read a calendar. September 4, the day after Labor Day, could not arrive soon enough. She was all excited about the first day of kindergarten. Mrs. Thornhill mentioned to Michelle several times that Tonya needed a new wardrobe.

Tonya's mother reminded Mrs. T that cute little girl clothes don't come cheap. "My grandma made most of my clothes, but she never taught me how to sew. Why does a garment with one-fourth the material cost as much as, or even more, than a blouse that fits me?"

Michelle wanted to do something special over the long holiday weekend, but she could think of nothing they could afford after buying school clothes for Tonya. On Saturday, mother and daughter went grocery shopping. On the way home, they picked up some barbecue. That southern delicacy was not as popular in Washington as it was where she grew up. Michelle was not sure if Tonya had ever tasted it. Not surprisingly, the girl loved it. At least, they celebrated Labor Day in somewhat of a traditional way.

On Tuesday morning, Tonya kept looking at the clock and rushing her mom. She did not want to be late on her first day of school. Backing out of the drive, Michelle thought to herself. "I should have taken her picture."

Cornfield told her mentee how nice she looked. Mrs. T had her camera waiting to take a photo of mother and daughter. After Michelle hurried on to work, Tonya got her picture taken again getting on the bus.

Cornfield was waiting when Miss Bizzy Belle came bounding through the basement door. "And how was my little butterfly's first day at kindergarten?" The rest of the kids were down for a nap so a lap was waiting.

Tonya told her all about her teacher, Ms. Joy. She remembered most of "the rules" that the teacher went over.

"Did you make any new friends?"

Mrs. T was not surprised when a boy's name came up first.

"Kermit sat right next to me. I called him 'Kermit the Frog,' and he tried to kiss me."

Cornfield did some envisioning as the girl droned on. "I wonder how many frogs that girl will have to kiss before she finds her Prince Charming."

K-9

Joyce wanted to go shopping again, but Michelle lamented that the cookie jar was empty. Her co-worker chided her. "Shopping is not about buying things, girlfriend."

Even so, Michelle did not remember being off with her when Joyce did not come home with an armload. She thought to herself how nice it must be not to worry about money.

Joyce pressed her. "Anyhow . . . I miss our chats. What do you say? I'll get a babysitter for Melissa and Tonya."

The last stop at the mall was at a pricey department store. Michelle was well aware that she was just along to keep her friend company. Everything was way out of her price range. After trying on a couple of party dresses, and not being able to make up her mind about either, Joyce indicated that she was ready to go. On the way out, she came to a screeching halt. Michelle was several strides behind her.

"That's you!" Joyce was holding out a colorful fall dress when Michelle got to her. "These could not be more your colors."

Michelle kept walking. "I can't afford anything in this store."

"At least try it on. That won't cost anything. It's on clearance and marked way down. You haven't bought a thing all day."

When Michelle took the garment off the hanger in the dressing room, she looked at the price for the first time. Even at 60 percent off, it was more expensive than anything that she had ever owned. When she stepped in front of the mirror, she had to admit that the dress looked good on her, though.

Joyce cheered her on. "Go ahead. Treat yourself. When you look good, you feel good."

Michelle was glad that her friend had walked away when the cashier asked if she had another credit card. She had inadvertently given her the one over the limit. She had mailed a payment for the other one she handed her, hoping that it had been posted. Apparently, it had.

As they drove out of the parking lot, Joyce looked over at her. "Don't you feel better already? Let me tell you what I'm going to do. I'll throw a little dinner party in a couple of weeks so you can show off your new threads. Do you have the right accessories for it?"

Michelle took a deep breath and exhaled. "I'll just have to make do. I can't afford anything else."

As they were approaching the La Russo residence, Michelle saw it first and was uneasy. The front door was closed and a note was tacked to it. Concern showed on both of their faces. Marc had posted it. The message said that he was at the hospital, and to get there as soon as possible. No mention was made of the daughters, and no one was at home.

Being a nurse only intensifies the anxiety when somebody in your family might be in trouble. Michelle forgot all about her dress and her friend, and she sped away in the X.

When she went charging into the ER, Tonya was sitting in the waiting area with the babysitter looking at pictures in a magazine.

"What happened?" She wanted to know.

About that time, Melissa's father came out of a phone booth.

"Where's Joyce?"

"She should be here any minute. I guess I took off and left her."

He assured Michelle that everything was going to be all right. "Melissa is getting some stitches put in. She had a run-in with a very bad dog."

After Joyce arrived, Marc tried to get the babysitter to tell the mothers what had happened. The girl was still so shaken that she asked Mr. La Russo to explain it.

As he understood it, the three were playing in the yard when a man walked by with his dog. Marc had seen the new resident walking his full-grown Rottweiler, always on a leash.

At that point, he turned to Michelle. "Please know that we don't blame Tonya for what happened."

Why did he say that? She looked at him puzzled.

He gestured to the babysitter and told her to correct him if he was wrong. "From what I have been told, the man allowed Tonya to pet the dog. When Melissa also wanted to pet it, the Rottweiler attacked her for no apparent reason. Before its owner could pull it away, it bit her on the cheek."

As her blood pressure began to rise, Joyce wanted to know if he had seen Melissa.

"Yes. The doctor doesn't think that there will be any permanent scarring, but he said it could be corrected with surgery if it became a concern."

She snarled. "We'll sue the man. Has anybody checked to see if the dog had its rabies shot?"

"Of course. That was one of the first things they did."

"Has the dog been put down yet?"

"Not that I'm aware of. I'm not sure that will be necessary."

"Oh, it will be necessary all right."

She looked down at Michelle, spitefully. "None of this would have happened if your daughter had left that dog alone."

Joyce stalked away. She went to the desk brandishing her nursing credentials. After identifying herself as Melissa's mother, she was ushered back. Michelle sat with Tonya.

After about thirty minutes, Joyce came through the doors. She was not as optimistic as her husband had been about the severity of Melissa's wounds. She also expressed concern for how the scarring might affect her daughter's looks. She then turned and started quizzing her husband.

"How did you find out? I thought you were playing golf today?"

Michelle looked up to see how he was going to answer that.

"I had to cancel my golf game. We have a bank audit coming up soon, and I had to go over the books while I had some peace and quiet. The hospital called me at the office."

"You didn't mention that to me this morning."

"I didn't think it mattered."

Joyce was seething. It mattered all right.

Michelle asked if there was anything that she could do. Joyce just shook her head, but Michelle was rather certain about what she was thinking.

Marc thanked them for staying and said they would be in touch. Michelle wondered if she was about to get hit with a lawsuit as well. She left without any mention of the dress.

Once buckled up, she turned to Tonya. "Are you okay?"

Without answering her question, she started explaining what really happened. "Mommy . . . That was such a nice man. Buddy is a really sweet dog. He only bit Melissa because she started pinching him and hitting him in the face. They are not going to punish her, are they?"

Michelle thought but did not say. "No. Their darling daughter was not the one who would be punished."

"Mommy?"

"Yes, baby?"

"I don't like Melissa. She's no fun to play with. Please don't make me go back there."

"Don't worry about that, my sweet little girl. You'll never have to go see them again."

Michelle remembered what she had thought earlier about being envious of those with no financial woes. She reached across the seat and took Tonya's hand. She would not trade places with Joyce La Russo for all the money in Marc's bank.

On Monday morning, Tonya told Cornfield that she had something really important to tell her after she got back from the church school. They usually had a little time to themselves before the other kids started waking up from their naps. A few days after she enrolled, Tonya started taking a seat at one of the tables for their gab sessions instead of sitting in the woman's lap.

After telling her about the dog incident, Tonya looked across. "Mrs. T? Why are some people mean?" It was the first time she had ever addressed her that way when she was speaking *to* her and not *about* her.

"I don't know the answer to that question." As they sat looking at each other, a little tear was streaming down both their cheeks. Miss Bizzy Belle was a big girl now, but one more lap hug was okay.

Joyce tried to ignore Michelle all Monday morning. Near lunchtime, her coworker blocked her path in the hall. "How's Melissa?"

"The swelling has not yet gone down. I'm afraid her wounds are going to get infected. And she keeps running to the mirror and crying."

"Joyce, I'm so sorry . . ."

Before she could finish what she was trying to say, the other office nurse pushed past her.

About mid-afternoon, the nursing supervisor stopped Michelle in the hall. "I think there's something of yours in my office."

When Michelle got home and took the dress out of the bag, she had already made up her mind to take it back. Then, she looked at her receipt. The clearance item was marked, "All sales final."

A few weeks later, the supervisor asked Michelle to stop by her office. She told her that she was retiring at the end of the month.

"I've already recommended you to take over my position. You're the most qualified, but Joyce wants it badly. As I'm sure you've noticed, she and Dr. McFeely have gotten kind of cozy. So, my opinion might not carry much weight."

Michelle waited for someone to approach her about the promotion. On the last day of the month, Joyce was sitting behind the supervisor's desk. A farewell dinner had been planned at a local restaurant to honor the retiring nurse. Despite the fact that there was never another word about Joyce's big bash, Michelle got to show off her pretty new outfit after all.

90 K

Mrs. Thornhill was keeping tabs on Miss Tonya. About a month into the school year, she asked for an update at church one Sunday. Ms. Joy said the little girl was different from any child that she had ever taught.

"How so?" Mrs. T wanted to know.

"It's a little hard to put your finger on. She's the most persistent little lass I think I've ever seen. At the same time, she's unusually thoughtful and helpful. It's not as though she's trying to get you to brag on her. In fact, she seems hardly affected by praise."

The teacher's expression changed. "Let me see if I can explain it another way. Tonya understands the rules perfectly. She even goes out of her way to help other kids stay in line. But, it's as if the rules don't always apply to her. She's not defiant, mind you. Tonya is the best team player I have. At the same time, I have a feeling that she always has her own little game going on the side. If I try to close ranks, she's already a step ahead of me. Does any of that make sense? Why are you laughing, Mrs. Thornhill?"

The X started making funny noises. After Michelle moved to Fairfax, she turned the care of the vehicle over to Joe's Garage. Each time she brought it around, Joe chided her for letting it go so long. With 90,000 miles on it, the engine needed a complete overhaul. He told her that it would have lasted much longer if she had taken better care of it. With numerous other bumps and bruises, the mechanic was not sure that the car was worth fixing.

He reminded her of what a shame that was. "A few years from now, the AMX will be a classic. It would have been worth far more than you paid for it."

Joe had taken an interest in Michelle. He especially enjoyed sporting with Tonya. He said as they were leaving one day. "If you ever get tired of that little girl, bring her over here. I think she'd make a top notch grease monkey."

Michelle did not know what to do. She did not have the money for the repairs, and she was afraid her credit was not good enough to buy another car. But there were no two ways about it. She had to have a way to go to work.

Joe made her an offer that she couldn't refuse. A black four-door Dodge Dart had been unclaimed for several months. The owner had apparently moved away. Since the vehicle had been abandoned, Joe could take possession of it and sell it for what he had in it. He said that he would trade even with Michelle and keep the AMX until he had time to restore it. He also told her that the Dart was a tough little cookie with many useful miles left in it if properly maintained.

"Hint." "Hint."

"Well, kiddo, off we go in the wild black wonder."

Before they even got back to the apartment, Tonya had already named the vehicle, "Black Bart the Dart." This new mode of transportation would take some getting used to. Already Michelle could tell that she was going to enjoy having more space, but she surely was going to miss her fun little driving machine.

TKO

Michelle had a new supervisor at work and things were touchy. Joyce handpicked a nurse to fill her old place and they were bosom buddies. As Dr. Payne's RN, Michelle did her job and kept her mouth shut. He seemed oblivious to any office politics, but she could not ignore the cold shoulder that she was getting.

Through Dr. Aiken's nurse, Michelle found out that Melissa's injuries were minimal. The stitches had been removed, and so far as she knew, the hysteria had subsided. She knew no details about what might have happened to the Rottweiler, or if any legal action had been taken.

The new nursing supervisor started becoming more and more critical of Michelle. When she brought the matter to her boss, Dr. Payne made it clear that he wanted no part of it. His stance was that the two nurses needed to work it out. He also reminded Michelle that he had hired her, and only he could fire her.

Clearly, Joyce's strategy was to make Michelle's life so miserable that she would leave on her own. The stress mounted. Michelle remembered a time when she had looked forward to going to work. But no more.

Miss Bizzy Belle

Then, she toughened herself. She had done nothing wrong, so why should she allow Joyce to push her around? Two could play that game. If she turned the tables, then maybe Joyce might leave, and she would get the position that should have been hers, to begin with.

Patients generally have no idea what goes on behind the scenes. That was certainly the case at the practice of Payne, Aiken, and McFeely.

One of the main reasons that Michelle was recommended for the supervisory position was because she was conscientious, and she consistently went the second mile. The nurse did not rush out at closing time like the others did. She stayed behind to tidy up, restock supplies, and to make sure that all of the instruments were properly sterilized and ready for the next day's use.

One morning while the new nurse was still in training, Michelle got to work a few minutes late. She had been delayed by an accident that shut down all lanes. Hurrying to get to her post, she was intercepted by Joyce. In front of the trainee, she was dressed down for her tardiness.

"We have strict hours here, and we don't make exceptions. In the future, leave early enough to allow for emergencies."

Michelle apologized and promised to abide by the posted time schedule. She walked out that afternoon with the rest of them, exactly on time. The next morning, Joyce was met with complaints, and a meeting was called.

"Things were not in order this morning. Who shirked their duty?"

Michelle was ready. "That's the responsibility of the supervisor. The rest of us have been instructed to follow precise time guidelines. At closing time, we have to leave."

If looks could kill, there would have been casualties.

Dr. Payne had already assured Michelle that Joyce could not fire her. She was not going to let the woman squeeze her out, either. If and when she left, it would be on her own terms. She had delivered a TKO in the war between Florence Nightingale's feuding fledglings.

K-7

About the time of the spring equinox, Dr. Aiken's nurse shared something with Michelle that grabbed her attention. She told her about a job that she had interviewed for but ultimately decided not to take. A large elementary school was creating a new school nurse position. Michelle wanted more information.

Mulling it over on her way home, one critical advantage to becoming a school nurse intrigued her. Once Tonya started public kindergarten, their hours would coincide, and she would not have to find a place for her daughter to stay after school.

The career nurse also liked the idea of having holidays and summers off. When she went by the school to check it out, she was surprised to find that her salary would actually be a little more than what she was already making. The benefits were better, too.

The process was all new to the administrators. They were not exactly sure what they were looking for. The position had been mandated by the school system, and the facilities were scheduled for retrofitting during the summer to accommodate a nurse on the premises. Since the new staff member was not to begin her duties until the next school year, the principal seemed in no hurry to fill the position.

Michelle did everything required and just had to sit tight. Mum was the word at work. She feared that if Joyce found out, she would put in a bad word. After months of playing cat and mouse, both were resigned that neither was going to get the best of the other. Michelle did not want to give Joyce any opening for a parting shot.

As the time for the Ferndale retreat was drawing nigh, and she had not heard from the school, Michelle was a little anxious. Concerned that the principal might try to get in touch with her while she was on vacation, she decided to pop into the office and leave Granny Addie's phone number.

Surprisingly, the receptionist acted as though she was expecting her. She buzzed Principal Carswell to let him know that Nurse Bell had come by. He came bounding out of his office with his hand extended.

"I'm so glad to see you. I was about to put a contract in the mail for you to look over and sign if you still want the job. Here . . . Just take it with you."

Michelle surmised that more effort had been put into Tonya's kindergarten graduation than into her own high school's. The five-year-olds wore caps and gowns. The sanctuary of the Methodist Church was filled. For once, the proud mother did not forget her camera. Mrs. Thornhill sat with her during the ceremony, and they shared her little packet of tissues.

Tonya was in no hurry to leave after the formalities were over. She was sporting with her pals, seemingly unaware that she might never see any of them again. Michelle was flabbergasted by how her daughter was right in the middle of everything.

After Ms. Joy had spoken personally to the other parents, she approached Michelle and Mrs. Thornhill. Tonya was busy taunting Kermit the Frog.

"I cannot begin to tell you what a remarkable daughter you have, Ms. Bell. But I'm sure you already know that. I just want to say that I know it, too. She has been so delightful."

When no one commented, she went on. "There are times I feel certain that she can read, but she does not want me to know it. I can hear her pretending to be reading to others gathered around her. Most kids have some familiar stories mostly memorized. When she thinks I'm not listening, every word is clear and distinct. If I walk up, she starts stumbling on some and asks me to say them."

No one was looking at Mrs. Thornhill who was beaming. The kindergarten teacher tried to sum it up.

"I'm not sure where she's headed. She's very good at drawing so perhaps she is going to be an artist. With her verbal skills, she could well become a writer. I do hope she will come back to see us. You can rest assured of something else, too. Whenever Tonya sets her mind to something, she will do it her way."

Michelle was a bit dumbfounded. It was a little hard to wrap her mind around what the kindergarten teacher was saying. She finally found her voice.

"Tonya has certainly enjoyed being in your class. She rushed me every morning so that we wouldn't be late. Make a deal with you. I won't believe half the things she told me that happened at kindergarten if you won't believe half of what she said happened at home."

"Deal."

Nobody noticed the little tear that was slowly making its way down Mrs. Thornhill's face.

Tonya told Ms. Joy goodbye for what she thought might be the last time. She knew that she would be seeing Mrs. T again, though. Mrs. Thornhill had agreed to keep her during the summer. Michelle had not told the woman about her new job, but it wasn't necessary. Tonya already had.

On the way home, Michelle thought back over the conversation with the teacher. "I'll bet Ms. Joy says something like that to all parents."

The extra room in Black Bart filled up fast as they loaded their belongings for the annual retreat. Mother and daughter really had outgrown the X. The new wheels came with a few other fringe benefits as well. It was not nearly as thirsty, and insurance rates were significantly lower. Black Bart also blended right into the scenery. Old Smokey could just keep on taking his nap.

Tonya carved out space in both the front and back seats. She brought along books to read and color. Mrs. Thornhill had taken her shopping and let her pick out several for the trip.

The concentrated time together during vacation was important to Michelle. It was not just hundreds of miles of togetherness, but it also marked critical milestones in their larger journey.

The mother took stock of how much her daughter had changed from year to year. She also got annual feedback from the child's great-grandparents.

Upon arrival in Ferndale, Tonya ran to Granny Addie. She started telling her all about Black Bart and the trip. The other two did not even think about their customary greeting ritual. When Tonya was in the mix, things had a way of getting rearranged.

K-1

On the first day back from vacation, Joyce pulled into the parking lot ahead of Michelle and waited for her at the door. "I hear you're leaving us." Whatever Nurse La Russo was or was not, she was well connected.

Michelle answered with a half-truth and then an out and out lie. "As a matter of fact, I have been offered another job, but I haven't decided what I'm going to do. I like working here so much that it is going to be hard to leave."

The supervisor responded, with a little subterfuge of her own. "Please let me know as soon as you make up your mind. You know that there's a nursing shortage around here, and I need time to find your replacement."

Michelle realized how naïve she had been to even imagine keeping her new job a secret. She still held the trump card, though. As prescribed by the physicians in the employees' handbook, she would follow the letter of the law and give only a two-week notice.

It annoyed Joyce that Michelle asked to leave early a couple of times without giving a reason, yet she was powerless to do anything about it. The soon-to-be school nurse had to go to the superintendent's office for conferences. Since the position was a pilot program for the entire system, they were figuring it out as they went along.

Michelle was required to begin two weeks earlier than the other teachers to get the infirmary set up. On July 18, Joyce found a letter of resignation on her desk. On August 1, 1974, the new school nurse reported for duty.

Miss Bizzy Belle

Dr. Payne insisted on giving Michelle a going away party. She wore her little black dress. If she had not purchased it while still getting rid of some baby fat, she would not have been able to get into it.

Tonya's last full day with Mrs. T was August 23. None of them knew what to expect when Michelle went to pick her up that Friday afternoon. She arrived before the other kids left. Tonya went by and told each goodbye, including the babies who had no idea what was going on.

She asserted emphatically to Cornfield. "I'm not telling you goodbye because I'll be back." Mrs. Thornhill was not so sure.

Part II: It's *Tone-yuh*

Okay

The excitement had been building all summer. Finally, the big day arrived. Mother and daughter were greeted at the front door on Tonya's first day of public kindergarten. The new student was assigned an escort to take her to her room. With a skip in her step and a strut in her stride, she pranced down the hall and never looked back.

Michelle's job description was a work in progress. Since teachers did not want the burden of managing their pupils' medications, it was the first responsibility handed over to the new school nurse.

Launching the position, Mr. Carswell asked her to make rounds, visiting a class or two each day. The principal thought this a good way for the kids to became familiar with the new nurse. The educators were also encouraged to invite Nurse Bell back to their classrooms to talk about health issues and simple first-aid measures.

The best way for the school nurse to keep track of the rooms that she visited was to start at the bottom and work her way up. About mid-morning, Mrs. Walters, Tonya's kindergarten teacher, told the class that they would soon have a visitor.

Tonya raised her hand. When the teacher asked what she wanted, she motioned for her to come to her and whispered in her ear. "Don't tell them she's my mother."

Michelle wondered how her daughter might react. She should have braced herself. After Mrs. Walters introduced the nurse and let her briefly describe why she was at the school, she asked if there were any questions. Most of the new kindergarteners had been still about as long as they could. One girl's hand went up.

Mrs. Walters recognized her. "Yes? Tanya?"

With no show of emotion, the kindergartener rose to her feet. "Mrs. Walters . . . My name is *Tone-yuh*."

Before the teacher had time to respond, the student turned her attention to their guest.

"Nurse Bell. I have a question. Why do you wear a hat?"

Their eyes met. *Tone-yuh* did not blink.

Mrs. Walters saw the query as a teaching opportunity. She asked the new faculty member to tell the boys and girls how she became a nurse, and yes, to explain the significance of her cap as well as her pin.

Michelle made her way to Tonya's room just before the final bell. The teacher said she was glad that she came by and apologized for getting Tonya's name wrong. She said when she printed the name tags that she had

Miss Bizzy Belle

inadvertently misspelled it.

"And then after I corrected it, I still mispronounced it. I'm glad she set me straight."

Her mother conceded. "She's good at that."

When they got to Black Bart, Michelle turned to her daughter. "Tonya? How did your first day go?"

"My name is *Tone-yuh*."

"Well . . . *Tone-yuh*. How did it go?"

"Mother . . . It was fine."

Michelle took in a quick sharp breath. That was the first time her daughter had ever called her anything other than "Mommy."

"What did you do?"

"Oh . . . Just some crazy stuff."

In bed that night unable to fall asleep, Michelle thought more about Tonya's day. Did the kindergarten teacher ask the kids about their families? She remembered how unnecessary that was when she started to school. Everybody already knew everyone. Might her daughter make note that most of them had both mothers and fathers? Nothing more had been said about Tonya's daddy since the incident when she was three. Now, she would be saying a form of his name every day.

After letting the kids get settled in on day one, it was time to get to work the next. "How many of you know the alphabet?" All hands went up.

"Who knows how to write your name?" It was unanimous again.

"I want you to show me. We're going to write our names on the board." Mrs. Walters had a twofold purpose. She could get her first glimpse of her students' performance levels. It would also help them to learn each other's names.

The teacher went first. She then started on the opposite side of the room from where Tonya was seated. "First . . . Say your name to the class. And then print it on the board."

She erased some of the efforts that were barely legible and wrote them herself. She then helped with a do-over.

When it became Tonya's turn, she bounced up, said not a word, and wrote, "Tonya Willa Bell" in perfect block letters. She turned to the class and said. "*Tone-yuh*, my name is *Tone-yuh*. I was named after a Russian heiress."

Nurse Bell was unable to visit classrooms on day two. One by one, teachers brought students to her with their medicine bottles. The school nurse took a Polaroid picture of each pupil, and then made out charts with their schedules. She then had to call each to the office over the intercom when his or her meds were due. How times had changed. If any kids took medicine when she was in school, she was not aware of it.

Michelle also had her first patient. A little girl with a big frown was brought to her. "What's the matter, dear?"

With her lips quivering a bit, the fourth grader explained. "I have a headache. Mommy always gives me Tylenol."

"Let's try something different this time. I think maybe all the blood has run to your toes. Lie down on the cot. Let's prop your feet up, and see what happens."

The nurse left the girl alone and went back to what she was doing. After about five minutes, she asked if she was feeling better. With a smile on her face, the girl sat up and was declared cured.

"Tell your mother to do this the next time you have a headache."

Michelle thought to herself as the fourth grader went through the infirmary door. "I wish all my headaches would go away that easily."

Tonya came into the kitchen one evening, with ponder on her face.
"Mother? Why don't I have a father?"

Michelle answered her question with a question. "Why do you ask?"

Holding up a book, the girl set forth her case. "In this story, there's a Papa Bear, a Momma Bear, and a Baby Bear."

While Momma Bear was trying to figure out which way to go, Baby Bear raised the stakes. "Most of my friends have mothers and fathers." She asked again. "Why don't I have a father?"

Michelle forgot all about the numerous things that she had rehearsed.

"God didn't make us all alike. He created some large families and some small families. Lots of parents have several kids, and others have only one. Some homes have both fathers and mothers, and other children have only one parent. Did you know that a few boys and girls have only a daddy?"

Whew! That seemed to satisfy her, at least for now.

She thought as Tonya walked away. "Yeah, right, Michelle. Blame it on God. Doesn't everybody do that?"

Nurse Bell found a flier in her box one morning about a month after the start of school. The state was exploring the possibility of organizing a School Nurse Association. Principal Carswell had circled the date and penciled in that he thought Michelle should go. According to the school calendar, the meeting in Richmond coincided with two in-service days for teachers in October. When Mrs. T agreed to keep Miss Bizzy Belle, the school nurse started making plans to attend.

Tonya was far more excited than her mother was. She really missed Cornfield. Michelle dropped her off after classes on Wednesday in order to get an early start the next morning.

After the other kids had all been picked up, the old friends went upstairs. Mrs. T wanted to know everything about kindergarten. As she was tucking the girl in that night, Tonya patted the side of the bed. Mrs. T took a seat.

The girl looked up at her. "Mrs. T? Do you have a father?"

"I had one, but he died several years ago."

"Do you have a mother?"

"I did. But she's no longer with me, either."

"Mother says that some kids only have a father, and others have only a mother. Is that true?"

"Tonya? What do you think?"

"I think everybody has a father and a mother. Mrs. T? Do you know who my daddy is?"

"No . . . I do not. Your mother has never told me."

"Did she say anything about him?"

"All she would tell me was that he didn't know anything about you."

"Thank you, Cornfield."

"Sweet dreams, my dear child."

In an evaluation conference before the Christmas break, Mr. Carswell told Michelle that she almost did not get the job. The central office preferred a nurse with a college degree. He said that the selection boiled down to her and a recent grad who had earned her bachelor's.

"I persuaded the superintendent to go with you because I knew that your experience far outweighed those extra days in the classroom. First, Walter Reed, and then working with that bunch over at the doctors' building—you can't be much more experienced than that."

The principal then gave Michelle some advice. "If you want to keep this job, or even stay in education, let me encourage you to go back and get your degree. The nursing schools near here have curricula designed for first-time students, those with associate degrees, and for ones like you with a professional diploma. They can help you move up to the next rung or even all the way up to a doctorate. They have both night classes and a full summer schedule to accommodate working nurses."

Nurse Bell reminded him that she couldn't take night classes because of her daughter.

"What about summer school? You might be able to get your degree in about three semesters."

When Michelle was explaining all of that on the phone, Granny Addie had another suggestion. "Why don't you and Tonya spend the next few summers with us? I'm sure you can get the same thing at Ephesus State."

Michelle sent for the admission forms, filled them out, and returned them. She requested that a transcript be forwarded from her nursing school. Only one thing was pending. The department required a personal interview before full acceptance into the program.

After taking Black Bart to Joe's Garage for full service, mother and daughter headed to Ferndale during the spring break. Michelle had a favorable impression of the university in general, and of the Nursing Department in particular. She was given her letter of acceptance before she left the campus.

Papa Doc was slipping away. At times, he seemed to recognize Michelle, and at others, he thought she was her mother. As they were about to leave, Granny Addie held Tonya especially tight and told her how she was counting the days until school was out.

Not too far out of Ferndale, two vehicles met on the highway as though ships passing in the night. Someone else had slipped away. Walt Williamson was on the way to bury his beloved friend, Mrs. Pauline Neumann. At the conclusion of the service, he learned that he owned a home in Ephesus, North Carolina.

More than anything, kindergarten was just fun for Tonya. Fun did not always have the same meaning for her that it did for other children. Opportunity never had to knock twice, either.

Mrs. Walters admitted to one of her associates that she was more than a little concerned after the girl's drama about her name. With her mother working at the school, she was also afraid that Nurse Bell might be one of those parents from hell. She admitted that things had worked out well.

What Tonya was proudest of was that she went all the way through the year without her teacher ever discovering how well she could read. She did not care as much for Mrs. Walters as she had for Ms. Joy, but that was okay. The six-year-old was moving up to real school.

Black Bart was loaded for bear and headed for North Carolina. If Michelle still owned the X, she would have needed a Me-Haul. Mother and daughter were not just going on vacation. They had packed for the summer.

Miss Bizzy Belle

Michelle was more than a bit apprehensive about returning to the classroom. She took some comfort in the realization that she would be competing with others her age. Since she had received college credit for much of her work, the nursing student could complete the requirements for a degree in three summers.

The Bakers' bungalow only had three bedrooms on the main floor. Papa Doc had moved into one of them some time back because he said Adeline snored. She claimed it was the other way around. Tonya decided after the first night that both were right.

Years earlier, Michelle's grandparents had installed a disappearing stairwell to the attic. Another unfinished bedroom was set up for the overflow when families visited. Grandchildren fought over it. Tonya had never been up there.

Rather than sleep in her mother's room, she claimed it. It got a little hot during the day, but it cooled off nicely at night with the window open. The view overlooked the back of the property, and mountains were visible in all directions. If Tonya was not sitting on the top of the world, she was looking out at it.

With the commute, lengthy classes, and clinical work, Michelle was gone much of the day. Nights were spent in her room pouring over her work. She had always been a good student, and that was not going to change. It occurred to her that she was working on a degree at the same school where her parents met and graduated. She had no clue that the father of her child also got his master's degree at the same institution.

Tonya was left alone with her great-grandparents. Granny Addie was concerned that the little girl might become bored. The first week, she planned several activities. One outing took in Canyon Creek Falls. Granny Addie wanted to know whatever happened to Watt.

"I don't take him with me everywhere now. But when I make my bed, I fold him and put him on top of the pillow. When I'm trying to figure something out, I still talk to him."

Tonya helped squeeze lemons one afternoon while Papa Doc was taking a nap. The girls were soon sitting and sipping lemonade on the veranda like grown folks. Out of the blue, Tonya asked Granny Addie a question. "Are my grandparents in Heaven?"

Michelle had not mentioned Tonya's inquisitiveness about her ancestry, so Granny did not know quite how to answer. Needing more information while trying to figure out how to respond, she probed further. "Has Michelle not discussed that with you?"

"Mother said that God didn't make everybody alike. She told me that some people only have a mother or a father, like me. I asked Mrs. T what she thought about that. Then, I asked her if she had a mother and a daddy.

She told me that both of her parents are dead. Are my mother's parents dead?"

"How did Mrs. T answer you when you wanted to know what she believed about a kid having only one parent?"

"She asked me what I thought."

"And what do you think about it?"

"I think everybody has both a father and a mother. Do you know who my daddy is?"

"Let me put your mind at ease. I don't know who your daddy is. But I'm not sure I should be talking to you about this without your mother present."

"She won't talk to me about it."

"Let me discuss it with her."

"Okay."

Walt Williamson was weary when he took a break at Ferndale. He was struggling with his job. Still grieving the death of Mrs. Neumann, the bequest of her house had, nevertheless, given him some renewed hope. Walt was not cut out to idle his life away amongst pretentious people always posturing for advantageous positions but refusing to take ownership of their lives.

As the musky aroma invaded his olfactory receptors, he recalled just weeks earlier standing on that very spot with Mrs. Neumann. This was his first visit back since her death. Regrettably, he could not stay long this trip, but he would be moving from his basement apartment to the upstairs.

Once back on the road for the last leg of his emotion-wrought journey, he looked over at the house where he once saw an old man and a toddler on the way to the mailbox. A woman and a little girl were sitting on the front porch. With a pitcher between them, he imagined that they were enjoying fresh squeezed lemonade. He wondered if it might be the same child. He did some calculating and decided that she was now just about that age.

His own little girl would have been about that old, too. He had thought about telling Mrs. Neumann about Michelle, but he did not want to trouble her. That was but another burden that he had to bear alone.

In the building that housed the Nursing Department, the Psychology Department was on the left, and Guidance and Counseling was on the right of the ground floor. An elevator operated between the two wings.

Miss Bizzy Belle

As Michelle was coming into the building one morning, the elevator door was closing. After pushing the button, she glanced casually to her right and let out a little shriek. Inside the glass window talking to the receptionist stood Walt Williamson in the flesh. That was the first time that she had laid eyes on him since the day he left. What in the world was he doing there?

Michelle was in no man's land. Class time was only minutes away. She could not go back out and watch for him to leave. If she took the stairs, she had to walk straight toward Walt to get to the door. If she turned her back toward him, there was no way to shroud her distinctive red hair.

Why was the elevator taking so long? As a few others started gathering, she positioned herself so that a taller male student shielded her from Walt's view. About four lifetimes later, the door finally opened. Michelle rushed in, pushed number six, and stepped to the back. She breathed a big sigh of relief as the door started closing.

Abruptly, it reopened. Another passenger saw someone rushing to get on and held the elevator. Another exhalation. It was a man, but it was not Walt.

Had he found her? Was he just waiting downstairs until she got to school? If so, he was not keeping a close eye on the elevator. Was he applying for a job? Maybe he was enrolling to work on another degree.

Michelle had a hard time concentrating on her work. When the class broke for lunch, she held back and then ran for the elevator when it was about full. If Walt was still around, maybe she could find safety in numbers. He was gone.

Every day for the rest of the summer session, she approached the building cautiously. Mercifully, she saw nothing else of the father of her child. She wanted so much to go inside that door and ask some questions. At the same time, she was afraid that she might blow her cover.

It was not easy keeping a lid on the past, a latch on the present, and a lock on the future. Life was about to get even more complicated because her sly daughter was on the prowl.

Michelle saw nothing okay about her granny talking to Tonya behind her back. Granny Addie asked in her own defense. "What was I to do? She brought it up. If you'll get down off your high horse, I think you'll see that I handled it just about as well as I could have."

"I'm sorry, Granny. That was wrong of me to snap at you. Maybe I should have better prepared you because Tonya isn't going to let this go. I don't know what to do. I don't know what to say."

Granny weighed in. "You've told me that her daddy was none of my business. I don't like it, but I have respected your wishes. Now, she wants to know about your parents. One of them is my daughter, so now it *is* my business. Michelle? What are we going to tell her?"

"I don't know Granny. I just don't know." As she went to her room to study, Michelle wondered if maybe spending the summer in Ferndale was not such a good idea after all.

Tonya had more questions but they were not as disconcerting. She wanted to know when she was going to ride the tractor again. Michelle placed a call to Pa Bell to see when they could head out that way.

"Pack little Peanut's bag when you come. Let her stay with us a few days. It ain't like she's gonna put us in the poor house or anything." Then he chuckled. "We're already in it."

"I don't know. That girl is a handful. Are you sure you're up to it?"

"I didn't ruin you, and I did just about everything I could think of to spoil you rotten."

"Let me talk to her about it. Either way, we'll see you Sunday."

"Come on in time to go to church with us."

"Pa Bell . . . I can't . . . I just can't."

"Get here by lunchtime, then."

How could this get more complicated? Granny needed a rest. That much was for sure. The seventy-four-year-old woman was not used to having a six-year-old girl under her feet. Furthermore, Papa Doc was not his old self, and he no longer took up time with Tonya.

If she let her daughter stay a few days with her other great-grandparents, what questions might she ask them? She trusted Pa Bell up to a point, but she was not at all sure about Mama Myra.

Pa Bell might roll up his sleeves and fix things with her parents. He was the only one with the gumption to do so. There was one big obstacle in his way, though. Tonya's granddaddy was also Mama Myra's son. At least her grandpa did not think that Michelle was "ruined," or if so, he didn't do it.

Not surprisingly, Tonya was all for staying a few days. She lay in bed thinking about the visit. She would not only be the apple of the old man's eye, but she also saw the old woman as an interesting challenge. What would her strategy be? She could get under her skin. That would be too easy. Should she try to charm her? That would take some doing. The imaginative girl mentioned her little game playing on the side to no one, not even Granny Addie. If she had, Granny might have put still more ideas in her head.

KO

Buford Bell greeted his granddaughter and great-granddaughter as they came in the back door. "There's my Peanut. And I'm so glad to see she's toting a bag."

As they were taking the things to her room, he asked Tonya something. "Do you know what I used to call your mother?"

Michelle pleaded with him. "No . . . Pa Bell . . . Don't go there."

"Why, 'Copper Head.' I never knew you were sensitive about your name."

Tonya laughed.

"I think Elmyra has dinner about ready, and I'm hongry."

Michelle consented to stay through lunch, but after gobbling down a few bites, she pushed away from the table. "Keep your seats. I'm just going to slip out, and get back to work."

Tonya hollered to her as she went out the door. "Bye, Copper Head."

Pa Bell lamented that Michelle had to leave before dessert. "Elmyra made a nanner puddin with calf slobber all over it. I want some coffee with mine. What about you, Peanut?"

Tonya turned up her nose. As she got up to start the coffee, Mama Myra made a face, too, but nobody saw it.

She might have been out of school for the summer, but Tonya had assigned herself some homework. After mulling it over, she decided that the best way to win Mama Myra over was to kill her with kindness. For starters, she would be a model citizen. That began with helping clean off the table. The girl was careful not to break anything. The woman was a bit puzzled.

She then said that she would wash the dishes. That caught the old woman even more off guard. "Do you have a stool I can stand on?"

"Oh, that's all right. I can wash them."

"May I dry them for you?"

"You go on and entertain your grandpa." Tonya noticed a softening in her tone.

Round One: Tonya.

"Peanut? What'cha wanna do first? Pick cotton, pull corn, bale hay, dig sweet taters, or slop the hogs?"

"You know what I want to do first, and it's none of those."

"I think the battery's dead on the tractor, and it may be out of gas. There's only one way to find out. But first, you'll have to whistle for me."

Tonya puckered her lips. Nothing but air came out.

As she kept trying, Pa Bell said to her. "I taught your ma how to whistle."

Tonya stopped the hissing sounds long enough to say that she never heard her.

"What a shame. Here . . . Let me show you again."

The little girl's eyes glistened as she made her first whistling sounds.

"Would you look at that?" The old Allis-Chalmers began chugging on the first pull of the starter.

"Think you can handle it by yourself?"

"I think so."

Pa Bell slid off and Tonya took the tractor round and round the yard. As he climbed back on the seat with her, he said in her ear. "I'll have you plowing by next spring."

As they headed back to the house, the girl made a suggestion. "Can we pick some flowers and take them to Mama Myra?"

"I think that's a lovely idea. The old girl could use some cheering up."

Tonya had the old man wrapped around her little finger. "I want to give them to her."

There were only a few flowers to pick from. The jonquils were long gone. A few daisies were in their glory, and the zinnias and marigolds were just beginning to bloom.

When Miss Bizzy Belle strolled into the living room where Mama Myra was stretched out on the couch, she proudly extended her handful of flowers.

"Why did you pick those? I was letting them grow to put on the communion table at church next Sunday."

Round Two: Mama Myra.

As the three were gathered around the supper table for leftovers, Tonya turned to her great-grandpa. "Has she always been this good a cook?"

"Why, Peanut. I can't remember when she was not a good cook. If she did poorly when we first got hitched, I guess I was just too much in love to notice."

Then, she turned the other direction. "Mama Myra? Do you also sew? Did you make your children's clothes when they were growing up?"

The old woman was flattered. "I've done a few stitches in my time, but I don't do much anymore. I made some of your mother's clothes."

Her husband told her not to be modest. "Elmyra . . . You know you were the best seamstress in the county. Tell Tonya how many ribbons you won at the fair."

"I think there were about twenty-three."

Tonya's eyes lit up. "Will you show them to me sometime?"

Round Three: Tonya.

The girl pushed the envelope a little closer to the edge. "I'll bet it was fun growing up in a home with parents like you. How many children did you have?"

The woman frowned, but Pa Bell went right along. "We had three wonderful children."

Tonya made her calculated move. "Are all of them still alive?"

The old woman just glared at her. Pa Bell knew that it was best to keep quiet.

Round Four: Mama Myra.

"I knew the little brat was up to something, trying to smooth talk me and such. She's been picking us to see what she can find out about her grandparents. If her mother would just do the right thing, then she could see them."

"Now, Elmyra. Don't be so hard on Tonya. She has a right to know some things. I'm sure Michelle don't know what to tell her. I'm a good mind to load her up while she's here and go pay Tolbert and Connie a visit. Just look at what they're missing not knowing their only grandchild."

"Buford Bell . . . You'll do no such thing. Michelle sinned against Heaven and Earth. She tarnished her family name. Her father raised her to be a fine Christian woman, and she has disgraced him. She turned her back on the church that nurtured and succored her. She's the one who must make amends. I've seen nothing repentant in her."

"Let he that's without sin cast the first stone."

Round Five: Pa Bell.

Buford Bell reached for his wife's hand as they crawled into bed. She pulled away from him in a snit.

Round Six: KO

Hairy situations

Tonya was getting excited about starting first grade. She got to stay with Mrs. T while her mother was in pre-planning. The daycare owner refused any pay. She said that she would take it out in trade. Mrs. Thornhill confessed that she did not know how she had been getting along without her helper. Tonya was showing up just in time to help break in her own new class.

Mrs. T was understandably inquisitive about the summer, but she waited for Tonya to come to her. The first day or two, she said little. One night at the supper table, the girl just blurted out. "I still don't know if my grandparents are dead or alive." She then explained to Mrs. T what little she had found out with her prodding and probing.

"They can't shut me out forever like I don't matter. Somebody's going to let their guard down someday."

The look that then took over Tonya's face was one of the things that Mrs. T missed the most. "At least, I had fun messing with Mama Myra."

On the first day of school, Michelle made a suggestion. "How about I walk you to your room?" In response, she got a patented *Tone-yuh* look.

"Mother . . . I know where my classroom is. I can get there by myself."

On the way home, Michelle was inquisitive. "Well, kiddo, how did it go?"

"I like Mrs. Berger. I think we can be friends. I'm not sure about Mrs. Harbaugh, though." She was referring to the teaching assistant.

"Why do you say that?"

"I guess I was not paying attention when Mrs. Berger introduced her. I called her Mrs. Hair Ball."

Michelle rolled her eyes. "You did what?"

"She does wear her hair up on top of her head in a ball."

An encore of the eyes.

The next day while the first graders were practicing writing numbers, the assistant pulled a chair alongside Tonya. She talked in hushed tones so that nobody else could hear.

"Yesterday, I thought it was really funny when you called me Mrs. Hair Ball." Cradling the hair bun with her hands, she went on. "And it sort of fits, doesn't it?" They shared a smile.

She then got serious. "Tonya . . . You need to be more careful about what you say to people. Some folks might get their feelings hurt."

"I know that Mrs. Hair Ball."

The first day of school when the teachers were being introduced was by no means the only time that Tonya was not paying attention during first grade. Mrs. Berger mentioned it to her assistant one day. "Sometimes, she's the best student I have, and at others, she's my worst." If Tonya had overheard that conversation, she would have smiled.

When Mrs. Harbaugh told the teacher what Tonya had called her, they both had a good laugh. "As far as I know, that's her own little thing. None of the other kids have called me Mrs. Hair Ball." Mrs. Berger said that she was not sure if she wanted to know what Tonya called her. Mrs. Booger was right.

Miss Bizzy Belle

It was nearly impossible to keep hiding her reading skills. Sometimes, she just could not help herself. When some kid was showing out, she coolly showed him up and then went back to sandbagging. Mrs. Berger could not get a fix on her. Every time she thought that she had Tonya pegged, the first grader scrambled the board.

Arithmetic was different from reading. Tonya obviously knew her numbers and how to count, but she had never thought much about how numerals had additional uses like letters did. During math, was about the only time that both sides of her brain were not fully engaged at the same time.

Nurse Bell found that her workload had increased considerably over the summer. She ran out of film for the Polaroid before the end of the third day. Teachers kept telling her how grateful they were that they did not have to deal with the bumps and bruises on the playground. They no longer had to make the call concerning sending a puny child home. The faculty members were particularly relieved that they did not have to keep up with medications.

It felt good to know that she was appreciated by the staff, but that was not always the case with parents. A few became irate because of the inconvenience of making arrangements for ill offspring. Some kids were sent to school running fevers. Viruses spread because others did not keep their children home when they had obvious symptoms.

It was not too early to start thinking about the next summer. Michelle was not sure she could endure a rerun of the drama that she had just been through. She had anticipated questions from Tonya about her grandparents. Not in a million years would she have imagined seeing Walt. While she still felt a tad vulnerable in the greater D.C. area, what place could be safer than the mountains of North Carolina?

The nursing student decided to make contact with a local university and see about transferring. She knew that she could count on Mrs. T to take care of Tonya.

Michelle went by the one most convenient to Mrs. T's and started jumping through their hoops. She did not hear back until late February of the next year. She had been accepted, but some of her work would not transfer. It was almost like starting over again.

Michelle went by to appeal, but she found out how difficult it was to transfer credits when course descriptions were not worded exactly alike. The dean of the nursing school made a couple of adjustments, but it made little difference. If she was going to stay on her degree track, going back to

Ephesus State made the most sense.

One little item of business stood right smack in the middle of her path. It was worth the effort of a trip back to North Carolina during spring holidays to try to resolve it. She gave Tonya the choice of going with her or staying with Mrs. Thornhill.

Once the girl made up her mind, she called Mrs. T while her mother was in the shower. "Cornfield . . . I don't want you to feel bad, or anything, because I really did want to stay with you. But I'm going with Mother just in case I overhear something when nobody knows that I'm listening."

The first grader had already spent a couple of faculty work days with Mrs. T. When she told her what she called her teachers, Mrs. T shook her head, but not in a disapproving manner.

"Oh, Tonya. You're just too much." They both snickered.

After the long haul, Michelle went to the university admissions office and picked up the latest college catalog. She found a park bench where she scrolled through the list of faculty and staff. Three Williamsons were listed, but not one had a first name that started with "W."

The next move was tricky, but she had to risk it. Dressed in a nursing uniform to make herself look more professional, Michelle made her way across the campus, and then straightway entered the Office of Guidance and Counseling. When the receptionist realized that she was standing at the counter, she turned from what she was doing. Michelle stated her business.

"I'm trying to locate an old friend of mine from back home. I thought I saw him in here once, but I was late for class. His last name is Williamson. Do you have any graduate students currently enrolled by that name?"

"No, ma'am. I know all of the grad students, and there's not a Williamson in the bunch."

"Thank you. I must have mistaken him for someone else." It never occurred to Michelle to ask if there were any alumni by that name.

Certain it was Walt that she had seen, she must roll the dice and take her chances. The odds had just gone up considerably in her favor that he would not be back in Ephesus. She was right but for the wrong reason. At the university where Walt was employed, he did not have summers off and had little opportunity to spend time in his mountain home.

The snoop

Near the end of the last day of school, Nurse Bell paid a visit to first grade. She was not going in her professional capacity but as a parent.

Miss Bizzy Belle

Michelle wished to personally thank Tonya's teachers for playing a critical role in her daughter's life.

"There will never be but one first grade, and Tonya has made memories that she will carry with her for a lifetime." Her mother was right. Tonya would never forget Mrs. Booger and Mrs. Hair Ball.

After a week with Mrs. T during post-planning, Tonya was ready for another summer adventure. She was optimistic about finally getting some answers regarding her grandparents. While she doubted it at first, she now felt certain that no one else knew anything about her father. Her great-grandparents might keep things from her, but not Mrs. T.

The first grade graduate had discovered Nancy Drew. The elementary school librarian was not accustomed to pupils from the lower grades checking out books. Since Tonya's mother was employed at the school, she saw no reason to deny the girl the privilege. She asked Tonya if her parents were going to read to her. All she got was a quick shake of the head.

Tonya Willa Bell had found herself a heroine. Some of the words were challenging, but she could usually figure out what they meant from the context.

Clues just did not come as easily for Miss Bell as they did for Miss Drew. While in Ferndale and Bellville, the spy planned to get some practice snooping around. She might even set a trap or two.

Even so, the summer of 1976 was mostly unproductive for the budding detective. She tried to move about unnoticed, hoping to eavesdrop on some juicy conversation. She pilfered drawers and searched closets, always careful to put things back just as they were.

Her only big find was a photo album at Granny Addie's with a few pictures of her mother's family in it. None was labeled. In one, she recognized her mother when she was a little girl standing beside what appeared to be her parents. Tonya still did not know if they were dead or alive.

Michelle fared better. She improved her grade point average to 3.3. One more summer semester and she would have her degree. There were no more sightings of Walt. Seeing him before must have been one of those weird coincidences like you read about in suspense novels.

The highlight of the summer was the celebration of the country's bicentennial. On Independence Day, Michelle, Tonya, and Granny Addie went to Asheville to see the big parade. They stayed for the fireworks show that night. Somebody was always celebrating something in the D.C. area, so these were not the first fireworks Tonya had seen. It was, nonetheless, the first time that she had been directly underneath them. Papa Doc did not feel like going, but he said that he would be okay.

On the way to school the day Tonya was beginning second grade, Michelle had trouble believing how much her daughter had grown. The girl's legs were getting longer with every hop, skip, and jump. She had already outgrown the jeans purchased only a few months earlier. The girl also had to have new shoes.

Second grade would be memorable for Tonya but in ways very different from her first. Soon after the year started, a lice infestation made its way through the school. Being the daughter of the school nurse provided no protection. Neither did it soften the aggravation. Michelle thought that she was never going to bring the pestilence under control.

Tonya got the chicken pox right before Thanksgiving. What does the school nurse do when her own child needs to be quarantined, and the mother cannot take time off? The only alternative was to take Tonya to Mrs. T's where she had to stay upstairs away from the other kids.

The most unforgettable experience of the beleaguered year was reserved for not long before school was out. The phone rang one Thursday evening after Tonya had gone to bed. She popped up and cracked the door just enough to hear some of the conversation. The girl could tell that something was wrong but could not fit it all together. She heard her mother saying that she would try to get a flight out on Saturday.

Not about to wait until morning to find out what was going on, she tippy-toed into the den wiping her eyes as though she had been asleep. "I heard the phone. Is something wrong?"

Michelle knew that there was no need in putting her off. She said the call was from Uncle Charles, and that Papa Doc had died that afternoon.

"I want to go." "I want to go." "I want to go."

"Tonya . . . There's no time to drive. I'll have to go by plane if I can get a ticket to Asheville."

"Get me a ticket, too." "Please." "Please." "Please."

"I'm sorry, but it's out of the question. I'll call Mrs. T and see if you can stay with her this weekend."

"It's just not fair." "It's just not fair." "It's just not fair."

"Tonya . . . The older you get, the more you're going to realize that life isn't fair. Get used to it."

Mrs. Thornhill suggested that Michelle leave her car at her house and take a cab to Dulles. She said it was cheaper than the parking fees, and that she would not have to fight traffic. With Michelle's heart somewhere else, getting through the school day Friday was difficult. The steady streams of petty problems she had to deal with seemed so trivial. Tonya did not make saying goodbye easy.

Going through the checkpoints at the airport was surprisingly uncomplicated for the first-time flier. Once on board, Michelle wondered how many people take their initial flights under duress. The lone daily nonstop to Asheville was only loosely packed. After the captain turned off the seatbelt light, she found a window seat. Uncle Charles was meeting her in Asheville.

As Michelle looked down at the magnificent sight below, she regretted not bringing Tonya. Seeing the thrill in her daughter's eyes, and just having her along, would have been worth the price of a child's ticket. The mother realized how much she leaned on her daughter. The girl was fully capable of upsetting the apple cart, but she also knew when to pour oil on troubled waters.

The main reason that she did not bring Tonya along was because she was trying to protect her from any unpleasantness that might ensue with her own parents. There was no way to avoid an encounter this time.

The bottom fell out

Granny Addie had to be the strongest woman Michelle had ever known. On the flight, she wanted to be more like her daughter. On the ground, she wished that she were more like her granny. Michelle couldn't imagine why anybody would want to be like her.

She drove her granny to the funeral home in Ephesus for the time of visitation. Uncle Charles and his half-brother stood at the head of the line. Michelle stayed with her granny but hardly knew anybody who came by. That is, except for one couple. She saw her parents when they came through the double doors.

As Tolbert and Connie Bell made their way to the widow, Michelle stood between her granny and the casket. As her mother released the embrace with her mother, Michelle stepped aside. The decedent's daughter leaned over the coffin and started weeping profusely. The stoical son-in-law stood by.

Michelle looked at her father, but he refused to make eye contact. How could one man's gaze, while staring off into space, convey pride, pain, ire, and resolve all at the same time? Her parents turned to leave and never acknowledged her presence.

Michelle had never been in that funeral home before. As they were leaving after almost three hours of greeting well-wishers, Granny Addie stopped as they went by the chapel.

"I started to have the service here, but it's so inconvenient for our friends and neighbors. I decided to have it at the church, instead, even though Doc was not much of a churchgoer. That way, we can take your grandpa straight to the graveyard."

Michelle paused a moment to look at the beautiful chapel. A year earlier, Walt had stood at that very podium and delivered a beautiful eulogy. She had no idea where it came from, but she had a sudden inspiration herself.

On the drive back to the house, Granny Addie said to Michelle that she wished she would now seriously consider moving closer by. "I need you, and you can use some help with your little live wire. While you're here this summer finishing your degree, why don't you look around and see what the possibilities are?"

"I don't know, Granny. I've got to do what's best for my daughter. Let me see how things go tomorrow."

The body laid in state an hour before the funeral. The mortician came to the house to escort the widow and those waiting with her to the Ferndale United Methodist Church at a quarter till two. Other family members had gathered at the church.

As they stood at the door about to be seated, Michelle approached the minister. "If you don't mind, I would like to have a couple of minutes at the graveside." He nodded in agreement.

Hearing the wonderful tributes to her grandpa made Michelle honored to be his granddaughter. She just hoped that he would be pleased with what she was about to do.

As the family and friends reassembled under and around the funeral home tent, the director was keeping an eye on the skies. Thunderstorms were in the forecast. After the pastor read from John 14, he made a move that surprised everyone except Michelle. He said that she wanted to say a few words.

"I'm not a speaker. In fact, I have never done anything like this before in my entire life. I promise I will be brief for two reasons. For one thing, I don't want all of us to get blown away in a storm. And secondly, I don't want to miss my flight. That could well happen if I get as long-winded as a Baptist preacher."

The Methodist preacher nodded his approval as others grinned with theirs.

"For those of you who don't know me, I am Madison and Adeline Baker's granddaughter. For that reason alone, I count myself to be among the most fortunate and favored persons ever to walk this earth. You see. I'm a school nurse in a Washington, D.C. suburb. I see kids every day from nontraditional homes. Some have moved around a lot, and many don't even know their grandparents."

Granny Addie's head was bowed as her granddaughter continued. "I have been truly blessed. I was raised by very devout Christian parents who always had my best interest at heart. I also knew my grandparents. I really knew them. I would not be the person I am today if not for the tremendous influence they had on me."

Michelle paused and looked down at the casket. She needed a moment to regain control of her emotions. A hush fell over those hanging on her every word. The silence was broken with a rumble of thunder.

"Okay. I guess I'd better wrap this up before we all get wet. I watched my Papa Doc slip away. I was not around as much as some of you were to see his gradual decline. I only saw him a couple of times a year and the changes I noticed were far more dramatic. Now. He's gone."

She hesitated again, but not for long.

"We sometimes get so set in our ways, so caught up in what we're doing, that we forget why we were doing it, to begin with. We lose sight of what's really important, and we don't even notice how our own lives are slipping away, too."

Michelle looked down at the casket again. "I love you, Papa Doc."

She then looked at her granny. "I love you, Granny Addie."

She turned to retake her seat under the tent, but then she stopped.

"I love you, Mother and Daddy."

The bottom fell out on the way to the airport. Papa Doc might have said it was raining cats and dogs. Pa Bell would have called it a real frog strangler. Uncle Charles was worried about getting her to the airport in time.

Other passengers were already boarding when Michelle got to the gate. When she buckled herself in, the rain had stopped. The jetliner soon taxied to the runway. As it lifted off, she missed her daughter more than ever.

After Michelle's spontaneous and unsolicited eulogy, most of the mourners came by to shake her hand, and to give her an obligatory hug. She closed her eyes and put her head back. "I think Tonya might have been proud of me, too." As for how her parents felt, they never gave any indication one way or the other. Then again, that was an indication in itself.

Michelle's granny said a special prayer for her granddaughter that night. With her head on the pillow, the wise old woman wondered out loud. "Isn't it strange that we have such clarity when it comes to seeing the shortcomings of others, and then we can be so blind to our own?" She turned over and tried to get some sleep. Other than her husband just laid to rest, the person that she missed the most was her great-granddaughter, Tonya.

Michelle's fortuitous rendezvous with Walt in Ephesus the summer before was not nearly as coincidental as she presumed. There was no chance of crossing paths with him while home for Papa Doc's funeral, however. He was one state down just across the Georgia line. The mother who raised him was buried that same day. Like his daughter, Walt did not get to go to the funeral, either.

Tonya was already asleep when the taxi delivered Michelle to Mrs. T's. The girl roused just enough to crawl into Black Bart's backseat. By the time that she was back in her own bed, she was wide awake. All Michelle wanted was a hot bath, but little Nancy Drew had some work to do.

Her mother's suitcase was open on the bed. The junior detective started rummaging, careful not to leave anything in disarray. Her hand felt something that was not clothing, and she pulled out a newspaper clipping. It was Papa Doc's obituary.

The little sleuth's eyes skipped over the first part looking for survivors. There it was in black and white. Madison "Doc" Baker was survived, among others, by a daughter Constance "Connie" Bell, her husband Tolbert, and their daughter Michelle. Tonya was in such a hurry to put the paper back that she did not see her own name listed among the great-grandchildren.

She had just stumbled upon her first big clue. Her grandparents were alive. Now, if she could just uncover some evidence that would tell her if her own father was, too.

There was no possibility that Tonya would ever forget the names, Tolbert and Connie, but she wrote them down anyway. That was the start of her secret file. She would add to it as she discovered more clues.

The live wire

The end of school could not come fast enough for either Tonya or Michelle. The second grader was not sure that she would even remember the names of her teachers. They mostly did their jobs without singling her out. She doubted that they would ever think about her again, and that was fine with her.

During post-planning, Tonya finally got to see Mrs. T. She told her all about her discovery. The little investigator said that she might drop a name now and then and see if she got any kind of reaction.

Once the apartment was secured for the summer, the mother and daughter were on the road. Michelle was feeling a little better about her finances. She was able to pay all of her rent in advance without having to mail checks while she was gone. For the first time, she was in a retirement plan. It allowed her to match the school system's contribution, and it was taken out before her check was cut. The mother saw it as the start of an educational fund for her daughter.

Michelle still wanted to pay Granny Addie back, but that would have to wait. At least Granny was collecting interest on the loan.

As they moved in and out of range, Michelle switched the radio tuner back and forth between stations. She could not relate to modern music. In the sheltered environment of her youth, about all that she was exposed to, was what she heard in church. The lengthy sermons brought back no fond memories, but she really missed the old hymns. Occasionally, she stumbled upon a station playing that good old gospel music that fed her soul.

As the latest hit by a group called AC-DC was introduced, Michelle's mind went to Granny Addie's most recent assessment of Tonya. The mother could not help but smile. The eight-year-old was indeed a "live wire." One never knew if her next performance would be in AC or DC.

In DC mode, Tonya interrupted her mother's thoughts.

"Why did you not have any brothers or sisters?"

Caught completely off guard, Michelle scrambled to find a way to answer. She certainly could not say anything about the brother who died. Tonya charged on.

"I wish I had a brother. Mother? Can we get a baby brother? A boy in my class is named Constantine. I think that sounds so fancy. But Connie might sound too much like a girl's name. What do you think? I like the name, Bert, too. Maybe we should call my brother, Bert. Bert Bell, I like the sound of that. Or, we could get twins, Bert and Ernie."

"I've never heard you mention Connie before."

"Oh, Mother. We've been friends since kindergarten."

"Don't get your hopes up, kiddo. I have all I can handle just with you."

"Way more . . ." she muttered under her breath.

After a stop for some Turkey Fried Chicken, Tonya switched to AC mode.

"Mother?" What all are we going to do this summer?

Michelle spoke for herself. "I'm going to be very busy with my studies. I can't slip up and make any bad grades, or I won't graduate."

That was not really what the girl was asking. "What about me?"

"I want you to help your granny a lot. She has the garden all to herself now. She's lonely with Papa Doc gone."

"Can I go see where he's buried? I've never been to a graveyard before."

"Sure. You can go with Granny to put flowers on his grave."

"This summer, will I get to visit Pa Bell and Mama Myra?"

"I know Pa Bell is expecting his Peanut to stay with him for a few days."

"Do you think I might run into my grandparents while I'm there?"

Michelle's wires short-circuited. Tonya knew that she had tripped a breaker.

Tonya was chomping at the bit to get to Bellville. Michelle was finally able to see a little daylight and needed a break. Granny Addie had her bags packed, too, and went along for the ride.

After Tonya was safely deposited, and they were driving up to the house where Michelle grew up, Granny asked if she was coming in.

"No . . . I just can't go where I'm not welcome."

"Maybe I can work on your mother some, and we four girls can spend a little time together when you come back to get us." Granny was a tad overly optimistic, and she knew it. She just kept planting seeds with the hope that some might eventually sprout.

The spy was on an assignment, and she had a plan. While Pa Bell was taking his nap, and Mama Myra watching her soaps, the young gumshoe decided to make her move. The diminutive sleuth said that she was a little sleepy and thought she might go lie down for a few minutes. The grouchy old woman did not look up.

On the way through the hall, the agent slid the telephone book out from under its place. She tiptoed to her room and closed the door.

The yellow cover indicated that the directory had listings for several exchanges. Bellville was but the first. Tonya turned the pages until she got to the names that started with B. Her finger went down the column. She saw Buford Bell. Several other Bells lived in and around Bellville. They might be her cousins. Toward the end of the list, her eyes fell on Tolbert Bell.

Tonya reached for her pencil and paper. She copied her grandparents' address and phone number. She did not know what she might ever do with that information, but new evidence was added to her secret file.

About that time, she heard a commotion coming from the other part of the house. Pa Bell was stirring. Would he notice the missing phone book? Tonya cracked the door to take a look. Good. He was going into the bathroom. When he came out, the phone was again resting atop the directory as though nothing had been disturbed.

Michelle looked sheepishly toward the office on her right each time she approached the elevator to the Nursing Department. Why couldn't she just forget about it? Seeing Walt was a one-time fluke. Was she going to spend the rest of her life worrying about the man looking over her shoulder?

For the first time in her educational experience, Michelle Anne Bell did not graduate with highest honors. It hardly mattered. She was just glad to have her degree. Since her parents had gotten theirs, a new auditorium had been built. Michelle did, however, march across the same stage that Walt had only a decade earlier.

Granny Addie did some gentle prodding about them moving closer by. Michelle blew it off and alleged in her defense. "I just don't think the standards are as high around here as they are in Virginia. I want Tonya to get the best education possible."

Granny did not buy it. "I don't think it's going to matter where the girl goes to school. What she learns, she'll get mostly on her own."

"I've already signed a contract for next year. I'll think about it, though. I promise I will."

Granny got in a parting shot. "Just remember. None of us is getting any younger."

When Michelle reported for work, she was greeted with both good news and bad news. The good news was that she received a 10 percent raise after getting her degree. The bad news was that several more things had been put on her plate.

The central office was no longer certifying immunizations. That responsibility had been handed off to the nurse. Furthermore, the school would now be conducting a number of screenings. Initially, they included vision, hearing, and scoliosis. The principal expected more to be added to the list. Other professionals would come in to conduct the actual tests, but the nurse was responsible for handling the flow of the herd.

Even though she had just completed her degree, Michelle was not sure how much longer she wanted to work in education. Dealing with youngsters and their testy parents was fatiguing. The degree was certainly a plus if she decided to explore other options. She had no way of knowing it, but a looming phone call was about to put her next career move on the fast track.

By the end of the first week, Tonya was embroiled in a fierce power struggle with Mrs. Favor, her third grade teacher. Bell came just far enough down the alphabet to get Tonya a coveted back row seat. Constantine De Palma sat across from her. His father was a general or something at the Pentagon. Tonya and Connie were accomplices in their shenanigans. She loved it when she could put ideas in his head and then sit back and watch him have at it.

After a couple of warnings went unheeded, the students arrived one morning to find a new seating arrangement. The room had an extra row of desks with one less in each. Tonya was now on the front row. Connie was still at the back of the room. Mrs. Favor had done herself no favors.

Constantine decided to bring out the heavy artillery. If he and Tonya could no longer be seated next to each other, he claimed that his father would get the teacher fired.

Tonya was not packing nearly as much heat, but she was not above taking her best shot. "My mother's the school nurse. She'll get another job and we'll just move."

Mrs. Favor held her ground. As a precaution, she decided to discuss the matter with Principal Carswell. After mulling it over, he sized up the situation.

"I really don't think there's anything to worry about. On the other hand, we don't want the pot to boil over. I'd rather not have General Pain in the Butt, or whatever his name is, on my case. And I certainly can't afford to lose Nurse Bell right now. She's given me no indication that she's dissatisfied with her job. Hopefully, it will just blow over."

M. A. Bell

Walt Williamson was not in a good space. He had lost the woman who was more like a mother to him than the one who raised him. Then, Maude also died a short time later. The former left a bequest. Walt inherited the modest little home she lived in. The latter took to the grave the only thing that he needed from her.

Miss Bizzy Belle

Walt's heart was not in his work. He knew who he was, but he was not where he wanted to be. The counselor decided that it was time to heed his own advice and figure out where that was.

He, thus, submitted his letter of resignation to the Outer Banks State University, effective September 30, 1977. He packed up his meager belongings and headed to Ephesus with a new outlook on life.

Walt soon became a partner in a private practice counseling center. That was what he had initially trained for but had done very little of. Sharing duties with a recent female graduate, the workload was manageable. He took some time every week to go rambling in the mountains. The tightness inside was loosening. He decided that he was not reinventing himself, but rather redirecting himself.

The clients were about equally divided between couples experiencing marital difficulties and children with behavioral problems. Since neither Walt nor his partner Lynda was married or had children, they decided that they might be the most qualified therapists in the state.

About the time the leaves were in the midst of their spectacular fall transformation, a woman showed up late for her first appointment. When she was finally escorted to Walt's office, she had trouble opening up. Eventually, it spilled out. Five years earlier, his client had undergone an abortion, and she was still having trouble getting beyond it.

Walt listened but felt ill-prepared to offer any substantive assistance. He handed her off to Lynda, presuming that another woman was better prepared to help her. He walked her to the receptionist, and they scheduled her next visit.

Walt did not have another immediate appointment to distract him. Sitting in his office, his mind was transported back to the night nine years earlier when he returned Michelle's call. It was only a few weeks after he had moved on without her. The ominous words she uttered that night still haunted him.

"I took care of it."

When he got home that afternoon, he could not get Michelle off his mind. After supper, he dialed the operator and asked for long distance information. Walt was not sure if his former roommate was still living in Washington. The operator could find no listing for a Michelle Bell in D.C. The only thing that was close was M. A. Bell, in nearby Fairfax, Virginia. He remembered that Michelle's middle name was Anne and that her school chums used to call her Ma Bell.

After pacing and pondering, he could find no peace. He came back inside and nervously dialed the number. He heard someone say, "Hello," but the connection was not good. Phone service away from large cities still left a lot to be desired.

Walt asked if it was the Bell residence.

He thought he heard the person say that it was.

Not sure who he was talking to, he asked if it was the residence of Michelle Bell.

The individual on the other end did not answer his question but asked one instead.

"Who's calling, please?"

Walt identified himself. He said that he once worked with a Michelle Bell, and that he was trying to get in touch with her. He assured the one he was speaking with that there was no emergency or anything. An awkward silence followed.

Afraid that the person might hang up, he asked a favor. "Would you please take my number and have Michelle call me?"

"Just a minute. Let me get something to write on."

Walt thanked whoever it was that he had been speaking with, but nobody ever called back.

Since Tonya's eighth birthday, Michelle felt that her daughter was old enough to be left home alone, at least for short periods. She could get stuff done with far less stress if her daughter was not tagging along. Tonya hardly looked up when she came through the door with a couple of bags of groceries.

After she finished putting them away, she went into the den and propped her feet up. Tonya said rather indifferently. "You had a call while you were gone."

"Who was it?"

"I don't know. Some man."

"Did he say who he was?"

Tonya pulled the note from her pocket, handed it to her mother, and started for her room. Her eyes stayed behind.

Trying to remain calm and composed, Michelle called out. "Did he say what he wanted?"

"Nope. He didn't say much. Just left his name and number. I could barely hear him. Hope I got it right."

When Michelle unfolded the scrap of paper, Tonya had written Wyatt Williamson, but she knew who the caller really was. Tonya found the note in the trash the next morning in a million pieces. A good thing the little gumshoe made her own copy.

The elephant no longer lived behind the glass door at the university in Ephesus. It had taken up residence in a duplex apartment in Fairfax, Virginia.

The last thing Michelle wanted to do was to tip her hand, but she knew that she must take action. If she did anything to arouse suspicion, Tonya

Miss Bizzy Belle

would not miss a smidgen. She must go on as if nothing had changed. Nevertheless, everything just had.

Lying in bed, she wished that she had followed Granny Addie's advice and looked at job prospects. There was no doubt about it. They now had to move. Her granny gave her the only cover that she had to leave her job in the middle of the school year.

Michelle started plotting her strategy. It was only two months until Christmas. She hated risking that Walt might show up before they could relocate, but she had no choice. In her plan, she and Tonya would go to North Carolina for the holidays. If she could find a job and a place to live, she could resign her position under the pretext of going home to care for an elderly widowed grandmother.

Meanwhile, Michelle could not give Tonya any reason whatsoever to connect the dots between the phone call and why they were moving. One thing was for certain, though. Her daughter would not be left alone again anytime soon.

About a week before the holiday break, Michelle told Tonya that they did not normally go anywhere for Christmas, but she thought Granny Addie might need some extra company. The eight-year-old started getting excited.

"Can I buy her a Christmas present?"

"Of course, you can. Do you have anything in mind?"

"What about a big teddy bear? I think Granny Addie would love to go to sleep with a huggy bear." After Black Bart was deemed roadworthy, they were off.

Michelle said to Granny Addie as they were unloading the car. "Love your new glasses."

Tonya told her that she looked like Mrs. Claus.

"I guess if I'm going to be an old granny, I might as well look like one."

Right smack-dab in the middle of Christmas was not the best of times to be job hunting and one career option was not open. Appalachia had not felt a need for school nurses.

That left only a couple of other possibilities. Michelle had not particularly enjoyed working at a doctor's office. As for hospitals, there were three directions to consider. With the nursing school so close by, the one in Ephesus might not have any openings. Asheville had more than one fine hospital. Knoxo Springs, the county seat of Walthall County, had a small hospital that was only about ten miles from Ferndale.

With limited time to slip away without having to answer a bunch of questions, Michelle ventured to Knoxo Springs first. When she entered the lobby, she saw a poster announcing a nursing position. The director was out for the week, but the hospital administrator, James Griffin, was in his office. Not wanting a good prospect to get away, he invited her in.

Michelle had to admit that her credentials were impressive. She not only had roots in the area, but she also had the experience and education that did not walk in the door of that little institution every day. Seeing possible supervisory potential, Mr. Griffin hired her on the spot.

The administrator understood that it would take some time to work out a notice and then get moved, but he assured her that she could go to work the first day she was available. Michelle was okay with the idea of once again doing what she originally trained for.

Housing was the next issue. Tonya's educational fund might have to take a hit. Tired of renting, Michelle explored the main streets of the town and saw a couple of "for sale" signs. One charming little house, in particular, caught her eye. Accustomed to costs in the D.C. area, she could hardly believe the asking price when she lifted a flier. With what she had for a down payment, and with the security of a job at the local hospital, she hoped that she might qualify for a loan even with her credit card debt.

Michelle did not know how and when to start breaking the news, especially to Tonya. She decided to appeal to her daughter's vanity. She asked her if she could keep a really big secret. Tonya gave her word and her eyes got big.

"When we get back home, not a peep until I say it's okay. Do you understand?"

"Yes, mother. I won't tell a soul. Now? What is it?"

"Let's go for a ride."

Michelle's fears were unfounded. As soon as Tonya learned of the upcoming move, she made no connection at all between it and the phone call from Walt.

As Tonya was saying goodbye to her classmates, her teacher wished her well. With her nose in the air, Miss Smarty Pants uttered not a sound. She walked out the door with her head held high. She wanted Mrs. Favor to think that she had actually engineered the move because the teacher refused to put her desk back where it was.

Connie believed her. Mrs. Favor wondered. Mr. Carswell did not know what to think. Nurse Bell did not have a clue.

Saying goodbye to Cornfield was the most difficult part. Tonya was also distancing herself from the place of her birth, leaving behind possible clues about her father. She discussed all of that with Mrs. T.

"You'll be back. I want you to visit me every chance you have. And you know what? I'm thinking about retiring soon. I'm just not sure that I can run this place much longer without you. Maybe I can come see you, too."

"Oh, Mrs. T . . . I love you so very much."

Tonya put her arms around her and held on tightly. When her mother hugged her, she felt only arms. When Mrs. T hugged her, she felt what was inside.

"I love you, too, my precious."

Tonya walked away with a little parcel under her arm. "I'm not going to tell you goodbye, because I'm going to see you again."

The Villa Bell

If Michelle could barely come up with enough money to pay for the move from Washington to Fairfax, Virginia, she did not even want to think about what it might cost to hire somebody to get her things to Knoxo Springs, North Carolina. The only viable alternative was to rent a Me-Haul.

The man at the distribution center said that she might get all of her things in a two-axle trailer, but he was not sure if the Dart had the muscle. He convinced her that driving a small truck and towing the car was a better option. He reassured her that women did it all the time. New neighbors had recently moved into the other side of the duplex. They had a teenage son, interested in earning a few bucks, to help load the truck.

Michelle had spoken with the real estate agent by phone several times and had forwarded the necessary paperwork to the bank. Both assured her that she just needed to sign a few more documents after she got into town.

The agent promised to make sure the house was ready. Uncle Charles had lined up help to unload. Granny Addie was coming to assist with unpacking. Folks in that part of the world did business a little different from what she was accustomed to. Michelle was rather certain she could get used to that again.

Tonya was all excited about riding shotgun. Her chum, Connie, told her what that meant. Michelle was more than a little apprehensive about driving the truck. Exiting the lot, she cut too short and Black Bart went across a curb.

"So that's what the man meant about making long turns." Once out of town and on the open road, she got a little more confident.

The truck did not pull away until almost lunchtime. After mother and daughter were buckled in, Michelle said. "Well, kiddo, let's begin our new life. Knoxo Springs, here we come."

Driving straight through was out of the question. Tonya had never stayed in a motel and she got to choose the bed. It was an exciting time. Life was becoming one new adventure after another.

The next morning, they decided to take advantage of the free continental breakfast. Right out of the blue, Tonya asked her mother a question. "Have you ever been in love?"

Where did that come from? Michelle was never sure how to deal with her daughter's probing. On the one hand, she did not want to give her false information only to be busted somewhere down the road. On the other, she wished not to say anything that her enterprising offspring might hang her with later. Since they were in this colossal venture together, she decided that a little candor might bring them closer.

"As a matter of fact, I have."

Tonya followed up before she had a chance to reconsider. "Who was the lucky fellow?"

Without going into great detail or revealing his name, Michelle told her daughter about Grover. She said that he went off to war, and she never saw him again. That much was true. The mother saw no need in mentioning that he was killed in action.

Michelle should have known by then that one question brought on another and then usually another.

"Did you ever date any men besides Royce and Uncle Vinnie?"

Michelle saw nothing incriminating about telling her daughter about the policeman.

"You were too young to remember, but I went out with a cop."

"Mother . . . Tell me about it. Maybe I can't remember it because I wasn't born, yet?"

"Oh, yes you were. I was involved in an accident in the X on the way to pick you up at Mrs. T's. I was not hurt too badly, but I had to go to the hospital and be checked out. The policeman came to the ER to finish filling out the report."

"Did you ask him out, or did he ask you?"

"Why, Tonya. I would never ask a man out. I knew he had my phone number on the report. I did flirt with him, and told him that it was okay to call if he didn't get all the information he needed."

"Oh, Mother. This is so exciting. What was his name?"

"His name was Rodney, but his friends called him 'Hot Rod.' I guess he lost interest in me after a couple of dates."

Once back on the road, Tonya reached for the little purse that Mrs. T gave her as a going away present. It came already stocked with a roll of

Lifesavers, some lip gloss, a tissue packet, a little spiral tablet, and a couple of pencils. While her mother was keeping her eyes on the road, Tonya was scribbling.

When Michelle looked down, trying to see what she was doing, Tonya looked up. "Mother? Want a Lifesaver?"

Not long before sundown, the Me-Haul, with Black Bart in tow, pulled into Knoxo Springs and turned down Lane Lane. A welcoming party was waiting to greet them. The utilities were on and Mr. Clean had flexed his muscle.

The car was unhitched, and the helpers went to work. Tonya went straight to check out her new room. She meticulously placed her little pocketbook on the shelf in the back of the closet under Watt. Miss Bizzy Belle then appointed herself the doorkeeper and the traffic cop as the truck was being unloaded.

Uncle Charles and his son returned the rental truck to Asheville. Granny Addie stayed until almost bedtime. The first thing she did was help her great-granddaughter set up her bed and get her things unpacked. Tonya christened their new home "The Villa Bell."

Tonya had a question when Michelle came to tuck her in. "When am I going to start school?" Since the next day was Friday, her mother suggested enrolling on Monday. That was fine with her. The excited girl did not want to miss any goings on at the Villa while they were getting settled in.

Lying in bed with Watt beside her on the pillow, Tonya looked out the window. She saw the stars, felt an incredible connection with the universe, and was overawed by an aura of peacefulness. It was unlike anything that she had ever experienced in the big city.

From then on, bedtime was her favorite time of the day. Her window faced east and from it, she could watch the moon rise over the trees. During the summer months, she kept her window open and was lulled to sleep by the night sounds. She sometimes awakened to glorious sunrises painting the sky. The only thing that Tonya missed back in D.C. was Mrs. T.

In the other bedroom, Michelle was lying on her back looking up at the ceiling. Her body was weary, but a smile was on her face. She had done it. The schools might not be up to metropolitan par, but her daughter was now in a security zone. There was no way that Walt Williamson could find them in this remote mountain town.

Granny Addie was back bright and early the next morning. Tonya was the only one up and was sorting through her stuff. Granny came in with two sacks of groceries. While Michelle was still trying to clear out the cobwebs, the other two scrounged around in the boxes until they found some pots and pans. In no time, Mr. Coffee was perking.

While the ladies were still sitting around the breakfast table sipping coffee good to the last drop, Tonya went outside to look around. So this was going to be her home. The mid-January morning was cold, but it felt different from what she had always known. She took a deep breath. The air smelled so fresh and clean.

As she went skipping up the street, the girl started making herself right at home. "I think I'm going to like this."

The new resident of Lane Lane went all the way to where it ended at the top of the hill. Beyond, was nothing but woods. Tonya had never been to the end of any road. She thought all of them were connected like strands of a spider web. Little did she realize that one day she would settle at the end of another road several thousand miles away.

The explorer turned around and started back in the other direction, passing the Villa on the way. She looked at the homes on each side. Who would be her new friends?

"Roller skates. I've got to have roller skates. No. I think I want a skateboard, but Mother would never go for that." Neither was the first thing that she asked for. At the end of the street, she could see church steeples.

On Saturday, Tonya wanted to get a look at her new school. Black Bart had been used to haul breakable things that still had not been unloaded. The two carefully moved the delicate items inside and then went to investigate.

Knoxo Springs was somewhat of a typical mountain town. Each was distinctive in its own way, and that one was no exception. What most shared in common was a downturn in the economy. The second and third generation of the pioneers had gotten spoiled to having regular paychecks. Many manufacturing jobs had dried up as factories closed. Plants were driven out of business by cutthroat competition, or they were acquired by large conglomerates that did the dirty work.

The quaint little town had a population of about three-thousand. The railroad ran parallel to Main Street. Passenger service had been discontinued, and the terminal was in disrepair. Freight trains still made deliveries a couple of times a week.

The town center revolved around a park below two adjacent free-flowing limestone springs. Neither drought nor deluge seemed to affect their output. One flowed into a little pond stocked with trout. Picnic tables lined the downstream banks of the other. In the summer time, children and adults alike cooled off in the sparkling creek water. Nobody could remember how the springs got their name.

One of the town's landmarks was a rickety old one-lane wooden bridge over the tracks. Hardly anyone used it unless a train had the Main Street crossing blocked. Give and take bottlenecked traffic inched across. The creosote laden timbers caught fire several times when steam locomotives still ran the rails.

The city took much pride in restoring the bridge in 1976. The dedicatory celebration coincided with the nation's bicentennial. It included a picnic in the park, a parade in the afternoon, street dancing that evening, and fireworks after dark. Members of the volunteer fire department stood by, ready to protect the bridge or anything else that might incinerate.

Knoxo Springs' most revered town father was the late Dr. Winthrop W. Lane. During the first half of the twentieth-century, he tended to the medical needs of the residents in town, as well as to those out in the surrounding hills. He kept expanding his clinic until it became a small hospital. After his death, the town purchased it and named it the Lane Memorial Hospital.

The Lanes were long gone, but their name remained. The first house that they lived in was at the end of a dead end street. Before the town got around to putting up street signs, Mrs. Lane called it Lane Lane. Michelle and Tonya now lived on it.

The consolidated high school was the only one in the county. Three elementary schools still operated in the other incorporated burgs.

Knoxo Springs was home to several churches. As was typical, the Baptist and the Methodist had the largest congregations.

It did not take very long to go from one side of town to the other. It had charming little houses and a stately old courthouse that had been used a couple of times in movie sets.

The hospital was on the first street coming into town from Ferndale. Lane Lane was at the end of it going off to the left. Two streets over, the high school was on the side of a hill, and the elementary right down below it. Tonya's eyes were taking it all in.

As they went past the churches, she made a request that caught her mother off guard.

"Let's go to church tomorrow."

"Which one would you like to go to?"

Tonya responded, matter-of-factly. "I'm a Methodist."

Michelle gave her a quick glance.

"Mother? Have you forgotten? I graduated from a Methodist kindergarten."

As they approached the steps to the First United Methodist Church the next morning, Michelle looked up and saw a familiar face. Mr. Griffin was an usher waiting to greet them. He welcomed them to Knoxo Springs, and said he hoped that they enjoyed the church service. Michelle mentioned that she was planning to come by the hospital the next day.

"Wonderful . . . Drop by as soon as you can and go by the office. I know they have some paperwork for you to fill out. I'd like for you to meet Barbara Jobson, the nursing supervisor. When did you get to town?"

When Michelle told him, he offered some assurance. "I know it's going to take several days for you to get settled in. I suppose we can get along without you for a few more, but I hope you'll be ready to start by next week."

As she took her seat, Nurse Bell was struck by how accommodating the hospital administrator was. He understood that she was more than just a hospital asset. He seemed to appreciate her as a real person.

The mother was not sure how to prepare her daughter for school. She warned her that the kids might make fun of her because of her "Yankee" accent. She told her about the teasing she got at Walter Reed because of her southern expressions.

Tonya responded with a bit of attitude. "If they make fun of me, then I'll just mock them for the way they talk."

Michelle thought how terrified she would be if she were in her daughter's position. Even though she never changed schools, she dreaded facing new teachers each year. Tonya seemed to adjust no matter the circumstances. Michelle admired the girl's courage and self-confidence, but she just couldn't imagine where she got it.

Partners in crime

Tonya was up bright and early on Monday morning. "Mother . . . I don't want to be late." The third grader, starting a new school in the middle of the year, did not know what to take with her. She decided on a notebook and a pencil. As they stepped inside the main office door, Michelle introduced herself and Tonya to the secretary.

After exchanging pleasantries, the receptionist gestured toward the principal's office. "I'm sure Mrs. Wagner wants to meet you. Let me see if she's available." She soon returned and said that it would just be a minute.

A casually dressed woman with salt and pepper hair came through the door with a big smile. No business suits or cover up coloring for her. Customs and conventions were different away from the big city.

Mrs. Wagner's smile was beckoning. "Come in. I've been expecting you." Apparently, word was already out that Knoxo Springs had some new residents.

The principal looked down at the note that had been handed her and then across at the new student. "So . . . This is Tanya."

The new student corrected her. "*Tone-yuh*, my name is *Tone-yuh*."

"And I'll bet I'm going to be saying that name quite a bit." Mrs. Wagner thought.

She then addressed the girl's mother. "Did you bring her other school records?"

"Yes. I have them here in my purse."

"We'll need to see *Tone-yuh's* birth certificate, too. We'll make a copy to keep on file if she participates in any age-related sports. And I do hope she will. Around here, we think physical activity and sportsmanship are very important."

"I'll bring it this afternoon when I come to get her."

"Birth certificate? Did she say I have a birth certificate? You mean I have a birth certificate?" With everything else that was going on, the new student had a hard time focusing on anything else.

"*Tone-yuh*. Your teacher is Mrs. Hart. I'll go ahead and tell you. Mrs. Hart believes that third grade is one of the most important in all of one's schooling. If students start falling behind at that level, they might never catch up. What kind of student are you?"

"I make all A's." Tonya was a bit miffed that there might have been any doubt.

"I suspect that you and Mrs. Hart are going to get along just fine. Come on. Let me take you to your room. She already has a desk set up for you. Mrs. Bell? Would you like to walk with us, too?"

Tonya repeated to herself again going down the hall. "A birth certificate. I have a birth certificate."

Entering the door without knocking, the room grew quiet.

"Class. Let me introduce you to your new classmate. This is *Tone-yuh* Bell and her mother. They have just moved to Knoxo Springs from near Washington, D.C. Mrs. Bell is a nurse at the hospital."

At the back of the class, one boy looked at another and whispered. "Snob."

Tonya made eye contact with him as though reading his mind.

She thought to herself. "You little 'twerp'."

The principal and mother were soon out the door. A whole new phase in Tonya's educational experience was about to begin.

"Boys and girls. Let's take a minute or two to get to know our new student a little better. Now, remember. There's only one of her. She will have to learn all of your names."

The little "twerp's" hand went up.

"Did you ever see any famous people?"

"Oh . . . All the time. My best friend's father was a general who ran the army."

Tonya did not see it coming, but she was about to have rank pulled on her. Subsequently, she would be upstaged.

Twerp fired back. "That's nothing. My pa's a Walthall County sheriff's deputy."

Another classmate volunteered some information just to let the new student know that they were not awed by her. "We see movie stars around here. My Aunt Alice played a jailbird in a murder trial filmed at the courthouse. I'll bet you never even saw the movie."

Changing her tone and changing her tune, Tonya smiled at her across the room. "No. But I'd like to."

Without raising her hand, another girl brought up exactly what Tonya's mother had mentioned. "She sounds funny when she talks."

Mrs. Hart came to Tonya's defense. "Maybe we sound funny to her when we speak."

Tonya Willa Bell was on new turf. The rules of engagement were definitely different, but she was a quick study. It would not take her long to begin rewriting some of them.

A cute little blond-headed girl with pigtails smiled at Tonya and waved. When the break bell sounded, they went to each other.

"Hi . . . I saw you at church yesterday. My name's Samantha, but only my parents call me that when they're yelling at me . . . Which happens a lot. You can call me Sammie."

The new classmates sat together during lunch. As straight-faced as a poker player, Sammie asked Tonya a question. "Well . . . How do you like 'The Old Wag' and 'Mrs. Heartless' so far?" Sitting right across the table from the transfer student, was another girl cut from the same cloth.

The bonding was so natural that neither thought that there was anything unusual about it. On only her fourth day, the new girl in town already had a new best friend. Tonya Bell and Sammie Ringer would be inseparable throughout the remainder of their school days.

At the final bell, Tonya raced to the office hoping to get a glimpse of her birth certificate. Her mother was waiting for her so it was too late. On the short drive home, the girl's mind was in gear. "I don't think she carries it in her purse all the time. Maybe I can see where she puts it."

All her mother wanted to talk about was Tonya's first day of school.

Miss Bizzy Belle

She told her mom she did not think that she was going to have any trouble with her studies since they were going over material she learned in second grade. She also mentioned Sammie Ringer and said they were going to be best buds.

Michelle was going on with no seeming awareness that it was one of the most monumental days in her daughter's life. And it had nothing to do with school. All Tonya was interested in was something in her mother's purse. Just like that, everything fell apart.

"I forgot to take your birth certificate this afternoon. Remind me to get it in the morning. I'll take you to school again, but after that, there's no reason you can't walk."

Did her mother have any idea what she was saying? She was talking about her birth certificate like it had no special importance. Not wanting to go a whole night with it hanging over her head, Tonya made a suggestion.

"Why don't you go ahead and put it in your purse tonight?"

"That's a great idea. Why didn't I think of that? Now, go take your bath."

Tonya started the water but left a crack in the door. She could not see her mother moving about. The bathroom door squeaked as she opened it more.

Oops. Thank goodness. The sound of the water muffled it.

Moving against the wall like a cat stalking its prey, she circled toward her mother's bedroom. She stuck her head in the crack just enough to get a quick glance. Her mother was sitting on the bed opening a little lockbox. The novice spy peered again. Keys were beside her mother.

Bolting to the bathroom before being caught, she closed the door. Quickly into the tub, she turned the water off and started splashing just in case.

"So . . . My mother has her own secret file."

Barbara Jobson's prematurely gray hair was stunning. Nurse Bell felt immediately comfortable with her, but she was also more than a little envious. Michelle was certain that with her red hair and ruddy complexion, she would not age gracefully. During a walkthrough of the hospital, the nursing supervisor said that they did not try to do all things, but what they did, they strived to do well.

Much of the energy centered around the nursery. Dr. Lane had delivered many of the parents and grandparents of the current newborns. The mountain folks in the surrounding area had no need to go to some bigger facility miles away. Mrs. Jobson reminded her new nurse that the nursery was the hospital's happy place, but it did not bring back fond memories for this mother.

The supervisor continued with the orientation. "We don't have much specialization around here. Our staff has to help cover all bases. Dr. Ringer is our lone OB/GYN. His nurses assist with deliveries, but all of us have to pitch in at times."

As they approached the emergency room, the supervisor explained its function. "Our ER is little more than a glorified first aid station. The local ambulance service takes the critically ill straight to Ephesus or Asheville. We do have a couple of good surgeons, but then again, they know their limitations with the equipment here."

Having made the rounds, the two nurses paused in the hallway. "Please call me Barbara. Am I free to call you Michelle? We don't stand much on ceremony. I do hope you enjoy working here, and I'm so looking forward to meeting Tonya."

After only a week in their new home, snow was in the forecast. Tonya had no idea why everyone was so excited. Where she came from, the frozen precipitation was little more than a major inconvenience. Sammie helped set her straight.

"When the buses can't run, we don't have school. It's like a winter vacation. You do have a sled, don't you?"

When Tonya shook her head, her new friend continued preparing her for the snow event. "Then we can take turns using mine till you get one. The street you live on is one of the three or four best places in town. Because it's a dead end, we don't have to worry about much traffic. The city only plows a narrow lane if anybody calls and has to go out. They leave the rest for us to play on. The older kids like the steeper hill coming down from the high school."

As Michelle came in the door from the first day on her new job, Tonya called out to her. "Mother . . . I need a sled."

Tonya's new buddy was on both their minds when they went to bed. Sammie was a doctor's daughter. Michelle knew she did not have the kind of money that the Ringers' did. In the other bedroom, her daughter was also thinking. "I have so much to learn from Sammie. And . . . I suspect there's a thing or two that I can teach her as well."

There was something else that Tonya could not stop thinking about. Where did her mother keep the box that held her secret files? The sleuth had already done a little snooping around in her mom's closet and dresser, but she came up empty.

Miss Bizzy Belle

The weatherman got it right. Tonya had never seen such beauty when she woke up on Tuesday morning. All she had ever known was living in a place where just about everything was paved over. The snow was a menace, quickly turning gray and ugly.

"So this is what a winter wonderland is . . ."

The hospital had a four-wheel-drive Cherokee that it used to fetch stranded employees. Michelle gladly accepted a ride when it came up her hill.

Sammie was also right about the popularity of Lane Lane. The kids started coming around mid-morning after the wet snow was about four inches deep. She called Tonya and told her that she was on her way.

Near the top end of the street, the best friends staked out a stretch that had a nice drop before a dip. Tonya soon got her first instructions in the fine art of sledding. Neither girl could remember laughing so much.

After both were just about exhausted, they headed back down the hill. Another new experience was just ahead. A fierce snowball battle broke out with Twerp and his sidekick, Twit. Tonya got pelted while trying to figure out how to compress the snow just right. Sammie held her own.

Twerp started taunting Tonya saying she threw like a girl. The timing could not have been better. Sammie let loose with a big snowball that she had worked on especially hard. It scored a direct hit to the side of his head. It stung so hard it appeared that he was about to cry. The girls made a run for it with missiles falling just short. As they approached the porch, Tonya started fumbling for her key.

Defenseless, Sammie was cornered. "What are you doing, girl? Let's get inside." She then raised her right arm, pointed her finger in the ten o'clock position, and barked. "Private property." Obediently, the boys stopped in their tracks.

Once inside, Sammie asked Tonya what the key thing was all about. She told her that nobody around there locked their doors. This was the first of the countless times that Sammie would be inside those walls. After her friend left to go home for lunch, Tonya wrote a long letter to Mrs. T.

The school administrators wished that the snow had arrived on the weekend. The students were glad that it waited until Monday night. Thursday was the first possible day that the buses could make their rounds out in the rural areas. The school might be closed the rest of the week. Parents did not have to make any special arrangements for their children. The community was safe, and these mountain kids were adept at entertaining themselves.

Tonya asked her mother if she could go to Sammie's house on Wednesday after another round of sledding. "And I do want my own sled before the next snow." Michelle was trying to get used to the idea that her daughter and the doctor's daughter were already joined at the hip.

The hospital nurse got to meet Sammie's daddy before Tonya did. She quickly made up her mind about something, too. "The thought of . . ." She stopped herself from going there. When she needed the services of a physician of his specialty, she would get an appointment with a doctor in Ephesus.

The Ringers lived only four blocks away right in the middle of the residential area. There were a few stately old homes in Knoxo Springs, but none could be called mansions. Neither was there a single gated community anywhere in the county. Nevertheless, the town was not without luxury. It had a country club with a golf course that the local duffers called, "The Cow Pasture."

Sammie's home was a two-story brick with only a small stoop at the front door and a screened-in porch on the side. Both her bedroom and her older brother Stanley's were upstairs. The house also had a full basement with a sitting space in front of a fireplace and an activity area for games.

A basketball goal was at the end of the drive. The back opened up to a fenced-in yard where Dr. Ringer did his barbecuing. Tonya had no idea what a grill was.

Everything had been happening so fast that the girls still had not found time to talk about their folks. After Mrs. Ringer made some hot chocolate, they went upstairs. Tonya was envious of Sammie coming from such a family.

She confided in her friend that she didn't know who her father was. "But if it's the last thing I do, I'm going to find him."

Sammie then had something special to share. "Let me take you somewhere. We'll have to go through Stanley's room to get there."

A crude door was inside his closet that opened to space over the garage. Sammie discovered it when she was about four, and it had been her secret hiding place since.

That was just the right setting for Tonya to tell Sammie about her secret file. She mentioned her mother's own lock box but said that she had not yet located where she hid it. She just had to see her birth certificate and know what else might be inside.

"Need a partner in crime?"

It was as though they had known each other all their lives.

Ebb and Flo

Sammie's father was a third generation physician. His grandfathers were college roommates and lifelong friends. The son of one married the daughter of the other.

Stanley, three years older than his sister, was already talking about carrying on the family tradition. Sammie's grandfather said that she broke the mold when she was born.

Dr. Ringer's first name was Ebenezer. His friends and many of his patients called him Dr. Ebb, or just Mr. Ebb. The sport that he was, the doctor dressed up as Ebenezer Scrooge at Christmas. No matter how corny it sounded, somebody always had to remind him that he was a "dead ringer" for old Scrooge.

His wife's name was Florien. When Dr. Ringer decided that he did not want to practice assembly-line medicine in a big city hospital, they settled in Knoxo Springs not far from where she grew up. Most folks called her Mrs. Flo.

Ebb and Flo were highly thought of throughout the community. The fun-loving, civic-minded couple was generous with their resources. Pillars in the Methodist Church, they also made it a priority to spend time with their kids.

In Tonya's old city, the snow stuck around. In her new home, it came and went a lot faster. School was back in session on Friday. During lunch, the girls stared Twerp and Twit down. Sammie whispered in Tonya's ear. "Men and their wounded pride."

Granny Addie called and said that she was fixing supper Saturday night. She told Michelle to come on around the middle of the afternoon so they could get home before the temperature dropped below freezing.

Tonya asked if Sammie could go along, too. Her mother said that she guessed so if it was okay with her parents. It was more than okay. Mrs. Flo said that her daughter could also spend the night if she wanted to. Michelle begged off since they were hardly settled. Mrs. Ringer reminded her that Tonya was welcome at their house anytime.

Once inside, Tonya went by Granny's bedroom just to make sure of something. "Paddy" the Paddington Bear was sitting in the middle of the bed. She then took Sammie to her private bedroom up the disappearing stairwell.

While the girls were otherwise occupied, Granny said that she had some news to share about Tolbert. "I'm not sure what's going on. Connie wouldn't tell me much. I guess he 'bout went off his rocker."

Michelle had concern written all over her face. "What do you mean?"

"He's in a hospital in Huntsville. His doctor wanted to send him to the state institution, but Connie talked him out of it. Do you know anything about shock treatments?"

The nurse tried to explain the procedure as best she could.

Granny always had her own way of putting things. "Not long before Doc died, we were talking about Tolbert. Sometimes your grandpa could be far off in la-la-land, and then he could be clear as a bell . . . No pun intended. I remember him saying something like this. 'If you can't make some allowances now and then, you'll wind up in the nuthouse.' I guess that old man knew what he was talking about."

Michelle asked about his teaching job.

"They gave your daddy a temporary leave of absence and are trying to keep his condition hush-hush. I asked Connie why she didn't just leave the old goat and have a life of her own."

"Granny . . . I can't believe you did that. What did Mother say?"

"You might not want to hear this, but it is what it is. 'I was raised to get married before having babies, and to marry for better or for worse.' You know what I told her then? 'You were also raised to take care of your family.' She hung up on me."

"Would you have ever left Papa Doc?"

"If he had tried to keep me from my own flesh and blood, I would have left him in a heartbeat. I never once had to explain that to him, either."

Around the table, Granny suggested that the girls spend the night. She said that she could run them home the next day after church.

"Oh, Mother . . . Please."

"I wish I'd thought of that. Mrs. Flo said that she could spend the night, but we didn't bring any church clothes. Anyhow. They're expecting her home tonight."

"Maybe soon." Granny Addie assured them.

On the drive back to Knoxo Springs, the new best friends were giggling about something in the backseat. The driver was alone in her thoughts when she heard the voice droning in her head.

"Look what you've done now, girl. You've driven your poor old daddy crazy."

Code T

Michelle's initial excitement regarding the price of her house was quickly offset when she learned of her pay scale. Her salary was only about

Miss Bizzy Belle

three-fourths of what she had been making. It all seemed to balance out, though. At least there was some satisfaction in building a little home equity.

She was not the only one with her mind on the finances. Tonya waltzed in one afternoon and said rather stoically. "Mother . . . I think it's time I got an allowance."

Michelle frowned, but Tonya was not deterred.

"Now wait a minute. Before you get all bent out of shape, just think about how much better this would be for both of us. If I had an allowance, I wouldn't be so much trouble for you. I have to pester you for lunch money, and then I'm always hitting you up when we go to movies or the rink. I know how to take care of money, and I'd like to be able to save for things. I want to buy my own clothes, too."

Michelle knew that she had to hear her daughter out. "How much did you have in mind?"

"Oh . . . I don't know. How about a hundred dollars a month?"

"In your dreams, kiddo."

The more Michelle thought about it, the more she liked the idea. The next day she made Tonya a counter offer. "What about fifteen dollars a week? Half of it without strings—the other half you have to work for."

"You mean . . . Like chores?"

"That's exactly what I mean. Wash the dishes, help keep the house clean, do your own laundry. That sort of thing."

"But Mother . . . After I pay my lunch money, hardly anything will be left. How about twenty?"

"Deal."

Tonya walked away feeling like she got the better part of that bargain. She was already doing the things on the list, anyway. Now, she would get paid for them. Michelle figured that she came out on the plus side. Tonya was right. Her daughter would not be pestering her so much, at least about money.

Backing out of the drive, Michelle thought to herself. "If Tonya walks to school, I guess I could certainly walk to work." The hospital was only a quarter of a mile down the hill. She drove anyway since she would already be on her feet the rest of the day. The real reason was that she did not like the thought of the steep climb back to the Villa after she got off.

Barbara worked with her on her schedule. Michelle was assigned the first shift, but she had to work every other weekend and was on call the others. It was nice not to have to worry about daycare. At least she was saving that money.

If Tonya needed to talk to her mother about something, she stopped by the hospital on the way home. The girl quickly made friends with the woman at the information desk who promptly announced a "Code T" over the sound system whenever Tonya arrived.

Other staff soon figured out what the new code meant. They stopped by and chatted with Miss Bell while she was waiting for Nurse Bell. Michelle was reminded often of what a precocious daughter she had. She acknowledged that there were also other ways to describe the girl.

That precocious daughter was stymied, however, when it came to finding her mother's lockbox. She and Sammie decided that it must be in the trunk of the car. The next time Michelle came home with groceries, Tonya ran to assist her. Unless the boot had its own secret compartment, it was not there, either.

Tonya came out of her room one evening while her mother was preparing supper. Michelle instructed her to look in the bottom of the hutch and put out some different place mats. No way! It was right there in the kitchen. It never occurred to either junior detective that the little metal box might be hiding almost in plain sight.

Tonya could not wait to get her hands on it, but she had no choice. Her bedtime came first, and her mother was in no hurry to turn in. The next day after school the partners in crime got to hold the cache in their own hands.

The only thing between the girls and their booty was a lock worthy of protecting Fort Knox. They tried unsuccessfully to pick it. The only way to open it was with the key, which was on Michelle's key ring, which was always in her purse, which she kept in her bedroom. The young investigators had to lie in wait and bide their time.

Michelle had not had a medical exam since she stopped working for the doctors. She scheduled a mammogram and made an appointment with the new female gynecologist in Ephesus. Her vehicle was also in need of service, and she planned to get that taken care of on the same day.

Coming into town, she saw an auto parts place and thought maybe someone at the counter might recommend a reliable shop. The cashier referred her to Hank Farmer's Garage since it was near the hospital. She thanked him and turned to leave just as a man rolled out of the office area in a wheelchair. He nodded to her.

Running a little ahead of schedule, she approached him.

"Vietnam?"

He nodded again . . . Several times.

"I thought so." Michelle was not accustomed to sharing personal information, but the two of them had a connection that she decided to mention.

"I was a nurse at Walter Reed for almost four years, and I worked with wounded soldiers."

Phillip Parker's eyes lit up.

"I spent a few days there myself. You know. I felt bad after I was discharged and sent to a VA hospital here in the state. Guys like me were so angry at the time that we didn't appreciate the hard work people like you were doing. Maybe this doesn't sound like much, but on behalf of all the jerks like me, please accept our sincerest apologies."

Michelle was moved by the man's sentiments. She told him how much she appreciated the assistance that she had received from one of his employees. When she dropped her car off, Hank said that it would be ready before she got back. Only one oil change was ahead of hers.

All of Walt's graduate school classmates scattered to the four corners except for two. Eli Pierce became a chaplain and served at the Ephesus Hospital. The other was Hannah Parker, Phillip's wife.

Walt left his Toyota at Hank's one morning on his way to chat with Eli. As he entered the front door of the hospital, Michelle was not far behind him on her way to a doctor's appointment just across the street.

When he picked up Mary Lou, Hank told him the vehicle needed new wiper blades. Walt had to hurry back to the office for an appointment with a client. Later that afternoon, he went to the parts place just in time to see Hannah getting into her car. Phillip had no idea who Walt was, and he never told him about looking in on him when he was at Walter Reed.

Walt tapped the horn to get Hannah's attention. She spoke before he had a chance to.

"I just had an interesting conversation with my husband. He said that a nurse who used to work at Walter Reed came in this morning. Said she was redheaded, too. Wasn't your little diversion up there also a redhead?"

"You're never going to let me live that down, are you?"

"Not if I can help it."

"Did he get her name and number? Maybe I should look her up."

Hannah drove away with the look on her face that still made Walt flush.

The Holy Grail

When Michelle walked in the front door after work on a Friday with a wide-open weekend ahead, two munchkins were waiting for her. Tonya took her mother's hand. "Please come and sit down. Sammie and I have a big surprise for you."

She took the woman's purse and put it on the kitchen table. Before Michelle had time to react, her daughter continued.

"Mother . . . I know you're exhausted after a hard week at work. First, we're going to run a big tub of hot water." Holding up a bottle of bubble bath, she smiled innocently. "See what I bought with my allowance?"

Michelle returned the smile but still did not have a chance to say anything. "While you're soaking in the tub, Sammie and I are going to pop a pizza in the oven."

The perplexed woman finally found an opening. "Where did you get a pizza?"

"It was in the Ringers' freezer. Mrs. Flo said we could have it since it had been there for a while."

Actually. They had not asked, but there was little chance that it would be missed.

"You girls are so wonderful. You just don't know how much this means to me."

"Shall we start filling the tub? Let me put your favorite record on."

Michelle sank into the soothing water to the sounds of the theme from *Dr. Zhivago* filling the Villa while the co-conspirators moved forward with the two tasks at hand.

Sammie turned the oven on and started taking the pizza out of its wrap. Tonya retrieved the lockbox and instructed her cohort to keep an eye on the bathroom door just in case.

She went diving in the purse until her hands found the keys. It had to be the smallest one on the ring. With her heart racing and palms sweating, she inserted it into the lock. It turned, releasing its hold. The girls looked at each other.

Sammie whispered. "Go ahead . . . Open it."

As the lid came up, Tonya made a mental note of how everything was arranged. On top, was an official-looking envelope. She peered inside and pulled out two social security cards. "I didn't know I had a social security number."

A small snap-top box was over on one side. Tonya lifted the lid, looked inside, and held up a modest diamond ring. "This must be my mother's engagement ring."

Sammie said nothing but gestured for her to get on with it.

Miss Bizzy Belle

A couple of insurance policies were in the next layer. One was her mother's health insurance, but the other was a life policy. It had her name on it. Tonya looked at it and thought out loud. "Maybe it's not too late for Mother to change her mind."

Sammie was growing impatient. "Hurry up."

On the very bottom, were two birth certificates. The one on top was her mother's. Tonya held it up and looked it over. She took a deep breath. The other was hers. Tonya had found the Holy Grail.

She wanted to look, but at the same time, she was scared. Sammie urged her on. With hands trembling, she took another deep breath and then unfolded it. Tonya tried to hand the document to Sammie, but she pushed it back.

For so long, she had been waiting for this moment. With newly-found resolve, her eyes darted from place to place on the document. She already knew her name. She saw where her mother's name had been entered. She knew that, too. Her eyes finally came to the spot they were searching for. In the space reserved for the baby's father's identity were two words.

"Name withheld."

Each afternoon when the two girls came out the front door of the elementary school, the only thing they had to decide was whether they were going right or left. Right went toward the Ringers' house. Left went to the street the hospital was on, and then to Lane Lane. They had more privacy at Tonya's, but Sammie had more stuff.

Michelle had been pleasantly surprised that Sammie's parents were not overindulging their daughter. The physician made more money than many of the residents of Knoxo Springs, but he was still paying off medical school debt. The Ringers believed that earning was an essential part of learning. They did not want their children raised any differently from others in the neighborhood. Sammie also had her chores. To Michelle's amazement, the girl's allowance was about the same as Tonya's.

The single mom knew that she had made mistakes in her life. If she never did anything else right, however, moving to Knoxo Springs must have been inspired. The deep and powerful connection between Tonya and Sammie was proof of that. It was the closest that she had ever come to believing in serendipity.

The girl who lived on the dead end street had certainly come to another dead end in the search for her father. The resourceful little investigator shifted her mind back into gear. Tonya thought of yet another angle that might provide a clue.

Two Saturday nights later when her mother was not working the weekend, the dutiful daughter cleaned the table after supper, washed the dishes, dried them, and put them away.

Michelle was watching TV. Tonya came up from behind the chair she was sitting in, put her arms around her, and asked warmly. "Mother? Would you like for me to pour you a little glass of wine?"

"Only if you don't mention it to Twerp. We wouldn't want his daddy coming over here and arresting you for serving alcohol underage." Michelle was proud of herself. That was clever. "But only about half a glass."

Tonya followed her mother's instructions and then added another jigger. Michelle began to chill and relax. After a few minutes when she got up to go to the bathroom, the waitress freshened her drink.

Before her mother got too sleepy, the undercover agent made her move.

"Why did you name me Tonya?"

"Have I never told you that story? I thought maybe I already had. I went on a date a long time ago. I only saw the guy a few times. On our first date, he took me to see the movie, *Dr. Zhivago*."

The wine was slowly working.

"Are you sure I haven't told you this already? I really got into it. I hope I've not bored you to death playing the soundtrack. Remember when we first got the VCR and I rented the movie? We watched it together."

Tonya nodded for her to go on, but she must have been too small to remember.

"Anyway . . . The film had a girl named Tonya in it. I fell in love with the name that night and said that if I ever had a daughter, I would name her Tonya."

"Mother? Was that man my daddy?"

"Yes . . . He was your father."

Michelle got up and carefully made her way to the bedroom before she said anything more. Tonya fetched her secret file.

"Can I have a birthday party?" "Please?" "Please?" "Please?" "I've never had one before."

"What did you have in mind?"

"Mrs. Flo said we could have it in their backyard if we wanted to. She said that if we buttered him up a little bit, Mr. Ebb might grill hamburgers and hotdogs. All we would have to do is buy invitations and decorations for the basement. I want butterflies."

"Please?" "Please?" "Please?"

"Who would you invite?"

"Sammie and I already have the list made out."

"I'm just not going to be caught up in any kind of competition where everybody is trying to outdo everyone else."

"I don't really care about gifts. I just want to have a get together with some of my friends."

"Let me talk with Mrs. Flo about it."

"Thank you." "Thank you." "Thank you."

On Saturday afternoon, two days after her ninth birthday, Tonya had her first party. Mr. Ebb came through, and the group of all girls played some silly games.

Michelle was wearing a beautiful red rose the next morning when Mr. Griffin greeted mother and daughter at the church on Mother's Day. Tonya and Sammie had sneaked into a neighbor's yard and cut it after the party was over.

When they got back to the Villa, Tonya proudly presented her mother with a small neatly wrapped Mother's Day gift. It had taken months to save enough to buy the *Dr. Zhivago* video.

Michelle was obviously pleased with her present. "Do you want to watch it this afternoon?"

"Only if you want to, Mother. Remember . . . It's your day."

George King

Mrs. Hart turned out to be not so heartless after all. She was tough, but Tonya thrived on challenges. The teacher came to her defense a couple more times like she did on the first day.

The new student was still not so sure about the "Old Wag." Tonya overheard Mrs. Flo telling somebody that because Mrs. Wagner was the first woman principal in the county, she had something to prove. When Mr. Ebb and Mrs. Flo said something, they usually knew what they were talking about.

Tonya figured that she was off limits to the principal during her first year. After that, she knew she was fair game. She was afraid that there might be some issues between the two of them before it was all over.

151

Tonya tried not to make enemies, but when she was just being herself, she sometimes showed others up. Consequently, a line was always forming somewhere of those trying to get her in trouble.

The summer was ahead for now, and Knoxo Springs had a budding recreational program. Kids flocked to sign up for their favorite sports. Tonya never had anyone to play ball with her before. She was not sure how she was going to do, but she was eager to give it a whirl. When she told her teacher that she wanted to play soccer, the other students did not know what she was talking about. Knoxo Springs had a little catching up to do.

The first two weeks after school let out was considered family vacation time. The athletic activities began after that. The Ringers usually went to Florida. They invited Tonya to go with them, but Michelle declined, claiming that it would be too much trouble for them. Mrs. Flo was unable to convince her that it might actually be less.

Tonya's consolation prize was that she got to visit her great-grandparents while Sammie was gone. When Michelle dropped her off at Granny Addie's on the first leg, Tonya could tell that something was up. Conversations stopped abruptly when she entered the room, but she clearly overheard the name, Tolbert.

In bits and pieces, Michelle learned that her father was out of the mental health facility. He was making slower progress than what they had hoped for. The school had hired a substitute to finish out the year, but the math teacher planned on returning in the fall. Granny said he was much more subdued, and that he reminded her of a sleepwalker.

"I think they keep him doped up. I so much wish that you could be there to help your mother interpret things. I asked Connie about it, and she said that it would only upset Tolbert. Looks like to me that man's been digging his own grave for some time now."

Michelle was a little concerned about her granny. "Are you sure you're up for making the drive to Bellville?"

"Been making it about twice a year since before you were born. Doc went with me sometimes, but I usually made the trip by myself. Anyhow. I'll have company this time. I called the Bells and told them to expect Tonya. She answered the phone and didn't seem too excited, but when he figured out what was going on, I could hear him in the background."

Pa Bell greeted them. "There's my little Peanut. I've been a little down in the mouth lately, and you're just the tonic I need. Got more company on the way, too. My old friend George King is coming over tomorrow. Says he's bringing his missus, too, if she's able."

Then, Mr. Bell turned to Mrs. Baker. "I know Connie will be glad to see you. All of this has really been rough on her. And on us, too."

Tonya stood by taking it all in. She would have a lot to take in over the next couple of days.

As Granny Addie drove away, Pa Bell turned his attention to the girl. "You learned to whistle Dixie yet?"

Tonya puckered her lips, stuck her chest out, and did not miss a note. The old man then joined her as they did a Dixie duet. Pa Bell's torso also swelled a bit.

When they finished, he looked down at her. "I hope you brought some work clothes. We need to plow the garden this afternoon. I want it to look good when company gets here. You can sit in my lap and we can whistle while we work."

The Kings arrived not long after breakfast the next morning. George said there was no need in sitting around watching the clock. He reminded them that they gained an hour when they crossed the Alabama line.

Tonya stayed with the ladies most of the morning, but to her great disappointment, they did not discuss family in front of her. The men went to the barn and looked at the garden. Mama Myra had done most of the cooking the day before. All she had to do was make cornbread. Tonya helped set the table.

After lunch, she followed the men when they went to sit under the shade tree. They did not seem to mind at all.

"George . . . We've seen a lot of changes in our time."

Mr. King nodded in agreement.

For the next hour or so, Tonya was enthralled. She heard the distinguished southern gentlemen talk about hard times because of something called a "Depression." They spoke of wars and of their farming days. Realizing that she was listening in, Pa Bell explained some things to her so she could keep up.

Inevitably, the conversation got around to when they were first acquainted. The men talked about their trucks, the ornery mules they hauled on them, and the farmers they traded with.

"Buford . . . Those were the good ole days." Mr. King then turned and addressed the little lady.

"When I spent the night here one time, I thought your mother was about the cutest redheaded girl I'd ever seen. Is her hair still that red?"

"Just about. Except for the gray hairs that I've given her."

Both men laughed.

"I told my grandson all about your ma. I tried to get him to send her a letter. I reminded him that as the boy, he would have to make the first move. I thought they might become pen pals, or something, maybe even sweethearts. I guess he never got around to it. He was a bright kid, but always a little shy around girls. Buford. It's a shame that we never got those two together."

When Michelle came to pick Tonya up, her daughter was bursting at the seams.

"Did you know that Mr. George King wanted to fix you up with his grandson, Walt? He and Pa Bell said they were sorry that the two of you never got together."

Michelle felt the blood running to her toes. Afraid that Tonya was watching for a reaction, she tried to act indifferent.

"Who is Mr. King? How would you know anything about that?"

"Oh, Mother . . . You know who Mr. King is. Not long ago, Pa Bell told us about going to Georgia to see him. He and his wife came over here for a visit while I was here. Mr. King told me about seeing you one time and what a pretty girl you were. He talked about your red hair. Don't you remember him? He said that he tried to get Walt to write you or something, but he guessed he never did."

Before she could catch herself, Michelle let something slip. "Did Mr. King say anything about where his grandson is now?"

Tonya had a devilish little grin on her face. "Why? Do you think it might not be too late?"

Her mother was not amused. "No. That's not what I meant at all."

"To answer your question, Mother. Mr. King said that Walt quit his job at some college, and moved somewhere else. If he mentioned a town, I wasn't paying attention, but I believe he said that Walt stayed in North Carolina. Do you think we might be neighbors?"

"Girl! You've got some kind of imagination!"

On the way home, Tonya tried to tell her mom about some other things that she did. When she could not keep her attention, she gave up. "Mother . . . You must be really tired. You're sure not in a talkative mood."

"I'm sorry, Tonya. My work is very stressful, and I can't get my mind off some of the patients."

Tonya reached for a book.

What Michelle really had her mind wrapped around was that her daughter had sat at the feet of her two great-grandfathers. The troubled mother had presumed that the two old friends had finally grown apart and were no longer in contact. Now, she had something else to worry about. What if Walt's Grandpa told him about Tonya?

At least, the girl had only referred to Walt by his first name. So far as she knew, Tonya had never put the names, Walt and Williamson together, but she was never sure if her daughter told her everything.

Everybody's a winner

Sammie came back from Florida with a mild tan. She complained that she was still not as brown as Tonya was. Her best friend said she mostly had a good time, but that Stanley was becoming more and more of a pest. One night she got sick after eating seafood. "Daddy said it was too much grease."

Tonya was ready to get on with the summer. "Are we gonna go out for any of the teams?"

"I don't know. I'm not all that coordinated. Why don't we try out for softball?"

Most of the other kids played Tee Ball and then moved up to the next levels as their skills improved. On the first day of practice, Tonya ran up to the coach and asked him when they were going to get their "costumes." She did not see anything funny about it, but he surely did.

During practice, the coach showed her how to hold a bat, but it felt awkward. He then instructed her in how to stand squared to the plate. When he threw her some gentle, underhanded pitches, she just stood and watched the balls glide right over the plate. Exasperated, he told her to swing at them.

After Tonya's third swing and miss, she pounded the end of the bat to the ground, glared at the coach, and set him straight.

"You keep missing my bat."

The uniforms finally arrived. When the girls were back at Sammie's, they could not wait to try them on. Mrs. Flo took several pictures.

Once the season started, both girls sat on the bench. Each nagged the coach to put her in the game, but neither was really excited about going out and making a fool of herself. After the fourth game, they turned in their uniforms.

A big awards ceremony was held at the end of the season. Tonya and Sammie went because they had nothing better to do. The school auditorium was packed. When the recreation department director strolled to the microphone, he tapped it a couple of times. As the rowdy crowd settled down, he revved them right back up.

"Everybody's a winner. There are no losers." The crowd cheered.

Championship teams were crowned. A curtain then opened with a couple of long tables loaded with small trophies for each participant. As the volunteer coaches joined the moderator on the stage to hand them out, he repeated what he had said before with great emphasis.

"Everybody's a winner. There are no losers. We have no all-stars, just all stars." Once more, his words were greeted with rousing approval.

Tonya could not believe it when her name was called out. She had quit the team without ever entering a single game. They thought she was a winner? She ducked her head and refused to go pick up her cheap plastic trophy.

With her patented little whine, Tonya made her plea. "Mother? Can we please get a bird feeder?"

"I don't know. Do any birds stay around here during the winter?"

"They would if they had something to eat. Mother . . . If you'll get the feeder, I'll buy the seed with my allowance."

"Well . . . Let me think about it."

Tonya made sure that her mom did not forget it. When she finally dragged her to the feed and seed store, Michelle complained that the feeders were kind of expensive. The salesman tried to persuade her otherwise.

"It will be well worth every penny. This economy model doesn't even require a pole. It can be hung from a tree limb. I'll even give you a little piece of chain."

The clerk told Tonya that unlike big box stores, he sold only the kind of seed that the local birds liked, not worthless filler grain that they just threw on the ground.

He did his job well. "You're going to be surprised at how fast they will find the feeder, and by how many different species you're going to attract."

An hour later, the bird feeder was swinging from a limb outside Tonya's bedroom window. Before dark, it had its first visitor. Word spread quickly among the birdie residents of Lane Lane.

Two days later, Michelle was reminded again that with her daughter, one thing usually led to another . . . And often, even to another.

"Mother . . . I need a field guide so I can identify the birds."

Michelle just took a deep breath and sighed.

"And don't you think it's about time I got a little increase in my allowance?"

Tolbert Bell was a tormented man. He steeled himself just to get through each day. Most students shied away from his classes, but the ones going to college had no choice. The principal had to relinquish the math teacher's right to paddle students after some normally supportive parents complained.

Like a mathematical proposition, he had failed. Therefore, he was a failure.

The father had failed as a parent. He could not even produce a son strong enough to live. His only daughter turned her back on her raising, and she was now living in sin.

The husband had failed his wife. She had to live with the shame of having a companion who had been hauled off to a nuthouse.

The Christian had failed his church. His calling was to be exemplary. He failed as a man because he was supposed to be the model of human perfection. In so doing, he failed his God.

Above all else, the dutiful son had failed his own mother.

Stars fell on North Carolina

Knoxo Springs was abuzz. Rumor had it that another movie company was headed to town. When all contracts were signed, shooting was set to begin between court sessions in the spring of 1979.

Adults and kids alike speculated about the chances of becoming extras. Twerp said that his pa had already been asked to play a bailiff. If the class had taken a straw poll on who believed him, he would have gotten exactly two votes—Twit's and his own.

Wishing to put its best foot forward, the city council took the prospects as a mandate to hasten revitalization projects. Idled by a stagnant economy, construction workers eagerly sharpened their tools. There was not an unemployed painter for miles around.

This circus did not come to town in one long parade. Executives drifted in, followed by a steady stream of production equipment. Tonya and Sammie went across the tracks to the courthouse almost every day after school to check out the newest developments.

When the phone rang at the Ringers' one afternoon during spring holidays, Mrs. Flo said it was Mrs. Wagner, and that she was looking for Tonya. One could only imagine the faces of the two girls when they heard that news. Whatever this was about, there was never a doubt that Sammie would stand by her.

When Tonya said, "Hello," she heard the voice of the school principal say sternly. "Good. When I couldn't get you at home, I thought I might find you there. Can you come to the school as soon as possible? Your mother needs to come, too."

Period. That's all she said. Tonya had absolutely no idea what was going on, but she thought it was entirely possible that it was showdown time with the Old Wag. Several scenarios started running through her mind.

The girl called the hospital and told her mother all she knew. One could only imagine the look on Michelle's face.

Mrs. Flo decided to go along just in case Tonya was in big trouble and in need of an advocate. The two girls and the two mothers arrived about the same time. Mrs. Wagner stood expressionless at the front door of the school.

"Come on into my office. Tonya . . . There's somebody inside who wants to meet you."

The girl froze. The others were already through the door when they realized that they had left her behind.

Was it her daddy? Had he found her?

Was that why her mother had to come, too?

So far, everybody was batting zero.

Mrs. Wagner introduced a man in an expensive looking suit. Mr. Boyce was the executive director of the movie company. The man was a bit rotund and had big bushy eyebrows. Strictly business, he explained the situation.

Contracts had all been signed to start shooting the courthouse scenes except for one. It involved a ten-year-old girl who was going to play the part of an important witness. At the last minute, the temperamental child star's fickle mother had yanked her from the set. No one was sure if or when they might return. Mr. Boyce indicated that the actors and crew members could not sit idly by while the difficult mom indulged in a tantrum.

The executive said that he came to the school and explained the situation to Mrs. Wagner. He asked if she might recommend three or four girls to interview, and see if one of them might at least stand in during rehearsals while the touchy negotiations continued.

He walked over to Tonya and took her hand. "Mrs. Wagner said only one name came to her mind. That must be you."

One could only imagine the looks on four faces in the principal's office.

Mr. Boyce asked if that was something she might be interested in. Sammie, standing beside her, answered for her.

"Of course, that's something she's interested in. Where does she sign her name?"

"And you would be?"

Extending her hand, she introduced herself. "I'm Samantha Ringer."

"Miss Ringer . . . I do hope we don't have any problems working with

Miss Bizzy Belle

Miss Bell's agent. Yes. There are papers to sign . . . If we get that far."

The movie director looked over at Michelle. "What do you think about all of this?"

Tonya's mother did not have anyone to speak for her, and she was momentarily mute. Mr. Boyce was familiar with stage fright.

With all eyes on her, she was finally able to say something. "I guess it's all right with me if that's what she wants to do."

The agent had a question. "When do we get started?"

Meanwhile, the future academy award winner had not uttered a word.

Mrs. Wagner stepped forward. "I'm interested in hearing what Tonya has to say."

"Cool . . . Sounds like fun."

Mr. Boyce seemed more relaxed when he suggested that the meeting adjourn, and then reconvene at his portable office near the courthouse. He invited everyone present to come along if they wished.

Agent Ringer apparently spoke for all of them. "I wouldn't miss this for anything." The entourage made its way across the tracks.

As Michelle started the engine, she looked over at her daughter. "Well, kiddo, I think it's about time that I had a little raise in my allowance, and I want it to start with a new car."

The young witness in the script did not have just a minor part. Her testimony was crucial to the outcome of the trial. She would be grilled by both the prosecution and the defense before dropping a bombshell.

Mr. Boyce gave Tonya a script of the first few scenes. He asked her to familiarize herself with her lines. He reminded her that she was just filling in. It was fine if she read the lines during the rehearsal, but she must keep up and not disrupt the flow and momentum. She was assured that the other actors would also be reading in the initial walk through.

The director then turned to Tonya's agent. He was really addressing his remarks to Michelle, but he played along. He said that whether or not Tonya was ever involved in any actual filming, she would be compensated for her time on an hourly basis. In the rare event that she landed a bit part somewhere, she would be paid as an extra. The lawyers were already drawing up a simple contract just in case.

Agent Ringer asked the same question again. "When do we start?"

"How about in the morning? Eight sharp."

As those in the little gathering were getting up to leave, Mr. Boyce turned to Mrs. Wagner. He thanked her for providing such vital assistance. He then became more specific.

"As you know, we're going to need several extras. An announcement has already been posted that auditions will be held on Saturday morning. I can put you at the head of the line if you wish. How would you like to play the part of the jury foreman?"

Once back at the Villa, Tonya opened the screenplay and looked it over. Mr. Boyce only asked her to become familiar with her lines, which were highlighted for her, but she wanted to feel the action. After reading through the ten pages three times, she folded up the script, put on her pajamas, and told her mother goodnight.

Looking at the starry sky outside her window, Tonya addressed her co-stars.

"Hey, you guys. Looks like you might have some new competition. But don't get too worried."

She was sawing logs in about ten minutes. Michelle hardly slept a wink.

The film was never destined to be more than a B-movie. Its actors were mostly in the twilights of their careers. The producers and directors had yet to make their marks. The story had an offbeat plot, and the aim was to inject comedy into a dramatic circumstance.

While it was Tonya's first day on the job, the production crew had been working for weeks. Up to the time of the trial, the movie had already been shot elsewhere. Only a limited cast made the trek to film these episodes.

Mr. Boyce met Tonya and Sammie when they arrived. He introduced the actress and her agent to Mr. Wainwright, the associate director, who actually ran the show. He then presented Tonya to the crew as rehearsals were about to begin. They gave her a round of applause.

The executive director asked Tonya and Sammie to sit with him until the witness was called to the stand to be sworn in. He suggested to Tonya that she just relax and be herself. He did not know her well enough to read her mind.

It took a while for Mr. Wainwright to get everything arranged. The cameras had to be put into their places even though the film was not rolling. Lighting and sound crews tested their equipment and then made adjustments. The girls had no idea what all went into a production.

As Mr. Boyce had predicted, the actors playing the parts of the judge and the lawyers held scripts in their hands for the first reading. Tonya had hers ready. The action finally began.

The defense attorney and the prosecutor bantered back and forth with the judge. Abruptly, Tonya's character was called to the stand. Sammie sang out. "Break a leg." The stand-in, with her head high, and her hand on a Bible that the local bookstore had loaned, uttered the first words of her budding acting career.

"I do."

The judge instructed the witness to please be seated.

Mr. Boyce remained in the director's chair while Mr. Wainwright moved about sometimes just pointing, and at others, giving verbal instructions. "Action." He called out, and then he went to stand beside the executive director.

Tonya looked at the script a time or two, but she mostly followed the wrangling. As it was getting closer to her first lines, Mr. Wainwright became concerned that she was not following the dialogue. When she still did not look at the script, he made a move toward her to prompt her. Mr. Boyce reached for his arm and held him back.

The judge asked her a question. She looked up at him and said her lines, not missing a word.

The defense attorney then began grilling her. Without looking down, she answered each query with a little flair. The directors looked at each other.

Once that round of questioning was over, Mr. Wainwright declared a break. Tonya left the stand and went to join Sammie. They faced each other holding hands and giggling.

About that time, an assistant called out to Mr. Boyce that the prima donna's mother was on the phone. "Tell her that I will speak only with the agent."

Moments later, she hollered back that the woman said she had fired the agent, but that she was now ready to talk.

"Tell her I'm busy, and cannot speak with her right now."

The second scene followed the same script with Tonya performing flawlessly. By noon, they had walked through the entire section several times. Mr. Wainwright looked down at Tonya each time and said to her. "You're doing fine."

The actors were then dismissed to study their lines and to start preparing for the next scenes. Rehearsals would begin at the same time the next morning. Tonya was sent home with more pages to look over. The associate director made his way to Mr. Boyce's office.

"I think we've found ourselves a little jewel. I've already called our favorite stage mom and told her that she missed the deadline. She was livid and said that she would see me in court. Huh. I'm shaking in my boots."

Then he added with a chuckle. "I don't think we're going to have any problems at all dealing with Miss Bell's agent." They both lit a cigar.

Michelle got another phone call that afternoon. She was invited back to Mr. Boyce's office, along with her daughter/actress, and the agent. Shortly thereafter, they were introduced to a couple of professional looking people from the producer's office. The man was a lawyer. The woman wore her hair up in a bun and had on dark rim glasses. She was holding a pen and pad.

The woman's hairstyle did not go unnoticed by the actress. "Hmm. Ms. Hairball has a twin."

The man addressed his remarks to the girl's mother. "We're prepared to offer Miss Bell a contract to play the part of Claire." Downplaying the situation, he added. "We'd like to keep things as simple as possible. Are you on board?"

"I have no objection. She seems okay with it. But I insist that she use a stage name. I don't want people knocking on our door at all hours of the night wanting autographs."

Agent Ringer had a suggestion. "How about Miss Bizzy Belle?"

Tonya nodded in agreement. "Sounds perfect."

"Ms. Bell and Miss Bell . . . We can offer compensation at the rate of ten dollars per hour including all rehearsal times. Is that agreeable?"

Agent Ringer was on the job. "Twenty, and fifty for actual filming, and her agent gets 10 percent."

Mr. Boyce countered. "Fifteen, and thirty." He looked up at the accountant taking notes, and she nodded.

Tonya's agent raised the ante. "And 1 percent royalty."

"I'm afraid that's out of our hands. Since Miss Bell is not a professional actor, no royalties can be offered. Is there anything else?"

The agent was not through negotiating. "Yes . . . Ten dollars an hour paid to our teacher for private tutoring if Miss Bell has to miss school."

Again, he got the nod.

One more thing she added. "On the days of actual filming, the actress, and her agent will be picked up at my house by a limousine."

Mr. Boyce was loving this. "My personal driver will pick you up in my Mercedes."

"Done."

"Ms. Bell, and Miss Bell . . . If you'll come back in an hour, the papers will be ready to sign."

As Mr. Boyce rose from his chair, Tonya's agent had one more demand.

"When the credits are running and the actors' names are up on the screen, end the movie in larger lettering, 'And Introducing Miss Bizzy Belle, as Claire'."

Mr. Boyce sighed, took a deep breath, and extended his hand to the agent. Under his breath, he was thinking. "That might not be such a bad idea at all."

When the producer's accountant and attorney went to his office to give a report after the contract was signed, he asked how it went.

The accountant said with a big smile. "I think we might have just gotten the bargain of the century. If things go according to Hoyle, we should have some wiggle room to tack on a little bonus." She then described how enchanting it was working with Agent Ringer.

The producer was pleased. "How sweet and how refreshing. Maybe we can find a little spot for her somewhere in the film."

The attorney was equally delighted with the fortuitous developments. "Perhaps, we need to go ahead and put her on the payroll as an agent negotiator."

After his office cleared, Mr. Boyce propped his feet up on his desk. The sweet smell of cigar smoke soon filled the room.

Under his wings

Mr. Boyce felt protective of Tonya and took her under his wings. He had little sympathy for those who got bumps in their bank accounts and bruises to their egos when they knew the ruthlessness of the system before they signed up. The last thing that he wanted was for this girl to get hurt. When his new discovery arrived at the courthouse on day two, he called her off to the side.

"What do you think so far?" The executive director was not prepared for Tonya's response.

"I can do this. But some of my lines are kind of dumb and really boring. I thought this was supposed to be a comedy."

"Hmm. What did you have in mind?"

"Can I just be myself?"

"Hmm. Let me speak with Mr. Wainwright about this."

As rehearsals began, Mr. Boyce took his customary seat in the director's chair. Tonya glanced over at him. He smiled and gave her a nod.

Tonya gained more and more confidence. Each time she went through a scene, she adapted it more to her liking. Other actors had to start ad-libbing just to keep up with her. They all got so tickled a time or two that the rehearsals had to stop and start all over again.

Miss Bizzy Belle was holding court.

Alas . . . It all ended about as fast as it began. The Mercedes pulled up to the Ringers' front door no more than a dozen times, with Mrs. Flo's video camera always doing some whirling of its own. Tonya learned all about makeup, and when it was over, she got to keep her "costume."

Mrs. Wagner presided over a jury box filled with familiar faces. In a couple of shots panning the courtroom filled with locals, Sammie was seen sitting beside the defense attorney. She was staged as star witness Claire's best friend.

Twerp had new bragging rights. His "girlfriend" was a famous movie star.

Mr. Boyce said that he would be back for the opening at the Knoxo Springs Theater. He would round up as many of the other cast members as he could for the gala event. He told Tonya and her agent to look for checks in the mail.

On Tonya's tenth birthday, she declared herself a double-digit-pre-teenager. Just before school turned out, Mr. Boyce made good on his promise. When she saw the amount on the check, her eyes sparkled, but Michelle did not get her new car. She said that the $2000 was going straight to the bank and into a college fund.

Sammie cashed her checks. Her agent's commission was $200, and she got another fifty for being an extra. She hid the money in her secret cache and promised her best friend that it would be their mad money.

Tonya went to Florida with the Ringers, and some of that cash exchanged hands. The celebrities got back into town just in time for the season kick-off of the summer recreation program.

The best friends decided to take a shot at basketball. They thought they had a jump on the game since the Ringers had a goal in their backyard. On the first day of practice, Tonya's shots kept coming up short. The coach moved her a little closer to the goal. The ball then went sailing over the top of the backboard.

Tonya looked up at her coach with disgust. "That was a perfect shot. You just made me stand in the wrong place." The girls were kicked off the team before the costumes were even handed out.

After all the excitement of fourth grade, fifth was a big letdown. Only one date on the calendar mattered to Sammie, and she was not even sure when it was. Tonya shrugged the movie premier off as no big deal.

Miss Bizzy Belle

In early October, something else came in the mail for Tonya with a Hollywood postmark. When she unwrapped it, she was looking at a colorful movie poster. The marquee in the picture was much larger than the one at the local theater. The movie title was in bright lights. Underneath it in an inset, was clear evidence that having Sammie as an agent was paying dividends.

"Introducing Miss Bizzy Belle, as Claire."

The bottom half of the poster announced a premier showing in Knoxo Springs on Saturday, October 27, 1979. A note attached indicated that a large supply of posters would arrive in time for Tonya to autograph them that evening.

Mr. Boyce said that he was looking forward to seeing her again, and the release of the movie coincided with the peak leaf season. He was hoping for a sell out every night. He also told the actress and her agent to expect a surprise.

The weather could not have cooperated more for the local premier. Michelle made sure that she had the day off, and Granny Addie arrived about mid-afternoon. She said nothing short of a knock on the door by the grim reaper would stop her from attending Tonya's movie opening.

A reception was planned in the courtroom for all those appearing in the film. The director sent word to Tonya and Sammie that they would be picked up at their usual place. Instead of his Mercedes, a limousine pulled up at the Ringers' with Mr. Boyce already inside. One can only imagine the looks on the girls' faces.

As he took the podium, the executive director apologized that none of the other cast members were able to attend since most of them were busy on other movie sets. He thanked all of the film extras again before introducing somebody they all already knew.

"Let me present to you, Knoxo Springs' own Miss Bizzy Belle."

Decked out in a long dress that also arrived in a package from Hollywood, she received a standing ovation. The press was well represented, and Tonya was blinded by flashbulbs.

People were already lined up to get tickets when they got to the theater. The featured guest was escorted to a table with a stack of posters. Sammie greeted the fans and handed them out. Most people just wanted the stage name signature, but some asked for personal comments. The actress was pleased to comply.

Michelle told Tonya that she was going to take Granny inside so they could get a good spot. She reminded her daughter that she and Sammie did not have to worry about that. They had reserved seats with the big boss.

Walt Williamson met Chaplain Pierce for lunch on the Saturday of the movie premier. Eli asked if he would like to ride out and see the movie that had scenes shot in Knoxo Springs.

"I'm not sure if it's any good, but it might be fun." Walt was not doing anything else that afternoon, so they set off to check it out. The two guys were almost to the ticket window when the entourage arrived. Walt suggested that they go see what it was all about.

Soon, they were in another line. When Walt was finally standing in front of the girl signing posters, she looked up at him and asked if there was anything special he wanted her to write.

He said to her with a gentle smile. "Use my middle name and we'll rhyme." Tonya wrote, "To Othell, From Miss Bizzy Belle." As the men walked away, she turned to Sammie. "That man is so nice."

After the movie ended, the lights came on while the credits were playing right at the point where, "Introducing Miss Bizzy Belle, as Claire," scrolled across the screen. Mr. Boyce escorted Tonya to the stage where a dozen red roses were presented to her. Those not already on their feet ready to leave soon were. Miss Bizzy Belle took several bows as though she had been doing that all her life. She waved at her mother and Granny Addie as they were leaving trying to get ahead of the stampede.

By the time that Walt and Eli got inside the theater, all of the aisle seats were filled and the lights were already dimmed. They were stuck in the middle and could not leave immediately. When he was finally able to move, Walt turned toward the stage. He thought the girl might be looking at him so he blew her a kiss. She smiled and waved back.

After the men got to the car, Eli remarked that the movie was not destined to become a blockbuster, but Miss Bizzy Belle sure stole the show. He added that she was ten times better than that famous child actress, what's her name.

Walt agreed. "I know this place around here is really proud of her. I wonder if we'll be seeing her again."

When the limo delivered the celebrities back to their homes, Mr. Boyce told Tonya that several agents had already contacted him about representing her.

"I don't think so. I already have the best agent in the world."

"If you ever change your mind, let me know." He gave both girls a polite hug, and then shook hands with their mothers.

After the Bells were safely back in the Villa, Tonya turned to her mother. "Do you think my daddy will ever see the movie?"

"Why would you be thinking about something like that right now?"

Ignoring her mother's sidetracking question, she went on to her next. "Do you think he would be proud of me?"

Michelle took her daughter's hand. "The thing that would make your daddy the proudest of anything in the whole world is for you to be proud of yourself."

Tonya then asked her mother. "Is your father proud of you?"

"No. I'm afraid he's not."

"Mother? Are you proud of yourself?"

"No, Tonya. I'm not. Sometimes I think the only thing I've ever done right in my entire life was having you. And when I think of how close that came to not happening, it scares me to death."

She took both of her daughter's hands and faced her squarely.

"Tonya . . . I am so proud of you. I'm sorry that I just don't always know how to say it, or how to show you."

"I know . . . Mother."

When Mrs. Thornhill went to check her mail, a parcel too large for the box had been put on her front porch. She recognized Tonya's handwriting, immediately. Careful not to damage the contents, the movie poster opened up in front of her eyes. It was one of those moments that an individual never sees coming but is, nonetheless, forever engraved in the heart. A special notation was imprinted on the poster.

"To Cornfield, From Miss Bizzy Belle."

Mrs. T.'s mind went back to when she first pinned that moniker on Tonya. It was just about the same time that the toddler started calling her by her nickname. Now, "Miss Bizzy Belle" was up in lights.

A letter and two photographs also came along in the parcel. After a long and exhausting day, Mrs. T was grateful for the unexpected delight. She went inside, took a seat in her favorite chair, and began savoring every syllable.

Tonya had written months earlier saying that she had been given a minor part in a movie. She said that she portrayed a witness in a murder trial, and her mentee went into some detail describing what the production was like. Tonya told her at the time that she was not sure if the movie would ever be released, but she would keep her informed.

In the letter Mrs. T now held in her hand, her protégée told her all about the opening night. One photo was of her signing posters in front of the theater. It was taken at just the right angle to include the marquee in the background. The other was when she received the red roses on the stage. The letter concluded with Tonya saying how much she missed her, and how badly she wanted to come up for a visit.

"How my little girl is growing up."

The woman retrieved the morning newspaper that she had already read and discarded. She scoured the cinema listings and finally found where Tonya's was playing in a small theater. The next Saturday afternoon, she made her way across Washington and joined a little group of theatergoers already inside.

The movie had some lighthearted moments during the first several minutes. Eventually, it got to the trial. The patrons had been very quiet until Miss Bizzy Belle took the stand. Then, laughter broke out.

After the film finished playing, the others got up to leave. Mrs. Thornhill was unable to move. She overheard some people raving about Tonya's performance. She looked back up at the screen just in time to see the trailer. "Introducing Miss Bizzy Belle, as Claire."

A brush with the law

Halloween was just four days after the movie's opening night. Some in the town were still riding an emotional high. The police chief warned his officers that trick-or-treating might be more spirited than usual.

Sammie dragged Tonya along with her to hit a few houses. While out, the girls learned of a prank being planned. A group was going to gather at Mrs. Wagner's home and "roll" it. Tonya had no idea what that meant. She was skeptical, but Sammie assured her that it was just innocent fun.

"What happens if we get caught?"

"Oh . . . The worst thing is that we might have to clean up the mess. But we've never been caught before."

After the streets started clearing of little ghosts and goblins, some of the older kids slipped back inside their houses and ripped off a roll of toilet paper or two. Not to arouse suspicion, they tucked them under garments and avoided moving in any sizable numbers.

Mrs. Wagner lived on the end of a street at the edge of town. The excitement was building as the kids started congregating on the dark vacant lot across from her house. They waited until about ten minutes after the lights went out. Unbeknownst to them, the Old Wag was watching.

Just above a whisper, Twerp gave the go ahead. "Let's do it."

It was hard to keep their voices down. Sammie was right in the middle of it, but Tonya was wary. Her eyes caught a glimpse of something. Squinting, she could see a patrol car inching its way up the street with its lights out.

Miss Bizzy Belle

The girl pitched the roll in her hand to Twit and slipped away into the darkness. She raced for home through unlit back streets and alleys.

Tonya and Sammie had made a pact that if either was caught and one got away, they would cover for the other. Sometimes, things actually do go according to plan.

A spotlight came on startling the mischief makers, and they were like deer caught in the headlights. The officer ordered them into a tight circle and radioed for backup. The chief soon arrived. He started taking names and collecting information.

"Who else was involved in this?"

He was greeted with blank stares.

"Why should you take the rap for this and let the others get away?"

Twerp finally spoke up. "Tonya Bell was here."

Sammie snapped at him. "No, she wasn't. She had homework due tomorrow, and she went to work on it after we finished trick-or-treating."

Twerp held his ground, insisting that she was.

"Officer. Don't pay any attention to him. This boy always blames Tonya when he gets in trouble, and now he's just trying to get even."

"Okay, Miss Ringer. We'll check out your story." He asked for Tonya's address and sent another officer to her house.

The other part of the plan was for the one apprehended to inadvertently give out her own address to buy some time. When the policeman knocked on The Ringers' door asking for Tonya, Mrs. Flo said that she was not there. She added that she did not think the girl was spending the night with her daughter.

"You mean this isn't where Tonya lives?"

"No. She lives over on Lane Lane. Why? Is something wrong?"

"Just a little Halloween prank that we're dealing with."

Mrs. Ringer thought to herself, but not very confidently. "I surely do hope my daughter isn't involved."

Tonya was out of breath running the last leg of her marathon up the hill to the Villa. Michelle was already in bed when she slipped in. Hoping for a clean getaway, she quickly slid into her own pajamas. Then, she saw headlights. Maybe it was a neighbor coming home. Not. The vehicle stopped in front of her house. She met the officer at the door before he had any chance of knocking and waking her mother.

"Sir? How may I help you?"

"Are you Tonya Bell?"

"It's *Tone-yuh*."

She thought to herself. "Not much of a movie goer."

"Is your mother home?"

"She's asleep. She's got to get up early in the morning and go to work.

She told me not to disturb her when I came in."

"Oh! So you've been out tonight?"

"Yes, sir. I went trick-or-treating with some friends, and then came home to prepare for a test tomorrow."

"Are you saying that you had nothing to do with Mrs. Wagner's yard getting rolled?"

"I'll be honest with you, officer. I did hear the rumors, but my mother doesn't let me run with the wrong crowd."

"How do I know that you're not the wrong crowd?"

"Look at me. Sir. Do you see me across town at Mrs. Wagner's house?"

The police officer left with no doubt in his mind that he had been duped.

Grace not always greater

After the final bell on both Thursday and Friday, Tonya went straight to the mailbox. On Saturday, she watched for the postman. Each time, there was nothing for her. Sammie wanted Tonya to go home with her after school on Monday, but the anticipated delivery was way more important. Charged with excitement, she ran all the way home. At last, it had finally arrived!

Tonya tore open the envelope. In her hand, she held a round trip ticket from Asheville, North Carolina to Washington, D.C.

It was not easy getting her mother's permission. When Mrs. T offered to foot the bill for a Christmas visit, Michelle did not think that her daughter was mature enough to fly alone.

"Mother . . . I'll be eleven next year."

Michelle was in a quandary. She mentioned it to Mrs. Ringer when she went by to see a science project that the girls were working on together. Mrs. Flo tried to reassure her.

"Oh, she'll be fine. The flight attendants will treat her like she's a little princess, which she is, by the way, in case you haven't noticed."

Friday, December 21, 1979, was Tonya's big day. School was out for the holidays, and she was on her way to see Mrs. T. The flight left Asheville just before six in the evening. Michelle checked her daughter in, walked her to the gate, and gave her all of the motherly advice that she could think of before throwing her to the wolves.

As she waved goodbye, Tonya called out some instructions of her own.

Miss Bizzy Belle

"Don't forget to fill up the bird feeder."

Michelle stopped to get a bite to eat on the outskirts of the city. Once seated, she grasped the edge of the table trying to steady her wobbly nerves.

Except for fast food, she could not even remember the last time that she had eaten out. Her mind drifted back to when she stopped at the little diner the day after she found out that she was expecting Tonya. More than a decade had passed, and she was anxious about being alone during the holidays without her daughter. Work might keep her busy during the days, but she dreaded coming home to an empty house in the evenings.

It was eleven Christmases earlier when Michelle made the long journey back home in the X. She had seen her parents only once since then—at Papa Doc's funeral. She worried about her father and wondered how he was handling the holidays.

By the time her food arrived, Michelle had lost her appetite. She grazed on the salad and nibbled on the meatloaf. She was soon back on the road to Knoxo Springs with the rest of her uneaten supper in a takeout box.

How the mother envied her daughter. Tonya was spending Christmas with someone that she could share anything with. Michelle wished that she had somebody to talk to, but it really didn't matter. All the really important stuff was taboo.

After the forty-minute drive, the despondent woman poured a glass of Sin Infidel. She had to limit herself because the next day was a workday. Why did none of this make sense? The most courageous decision that she ever made was to keep her baby. Why was it that the one thing she did right tore her family apart?

The previous Sunday, Michelle and Tonya went to church. The Ringers motioned for both to come and sit with them. Tonya went to join Sammie, but Michelle took a seat near the back.

The minister's topic was, "The Grace of God." As she sipped, Michelle revisited the essence of what he said.

"God takes the mistakes of our lives, the messes we have made, redeems them, and turns things around for the good." She felt like he was speaking only to her.

Michelle's own religious upbringing dwelt on confession and repentance of sin. When misfortunes struck, it was because of transgressions. Those who suffered did so because of unconfessed sin.

What else did she have to confess? What did her parents expect of her? Why could they not see that their granddaughter was the very embodiment of God's grace? Why did they continue to turn their backs on both of them? How much more did she need to be punished?

The kindly parson also said that "Jesus is the reason for the season," and that God's Son is "The Prince of Peace." He closed with the assertion that

171

Christmas is when people everywhere celebrate "the peace of God that exceeds all understanding."

Why then was grace so out of her grasp? Why was no peace in her heart?

Pa Bell rang the bells on Christmas Day in Bellville. His son, Tolbert, put his hands to his ears and could hardly wait for them to stop. The man had been fighting for so long. No truce was imminent, but one thing was indisputable. He was not winning the battle. Yet, compromising was out of the question for those like him committed to uprightness. Standard-bearers who march under the banner of the TRUTH never have it easy. All the troubled man knew to do was keep on fighting—even if it killed him.

More chairs would be empty around the Christmas dinner table. Tolbert told Connie to go on without him, but she said that her place was with her husband. She took the gifts over before anybody else arrived. Mama Myra fixed plates and sent them back with her.

During his Christmas blessing, Pa Bell remembered his eldest son and wife. He prayed that they might receive divine wisdom and guidance. An inflection was in his voice when he mentioned his little Peanut in his prayer. He then asked the Good Lord Above to bless Michelle and Tonya, wherever they were, not only during the Christmas season, but also throughout the coming year.

All eyes were closed except two. Elmyra's were glaring at her husband.

On angel wings

The agent announced over the intercom that boarding would begin soon. He then asked Miss Tonya Bell to come to the counter. He informed her that the plane was fully booked with holiday travelers, but one passenger was unable to make the flight. Miss Bell had been upgraded to a seat in first class. He said that they were putting her there just in case her designated flight attendant got bored and needed some conversation.

"Here she is right now." The passenger was escorted aboard and shown to her front row seat by the window. Her new friend gave her some gum to chew to help her ears pop.

Miss Bizzy Belle

It was already dark outside. Take off made her insides feel a little funny, but the attendant had her own little fold down chair right in front of her and held her hand. They both smiled. Tonya felt the plane lift off, and she watched the city lights fall beneath her.

About half an hour into the flight, the girl got a message from the captain. She was ushered into the cockpit, and asked if she wanted to fly the plane. The copilot was taking a break, so she took his seat. Wow!

"Hold it steady." After about five minutes, the captain gave Tonya her wings.

Mrs. T was waiting in the terminal when the plane pulled up to the gate. She did not have to wait long. Tonya was the first passenger to come down the ramp. The two embraced, and then headed to baggage claim.

"Did you see my wings?" They just picked right up where they last left off.

When the two got back to the daycare center, Tonya wanted to go straight to the basement. Many of her earliest memories were made right there. The first thing she saw was something that was not there when she left. She gave Mrs. T a smile bigger than usual when she looked up at the movie poster. It was already late, and Mrs. T tucked her in like old times with a customary bedside chat.

"Sunday night is the Christmas pageant at the church. You'll get to see some of your old pals from pre-K. And they have saved a special part for you."

"What is it?"

"An angel—you couldn't be anything but an angel. Tomorrow, we'll try on the costume I've made for you. You'll have another set of wings."

On Saturday, they went Christmas shopping to buy Tonya some new clothes. Mrs. T explained something on the way. "I wanted to surprise you, but I just couldn't imagine how much you had grown. I waited so you could go with me." Tonya tried on several outfits and modeled them for Mrs. T. They went home with three.

Tonya's smile was replaced by a frown in the middle of a sentence. "These are the prettiest dresses I've ever had, but I didn't bring you a Christmas present."

"Yes, you did. You brought me the best Christmas gift ever. You." The smile was back.

Ms. Joy was the first to greet them at church the next morning. Tonya wore one of her new outfits.

Kermit the Frog was Joseph in the pageant that evening. He had his own guardian angel watching over him. As Tonya fluttered her wings, she told Cornfield that she felt more like a butterfly than a cherub.

Mrs. T had closed the daycare center for a week so that she could spend all of her time with Tonya. The two busied themselves preparing Christmas eats and Christmas sweets. At bedtime on Monday, Mrs. T asked Tonya if she had been a good girl that year. She answered in precisely the manner that was in no way a surprise.

"That all depends on what you call 'good'."

"I surely do hope you're not on Santa's naughty list. It would be a shame if he just passed us by tonight."

Books, books, and more books were under the tree the next morning. So was a new sled.

On the way back to the airport, Mrs. T reminded Tonya that she was still planning to retire within the next year or so. "I've got places I want to go, and things I want to see. I'm hoping you can travel some with me."

"Oh . . . That would be so wonderful."

The ticket agent greeted Tonya as she walked up to get her boarding pass.

"I see you've already earned your wings. Have a nice flight."

"Mrs. T . . . I've had so much fun. This has been my best Christmas ever."

"Mine, too, child. Please say hello to your mother, and thank her again for letting you come."

As they hugged, Tonya puckered up her lips. "I'm not telling you goodbye. I'll see you again." That was certainly not the first time that she had uttered those words. Nor would it be the last.

Tonya's first flight was at night, but when she returned, the sun was shining. She did not get the same royal service going home as she did on the way up, either. The flight attendant was a bit annoyed at having to stash the sled.

Michelle was getting panicky when the passengers had stopped coming, and there was still no Tonya. Her daughter was the last one off. The girl had to wait until everyone else cleared to retrieve her sled.

Relieved, the mother greeted her daughter with a question. "Is that what Mrs. T gave you for Christmas?"

Tonya nodded but made no mention of the books stowed in her luggage.

"How was your Christmas, and how is Mrs. T?"

"It was nice, and she's fine."

Michelle then surprised her. "Santa Claus came to see you while you were gone."

"He did?"

"You'll just have to wait until we get back home to see what he brought you, though."

Tonya ran into the house but did not see anything new until she went into her room. A much bigger bed was where the old twin had been.

Her mother told her that Mrs. Flo called and explained that they were getting a new waterbed. She wondered if we wanted their old queen.

"I started to put it in my room, and give you the double, but then I realized that you'd be the one having sleepover company."

"Can I call Sammie, and see if she can come over tonight? What's a waterbed?"

One of Dr. Ringer's golfing buddies was curious after a round at The Cow Pasture. "You and Flo been making waves on your new waterbed?"

The foursome was enjoying a drink at the clubhouse. Technically, Walthall County was dry, but somehow the club had found ways around it. Ebb took another sip before answering.

"You know what they say. Two things are better on a waterbed . . . And one of them is sleep."

"Well . . .?" His friends waited.

"I'm not sure that either of us is sleeping any better. Every time one of us moves, the sloshing sounds a lot like what I hear when I put a stethoscope to a woman's belly. It also makes me want to get up and pee."

"And . . .?"

"I named the bed, 'Lake Superior,' but Flo says it's more like 'The Dead Sea'."

When winter finally started loosening its grip, Tonya did some spring cleaning. She walked into the kitchen and put in a request.

"Mother . . . I need a bookcase. The stack of books in the corner has grown so tall that it keeps falling down."

"Let me see what I can do. I think the hospital has used desks and other equipment in storage. An old bookcase might be in there."

A couple of days later, a Code T was issued. Tonya went by the hospital to remind her mom to investigate the bookcase situation.

When she got home from school one day about a week later, the girl found just what she wanted on the porch. A maintenance worker had dropped it off. When Michelle came home from work, Tonya was waiting.

"Thank you, Mother. But I must paint it before I can use it." The next day, Tonya told Sammie about her new acquisition, and her friend offered to help. "I think we have some old paint in the garage." When Michelle got home, a piece of bright red furniture was drying on the porch.

Most of the books that Tonya had gotten for Christmas went on the top shelf. In the batch, there were three junior mysteries and a selection of field guides to help identify birds, trees, rocks, wildflowers, and butterflies.

The thoughtful mentor had also included a couple of books that the preadolescent might find especially helpful as her body was poised on the brink of some significant changes. They were kept out of sight.

Tonya never said anything to her mom about the health and hygiene books. Of course, she shared them with her best friend. The girls approached the subject matter cautiously at first. Then, they could not soak it up fast enough. Sammie commented one day as they were holed up in their secret compartment using flashlights.

"My mother would kill me if she caught me reading this kind of stuff."

Tonya looked up at her. "Sammie? How long have we known each other?"

"I don't know. Maybe forever."

"And I still haven't taught you that the secret is not getting caught?"

"Girlfriend. I don't know how you do it. I can't get anything by my mother. She seems to know what I'm going to do before I do."

Then, she veered. "I still don't know how you got away on Halloween. And you made it all the way home without even getting caught."

Tonya's eyes were glowing in the dark. "You should have seen how I had that haughty cop eating out of my hand."

Sammie sidled up to her best friend three days later. "Go home with me after school. I've got something really wicked to show you."

"What is it?"

"Can't say it right here. Somebody might overhear me."

"We'll have to hurry, too, before Stanley gets home from band practice." This had to be something juicy.

The girls spoke to Mrs. Flo when they went in, and she asked if they wanted a snack. They declined and went straight upstairs.

"How did you find this?" Tonya wanted to know.

"I kind of figured if Stanley had anything to hide, it would be under his mattress. I was right."

The friends took the girlie magazine to their secret hiding place. Both of their mothers were very modest, and neither girl had ever seen a naked woman. They whispered and giggled as Sammie turned the pages.

Tonya observed. "I know my boobs will never be that big."

Sammie wondered. "Do you think I'll ever have that much hair? Mine might be so light that it won't even show up."

Tonya exclaimed. "Look. There's a blond and her hair's darker than what's on her head."

Sammie wished. "Now if we could just get our hands on a magazine with men's pictures."

Miss Bizzy Belle

Reality set in. "Quick. Let's put this back. If Stanley were to catch us, he would stop putting things there."

The girls went back downstairs with cherub-like innocence painted all over their faces. They wanted a snack after all.

Whatchu looking at, boy?

For her eleventh birthday in 1980, Tonya did not want a party, and she requested no gifts. That was all she would tell her mother. It was the first time the girl could remember that her birthday fell on Mother's Day, as it did the day she was born. May 11 would be all about the one who gave birth to her. Well, almost. But not quite.

Tonya appealed to Granny Addie for help, and she was delighted to do her part. The widow began by putting in a request for Tonya to spend the weekend with her. Michelle was invited to join them for lunch on Sunday. Granny offered to come and get her great-granddaughter after school on Friday.

Taking her mother out to lunch on her day was just not an option. Everybody did that. This had to be something really special. As the plans were taking shape, Tonya mentioned something else.

"We can't bake her a cake. She'll think it's for my birthday."

Tonya puffed out her lips. "I just wish my daddy could be here, too."

The brainstorming continued, and they both came up with it at the exact same time—a picnic at Canyon Creek Falls! Granny didn't have everything on hand, so they decided to go into Ephesus on Saturday morning. Tonya always enjoyed getting groceries with Granny.

Before they left, the girl went to the chicken house to gather the eggs. After Doc died, Granny only kept four laying hens. That gave them just enough for the potato salad, but it left them short for deviled eggs.

Tonya pushed the cart and Granny filled it. Taking advantage of the opportunity, she stocked up on other things that she needed. While in the checkout line, Tonya looked up and saw somebody coming in the door.

"Isn't that the man who blew me a kiss at the movie premier?" She was about to blow him a kiss, but he turned right with his buggy and did not look her way.

Granny just could not imagine a picnic without fried chicken. She bought a whole fryer because it was cheaper, and Tonya watched as she cut it up. They floured it, peppered it, and carefully put the pieces in the hot skillet.

Tonya grated a cabbage and carrots for slaw. Together, they peeled, diced, and boiled the potatoes. In another pot, they boiled the eggs. More than once, Tonya exuded out loud.

"This is so much fun."

Michelle arrived just in time for church. When the minister mentioned something about it being Mother's Day, Tonya looked at her mom, grimaced, and snapped her fingers as though it had slipped her mind. Nothing was said about lunch on the way home. When Michelle came out of the bathroom after washing up, the other two were holding a picnic basket.

"Surprise!"

The weather cooperated marvelously. Three of four living generations partied and picnicked with the roar of the falls providing a reverberating backdrop. As they were packing up to leave, Tonya had something to say. She told her mother how special it was to be born on Mother's Day. She added that she never wanted her birthday to take the spotlight off the one who had given her birth. After giving her mom a hug, Tonya wiggled free.

"Now . . . What did you get me for my birthday?"

Four eyes turned to her.

"Just kidding."

Tonya was not left out after all. When she came home from school the next day, a package was on the porch with a Washington, D.C. postmark. The girl tore into it. First, she read the note.

> *Dear Tonya,*
> *I hope your Mother's Day surprise went well. What a joy you must be to her. I know you said that you didn't want any birthday presents this year, but you'll just have to forgive me. I am sending you some things that you might need soon. One item is for whenever you are ready. The other supplies you can keep in your purse so you can be ready when the time comes.*
>
> *I love you,*
> *Mrs. T*

Tonya was overjoyed when she saw what was in the box and went straight to the phone. "Sammie, you've got to come over. I have something really exciting to show you."

Her best friend was not going to be outshone. She convinced her mother that if Tonya had a bra, she needed one, too. Sammie and Mrs. Flo went shopping the next day. Neither mother let her daughter wear the new undergarment right away, but by the middle of summer, they gave in.

Sammie was upbeat the first day they went out dressed like young ladies. "I can't wait for school to start. I wonder who else will be wearing a bra."

Tonya mentioned that the Wilder girl was already wearing one before school was out. "But she's a little 'stout' anyway."

The less diplomatic Sammie countered. "No, she's not. She's fat."

During lunch on the first day of sixth grade, the best friends circled all of the tables under the guise of welcoming everyone back. What they were really doing was conducting a little survey. To their surprise, most of the girls had also upgraded their wardrobes over the summer.

During the break, Tonya caught Twerp looking at her chest.

"Whatchu looking at, boy?"

"You don't need that thing, TB."

It was a few days later before she found out that his comment had nothing to do with her initials.

The Naturalist

During her sixth grade year, Tonya became more fascinated with the natural world. The middle grades shared a science lab. Teachers and students alike often brought interesting items to exhibit. One of the most popular displays was the butterfly nursery.

The pupils learned about pupae. They witnessed caterpillars morphing into cocoons, from which butterflies eventually emerged. Tonya was enchanted by the process and went by every day to watch the progressions. Mrs. Baylor asked the class if they had ever thought about how the term pupil might have been derived.

Twit boasted. "I'm not a pupil. I'm a *stud*-ent." The class groaned collectively.

Twerp said that he could bring a wasp nest if his classmates wanted to see things hatch. Mrs. Baylor called his bluff and pointed to an enclosed wire pen where he could put it. The next day, he said that his daddy wouldn't let him because he was going to use the grubs for fish bait.

Mrs. Baylor was different from other teachers, and she reminded Tonya of Mrs. Thornhill. The teacher did not just teach subject matter. She illustrated how it applied to the students' lives. Tonya knew she was her favorite, but that was their little secret. She was not about to be called a teacher's pet.

When studying arithmetic, Mrs. Baylor not only put them through exercises so that they could gain proficiency, but she also explained why math mattered. She used coins to illustrate tenths and fractions. They went on imaginary shopping trips using Monopoly money.

During science, Tonya was fully engaged. The teacher was pleased to give special attention to a student for a reason other than because of falling behind.

Notwithstanding her studiousness, Tonya was not always a model citizen. Her mischievous quotient always ran in parallel to her IQ.

Tonya's interest in the environment extended well beyond the classroom. A seldom used hiking trail led into the forest at the end of Lane Lane. She ventured a little farther with each exploration. Sounds from the highways grew distant. As the path continued on an incline, the breezes increased. Birds rustled in the bushes. As the wind blew through her hair, she experienced a special kind of exhilaration.

The field guides from Mrs. T were put to good use. Already, Tonya had observed more than twenty kinds of birds at the feeder. She really got into identifying and pressing the leaves of twenty-five different species of trees for a school project.

When at Granny Addie's, Tonya was at last old enough to walk to the creek by herself. Her great-grandparents had been taking her to see the ferns of Ferndale for as long as she could remember. She was fascinated with how they all disappeared during winter, leaving the banks barren, only to return again every summer in all of their floral splendor.

Granny took her to ride on unpaved roads to see the rhododendron and mountain laurel in bloom. She also pointed out wildflowers, and Tonya started learning their names. One of her favorites was goat's beard. They went wild berry picking and made cobblers and jellies.

Tonya learned that food does not just automatically appear on grocery shelves. Both her Pa Bell and her Granny Addie helped her plant seeds. She got to watch the sprouts break through the soil. The girl learned the importance of cultivating the plants, and she also helped pick the vegetables when they were ready. Few things compared to the joys of a tomato sandwich, especially when the tomato came straight from the garden.

Some nights, Tonya put her pillow at the foot of the bed. As she looked up into the night sky, the vastness of the universe fascinated her. She was just a tiny speck on a little planet amongst millions of stars. Nevertheless, somehow she knew that she mattered.

"Who am I God? Why was I born in one place, and now live in

another? What will I be when I grow up? And one more thing, God. Why won't my mother tell me who my daddy is? If he doesn't know about me, please tell him. Please keep him safe until I find him."

A pain in the patootie

Around the dinner table, Mrs. Flo shared an observation. "By next weekend, you won't be able to stir the leaf-watchers with a stick." Mr. Ebb mentioned that people from the mountains go to Florida, and folks from Florida come to the mountains.

"I guess the residents down there resent us coming about as much as we hate having our roads all clogged. But it's good for the economy."

Tonya and Sammie were unusually quiet. They were waiting for Stanley to leave. He had already announced that after he finished eating, he was going to a friend's house. The girls needed to get into his room.

While at the beach, Stanley had bought a sack of miniature noisemakers at a novelty store. The little round balls exploded with a pop when they were thrown against a hard surface. Sammie and Tonya were hoping to find another use for them.

After the table was cleared, the brother had vamoosed, and the parents had retreated to the screened-in porch to relax in the cool of the day, the girls went upstairs.

Sammie whispered. "I hope we can find them."

Tonya added. "And I hope it works."

When only about a dozen of the snap pops were left in the drawer, the lad's sister conjectured. "Maybe he won't miss any of them. Anyway . . . What can he do about it?"

After confiscating five, it was time to get down to business. "Okay. Let's see if our plan's going to work. We'd better do it in here because my bedroom is too close to the porch."

Tonya tipped a chair back, and Sammie put one of the balls under a leg. Carefully, the chair was lowered. Nothing happened. So far. So good.

Sammie then plopped down in the chair with her full weight, and "pop" went the snap.

Twerp and Twit were a pain in the patootie. Each endlessly accused the other of liking either Tonya or Sammie. That was always met with contorted faces and disgusting utterances. It was payback time.

When the first break bell sounded the next morning, both girls pretended to be finishing some work. After the room emptied and Mrs. Baylor left for the teacher's lounge, Tonya stood guard. Sammie put snap pops under both front legs of Twerp and Twit's desks. They then went out and mingled with an air of frivolity.

The targets of the prank were always the last to return to their seats. As the teacher was trying to get the class settled back down, first one, and then another loud POP got everybody's attention.

"Boys . . .? Where did you get those things? You know they're not allowed at school. Now go straight to the office."

"But Mrs. Baylor . . ."

"But Mrs. Baylor nothing. You heard what I said."

The studious girls kept their heads buried deeply in books. They could not look at each other. Nor did they dare make eye contact with the boys glaring back at them as they skulked out the door. Neither did they see the teacher watching them.

Mrs. Baylor was not only a gifted science and math teacher, but she also strived to help the mountain boys and girls learn grammar. Most students continued repeating the bad habits that they had picked up at home.

That was made painfully clear one day when Twerp mocked the teacher on the playground. "I seen all those 'isn'ts' crawling on the ground." Even so, she remained diligent in her efforts for the few who wished to improve.

In one lesson, some of the kids were struggling with the differences between drug and dragged, and laying and lying. Twit said that to him lying meant telling a lie. Mrs. Baylor thought to herself that he would know. The boy could not understand how lying could have anything to do with a person laying on a bed.

Up went Tonya's hand. Her teachers always grimaced when that happened. Sometimes, she surprised them with a particularly keen insight. At other times, she just surprised them.

Mrs. Baylor was very apprehensive. There was no way of telling what was going through the girl's mind. Was Tonya going to ask her if this had anything to do with getting laid? The teacher took a deep breath before gesturing to her.

"Mrs. Baylor?"

"Yes, Tonya?"

"How do chickens *lay* eggs?"

About the time the calendar turned over to May, Tonya got Michelle's attention. "Mother . . . I know what I want for my birthday."

"What did you have in mind?"

"A 'tween party.' Cause next year I'll be a teenager."

Michelle just looked at her, knowing that whatever her daughter was thinking would not have to be pried loose.

"If you'll just give me twenty-five dollars, Sammie and I will take care of everything."

"Exactly, what do you mean by everything?"

"I was thinking of a slumber party and having pizza delivered." Then, she said with a grin. "We might sip a little of your Sin."

"I'll let you have the party, but not the Sin. That's all mine. I'll have my own party."

Michelle knew that Tonya was going to be persistent so she conceded. "No more than five of you. And it will need to be on Friday night because we're going to Granny's for Mother's Day."

"Can we stay up all night?"

"No. Lights out at eleven."

"I was thinking more like one."

"Okay. Midnight then."

The next morning, six sleepyheads had serious hangovers. For five of them, the cause was a lack of shuteye.

Tonya was still dragging on Sunday morning. She begged her mother to let her sleep in, but Michelle insisted that she go with her to Granny Addie's. In the end, she was glad she went because a big surprise was awaiting her. Tonya's grandmother, Connie, had been by the day before and dropped off a couple of gifts. One was for her mother on Mother's Day. The other was something for Tonya's birthday. Michelle could not help but notice that she was the one left out.

On a lazy, hazy, spring Sunday afternoon in the Smokey Mountains of North Carolina, Tonya was home alone. Her mother was working the weekend shift, and Sammie had gone off somewhere with her parents. Tonya thought it was still there, and it was. She loaded the cassette into the VCR and made herself comfortable. She had watched the movie earlier with her mother, but she wanted to revisit a few scenes.

Tonya gave her mother a chance to shower when she came in. After being at the hospital all day, it was always the first thing that Michelle wanted to do. When she came back in the living room, her daughter was waiting for her.

"Here . . . Mother. Have a glass of Sin, and just relax."

Since Walthall County was dry, Michelle restocked her booze when she went to Ephesus or Asheville, insisting that it was for medicinal purposes. Her observant offspring had figured out that it took about half an hour for the stuff to take full effect.

Michelle was appreciative of the gesture. "Oh, that's so good, and you are so thoughtful."

Soon, the glass was empty. Tonya was afraid that her mother might fall asleep, so it was time.

"So . . . You are a nurse like Lara was. Was my father a physician like Dr. Zhivago?"

That was sobering. "Of all things, why would you ask me that?"

"Well . . .? Was he?"

"Tonya . . . I've told you that I will not discuss this with you. But just this one time, I'll answer your question. No. He was not a doctor."

"Was he a married man? Is that why you can't tell me who he is?"

"Please don't do this to me. But no. He was not married."

"Was he a poet?"

Michelle got up and went to bed.

After her mother was asleep, Tonya opened her secret file. Regrettably, she could add nothing to it. It did not appear that the cop had anything to do with her birth since she was already a baby when they met. Uncle Vinnie was a creep. She certainly had no connection to him.

She never heard anything more about the man who called when she was eight. She would keep his name on file just in case anything ever turned up. One other possibility had not been fully explored. While she had the file out, she copied a Bellville address on an envelope.

Look what I've done to my daddy

Connie Bell had bus duty on Friday afternoon, the last day of school. Already, she was dreading, not just the weekend, but the summer. Tolbert went on home ahead of her.

Driving home, she was aware of just how weary she was. All she could think about was getting in the house and out of her clothes. Her husband met her at the door waving something in his hand. She had never seen his face so red.

Holding up a piece of mail, he bellowed. "What is the meaning of this?"

Miss Bizzy Belle

Connie tried to settle down the agitated man. "Well . . . Let me see."

Tolbert held it out but jerked it away as she reached for it. She got just enough of a glimpse to see that it was from Tonya.

"Did you open my mail?"

"We are husband and wife. We have no secrets. At least I thought so until I got home."

She glared at him. "Give me my mail this instant."

He responded with a determined resolve. "Not until you explain why you got a thank you note from Michelle's illegitimate child."

"Calm down, Tolbert."

"Calm down? Calm down when my own wife has turned against me and gone over to the other side?"

"Stop it! This is not about choosing sides. Michelle is our daughter and Tonya is our own flesh and blood. We are all on the same side. We are family."

Quick as a wink, Connie snatched the envelope, went into their bedroom, and locked the door. She read Tonya's sweet little letter thanking her for the birthday necklace and bracelet. Tears filled her eyes. She felt like she was on the brink of a breakthrough.

Tolbert made no attempt to break in on her. Connie took a deep breath and made her way to him. She found him sitting at the kitchen table with his head in his hands.

The words that had been welling up for years issued forth, but they did not spew out in indignation or rage. Her sentiments were rather measured with calmness and composure.

"Tolbert Bell. I will no longer let you keep me from my daughter and my grandchild."

The man made one feeble attempt to hold on. "Parents must stand together. That's what's wrong with the world today . . ."

The man's wife interrupted him before he could go any further.

"I've stood with you long enough. What did it ever get either of us but pain and misery? It's about time for me to stand up for what I know is right."

The battle was over. The stalwart had gone down in defeat. He had lost the war.

The disconsolate man, humiliated and disgraced, got up and walked away without saying another word. His daughter had shamed him, and now his own wife had betrayed him. Connie heard the truck start up, and she presumed that he was headed to his mother's.

Tolbert's head started throbbing with searing pain. The vehicle lurched and surged as his body convulsed. The pickup veered off the road and into a ditch. The engine kept running, but a rear wheel was off the ground.

After her husband had been gone for about an hour, Connie was worried and went looking for him. She saw flashing lights ahead not far from the house. The terrified woman rushed up just as her husband was being loaded into an ambulance. He was unconscious but alive. The EMT told her that the man apparently had a stroke.

Tolbert Bell would now live out his days peering at the world from hollowed out eyes, seeing faintly but unable to comprehend, hearing sounds but unable to speak. He was totally dependent upon others for everything and was in control of nothing—not even his own bodily functions.

Michelle was looking forward to a quiet weekend. Tonya went home with Sammie after school and planned to stay through Sunday. Getting out of her uniform and into a hot bath was about as far ahead as the weary nurse could see. Soaking in the tub, she sipped her second glass of Sin.

Soon relaxed, Michelle closed her eyes. She imagined her routines as an endless elevator ride, going up and then coming back down. She didn't know which floor to get off on and was petrified by the thought of who might get on every time the door opened.

Suddenly, somebody hit the panic button. The alarm went off and the elevator stopped between floors. Had she dozed off? Was it the wine?

No. It was the phone. Rousing herself from the semi-stupor, she grabbed a towel. Thinking it might be Tonya, she picked up the receiver. Rather, her granny was on the other end of the line.

"Have you already had your supper?"

Michelle told her that she hadn't. She then lied and said that she was about to go to the kitchen.

"Come eat with me. I'm just about to put some leftovers on the table."

"Oh, Granny. I appreciate that so much, but I'm kind of tired tonight."

"Michelle . . . Come anyway. I have some important news that I need to share with you, and I'm not very good talking on the phone. Is Tonya home with you?"

"No . . . She's at Sammie's."

"Good . . . Then, come prepared to spend the night."

"Give me about an hour."

Not sure how much she had consumed, Michelle made coffee. The days were getting longer, but she still did not get to Ferndale before dark. She wondered what was so urgent, but Granny had given her no clues.

There was no way to break the news gently. When informed of her daddy's stroke, Michelle screamed.

Miss Bizzy Belle

"It's all my fault. Look what I've done to my daddy."

Granny Addie grabbed her granddaughter and shook her.

"No, Michelle. You're not to blame. Your father brought all this upon himself. He chose to live in bitterness and anger. He turned his back on you, and not the other way around. There's no reason that he should not have been proud of you. Tonya could have been his pride and joy. Instead . . . He preferred to be miserable. Now, his body has turned on him."

Michelle sat sobbing holding Granny Addie's hand. Finally, she was able to ask. "Is he going to live?"

"The doctors say it's too early to tell. The critical time is the next forty-eight to seventy-two hours. If he survives, Connie said the stroke was so massive that he will likely never walk again. If you ask me, I think it would be a blessing for him to just go on."

"Oh, no. Granny. Don't say that. My daddy can't die."

It would do no good for the wise old woman to say what else was going through her mind. She just sat and held her granddaughter's hand. Michelle finally was able to speak.

"I want to go see him, but I can't. I'm afraid it might upset him. I'm afraid seeing me would put him in his grave."

"Listen, child. Your daddy now has no choice but to practice what he has preached so sternly for as long as I've known him. You've heard him say it many times. 'When you make your bed, you have to lie in it.' He's made his bed, of whatever sort that turns out to be. And now he will have to lie in it."

Neither Granny nor Michelle knew anything about Tonya's thank you note.

Michelle just wanted to go home, but Granny Addie insisted that she stay. Rest, what there was of it, did not come easy. Up early the next morning and afraid that she might disturb her granny, she quietly slipped out the front door. It had been years since she had seen the ferns. It had been even longer since she had attempted to pray. How could she pray for what was best when it might also be what was the worst?

The aroma of coffee filled the house when she returned. Granny thought her granddaughter was still sleeping and was surprised when she came in the door. With few words between them, they prepared breakfast. Around the table, the woman picked up where she left off the night before.

"Michelle . . . Your daddy has always been right about people and their beds—although I'm not sure he ever understood that it also applied to him. It might be too late for him now, but it isn't for you. I've never tried to tell you how to live your life. Well, maybe I did a time or two. Listen to me. You cannot judge yourself by how anybody else feels about you. You can never be what others want you to be. Forget about trying to get

Tolbert's love and approval. As Doc used to say, 'You can't get blood from a turnip'."

Michelle heard what her granny was saying but the words just didn't jive with what she had always believed.

The woman went on trying to get through. "Don't ruin your health worrying about things you can't control. You're going to blink a couple of times, and your daughter is going to be grown. I'm not saying that your life is always going to be a bed of roses, but you're still young enough to make of it what you want."

"I know, Granny. I know."

Granny also knew that the apple doesn't fall far from the tree. Redirecting, she asked if Tonya would be okay the rest of the day.

Michelle said that she was going to stay at the Ringers' until after church on Sunday.

"Good . . . Let's get ready to go to Alabama."

"Granny . . . I can't."

"Oh yes, you can. Your mother needs you. I've already talked to Connie this morning. There's been no improvement, and they've moved him to Huntsville. I need you to take me, and I'm going prepared to stay a few days. You can come back and get me the next time you're off."

Michelle was not very talkative on the two-and-a-half-hour drive. Granny left her granddaughter to her thoughts. As they entered Huntsville, Michelle spotted a sign pointing to the hospital and said that they were almost there. Once inside, they followed the directions to the intensive care unit.

Granny Addie forged ahead but Michelle held back. Connie saw them as they approached the waiting room. She went and hugged her mother and then turned to her daughter standing sheepishly in the hallway.

"I'm glad you're here, but I was not sure you would come. I wouldn't have blamed you if you hadn't."

Michelle skipped right over what her mother had just said and asked about her father. "Has Daddy regained consciousness? Is he any better?"

"It does not look good. Sometimes he can squeeze your hand just a little. He's still in there, but I'm not sure for how much longer. Come. I want you to go with me to see him."

"No." "No." "No." Michelle was still fighting her own battle.

Connie turned away from her daughter. "Mother? Will you go with me?"

Michelle was left alone in the crowded waiting room. The only empty seat was the one just vacated. Sitting where her mother had sat, something came over her. What must it be like for her mom?

She got up and made her way to the ICU. Granny Addie was standing just outside her daddy's door. She motioned for Michelle to go in. Connie turned to see who had entered and then reached for her. They locked arms and went to the bedside.

Even as a nurse, it was hard to recognize the man who raised her amongst all the wires and tubes. Her father's eyes were closed, his face drawn, and his body twisted. His daughter studied the monitors and frowned.

The man's wife spoke to him. "Tolbert . . . Look who came to see you." If there was any recognition, Michelle could not detect it. Connie placed her daughter's hand in his. "Squeeze Michelle's hand if you recognize her." Once again, there was no apparent response.

Michelle was soon beset with a familiar kind of tug of war. She wanted to stay near her father in the event that he rallied, but at the same time, she was suffocating. Back on the elevator, she did not know which number to push. After about an hour in the waiting room, she said that Tonya had no idea where she was and that she needed to get home and talk to her.

Her mother asked if she wanted to see her daddy again before she left. Michelle shook her head.

The drive back to Knoxo Springs was long, lonely and exhausting. The internal battle raged on.

When Tonya came bounding in after Sunday lunch, she immediately detected that something was wrong. She listened intently, had some questions about a stroke, and then announced emphatically. "When you go back to get Granny, I'm going with you."

"I'm not so sure about that, young lady. Have you forgotten that I still make some decisions around here?"

"Mother . . . I'm going."

School did not let out in Knoxo Springs until Wednesday. Granny Addie was ready to come home so Michelle arranged to be off on Thursday and Friday.

She had no idea how to prepare Tonya. This would be the first time that she had ever seen her grandmother. When they got to the waiting area, Connie greeted them. Tonya held her chin up and her arm out just a little so that her grandmother could see that she was wearing the necklace and bracelet. Nothing else was necessary.

Connie stayed with Tonya when Michelle went to see her daddy again. So far, he had beaten the odds. That is, if not dying from a massive stroke was considered the winning prize. She thought perhaps he looked gaunter than before. If there was any recognition of her, she could not sense it.

After her mother came out, Tonya insisted on going back. Michelle stood firmly against it, but her mother took a different approach. She took the girl's hand, and Michelle followed behind. When they entered the room, Tonya took a moment to size up the situation. She looked up at the heart monitor, and then at the other equipment. Then, she made her way to the side of the bed.

Not knowing what else to say, her grandmother whispered softly. "He has not always looked like that."

Tonya looked up and reassured her. "I know. I've seen his picture."

Michelle shot her daughter a questioning look. Tonya shrugged. "Well . . . I have."

Without instructions from anyone, the girl took the man's hand. She squeezed it a time or two, looking for some reaction. When none came, she released her grip and began to speak.

"Hello, Granddaddy. I'm Tonya Willa Bell, your granddaughter. I'm so sorry that you are sick. I do hope you're going to be okay soon because I've been so looking forward to meeting you. Granddaddy Tolbert. I say a prayer for you every day, and I love you very much."

When Tonya turned, her mother was scrambling to get out of the room. Grandmother Connie put her arms around her. The man on the bed opened his eyes for a couple of seconds, but no one was sure if he saw anything.

To save time, Granny had brought her things to the hospital from the motel room. She told her daughter to call if there was anything she could do. Michelle found herself again at a loss. Tonya gave her newly-found grandmother a big hug and told her that she would be back again as soon as she could get a ride.

Granny Addie and Tonya both offered to sit in the backseat going home. When neither gave in, they decided to settle the matter by sitting in the back together. Michelle went through the motions of driving while her emotions were racing far faster than the mile a minute the car was going.

Over and over, she kept asking herself. "How does she do it? How could Tonya not think that something was wrong with *her*? Why would she not believe it was her fault that her grandparents never had anything to do with her?"

A grave insight

The doctor informed Mrs. Bell that a decision was imminent, and he explained the situation to her. She knew what she was up against.

Tolbert was already on life-support when he was admitted. He had thus far survived the stroke, but his prognosis was bleak. There had been little brain activity for several days, which essentially left no hope for recovery. He could be kept alive indefinitely, but he might well remain in a vegetative state. There was no way of knowing what might happen if support was removed. If he lived, he would be put in a nursing home.

Connie did not discuss any of that with Michelle on the phone but requested that she come as soon as possible. Supervisor Jobson understood that family always came first, and she assured her nurse that her shifts would be covered for as long as she was needed elsewhere. Granny Addie decided not to go, and invited Tonya to stay with her, but there was no way the girl was going to be left behind.

Alone in her thoughts, Michelle went over the various possibilities facing her family. She wondered how her daddy's parents were holding up. The passenger brought a book to read and was absorbed in it for the first hour. Apart from any apparent context or setting, Tonya looked up and had a question.

"Where's Grover buried?"

Of all inquiries that Michelle could have ever imagined, that one was not anywhere on the list. As she was prone to do, the woman twitched her head, searching inside her brain for how to answer. No need in brushing her daughter off. The girl would keep coming at her until she got an answer. Why was that important to her with so much else going on?

Tonya just kept looking at her. Michelle was finally able to respond. "He's buried in the cemetery of the church near where he grew up."

Not surprisingly, that did not satisfy her.

"Where's that?"

"It's just outside a small town between Birmingham and Huntsville."

"Do you ever go visit his grave?"

"I've been a few times."

"When was the last time? Have you been since I was born?"

"It's been several years. And no. I haven't been since you came along."

"Mother . . . I want to go see where Grover is buried. Can we go? Maybe it will do you good with everything else that's on your mind right now."

Michelle's head twitched again. What was this about? Abruptly, she realized something. She was certain that she had never mentioned Grover's name in front of her daughter, or that he was killed in Vietnam.

The news at the hospital was no different. Michelle wanted to be respectful of whatever her mother's wishes might be, but Connie was waiting for Michelle to advise her. The matter was further complicated because Tolbert had no living will.

The nurse's medical training was geared toward keeping people alive. Yet, she had witnessed so many patients and their families put through the mill when there was no hope for a recovery with any quality of life. This was different, though. This was *her* daddy.

One part of her knew that he would not want to linger once he had lost his dignity. The other side wanted to hold on forever in case there was any possibility that he might rally and give her the faintest smile.

The hospital could not take him off life-support without the family's consent. The doctors gave them until the next day to decide. The social worker went over the insurance details for both scenarios. If they pulled the plug and his main organs continued to function, then he would be moved out of the ICU. If still alive after a week, he would go into a nursing home.

Michelle asked for some privacy with her daddy. She held his hands and poured out her heart. She thought that she detected a slight change in his heart rhythm on the monitor, but she could not be sure.

She did not relish the thought of hanging around the hospital all day. Tonya's suggestion was now more appealing than ever. How did her daughter always seem to sense things like that? Maybe she could find some strength and resolve at the foot of the grave of the only man that she had ever loved.

Tonya returned to her book during the forty-minute drive south. So many "what ifs" played in Michelle's head. Since the day Grover received his draft notice, nothing in her life had turned out as she imagined. What if he had returned from the war? What if they had gotten married? Then again, if that had happened, her daughter would not be sitting in the seat beside her. What if she and Walt had stayed together?

That daughter broke the silence. "Are we almost there?"

"Only about ten more miles."

The picturesque church was the kind that could have been on a funeral home fan. Several more graves had been added since Michelle was there last, and it took a minute for her to find the lot she was looking for. She let out a vocal sigh when she came to it. Grover's father was now buried beside his son. No one had bothered letting her know. She wondered if her parents were informed and did not get the word to her.

Tonya perused the markers. Her mission accomplished, she turned to her mom. "Mother . . . I know you need some time alone. Don't worry about me. I'll be fine."

The girl went walking among the other graves. Her mother's fiancé was not her father. He died more than four years before she was born.

As they started back to the hospital, Tonya asked a question. "Do you know the difference between a cemetery and a graveyard?"

"I've never thought about it. Aren't they two ways of saying the same thing?"

"No, Mother. A graveyard is at a church, like where Grover is buried. It's in the *churchyard*. But a cemetery is off somewhere else. Do you know how cemeteries got started?"

"I've never thought about it."

"During times of plagues, community leaders decided to bury the dead away from population centers to try to stop the spread of germs."

"Well . . . I guess that makes sense." Michelle wondered how her daughter came up with stuff like that. It still puzzled her why Tonya wanted to go to Grover's grave, but she had far too much on her mind to dwell on it.

Tonya was relieved that Grover was not her father. Her daddy was alive. She just knew it, and she would find him one day.

Michelle's father was alive, too, but barely hanging on. She was no closer to deciding how to advise her mother than before they left. Her head was pounding and regrets were hounding. Why did she not heed Granny Addie's ongoing advice and make the first move with her parents? Why did she allow fear to paralyze her?

She did not have one regret, though. Tonya would never have to go through anything like that with her own daddy. Michelle did not understand just how right she was, but for all the wrong reasons.

The family meeting was set for the next morning at nine. Michelle told her mother the night before, and reconfirmed it the next day, that she would have no part in making the decision. Connie made the call. She also placed a call to her pastor and asked him to be by her side.

When the minister arrived, she introduced him first to her daughter, and then to her granddaughter. He shook Michelle's hand and then turned to the girl.

"Hello, Tanya. I've heard about you."

"It's *Tone-yuh*, and I've never heard of you." Something about the preacher made her feel a little funny—as though he thought he was better than she was. He might have heard of her, but he obviously did not know much about her. Otherwise, he would have realized that it was very much in his best interest to be a bit more conciliatory.

Wife, daughter, and granddaughter were given a few minutes alone with the husband, father, and grandfather. The wife spoke to the unresponsive man as if he was hearing her every word. She praised him for his strength and integrity, and she thanked him for the many years they had spent together.

Michelle sobbed, unable to speak.

When Tonya told her granddaddy that she loved him, his eyes opened. Michelle let out a gasp. The physician standing by looked at the heart monitor. Nothing had changed.

The minister offered up a prayer. Tonya could not see what any of that had to do with the Lord's will, but he seemed pretty sure that it did.

The family was given the option of remaining in the room or waiting outside. The wife and minister chose to stay. Michelle took her daughter's hand, and for once, gave her no say so in the matter.

In the waiting room, Michelle wept profusely. Tonya held her mother's hand and tried to console her. After several agonizing minutes, a doctor came out and told them that the man was breathing on his own.

Connie was solemn when she came through the door. The preacher asked the family to go with him to the hospital chapel. Michelle said that she needed a restroom break first. Others nodded. They agreed to reassemble in the chapel.

Michelle and Tonya were seated in the front pew when Connie and the minister came in. Somebody had been a little careless and it did not go unnoticed.

On his knees this time, the preacher prayed long and he prayed loud. Tonya slipped away and closed the chapel door to keep from disturbing others in the lobby.

When he finally finished, the pastor said his goodbyes to Connie, shook Michelle's hand politely, and turned his back on Tonya. He had no idea that when she wanted to be invisible, she did it on her own terms.

As the not so humble parson turned to leave, she abruptly informed him of his oversight.

"Hey, Preach. You forgot to zip up your britches."

On the way home, Michelle looked over at her daughter and shook her head. "Tonya . . . I can't believe you did that."

With a characteristic *Tone-yuh* look on her face, she explained the situation to her.

"Mother . . . I knew he needed to know. And I didn't feel like it was your place, or grandmother's to tell him."

"You could have at least just said XYZ, or you left the barn door open."

Miss Bizzy Belle

"He's such a pri . . ., uh prude, I doubt that he even knows what those things mean."

Granny Addie had supper waiting when Michelle and Tonya stopped in Ferndale to tell her the news. This time, the saintly woman mostly kept her thoughts to herself.

Tonya didn't, though. She told Granny privately all about the preacher's zipper. When the woman snickered, they both got tickled.

Hours stretched into days and days into weeks with no change. Fortunately, Connie was able to get her incapacitated husband into a nursing home just outside of Bellville.

In the nick of time

Michelle was in the kitchen when the phone rang and heard her daughter call out. "I'll get it . . . Hello, Mrs. T."

It was still a month before school started, and Mrs. Thornhill wondered if there was any possibility of her all-time favorite daycare kid coming up for another visit. Tonya put her mother on the line. A time or two, she thought that she was going to have to take the receiver away from her, but Michelle eventually capitulated. Mrs. T said the ticket would be in the mail in a jiffy.

As Tonya was checking in, the agent asked her if she had a frequent flyer number.

"This is certainly not my first flight, and I do hope it won't be my last. What do I have to do to get one?"

Speechless, Michelle just rolled her eyes and shook her head. "I don't know this kid."

The seasoned traveler told her mother that there was no need in waiting around. She knew how to get on the plane and find her seat. Just to make sure, the agent at the boarding gate asked Tonya if anyone would be waiting for her in D.C.

Michelle's nagging ambivalence was back. With the stressful summer, it was nice to have Tonya out of her hair for a couple of weeks. At the same time, coming home to an empty house seemed, at least for the moment, more than a little disconcerting. While in Asheville, she restocked her stash of Sin.

Someone was indeed awaiting Miss Bizzy Belle. While at baggage claim, Tonya began filling in Mrs. T on her granddaddy's condition.

"He's not going to make it, but Mother has not accepted that yet."

On the way to the house, Tonya also got Mrs. T up to speed on her detective activities. She sighed. "I'm back to square one."

When Mrs. T came to tuck her in, she said with a smile. "It's so good to be home."

"I know. I still miss you so much."

Mrs. T had some big news of her own. She had finally closed the daycare center.

"Do you still want to do some traveling with me?"

"Of course, I do. But you know school starts back when I get home. And I'm still not old enough to help you with the driving."

"How about we take a trip during Christmas?"

"Oh, Cornfield. That would be so wonderful."

Over the next couple of days, the "girls" got caught up on lots of things. At church, Kermit teased Tonya about being a hillbilly.

She shot back. "And you're a city slicker."

When they discussed that exchange later that afternoon, Mrs. Thornhill offered some advice. "He's sweet on you, you know. Have boys discovered you, yet?"

"Mrs. T . . . Boys are so stupid. They think they can impress me by showing out. I just can't help myself sometimes. I have to go ahead and knock the props right out from under them. They're so dumb that they think they won."

"Well . . . In a way they did. They got your attention."

"So, you think the best thing is just to ignore them?"

"That will only make them try harder, but after you pretend you don't even notice, they will soon get the picture."

"But what if I want a boy to notice me?"

"Tonya, my child. That will never be your problem."

"Mrs. T . . . Nobody else talks to me about things like this."

Another subject was on the woman's mind, and she wondered if anybody had talked with the girl about it. It was time for a chat over coffee.

Mrs. T wanted to know after Tonya took a sip. "How do you like it?"

"Ugh . . . How do you drink that stuff?"

"Did you get to read all the books you got for Christmas?"

"Yes . . . Sammie and I read some of them together."

Tonya described their hiding place, and how they used flashlights to read the really exciting stuff.

"Thank you so much for the books on health. If you hadn't given them to me, I don't know how I would have learned anything."

"Does your mother ever talk to you about those kinds of things?"

"It's funny that you would ask that. Sammie and I have talked about

Miss Bizzy Belle

this. Her dad is a vaginacologist and my mother is a nurse. But our parents won't even talk to us about the facts of life."

"Did you say a vaginacologist? Tonya . . . That's so clever. You did read those books, didn't you? Have you started, yet?"

"No . . . How will I know when it's about to happen?"

"You might have some pain in your lower abdomen, or you may have no symptoms at all. The main thing is that you are prepared. Do you keep some supplies in your purse?"

"Yes . . . And thank you again for the last package you sent me. I love you so very much."

They had the talk just in the nick of time.

When Tonya came walking down the ramp, she spotted her mother waiting.

"Did you have fun?" Michelle asked her daughter.

"No . . . I was bored to tears. I don't think I'll ever go back there again."

"What's new with Mrs. T?"

"She's retired now. We're going on a trip together at Christmas."

"I thought you said that you were never going back."

"She's going to come by here and get me."

"Anything exciting happen?"

"Nothing much. Got my first period."

Tonya skipped up the corridor toward baggage claim.

On the way home, Tonya asked about her granddaddy. She learned that he was still in a coma. The first thing she noticed when she got back to the Villa was a couple of empty wine bottles. She also observed her mother bringing in a bag of something that had been in the back floorboard. Without even unpacking, she went to the phone.

"I'm going over to Sammie's for a few minutes. I'll be back before bedtime."

With all that had been going on with her grandfather's stroke, and then spending two weeks with Mrs. T, the girls had not had any together time in a while. Sammie ran out to meet her. Simultaneously, they both called out the exact words.

"I got my period!"

Some serious calculating followed in order to establish which of them started first. Since they both started on the same day, they settled for a draw. The conversation continued in Sammie's room as they compared notes. Both of them had just passed another of those transitional milestones from which there is no turning back. The girls were now young women. Tonya went first.

"I'm really glad that I was at Mrs. T's. I don't know what I would have done without the books she gave me. The first night I was there, she talked to me about it, and then, she knew just what to do when I started. Tell me about yours."

"I noticed some stains in my panties, so I went to Mother's bathroom and put in one of her panty liners. I told her about it when she came in from lunch with the gals at the club."

"What happened then?"

"We lit a shuck to the store to get my own supplies. You know what she asked me on the way? She wanted to know why I didn't tell her that I thought it was about time. How am I supposed to know those things when she won't even talk to me about them?"

Tonya went into conjecture mode. "Sometimes, I wonder if my mother even knows how babies are made. She certainly didn't have me because she wanted me. She's made that as plain as the nose on your face. You'd think they taught that sort of thing in nursing school."

Sammie brought it closer to home. "I can't imagine my parents actually doing it. Can you believe my mom? Why would she marry a man who looks at women's bottoms all day? Don't you think the last thing he'd want to do when he comes home is to look at another one?"

Tonya wondered out loud. "Maybe they don't look when they do it."

Sammie's face contorted. "That's so gross!" She then changed the subject.

"I wonder what seventh grade is going to be like. Do you think any new boys have moved into town during the summer?"

"Probably not. But you know, next year is when the kids from the elementary schools out in the county will be coming to Knoxo Springs. I hope there'll be some cute guys."

Sammie speculated that they might be even scuzzier than the ones that they already had to put up with.

Tonya pulled rank. "Anyway . . . I already have a boyfriend. Kermit and I are going to write to each other."

Michelle was sipping a glass of Sin when Tonya came in. "Mother . . . Don't you think maybe you should go a little easy on that stuff?"

"I just need a little something to help settle my nerves until I can get over this hump. You just don't know what it's like for your daddy to be lying in a coma, and there's nothing you can do about it."

"You're right, Mother. You won't even tell me who my daddy is."

"Can't you see that I'm doing this for your own good? You'll never have to go through anything like that."

Miss Bizzy Belle

"But Mother . . . That should be my call, and his call, too. Not just yours."

Michelle lied as she got up to go to bed. "Anyhow . . . I wouldn't know how to find him if I tried."

Michelle knew that she was not being very supportive of her mother. She had not been to the nursing home with her and was not sure that she could. Labor Day weekend was coming up signaling the end of summer. Her teacher mom had no choice but to return to the classroom if she had any hope of keeping the debts from piling up. Maybe a family cookout might do them all good. Granny Addie was just happy to be included.

When Pa Bell heard about it, he insisted that the celebration be at his farm. He went whole hog and bought a ham, which he slowly cooked over hickory coals. A couple of late watermelons were out in the patch, to boot.

The garden had about run its course for the summer, but peas and tomatoes were still plentiful. Corn came from the freezer and green beans from a canning jar. It was too early for sweet potatoes.

Tonya winked at Pa Bell. "This is the best barbecue I've ever eaten."

With a wink of his own, he told her that she was the best farm hand he ever had.

Michelle offered to help with the dishes, but Granny said that she would do both their parts. She suggested that Michelle and Tonya go sit with their grandpa since they got to see him so seldom.

Tonya insisted on going to the nursing home on the way out, and Michelle decided to bite the bullet. Connie had already visited earlier that morning. Granny Addie waited in the sitting room.

The attendant at the desk told them that Mr. Bell was keeping his eyes open some. No one was sure if he was seeing or hearing anything. He could also grunt at times if he was trying to get somebody's attention. He was not very good at squeezing either hand, though.

Tonya was curious about something. "How does he eat?"

She was informed that he got his nutrition through a feeding tube.

Tolbert's eyes were closed when they entered his room. Michelle suggested that they not disturb him. Tonya ignored her mother. She took her granddaddy's hand. "Hello, Granddaddy. This is Tonya, your granddaughter. Are you feeling any better?"

The man's eyes opened, and his head turned a little trying to follow the sound of her voice.

Messing around

One thing different in seventh grade was that boys and girls were separated for an extra long class period. Some subjects were just not suited for a mixed audience. The girls' class was called health science. The boys studied livestock and shop-related things.

Tonya told Twerp that there was a chapter in his book about animal husbandry.

"I ain't gonna be no animal's husband." He liked it when others laughed at him.

Sammie said maybe somebody finally figured out that kids needed some kind of sex education. "I wonder if we'll learn anything we don't already know?" Her best friend suggested that they just play along and see where it might go.

When Tonya told her mother about the class, the nurse said that the school had to be very careful. "Some parents believe that a little knowledge is a dangerous thing. If you teach adolescents about sex, then it's like you're showing them how to do it. And then they will."

"Mother . . .?" Do you think I will?

"I have no idea what you'll do."

The girl thought to herself as she walked away. "And it's going to stay that way."

It was hard to keep up with the melodrama of seventh grade. Some boys and girls were open sweethearts. The grapevine was ever abuzz with gossip. Tidbits regarding possible liaisons, breakups, and who was jealous of whom were continuously moving up and down the line.

Several potential suitors courted Tonya, but she remained aloof. How many times did she have to remind the dudes that she already had a boyfriend? Twit demanded proof. Mrs. T had taken a picture of Tonya and Kermit, which she just happened to carry in her purse. The two had also exchanged school pictures. That only escalated the teasing.

She brought an envelope to school one day from a letter Kermit sent. Twerp snatched it from her hand with illusions of reading the letter aloud. To his disappointment, nothing was inside.

Tonya taunted him. "You don't really think I'd be that stupid, do you?"

Sammie, on the other hand, was fair game. She made it plain that none of her classmates met her standards. She was, nonetheless, flattered when eighth and ninth grade boys flirted with her after school. The best friends were already talking about such things as first dates and first kisses, but that would all have to wait a while.

Miss Bizzy Belle

The small isolated town had a skating rink, a theater, and a couple of fast food joints where the kids hung out. The churches were also gathering places for youth activities. Somebody was always having a birthday party, and inevitably feelings got hurt when certain ones were not on the guest list. It seemed as though some girl was always trying to get even with another.

The boys might have a friend or two closer than others, but they mostly moved about individually. Not so with females. Cliques of four or five girls dominated the social structure. Each had its own leader who kept the others in line. When one member got kicked out, another was invited in.

Tonya and Sammie had their own private peer group, and that was all they were interested in. That did not give them impunity, however. Ringleaders often taunted them for being stuck up. That sometimes bothered Sammie, but Tonya knew how to stick it right back.

Right about dusk one evening, Sammie had a glint in her eyes when she suggested something. "Let's go skinny dipping."

Tonya pondered that possibility with a sparkle in her own eyes.

"The spring water will be chilly, but the weather is still warm. Let's do it."

The girls put some towels in a bag and headed to Knoxo's fabled springs. Officially, the park closed at dark, but there were no gates to keep people out. The moon was almost full, and it had already come up. Charged with the excitement, they whispered while casing the joint. Cars were driving by out on the bordering street.

Sammie started getting cold feet. "You go first."

"Nope. This was your idea. You go first. I'll stand guard."

Slowly, Sammie started taking off her clothes.

"Come on. Nobody's around. Let's do this together."

The naked girls stuck their toes into the frigid water. They had come this far, and there was no turning back. It was hard to keep voices down and not make too much noise splashing around. Shivering in the moonlit pond, it was the most daring thing that either had ever done.

Yikes. Headlights were coming into the park, and they could see that it was a police car. The girls grabbed the towels and their clothes and looked around for somewhere to hide. Hurriedly, they retreated into the edge of the woods adjacent to the springs.

With teeth chattering from both the cold and the exhilaration, they started drying off. So far. So good. They squirmed as the garments did not want to go over the cold damp bodies. Finally, they were dressed. The cop circled and left.

The daring duo tiptoed back to the entrance and then started walking nonchalantly up the street. As cars went by, Sammie said with flair. "Just think. Those folks have no idea what we just did." Without warning, a vehicle came up from behind and pulled alongside them.

The officer rolled down the passenger side window and told them to come closer. "What you girls been up to?"

Tonya recognized him. "Just out for a moonlight walk."

"Haven't I seen you before?"

"I don't think so."

"You're the girl that lives over on Lane Lane, the one who denied being part of the Halloween prank. I know who you are."

Tonya just glared at him.

He continued the brief interrogation as Sammie tried to remain invisible. "What's in those bags?"

Tonya turned it back on him. "Why? Do you have a search warrant?"

"You girls go on home. And don't you ever go skinny dipping again. You hear?" The cop was trying not to let them see him chuckling under his breath as he drove away.

"Another rite of passage in this town. And those girls, like all the kids before them, think they invented it."

When Tonya came in from school one day, Michelle asked if anything interesting happened.

"Not much." And then her mischievousness got the best of her.

"Twit said he saw my panties when I was in the swing during recess."

Her mother was both concerned and curious. "How did you handle that?"

"I told him that he was a big fat liar."

"But what if he wasn't?"

"Oh, Mother. I knew he was lying through his teeth the whole time."

"How could you be so sure?"

"Because I wasn't wearing any panties."

"Tonya . . . !"

"None of that happened. I was just messing with you."

"Tonya . . . !"

The Methodist Youth Fellowship was planning a hayride for Halloween. The fright night came on a Saturday in 1981. Tonya suggested that they go. "Maybe the cops will leave us alone if we're with a church group."

The kids were beginning to think that it was going to be more of a trick than a treat when the truck was late. The old two-ton GMC eventually groaned its way into the parking lot. Surreptitiously, the boys had hatched up a little plan. As soon as the back gate opened, they ran and hopped aboard. When the girls climbed up, they found a gap between each guy. A mad scramble ensued, and the fruit basket turnover continued for a couple of minutes.

The girls outnumbered the boys, so some of them got to sit together. Tonya and Sammie claimed a spot between two eighth graders right behind the cab. The night was chilly and quilts were provided if needed. For the more adventurous, the wraps would serve another purpose as well.

The old mountaineer shifted the gears up and down as he hauled his cargo way back into the boonies. The curvy roads were just the excuse for leaning into each other. Some of the lassies kept falling into the laps of the lads.

Unbeknownst to the hay riders, some other plans had also been hatched up in the pumpkin patch. The truck pulled into the yard of an old abandoned church. The driver shut down the engine and then killed the lights. Faint glows started flickering from inside the old building. The girls screamed and the boys tried their best to protect them. Howling sounds came from the direction of the graveyard. More of the same.

Tonya sighted a figure coming out of the woods under a sheet. A dim flashlight was shimmering through the material.

She bolted to the back of the truck, pointed toward him, and shouted. "Get him."

Several jumped off and chased the poor man into the woods. Fortunately, he had the sense to turn the light off. Tonya stood at the back of the truck, observing with pride the spectacle that she had created.

At church the next morning, the pastor had a couple of Band-Aids on his face. At the Wednesday night family supper, his hands and arms were covered with poison ivy. He and Tonya had an undeclared staring contest. Neither of them blinked. She had managed to escape the gaze of the police, but not the watchful eyes of the parson.

Brad

With her father in a catatonic state, unable to be engaged in this world, but still not part of the next, the spirit of Thanksgiving eluded Michelle. Neither could she find any reason to look forward to the upcoming holiday season.

The mother was once again envious of her daughter. Mrs. Thornhill was flying into Asheville where Tonya would join her. The two were going on to Texas to spend Christmas with her grandson's family. Michelle offered to pay some of the expenses, but she tendered little resistance when the gracious woman insisted that the trip was her gift to Tonya.

For the first time ever, Mama Myra decided not to host Christmas dinner. She said there was no way that she could celebrate the season with her son stuck in a nursing home. Michelle felt certain that her grandmother blamed her for Tolbert's stroke.

Granny Addie invited her to Christmas dinner with her family. Michelle had not seen some of her aunts, uncles, and cousins from that branch in quite a while. The nurse was grateful to have a reason to decline when Barbara asked her to work.

Tonya, on the other hand, was genuinely excited about her first flight with a buddy. A whole new world was about to open up to her. Texas—she was going to Dallas, Texas!

Mrs. T's plane was a few minutes late, but Tonya still had time to show her around the much smaller Asheville airport. Michelle left after wishing both her daughter and Mrs. Thornhill a Merry Christmas. The DC-8 was packed with holiday revelers. After soaring over the mountains and bursting through billowy clouds, the day was clear. From her window seat, Tonya had a spectacular view of the magnificent scenery below.

Sara, the mother of Mrs. T's grandson, Brad, met them at Love Field. The Cartwrights lived in the Carrollton area on the northern outskirts of Dallas. Mrs. Thornhill had asked Sara to reserve a room at a motel, but when they arrived, she insisted that they stay with them as long as the two did not mind sharing a room.

Sara was a teacher and already on break. Her husband, Jason, was an accountant. He had limited time off from work with lots of year-end reports to deal with. Sara's parents lived in Plano, and they were hosting Christmas dinner. The visitors were sent a special invitation to join them.

At sixteen, Brad was four years older than Tonya. When he came in from basketball practice, he was hot and sweaty. Tonya felt her heart flutter. She would tell Sammie later. "What a hunk."

"So you're Miss Bizzy Belle, the little snotty-nosed kid I've heard so much about."

"And you must be Brat, uh Brad, the grandson Mrs. T is always making excuses for. You look nothing like the pictures I've seen, either. You must have gone out and had glamor shots taken."

Tonya served notice that she could take care of herself. The grandmother smiled.

On the plane ride, Mrs. T gave Tonya a heads up as to what she could expect. One surprise, however, she kept a secret. As a special Christmas present, she had booked four tickets for a matinee performance of "Swan Lake" at the Music Hall in Fair Park.

Sara, Brad, Mrs. Thornhill, and Tonya left early enough to do some touring around downtown Dallas. Tonya and Mrs. T got to see Dealey Plaza where President Kennedy was shot.

The theater was unlike anything that the twelve-year-old girl had ever experienced. From seats on the left near the front, she could see the pit. The orchestra director's head was bobbing and his arms were moving during warm up.

Tonya had never been to a live performance, and she was spellbound. Tucked between Mrs. T and Brad, she did not let her immersion in the production keep her from aggravating the boy on her right, though. They had an ongoing battle for rights to the armrest.

Tonya had only seen pictures of swans. She knew little about them but left with a determination to learn more. Her mind went immediately to a story that Mrs. T had read to her years earlier. When she got home, she would have to get her hands on a copy of "The Ugly Duckling."

When they crawled into bed, the tired girl turned to Mrs. T before she turned over to go to sleep. "Oh, thank you so much. Every time I get to spend Christmas with you, it's the best ever. I will never forget this day as long as I live."

Tonya was not the only one who expressed appreciation to Mrs. Thornhill. Brad called Gran-T off to the side the next day. He told her how honored he was to be invited. He reminded her that one of his earliest memories was of his parents taking him to that very theater to see "Swan Lake." He remembered that it was the last time his father was home before his helicopter was shot down in Vietnam. "And for you to plan all of that on my daddy's fortieth birthday was so very, very, special."

Then, it hit him. "You knew that the whole time, didn't you?" As they broke a Christmas embrace, he mentioned something else. "By the way, that's quite a kid you're helping to raise."

"Like you . . . She doesn't have her father around to see what a wonderful person she is."

"There's nothing wrong with that girl that a little growing up won't cure, but you're the one who's so wonderful, Gran-T."

Mrs. Thornhill roused the next morning to an occurrence not all that uncommon for her. Tear stains were on her pillow.

Brad volunteered to take Gran-T and her little protégée to the airport. He had only gotten his driver's license a few weeks earlier. Love Field was about three turns and twenty minutes away.

After checking in, Mrs. Thornhill told her grandson how much she wished that she could see him more often. He responded with some pride in his voice.

"There's something I've been waiting to tell you. I'm trying to get an appointment to the Naval Academy."

She beamed. "Oh . . . That would be magnificent. Annapolis is not that far from where I live."

"It's a long way from a done deal. My representative is a Democrat, and I'm not sure how much clout he will have with that Reagan bunch. I'm working hard to keep my grades up. The appointments will be made next fall during my senior year. My ultimate goal is to become a Navy SEAL."

"Your daddy would be so proud of you."

"If I get the appointment, I won't have a lot of free time. And I want to get one thing straight right now. If I do get a chance to come see you, now that you've closed the daycare center, I don't want any other scrawny kids hanging around."

"This one right here lives in North Carolina, and she hardly ever gets to visit me. But let me get something straight, too. She's always welcome at my house. Have I made myself clear?"

"Crystal."

Tonya was standing by, taking it all in, not saying a word, but never out of the picture.

Once in the air, the girl collected her thoughts. She supposed that she was in love when she first saw Brad. After a few days, it felt more like she had found herself a big brother. Then, something else grabbed her attention.

"It must be easier for people to say that your daddy would be proud of you when he's dead. I still don't know if my daddy is dead or alive. Will I ever know if he's proud of me? I'll bet I'd really be proud of him."

Michelle was not at the gate. Mrs. Thornhill had only a forty-minute layover, but she went to baggage claim with Tonya to see if her mother was there. She wasn't. They went to the airline's service desk to see if there was a message. There was.

Michelle had gotten lost on the way to the airport. When she realized

Miss Bizzy Belle

how close it was to the time for Tonya's flight to arrive, she found a payphone. It took some hoop-jumping, but she was finally able to leave a message. Tonya heard her name called over the intercom while she was reading the note. Her instructions were to stay at baggage claim until her mother arrived.

Mrs. T had to go. The farewell seemed so harried and unfinished after all that they had experienced together.

The agent went with Tonya to claim her bag and then kept her with him at the desk. About thirty minutes later, the girl looked up and saw her mother coming down the corridor. Michelle offered as an excuse that she almost never found a place to park. The airline representative started to remind her that it was the peak of the holiday season, but he decided that a little lecture about allowing extra time would be futile.

Neither Michelle nor her daughter was very talkative on the way back to the Villa. When they went inside, Tonya asked her mother if she had company while she was gone.

"Why do you ask?" Michelle wanted to know.

"I smell cigarette smoke."

"No one's been here. Not long ago, a coworker told me how much a smoke helped her get through the day. She offered me one. I've been smoking about one or two a day with her for a while. I bought a pack while you were gone."

"Mother . . . You cannot smoke in this house. I forbid it. Take your nasty cancer sticks outside. If you want to kill yourself, go ahead. But I'm not going to breathe your filthy secondhand smoke."

Tonya waited until they had eye contact. Her gaze was fixed. "Mother . . . I don't like you very much right now."

It was the first time the girl had ever said anything like that. Her own daughter hated her, too. It was now unanimous.

Back in her own bed, Tonya thought to herself that if not for Sammie, she would go live with Mrs. T. She would kiss her Kermit, and he could turn her into a princess, or a swan, or perhaps a butterfly. Although in separate sleeping quarters hundreds of miles apart, Tonya and Mrs. T shared something in common that night. Each slept on a tear-stained pillow.

The next morning, Michelle wanted to explain why she was late getting to the airport, but Tonya was still asleep when she went to work. When she got home, her daughter was at Sammie's.

She put it aside. "It's probably just as well. Tonya would never cut me any slack, anyway."

The situation did not just go away, though. When the girl came in just before bedtime, she confronted her mother. "Were you drunk last night?

Was that why you couldn't find the airport?"

"Tonya . . . Please let me explain. I left in plenty of time to stop and get a bite to eat on the way. I ordered a glass of wine with my dinner. The waiter insisted that I have another. I wouldn't call two glasses of wine 'drunk'."

"Mother . . . Look at what happened. You were drinking and driving. You got lost. Don't you ever do that to me again. If I even suspect that you've had anything to drink, I'll get out of the car and walk home if I have to. You can kill yourself with your pills, and your cigarettes, and your booze if you want to. But I'm not going to let you take me down with you."

"You just don't understand. You went off and left me. And when I went to see my daddy, he just looked off into space. It was just about more than I could handle."

"Are you going to work yourself up and have a stroke, too, like Granddaddy did?"

"Tonya . . . Don't say that. That's not fair."

"But, Mother . . . It's true."

"Tonya . . .? Is it that time of the month?"

"If anybody's on the rag, Mother . . . It's you."

The Ringers were planning a big New Year's Eve party. Sammie and Tonya went with Mrs. Flo to round up all kinds of munchies. Four card tables were set up for the adults in front of the fireplace with a roaring blaze warming the basement. The kids created their own fun.

Michelle accepted the invitation, but with a headache coming on, left well before midnight. Tonya was spending the night. After the fireworks, the best friends were weary of juvenile sporting. They were ready for bed, but still not ready for sleep.

Tonya vented first. "I'm not a 'pre' anything. All my life, it's been 'pre' this, and 'pre' that. First, it was pre-k, and now I'm supposed to be a pre-teen and a pre-adolescent. When I got back from Dallas, Mother actually accused me of having pre-MS."

Sammie weighed in. "I know what you mean. Sometimes, I just want to run away from home. My parents treat me like I'm still a baby. Stanley gets to do this. And Stanley gets to do that. But Sammie's not allowed to do anything."

Tonya threw something in for good measure. "We'll probably be seniors before they even let us date."

Sammie continued getting it out. "We can't get away with anything. Why did we get stuck in this mountain hick town where everybody knows

Miss Bizzy Belle

everybody, and everything you do beats you back home?"

"Sammie. If it weren't for you, I'd go live with Mrs. T."

"Oh, Tonya. Please don't go off and leave me."

The girls sat up in bed. It was time for a New Year's resolution. Tonya Bell and Sammie Ringer resolved to always be best friends. Always. No matter what.

Neither had any idea what "what" meant.

Tonya had never really gotten into Valentine's Day. She always received several but never bothered giving any. The February before her thirteenth birthday, she was in a quandary. Would it be too presumptuous to send Kermit one? Might it make him uncomfortable if he had not sent one to her?

If it came a day or so early, that would give him a chance to save face and get one in the mail. Picking one out was not easy. It could not be too mushy, but she wanted it to be more than just about friendship. Finally, she found one that was not perfect but would do.

Three days after she mailed it, a major surprise awaited her in the mailbox. Tonya's boyfriend had sent her a big beautiful red valentine with "Sweetheart" on the front in bold letters. She would save it forever. Maybe she should not mention this to Sammie. It never even occurred to her to say anything about it to her mom.

Monumental fun

Sammie's thirteenth birthday was about two months before Tonya's, and her parents wanted to do something special for this milestone marker. They asked for suggestions, but she could not think of anything that she wanted to do with them or without her best friend. When mulling it over, Tonya was just thinking out loud.

"We could always go see Mrs. T during spring break and let her show us around Washington. I was so young when we moved away that I hardly remember anything about the government stuff."

She then threw out another intriguing possibility. "I could look up my old friend, Connie, from grade school, and we could double date."

"Tonya . . . That's brilliant. I think my parents might really go for something like that, all educational and such. They never have to know that boys had anything to do with it. We could also tell them that we were celebrating both our birthdays. Our parents might resist a bit about not being along, but the more they think about it, I think the better they will like it. Are you sure Mrs. T won't mind?"

The girl knew the woman rather well. "I think she would love it."

Tonya knew how to work around her mother, but how could they sell Sammie's parents on the idea? What if Tonya was going to see Mrs. T during the break, and she invited Sammie to go with her? They could throw in the birthday angle later. The conniving girls' scheme started taking on a life of its own.

The Ringers never knew what hit them. They took the bait and swallowed it hook, line, and sinker.

Tonya blurted out as she burst through the door a few days later. "Mother . . . I only want money for my thirteenth birthday."

"Why would you say that now? That's still weeks away?"

"I want new clothes for the Washington trip, and I need my birthday money so I can go ahead and buy them now."

"Tonya . . .? Do you realize that you didn't even discuss those plans with me until after they were made? When Mrs. Flo called, I had to fake it that I even knew what she was talking about."

"Oh, Mother. I knew you would be glad to get rid of me. I guess I should have mentioned it, but your head was always somewhere else."

"Anyway . . . Mrs. Flo is taking Sammie shopping in Asheville this Saturday. I want to go, too, and pick up a few things." The girl then added to appease her mother. "You're free to come with us if you're off this weekend."

"No. I've got to work. How much money did you have in mind?"

"I think a couple hundred dollars will do it. Just think how cheap you're getting off. The Ringers are spending so much more on Sammie's birthday, and Mrs. T is paying for my ticket."

"I don't keep that kind of money around. I'll let you use a credit card, but only with Mrs. Flo's supervision."

"Are you sure you have one that's any good?"

"On second thought, I'm off tomorrow. I'll go by the bank. But don't forget this when your birthday rolls around."

"Oh, Mother. You're so sweet."

Kermit was given the assignment of locating Constantine De Palma. When he dialed the number of the second listing in the book, he hit pay dirt. Connie's mother and Mrs. Thornhill worked out some details. Since the boys knew their way around Washington, Mrs. T decided to let them take the lead and play tour guides.

Miss Bizzy Belle

Good Friday was the start of spring holidays, and Easter weekend could not come fast enough. The girls got permission to begin their vacation a day early since it was an "educational" trip. Mrs. Flo took them to the airport on Wednesday afternoon.

Kermit was with Mrs. T when she met them at Dulles. Tonya did the introductions.

"Mrs. Thornhill . . . This is Sammie."

"I'm pleased to meet you. I've heard so much about you."

"And Sammie . . . This is Kermit."

Kermit and Tonya held hands on the way to the car.

Neither of the boys' spring breaks corresponded with the girls', but both were out of school on Good Friday. It and Saturday were set aside to go downtown. The women had worked out for Connie's mother to bring him to Mrs. T's, and for him to spend Friday night with Kermit.

As they were lying in bed, Sammie sniggered. "See how things work out if we can just keep our parents out of the way." With stars in her eyes, she went on. "The 'Frog' is a dude, and I can't wait to meet Connie."

It had been four years since Tonya had last seen her old Fairfax pal. She was flattered that he even remembered her when he got the call.

Tonya said to Mrs. T in private. "This is so maddening. What if Connie and Sammie have no chemistry? What if I like him better than Kermit? What if Kermit falls for Sammie?"

The wise woman knew precisely what to say. "Just relax, and be yourself. Have fun. That's the main thing."

As Connie was getting out of the car when his mother dropped him off, Sammie whispered. "He's such a fox." Tonya did not know what to expect. He extended both hands, and then he looked her over.

"I've been trying to imagine what you might look like now. You're pretty."

He then turned his attention to her best friend. "So . . . This is Sammie." She was smitten.

Not wanting to deal with the hassle of parking, Mrs. T called a cab. She sat in the front, and the other four stuffed themselves in the back with the girls in the middle. The monumental fun was just beginning.

Connie was the alpha dog. Kermit was more enamored with Tonya than with the historical places that he had been to before. Sammie gave Connie her undivided attention. Tonya enjoyed sporting with Kermit. Mrs. T watched over the brood like a mother hen.

Sammie's parents had sent along an envelope with cash to cover the expenses. Their calculations did not include two extra tickets at each venue and two more mouths to feed. When the money started running low on Saturday, Mrs. Thornhill stepped in.

On Saturday evening, with emotions running in overloads, and with both egos and gangly bodies occasionally tripping all over each other, the four said their goodbyes. Mrs. T invited the boys back for dinner on Wednesday night before the girls had to leave the next day.

Mrs. T got a hug from both of her guests before they went to bed. Tonya thanked her and told her how much fun it had been. The woman responded with a pleasant little glint in her eyes. "I wouldn't have missed it for the world."

Soon after they closed the door to their bedroom, the phone rang. Mrs. Flo asked Mrs. Thornhill how things were going.

"Oh . . . I think they're having a good time. They're already in bed."

Sammie's mom was amazed. "You must be wearing the girls out for them to turn in so early."

"We've been busy. I invited some of Tonya's friends to join us, and that's making the trip even more enjoyable."

"Mrs. Thornhill. That's so nice of you. You are very brave hosting a bunch of giggling girls." Mrs. T offered no clarification.

Kermit sat between Tonya and Sammie at church on Easter Sunday. Nobody else could see it, but he slipped his hand under his girlfriend's purse and found hers. He also leaned against her when they were standing during a prayer. After the service was over, Ms. Joy came over and told them what a cute couple they were.

Wednesday night was a riot. With the awkwardness of the firsts behind them, the evolving personalities took turns sharing the spotlight. Mrs. T watched from the lamplight. Sammie and Connie promised to keep in touch. Tonya told Kermit that she hoped to see him again soon.

On the flight back to Asheville, the girls snickered and snorted all the way. Sammie said it was a good thing that she picked up some brochures because her parents would want a full report. Both of her parents were waiting for them at the gate. The gaiety continued in the backseat on the way to Knoxo Springs.

Mrs. Flo wanted to hear all about the trip. "What did you like most about Washington?"

Both girls tried to contain their giggling, and Sammie struggled to get serious.

"Hmm, let me think. I really liked the Lincoln Memorial and the

Miss Bizzy Belle

Washington Monument. We went to some good museums, too, but I guess my favorite place was the Smithsonian. I could have stayed in there for days."

Her mother suggested that maybe she could go back again sometime.

The girls looked at each other about to crack up. Sammie had not answered her mother's question.

"Mother and Daddy . . . Thank you so much for my thirteenth birthday present. You parents are the greatest." Neither could see the straight face that she was working hard to put on. Tonya then expressed her appreciation, as well.

Mr. Ebb had been quiet. From the driver's seat, he shared his perspective as the elder statesman. "We're so proud of both of you for taking such an interest in our country's history. Most girls your age would only be interested in boys."

He then added. "And by the way, your teacher is a patient of mine. She had an appointment during her break. She expressed great admiration for how you two decided to celebrate such a special birthday. She said that she would be expecting a full report next week to make up for the day you were absent."

Oops . . .

When her thirteenth birthday finally rolled around, Tonya decided to give herself a couple of presents. She purchased both a spiral notebook and a sketchbook. In a letter to Mrs. T, she mentioned that one day she might write a children's book and do her own illustrations.

With a penchant for naming things, she had to come up with something to call her journal. After considering several possibilities, she settled on "Willa-O-Wisps."

Tonya had no interest in merely recording her daily activities. She rather tried to capture the thoughts that occurred when she let her mind just be.

As for the sketchbook, she was once good at coloring. It was time to have a try at drawing. The first thing she sketched was a butterfly. Since Watt was her only critic, Tonya decided to call the art book, "Watt Not."

Nothing out of the ordinary happened on the actual date. It came on a school day, and Tonya spent the night with Sammie. If Michelle remembered, she did not mention it. The daughter did send her mom a Mother's Day card in the mail.

It was coming up on a year after Tolbert's stroke. The prospects of him surviving the summer were not good. Bedsores, pain medications, and recurrent infections had taken their toll, and his kidneys were failing.

Connie completed another year of teaching. She tried to keep her chin up, but her spirits were sagging. The joy in her life was the granddaughter denied her for so long. She invited Tonya to come spend a week with her as soon as school was out.

Michelle was sinking deeper into the depths of despair. Her prayers for a miracle recovery for her father had gone unheeded. She was torn continuously between holding on and letting go. What she needed from her father, he was no longer able to give—if he had ever been, to begin with.

Tonya took her pencil and pad to her grandfather's room. When she sketched his profile, she did not have to use her imagination when she added a tear creeping its way down his cheek. In her journal that night, she wrote.

Why do some people get stuck as caterpillars, never able to emerge from their cocoons and become butterflies?

She also spent a few of the days with Pa Bell while in Bellville. He taught her how to crank the Allis-Chalmers, where the gears were, the way to let off on the clutch, and how to shut it down. The tractor was the closest thing to a horse that she had ever ridden. Mama Myra was her cranky old self.

One day, the young teenager ventured all the way to the creek. For about an hour, she sat listening to the cascading water and watching the clouds. Dragonflies darted about, and one kept landing on her hand. She opened Watt Not and sketched it.

The girl had always worn her black hair long, but she told her grandmother that she wanted it cut short for the summer. Connie was hesitant to consent without first getting Michelle's permission. Tonya convinced her grandmother that her mother would not care one way or the other. Eventually, the persuasive teen's wishes prevailed.

When Michelle went to get Tonya, she noticed the change. "You've had your hair cut."

The sassy thirteen-year-old shot back. "Mother . . . You don't miss a thing, do you?"

"Well . . . I surely missed you while you were gone."

For a moment, Tonya thought her mom was going to come give her a hug. When their eyes met, Michelle turned away.

The prospects were dim for any further excitement during the summer. Tonya wanted to go back and see Mrs. T, but Michelle put her foot down.

Miss Bizzy Belle

She wanted her close in case anything happened to her granddaddy.

Sammie was going off with her folks on a longer than usual vacation. She told Tonya that her parents felt like it might be the last time that they would all be together as a family. Stanley's only interest in going was to do some of the driving.

Walt Williamson was in a funk. The most exasperating thing about being a counselor was trying to work with those who knew better. He found that the same professionals, good at telling others what to do, often had blind spots when applying the same standards to themselves. That really hit hard one day when he wondered if he might be guilty of the same thing.

The therapist smiled each time he remembered the session back at Ft. Benning with the major's wife. He had since added numerous things to his personal "fucket list." Approaching middle-age, some items were already appearing on the other list as well.

It was high time for the counselor to heed his own counsel. From the occasion when Walt realized that he was an ugly duckling, he fancied seeing swans in the wild. The thirty-nine-year-old man decided to make that happen. In a pickup truck with a camper, he set out on the quest. Little did he realize when the voyage began that he would venture all the way to Alaska. Neither did he have any awareness of what life-changing experiences were awaiting him along the way.

A night to remember

The church was encouraging junior high students to go to a religious camp for a week near the end of June. Sammie thought it over and suggested to her cohort. "I'll go if you'll go. At least we'll get to meet some new boys."

Mrs. Flo drove them to the assembly, set back in a beautiful mountain valley. After checking in, the girls rushed to their cabin to pick out adjacent bunks. Afterward, they sauntered around the campgrounds checking things out.

Age-graded Bible study classes were scheduled for mornings and music was featured during the evenings. The afternoons were free for recreational activities. When the dinner bell rang, they discovered that the girls outnumbered the boys.

Sammie did not see anyone that turned her head, but Tonya set her sights on one of the few boys just slightly taller than she. He seemed okay with her hanging around, and she made sure that they were walking together on the way to chapel the next morning. She confided in Sammie that before the week was over, she was going to get Kenny to kiss her.

The entire group worked on a musical to be performed for the parents on Friday night when they came to pick up their campers. After the final rehearsal on Thursday, Tonya whispered in Kenny's ear. "Let's slip away after lights-out and take a walk in the moonlight."

The staff was very much aware of the full moon and had tried to prepare themselves for more craziness than usual. The director had the added task of keeping an eye on his amorous assistants, as a budding romance was breaking out between the head boys' and girls' counselors.

Kenny was hesitant, but Tonya reassured him. "It's the last night. The worst thing that could happen is that they send us home."

The introverted boy was feeling his oats a bit in that he had attracted the attention of a popular female. He was certain that other guys were envious. Not wanting his good fortune to slip away, he ultimately consented.

Sammie agreed to cover for Tonya. In the event of a flashlight check, they rolled up towels and made it look like the bed was occupied. The bold and daring campers made plans to meet at the gate. Tonya was not sure if Kenny would show up, but he was waiting when she slipped out.

When she took his hand, it caught him by surprise. As they started strolling up the road, she gestured with her other arm. "What a beautiful night."

Kenny stopped in his tracks. "I think we should go back."

"Come on. Trust me. I promise to give you a night that you'll never forget."

Car lights heading their way startled them. Tonya had not counted on that, but she took charge. "Quick . . . Through the fence." Both received a rush in the excitement.

This was even better. About fifty yards into the pasture, there was no reason to beat around the bush. Tonya squared herself facing Kenny and shocked him yet again.

"Now, you can kiss me."

Perhaps, the gangly boy should have seen that coming, but he was oblivious to the wiles of the fairer sex. To make matters worse, he had no clue how to kiss a girl. He was a bright kid, though, and he started racking his brain to come up with a way to buy some time.

Miss Bizzy Belle

"Uh. I'm a Christian . . . And you know . . . They've been telling us all week that we need to pray about important stuff. Before I do this, I want to pray about it."

Tonya never saw that coming, either.

Without another word, Kenny dropped to his knees in the grass.

Not knowing what else to do, she knelt beside him. Her prayer was that his prayer would soon be over so hers could be answered.

The pasture was home to a flock of sheep. With Kenny and Tonya still prone, and with him silently and earnestly petitioning the Almighty for some guidance in this delicate matter, the resident ram in charge of the herd came to check on things. He simultaneously announced both his presence and his displeasure.

"Run!" Tonya called out. Kenny put legs on his prayers. The ram was more than willing to escort him to the fence. Tonya took cover behind some bushes.

"Oh, s_ _ _!" The suddenly not so reverent camper let the expletive slip when he stepped in a pile of sheep dung. With the battering ram hot on his tail, the poor boy tore his shirt getting through the fence.

Kenny had lost complete sight of Tonya. Since he was not much of an athlete, the boy presumed that she had outrun him. Once back on the road, he wiped his feet on the grass in an effort to clean his foul-smelling shoes, but no matter how fast he walked, the stench kept pace. He was not a happy camper.

As the lad approached the spot of the ill-fated rendezvous, he was trying to figure out how to slip back into his cabin. For certain, he had to find a place to stash his shoes.

With the campers bedded down, the head counselors were in the shadows having a little prayer meeting of their own. Wary of somebody sneaking up on them, they saw Kenny coming through the gate. Tonya was not far behind him, but she kept out of sight.

The boy's counselor intercepted him and queried him. "What are you doing out of your cabin? And where have you been?"

The busted camper was quick on his feet. "I had a big decision to make in my life, and I needed to slip away and pray about it."

"Did you?"

"Yes . . . I got down on my knees out in the pasture."

"Did you get an answer?"

"Just about the time I thought I knew what I should do, the ram came and chased me through the fence. See . . . I stepped in mess, and I tore my shirt."

"I don't know what you're dealing with, Kenny, but I do hope you find direction. You're a fine young man. Now, go clean up your shoes, and get back to bed."

As they sniggered in hushed tones, the youth worker put his arm back around his girlfriend and whispered in her ear. "Can you believe that? At least one kid has gotten something good out of this week."

The counselors could not say a word about the incident to any of the other staff. It would raise questions as to why they were not on duty in their respective cabins.

The other party to the mischief heard everything without being seen. Since she had her counselor in the crosshairs, she was in no hurry to get back to the cabin. Sammie was sound asleep when she finally slipped in.

While Tonya was inaccurate in her prediction of getting kissed that night, she, nonetheless, delivered on her promise. Kenny would never forget that night the rest of his life.

A field trip was planned before the next morning's Bible study. Kenny stayed as far away from Tonya as he could. The class took a hike to view the flock of sheep. Most of the campers had never seen one, and none as up close and personal as Kenny had. The farmer and his Border Collie corralled the ewes and the lambs to a place near the fence. The man then talked to them about sheep and herding.

The ram kept his distance. Tonya slipped away from the group and went up the road in his direction. He came over to her, and she reached in and patted his head. A piece of cloth was caught in the fence right under her arm. She freed it and took it for a souvenir.

When the junior high students returned to the chapel, the camp pastor led a discussion based on Psalm 23 from the Old Testament and teachings about "The Lamb of God" from the New.

Tonya took out her sketch pad. Her counselor was curious and went over to investigate. The camper held up the drawing of a ram's head. The college girl commended her and said that it was worthy of framing.

Tonya motioned for her counselor to lean in, and she whispered in her ear. "Is he a good kisser?" Oh, what fun it was to watch her blush.

Before she closed Watt Not, Tonya added a title to her drawing.

"Camp Rambunctious."

When the Bell tolls

On the first day of August, Michelle got a call while still at work. Her daddy's demise was imminent. On her way out, the nurse went to the hospital pharmacy and picked up some meds. She and Tonya packed enough clothes to stay several days. The man in the hospital bed was hardly recognizable.

Tolbert Bell lingered two more days and died in the wee hours of the morning after everybody had gone home. Michelle was relieved that it did not happen on her watch.

At his funeral, before a packed house overflowing out into the yard, tribute was paid to Mr. Bell for upholding the highest of moral standards and for sustaining the courage of his convictions to the end. He was extolled as a paragon of virtue. The man's life was held up as an exemplary model for others to pattern theirs after. The preacher compared the deceased to Job in his suffering, and he said that Tolbert had now gone home to be with the Lord where he had been fully exonerated.

Music rang from the rafters. The choir sang of kneeling at the cross in the sweet bye and bye with holy manna being spread all around. The brethren in the amen corner chimed in, and some of the sisters wailed.

After the funeral was over, Michelle could barely remember anything about any of it. In the backseat on the way back to the house, Granny Addie was thinking out loud more than anything else. "The big difference was that Job didn't bring his problems on himself." Then she added. "But I suspect the preacher didn't think that Tolbert did either."

Tonya inquired if her granddaddy was ever in the army.

"Why would you ask that?"

"The preacher said that he was 'a pentagon of virtue.' I figured that must have been some kind of medal he was awarded."

"Oh, Tonya."

Pa Bell asked if Tonya could stay a few days with them. The old man and the young lady took short walks and had long talks. They whistled a lot. In addition to the tractor, she drove his truck around the farm.

Mama Myra took to her bed. The last thing that she wanted was the shameless brat who caused all of the trouble in the first place back under her roof.

When Michelle came back to get her, Tonya was still trying to process things. "You know Mother . . . Pa Bell's a fine old man. Why was his own son so different from him?"

"I wish I could answer your question, Tonya . . . But I really don't know."

Larry G. Johnson

The meltdown

During eighth grade, perhaps more than at any other time in their lives, Tonya and Sammie felt stuck between two worlds. They were no longer children, but still not adults. They had boyfriends, but could not date. The adolescents had no desire to go back, but they were not always confident of what was ahead. Bodies were changing in front of their eyes, and they were sometimes self-conscious about how other eyes were assessing.

Where they were in their education, illustrated that predicament. The pupils had finished elementary school, but they were not yet in high school. It seemed to them that the teachers were trying to review everything they had studied up to that point, so the students were better prepared for the next year when grades started counting toward credits for graduation.

For those at the top of the class, it was endlessly boring. Tonya did not do boring very well. All of her life, she had honed her skills for not getting caught. One day toward the end of the first semester, her math teacher asked her to stay during the upcoming break. Tonya started reviewing a laundry list of things that the unscheduled session might be about.

A couple of students wanted to remain in the room to study, but the teacher ordered them out and then locked the door. Tonya started practicing her "Miss Innocence" look.

Without any preliminaries or pretext, the woman began pleading her case. "Why do you keep doing all this to me? I'm trying so hard to work with these students and keep them in school. All you seem to want to do is make my life miserable."

Tonya looked down and did not utter a word. When the silence endured, she looked up. Her teacher was crying. The disruptive student went and put her arms around the disconsolate teacher.

After a brief interval, she wanted to make amends. "I'm so sorry. I'll do better. I promise I will. You really are a terrific teacher."

"Go. Get out of here. And don't you ever mention this to anybody."

The eighth grader smirked as she went out the door. "I made her cry." Then, she glanced back at her teacher trying to straighten up her face and felt sorry for her.

"Lighten up, girl. Sometimes you forget what effect you have on people."

Sammie was waiting outside and wanted to know what happened. Tonya told her that the teacher just wanted to go over a math problem with her. Sometimes even best friends don't have to know everything.

Sammie was valedictorian and Tonya salutatorian at the eighth grade graduation. Nothing else was ever said about the day the teacher had her meltdown.

Miss Bizzy Belle

The Ringers and Mrs. Thornhill all had some big end of school news. The doctor and his wife had bought a little cabin up on a lake. Mrs. T had purchased a new car.

Sammie's parents threw a graduation party for the girls at their new retreat. They decided to forego a vacation to spend as much time as possible fixing up the place. A little beach and a swimming area were nearby. Mr. Ebb promised to get a boat but said that would have to wait.

Tonya had never been around water much and did not know how to swim. She vowed to take care of that soon.

The fourteen-year-old had promised both her Grandmother Connie and Pa Bell that she would spend a couple of weeks out their way. She had also been neglecting Granny Addie and wanted to see her. With all of that already on the docket, Mrs. Thornhill invited Tonya to take a road trip.

Family first, the teenager decided. She got to D.C. in time to take the train with Mrs. T to Philadelphia for Independence Day. Kermit was invited to go along and they cavorted. During the fireworks, he kissed her. Tonya was glad that she had saved herself for him.

Two days later, the females were in the maroon Volvo headed in the other direction. The old blue car was still in the garage. Mrs. Thornhill said that they allowed her practically nothing for it.

The driver turned the new vehicle toward the Outer Banks of North Carolina. Tonya had no way of knowing it, but she walked in her daddy's footsteps. The carefree gals went on to Myrtle Beach for two days, to Charleston for another couple, and then to Savannah for three. They took horse-drawn tours of the historical areas and enjoyed seafood at least once a day.

Tonya had saved as much as she could from her allowance. Pa Bell slipped his great-granddaughter twenty dollars. Granny threw in another ten. Tonya kept a pocket calculator with her, and she insisted on leaving the tips with her own money.

From the Georgia coast, they went back through Atlanta on the way to Knoxo Springs. That was Mrs. T's first visit to the Villa Bell. Tonya pointed out something before they got there. "I'll have my learner's permit next summer, and I can help drive." She and Mrs. T began planning a trip out west.

The Ringers were excited about meeting the woman that they had heard so much about, and who had entertained their daughter for her thirteenth birthday. Mrs. T was the guest of honor for a full weekend at the lake.

Michelle had used up her vacation time during her father's demise.

She got stuck working and hardly saw Mrs. Thornhill. She offered to cover some of Tonya's expenses, but Mrs. T said that she should be paying the girl for being her personal valet.

As they were saying their goodbyes, Tonya was concerned. "Are you going to be all right driving back to Washington by yourself? I could go with you and then fly back. I have some money left over that I could put toward a ticket."

"Oh . . . I'll be fine. And again, thank you so much for going with me. I would have never done this by myself."

"Me, neither." The girl had done some serious growing up during the summer. Watt Not was full, and her Willa-O-Wisps journal was bursting at the seams. When Mrs. T had her pictures developed, she always got double prints. Some of Tonya's spending money was earmarked for a photo album.

Up the hill

It was groundbreaking when the students in Knoxo Springs "went up the hill." The high school was only about forty feet higher in elevation than the elementary one right down the street, but that was rarified air for a ninth grader. The only downside was that freshmen went from the top of the heap to the bottom rung of the seniority ladder.

Girls liked it best. Boys in upper grades did not have to degrade themselves if attracted to females beneath them in school. All were now in the same building.

The class size just about doubled with the new students bussed in from the feeder schools. Tonya and Sammie had done some class switching in eighth grade, but ninth was the first year that they moved from one room to another for each subject. They also had their first male teacher, an assistant coach who taught civics.

Sammie was not doing too well in the boy department. She and Connie had corresponded a couple of times, but neither were interested in a long distance romance. Guys seemed to be intimidated by her stunning good looks. As a blond with brains, she defied the stereotype. Neither did being a doctor's daughter help her case. Behind her back, some of the kids called her "Barbie."

Boys were not exactly falling at Tonya's feet, either, but it had little to do with her looks. If some dude was giving her unwanted attention, all she had to do was glare at him, and he disappeared back into the woodwork.

Possible prospects from among the newcomers gave both girls hopes. While the newbies checked them out, neither girl saw anything that even turned her head, much less turned her on.

Tonya overheard Twerp telling one of the new students. "Don't mess with her. She'll bite your head off." She also knew full well that her old nemesis had an ulterior motive. From the way he looked at her, she could tell that he would love nothing more than to lay his eyes on what was hiding underneath her clothes. She thought about shocking him. It would almost be worth it just to hear the other boys laughing at him for lying when he bragged about it.

Tonya wanted to take art lessons, but the country was trying to pull itself out of a recession. Those kinds of "non-essential" classes were first on the chopping block. Instead, she enrolled in a swimming class at the rec department.

The quickie

Stanley was a senior during the 1983-84 school year. Sammie felt empowered with a big brother looking after her, but she was also looking forward to having the upstairs all to herself when he went off to college.

"Mr. Everything" at KSHS, Stanley was studious without being a geek. He had broken several girls' hearts without ever going out with them. Determined to go to medical school, he had no intentions of getting serious with any one female. At the same time, the well-rounded student was all male.

Sammie and Tonya were in his room one day searching for anything salacious when they heard voices coming up the stairs. Blocked from getting to Sammie's room, they dived into their secret bunker. Through the tiniest crack, they could see that he had brought a girl with him.

Serious bribery material was in the making. The inadvertent voyeurs had a front row seat in a sex education class. The instructors, however, had no idea that they were providing a laboratory exhibition. The crash course was over so fast that the students did not even have time to take notes.

Tonya quipped after they were gone. "I guess that's what you call a 'quickie'." Sammie wanted to know where she learned that word. Fluttering her eyelids, she claimed that she had just made it up.

On second thought, the girls decided that it was best not to harass Stanley. He might be more careful in the future.

WOWs

With summer relenting and a touch of fall in the air, the girls spent most weekends at the cabin. They went to an occasional football game to end the school week. Tonya had a chance to work on her swimming skills until the water in the lake got too cold. She never went without her new Watt Not or her second journaling notebook. Instead of writing "Willa-O-Wisps" across the cover of the latter, she abbreviated it to WOWs.

Flocks of honking geese flying south for a warmer winter clime always caught her attention. The ducks on the lake were already gone until spring. "Where do the butterflies go?" Tonya wondered.

She could identify with migratory instincts. Her main home was in the mountains of western North Carolina, but she trekked back and forth to the place of her birth. One thing about that really puzzled her. She knew that she was born in D.C., and she had no reason to suspect that she was not conceived there. Yet, she felt no connection with her father when she was in Washington.

Tonya lived among peers, many of whom had never been out of the state. She got along well with most of them but had little in common with any of them, even her own mother.

She wrote in WOWs:

> *Birds of a feather flock together, each birdie feathering its own nest.*
> *Furtive butterflies flutter by, flirting with a hand upon which to rest.*

Tonya just blurted out as she came out of her room one Sunday afternoon. "Mother? Have you ever been on a cruise?"

"Why would you ask me that? No. I've never been on a cruise."

Michelle braced herself. She had learned that her daughter rarely asked a stand-alone question.

"How many states have you been in?"

"I don't know. I suppose just the ones between Alabama and Washington. You've already been in more than I have."

Tonya needed to be careful. She did not want to give her mother any hint as to the nature of her line of questioning. Michelle was trying to figure out where it was going.

"What's the most exciting place you've ever visited?"

"Why are you so interested in me all of a sudden?"

"Oh, Mother. I just want to get to know you better."

Michelle was flattered. "To answer your question, I've never had much excitement in my life, other than never knowing what you're going to come up with next."

"Now wait a minute, Mother. When I was born, you had the X. You must have had lots of fun before I came along."

"I did enjoy driving it, but that car was never me."

"Then, why did you buy it?"

"Grover's parents gave me his old Falcon Wagon when he died, and it was already about worn out. When it reached the point of costing more to fix than it was worth, I took someone from work with me car shopping. I let that friend talk me into buying the X, but I always thought that it was out of character for me. Look what I'm driving now."

"Did you take any vacations in it?"

"No. The first time I drove it out of Washington was when I went back home for Christmas the same year I bought it. The next trip, you were with me."

"Black Bart is about on its last leg, what are you going to get next?"

"You keep me in the poor house all the time. I'll drive it as long as I can."

"Mother . . . You need to get out more and have some fun."

Michelle was baffled again. What did any of that have to do with anything?

As Tonya went back to her room, she muttered to herself. "I guess my mother just had a quickie."

Driving him crazy

The hype about high school was just that for Tonya. Only two things mattered during her ninth grade year. One was getting her learner's permit when she turned fifteen, and the other was the day school was out for the summer. She and Mrs. T had plans.

Tonya's birthday was on a Friday, so she just had to wait one day. The office for new drivers was only open on Saturdays. Michelle informed her that she was scheduled to work that day.

"No problem, Mother. Only one parent is required to sign for me. Call my daddy. I'll bet he'll be happy to go with me. And don't forget that I'll need my birth certificate."

On Wednesday, a Code T went out over the hospital's speakers. Tonya told the receptionist that she would go to meet her mother when she came down the hall. Instead, she went to Mrs. Jobson's office. When the girl finally found her mother, she told her that everything was all set. Barbara had switched her days so that she could be off on Saturday.

Michelle assured Tonya that she had the birth certificate in her purse, wondering if her daughter might be inquisitive about it. She didn't know that the girl already knew what was on it.

When asked if she was nervous about getting behind the wheel, Tonya said, confidently. "I already know how to drive."

Michelle was curious. "What do you mean by that? Driver's Ed classes were eliminated with the budget cuts."

"Mother . . . Pa Bell taught me how to drive several years ago."

"You never told me about that."

"I probably did, and you just forgot."

It took over an hour, but ultimately Tonya strutted to the car with an official document in her purse. She was sitting in the driver's seat when her mother caught up with her.

Michelle voiced her concern. "I don't know if my nerves can handle this."

"Mother . . . I need to get all the experience I can so that Mrs. T and I can take turns driving on our trip." She started up the car and waited for her mother to buckle up.

Tonya's bags were packed, and she was ready to go when Mrs. Thornhill arrived at the Villa two days after school was out. They spent several minutes looking at a road atlas the night before they pulled out. Mrs. T had highlighted a number of possible destinations, but Tonya was informed that she had been appointed the navigator. The first stop was Dallas, Texas.

Brad did not get into the Naval Academy as he wished. He conjectured that it was just too much politics. Instead, he went to college and had finished his first year at SMU.

Mrs. T waited to let Brad tell Tonya that he was going to accompany them for a few days and then fly back home. The fifteen-year-old girl decided that might be fun, but she did not let on.

Mrs. T drove all the way to Dallas. She reminded Tonya that there was a big difference between tootling around on a farm and being out on the open road. The surprise had a part two. Brad was going to give the girl driving lessons.

She wrote in her WOWs. "Wow! I may have trouble thinking of him

Miss Bizzy Belle

as a big brother."

Brad had muscled up in the two-and-a-half years since Tonya had last seen him. Then again, she was no longer a beanpole, either. When they were alone in the den, she started priming him. "I sat in Pa Bell's lap when he first let me drive. Are you going to let me sit in your lap?"

"Sure. Just as long as you have permission from the vehicle's owner."

Tonya was not about to make it easy. "Do you know how to drive a stick shift?"

"No. I've only driven automatics."

She continued flirting with him. "I may have to teach you a thing or two. I know how to pop the clutch and peel rubber."

Wondering what he had gotten himself into, Brad conceded. "You probably know how to get us all killed, too."

Mrs. T preferred going ahead and getting a ticket for her grandson's flight back to Dallas, but Brad wanted to keep his options open. If he found the girl insufferable, he could bail earlier. If on the other hand, all of them were getting along well, he might hang with them longer.

Brad was at the wheel when they got an early start to get ahead of the traffic. Tonya sat in the back. About an hour beyond Dallas, they stopped for breakfast. On the way back to the Volvo, he handed Tonya the keys. She held them out with a funny look on her face.

She was trying to rev him up. "What are these?"

"Keys . . . You dummy. Do you want to drive?"

"He called me a dummy. He shouldn't have done that."

Tonya went into robot mode. She waited for every instruction and then moved stiffly and mechanically like a mime. Mrs. T was sitting in the back trying not to laugh.

In utter exasperation, Brad was stymied. "Stop the car."

She slammed on the brakes so hard that he had to brace himself.

After letting the vehicle coast into the emergency lane, she extended her hand to the now reluctant instructor and offered. "Truce?"

"Out! This driving lesson is over."

"Boo Hoo. Poor Brad."

Buckling up in the passenger seat, she thought to herself. "I'll bet Brad's thinking this would be a lot more fun if I had let her sit in my lap." She was wrong. He was calculating how far it was to the next city with an airport.

After lunch and miles on down the road, Tonya called out from the backseat. "I want to go to Mexico. Let's head toward El Paso."

Brad responded from the passenger seat. "Who asked you?"

"Sir. Maybe you are not aware of our travel arrangements. I've been assigned the role of the navigator. We go where I say we go."

Mrs. T grinned from the driver's seat.

After almost ten hours of west Texas, Tonya made another pronouncement. "I don't care where we stay tonight, just as long as it has a pool."

The two in the front seat started looking for billboards. Ten miles later, Mrs. T went into a motel lobby to check in.

As Brad was unloading the luggage, Tonya issued a challenge. "Last one in the pool's a rotten egg."

He yelled at her when she ran into the bathroom and closed the door. "That's not fair."

"All's fair in love and war."

Brad told Gran-T just to close her eyes, and he hastily put on his swimming trunks. He was sitting on the side of the pool with his legs dangling in the water when Miss Bizzy Belle came out. Tonya had rotten egg on her face.

Proud of her swimming skills, she started sporting with him. Before he realized it, he was having fun with her. El Paso was still a couple of hours down the road. Maybe he could make it to Tucson, or Albuquerque, or wherever the little princess decided they were going.

Mrs. T handed the keys to Tonya the next morning, and then she crawled in the backseat. This time, the student driver listened intently to her instructor. He wanted her to know more than just which pedals to push and how fast to take a corner. He enlightened her about the physics and the mechanics of operating an automobile. With every passing mile, Tonya felt her confidence soaring. She was also learning how to drive.

About the only two things, the party of three could say after walking across the border into Juarez, was that they had been to Mexico, and they had eaten real Mexican food. At Tucson, the navigator had a tough decision to make. Part of her wanted to go toward San Diego and then up the California coast.

Tonya still had not gotten used to the scale of maps for the larger states and had no idea how long that would take. She most definitely did not want to miss the Grand Canyon. Without even realizing that Mrs. T had done a little steering, Tonya directed Brad to make a right toward Phoenix. Mrs. Thornhill also kept pulling back on Tonya's throttle.

In this new territory for all of them, the navigator took it upon herself to elucidate the other passengers about information gleaned from the atlas. The driver was always responsible for keeping an eye on the fuel gauge.

The desert was hot, hot, hot. The pool water each evening was cool,

Miss Bizzy Belle

cool, cool. Tonya decided that Mrs. T's grandson was both.

The Grand Canyon was so much grander than even the promotional materials promised. It was the first place Tonya had ever been that was already calling her back. The travelers were also beginning to grow weary of being on the road, so Mrs. T made the call to start back toward home. She did not have to purchase an airline ticket for her grandson after all.

Following lots of horseplay with Brad in a motel pool in Colorado, Tonya went in to shower. Then, she went back out with her pad and pencils.

Coming up from behind her, Brad surprised her. "What are you drawing?" Before she had time to conceal the pad, he saw his own caricature.

"May I have it?" Tonya ripped it off and handed it to him. She could always do another for herself.

The Grand Canyon experience opened the budding artist's eyes to something else. Wonders of the world could not be sketched adequately in black and white. She was ready to experiment with oils.

Saying goodbye to Brad in Dallas was a little clumsy. Mrs. T watched with amusement. Tonya extended her hand, and then blushed when he pulled her into a hug.

Before depositing Tonya back in Knoxo Springs, the retired woman, and the blossoming teenager discussed some possibilities for their next trip. Mrs. T asked Tonya what she thought about a cruise to Alaska. Her body language required no verbal response.

Self-esteem

On the Tuesday after Labor Day, Michelle decided not to go outside during her break. She was trying to quit smoking. For the time being, caffeine would have to suffice. She poured a cup of coffee, picked up a copy of the Ephesus newspaper, and let out a gasp. A photo of Walt Williamson was on the front page.

Because of the holiday weekend, the paper sent only a photographer to cover the story, and the information was sketchy. About all Michelle could find out was that Ephesus State now had a University Press, and it had selected the book of a former North Carolina resident, now living in Alaska, for its inaugural publication. It did not mention that the author also had a degree from the same institution and that he had a second home across town.

It was not too late for that smoke. So. That's why Walt was at the university on the day she saw him there. He was looking for somebody to publish his book. In the picture, an unidentified woman was seated beside him as he autographed copies of *I. D. – The Identity Dilemma*.

Other thoughts raced through Michelle's mind. "Walt was living in Alaska now. Good. That should keep him well out of the picture."

She just had to read the book, but Tonya must know absolutely nothing about it. As far as Michelle knew, her daughter still had never put the names, Walter, or Walt, and Williamson together. There was a bit of a scare when he called and left his name and number before they moved to Knoxo Springs, but Tonya wrote the first name down wrong and had never mentioned the incident since.

With the weekend off, Michelle decided to go shopping in Asheville. She was running low of several things and thought getting lost among strangers might lift her spirits. When Tonya found out, she announced that she was going, too, because she needed some new fall clothes. That thwarted any chance of picking up a copy of Walt's book.

About a week later, she went to the local bookstore just to check. The new volume was openly displayed. The owner told her that the author had become somewhat of a media sensation after appearing on a television show. He was making appearances all over the country, and the book was showing up on some bestseller lists. Michelle made a contribution to Walt's paltry royalties.

Priority number one was keeping Tonya's daddy's book out of sight, although there was no rational reason that the girl might make any connection. Neither, however, was there any logical explanation for her being so drawn to Watt.

Michelle did not suspect that her daughter ever meddled with her things, but she did not want to be careless. She wrapped the volume in an additional book jacket cut from a paper bag and placed it at the bottom of her dirty clothes hamper. That was one place she felt certain Tonya would not look. Each had been doing her own laundry for years.

When she started reading the book, Michelle had no preconceived notions about what to expect. She noticed Walt's offbeat humor immediately and wondered how many readers would even get it. This was the one part of the man that she missed the most.

She quickly discovered that the book was not just for amusement and entertainment purposes. The author identified himself as a "war baby." Since they were born the same year, she could relate to that. The way Walt described the times when both of them were coming of age made sense to her. She had witnessed the changes in society that he referenced as part of his premise. Maybe he really was on to something in how the "revolutions" of the 1960s and 70s created identity voids that were previously not as pronounced.

Then, it got knotty. If ever there was a person with an "identity dilemma," it was she. The book was left in the hamper for several days.

After reading only so far, more than ever, she knew that she made the right decision not to stay with Walt. She would have been no good for him. Pudgy Michelle could have never competed with that tall, attractive woman sitting beside him in the newspaper photo. On the other hand, he could have held her up as Exhibit A in how not to love yourself, and his daughter as Exhibit B to illustrate the mirror opposite.

Two weekends later when Michelle was off again, Tonya said that she was going to the cabin with Sammie's folks. She invited her mother to come along.

"Bring a good book to read if you're not interested in what the rest of us are doing." How could Tonya do that? Was there any kind of explanation for how she always seemed to know which buttons to push?

The invitation was declined, but the "good book" was reopened. Michelle's wide-ranging emotions duked it out in a slugfest. The man she once lived with and the father of her child always seemed so sure of himself. She hated him for that. She had always struggled with her self-concept. Why did self-confidence come so naturally for him?

What he said about how individuals go about resolving their own identity dilemmas was so simplistic that it made her mad. How dare he infer that it was all that easy. Walt believed that people can rise above their genetics, their upbringing, and their circumstances, and take charge of their own lives. All of her life, she felt trapped by those very things.

What astounded Michelle more than anything was that the daughter the author knew nothing about was the very personification of what he postulated. At the moment, she did not know which one she resented the most.

If the intention of *I. D. – The Identity Dilemma* was to inspire and motivate, in Michelle's case, it failed miserably. After reading it, her self-aversion went on steroids.

Without even saying hello, Tonya called out as she came through the door. "Mother . . .? What do you think 'self-esteem' means? The teachers keep harping on it, but I don't think they have a clue what they're talking about."

Her daughter had done it again. It was as though she had peered right into her mother's soul and knew precisely what book she had just finished reading.

Michelle struggled to right herself without stumbling. She reverted to the old answer a question with a question routine. "What do they seem to be saying when they use that expression?"

"They don't get it. If you don't like yourself, then why should you expect others to like you? The teachers think that if you keep bragging on people, and telling them how wonderful they are, they will start believing it and feel good about themselves. That's so ridiculous."

"Don't you like for others to appreciate what you do?"

Tonya really was trying not to be condescending. "Mother . . . There's a big difference between somebody admiring what I've done and appreciating who I am. Besides . . . Why should that even be important to me? I know whether or not I've done a good job. If somebody brags on me when I don't deserve it, how can that make me feel good about myself? It just lets me know that I can't trust their judgments."

"Tonya . . .? How do you know if you've done your best?"

"How can I not know? That's for me to decide. Sometimes I do a pretty good job. Other times, I mess up big time and I know it. You know what? I've learned far more when I 'misconscrewed' something up and then had to fix it than I ever did when I got it right."

Michelle tried to walk away, but Tonya would not let it go. "Tell me something, Mother. When you think about school, do you remember the questions you got right or the ones you missed?"

"Both of my parents were teachers. I was not allowed to get anything wrong."

"Mother . . . That's so sad."

Michelle just stood there like she was being dressed down. Tonya was not done.

"And another thing that bugs me. Nobody believes in punishment anymore. How stupid is that? We're handed out these little token rewards—kudos they call them—like a dog getting a biscuit if it sits and barks on cue—good little doggie. But then if we do something really dumb, nobody wants to point that out. It might damage our precious little self-esteem."

Michelle still did not know what to say, but she knew what she was thinking. "Tonya's daddy would be so proud of his daughter right now."

The girl was still not through. "I think about all the self-esteem movement has to show for itself is a bunch of whiners who become world-class manipulators to get what they want. How can that be called 'esteem'?"

Michelle tried one more time to wiggle free, but her daughter blocked

Miss Bizzy Belle

her path. "By the way, did you know they're calling my age group 'Generation X'? It's no wonder. The Baby Boomers' spoiled brats with all their self-esteem don't have a clue who they are."

"Tonya . . . Maybe you need to write a book."

"Maybe, I will."

First, it was Walt's book, and now Tonya's rant. Michelle felt like a punching bag. She went outside to smoke, and then came back inside and poured herself a glass of Sin.

Tonya said one thing that did make her stop and think. "I wonder if she thinks I've been too light on her. Maybe I should tighten up on the reins."

Sealed instructions

A note was on the kitchen table when Tonya got home from school on a beautiful Indian Summer afternoon. It said that Uncle Charles had called to check on Granny Addie and got no answer. He went to investigate and found that his mother had died in her sleep. It also said that Michelle planned on being home before bedtime.

Tonya said a prayer of thanksgiving that her granny did not have to suffer. The woman had been in decline for about a year, and she had made it clear that she was not going to a nursing home. Realizing that her time was getting shorter, the old woman had made sure that her business was in order.

When Michelle got home, she handed Tonya a sealed envelope and told her that personal messages were left for all of Granny's loved ones. She said that she had already read hers. With a sense of awe and reverence, Tonya went into her room and closed the door.

Granny Addie pointed out the special bond between the two of them. She asked her great-granddaughter not to mention that to other family members. She reminded her that they had always had secrets and always would. Tonya wondered what she meant by that. It would be a while, but eventually, she would have a better grasp of what that meant.

Michelle had spoken at Papa Doc's funeral. It was now her daughter's turn. Tonya did not volunteer as her mother had done. Granny Addie asked her to.

She said in her letter that one of the bad things about being in a small Methodist Church was that preachers didn't stay around long enough for them to get to know you. She had been unable to go to church in a while, and she indicated that the current pastor had only been to see her once. She knew that he would say the proper things, but she wanted somebody to say a few words who knew her heart.

Tonya wept.

This was undoubtedly one of the hardest things that she had ever been asked to do. Nonetheless, at the same time, it was one of the easiest. Little preparation was required. All she had to do was speak from her heart.

Tonya told those assembled that her granny was the wisest woman she had ever known. It was from her that she first experienced unconditional love and acceptance. Michelle winced, but she knew that her daughter was right.

In her eulogy, the fifteen-year-old recounted how her great-grandmother modeled for her a profound reverence for life and a genuine respect for all of God's creatures. She concluded with pride in her voice. "Granny Addie made me feel like I was her most special favorite." She paused and then added. "But I also know that she made every one of you feel the same way."

Somewhere, Granny Addie was surely smiling.

Transitioning

Tonya's grades were consistently near the top, but that did not always come without a tussle. Mastering the material was hardly a challenge. She kept getting tripped up in something called "feedback."

When the best friends were discussing it one day, Tonya verbalized her frustrations. "Why do the teachers all want us to like them? We have to fill out all these questionnaires. They need us to keep patting them on the head, and telling them what good little teachers they are."

No matter how anonymous the forms claimed to be, Tonya was never sure. That did not keep her from skewing the results now and then, and watching for a teacher to be in a foul mood the next day.

She observed similar traits in the parents of her peers. She saw most as so weak-kneed that they caved with the slightest hint of a child's disapproval. In WOWs, she scribed.

If the animals are running the zoo, then why don't they unlock their cages and set themselves free?

Miss Bizzy Belle

Transitioning from drawing to painting was also not without its challenges. No art classes were available, and she did not have a mentor to give her even elementary instructions.

Initially, she just dabbled with mixing colors. Her first painting with any resemblance of anything real was that of a rainbow. Her first with any semblance of a setting was a sunset over the lake at the Ringers' cabin. Tonya was astonished when Mrs. Flo wanted to purchase it.

"That would make me a professional artist." The amateur painter gladly gave it to her.

Transitioning from childhood into youth also came with plenty of trials, especially at home. Tonya knew that she had an attitude, but she was not about to let her mother take out her frustrations on her. She just wanted a parent to talk to her about things. The teenager went to sleep many nights looking at the stars and wishing that she could sit in her daddy's lap.

Michelle's feigned attempts to stop smoking never amounted to anything. Comfort food and caffeine had been added to the mix. Tonya wondered how she could be so different from her mother.

The best friends still did many things together, but Tonya knew more and more that Sammie understood her less and less. It troubled her that Sammie leaned on her so much.

The only person that Tonya could really confide in lived several hundred miles away. Mrs. T had given her a telephone credit card to use anytime that she wanted to call.

When she turned sixteen, Tonya got her driver's license, but she did not get a key to Black Bart. The occasion was marked by adding another notebook to her collection. Along with recording insights and observations, the high school student also started writing short stories for her own satisfaction and amusement. In tenth grade, she took a typing class and began saving her money for a typewriter. She also wanted her own camera to photograph things that she could paint later.

When absorbed in sketching, putting something on canvas, or alone somewhere scribing, the girl was freest to be herself. She was not trying to impress anyone with any of her compilations. Watt was the only critic that she consulted, and they laughed a lot.

When Tonya mentioned to Mrs. T that she had been unable to find an art class, her mentor proposed an intriguing possibility. Why not enroll in a summer art camp in D.C.? Mrs. T had waited too late to book an Alaska cruise. Perhaps, they could fly to Anchorage the next year and rent a car. Tonya agreed that might be more fun, anyway.

Michelle was never excited about her daughter going to the state where her daddy resided. She was both relieved and supportive of the girl spending some of the summer in Washington instead. Tonya noticed that the airline ticket was only one way. Was Mrs. T going to kidnap her?

When they went to the parking lot, Tonya was surprised to see Mrs. T's old blue Volvo instead of her new car. The woman said that she hardly drove it enough to keep the battery charged, and was hoping that Tonya could run it some while she was there.

The art camp was near Arlington. On the first morning, Mrs. T handed the keys to Tonya and told her that she would go with her the first day and come back and pick her up in the afternoon, but that she wanted her to drive. The woman waived Tonya off when she tried to give the keys back to her that evening.

Mrs. T gave Tonya written directions the next morning and asked if she minded going by herself. The sixteen-year-old was a bit awed but set out on her own.

Tonya had several options at camp. She decided to take drawing the first half and oil painting the second. She was not really interested in crafts, working with clay, or other alternative media. The director reminded the campers that the staff would be assisting two different kinds of artists—those who wanted to be professionals and the others who just wanted to do art for fun. Tonya knew which camp she was in.

She was the oldest student in the beginning drawing class. The instructor was surprised at how much natural talent she had. Tonya was just as mindful of how little she knew.

In the oil painting class, she was introduced to the color wheel and things that she did not know about mixing paints. She learned more about hues, tints, shades, and tones. Then, she picked up pointers in brush strokes, using a palette knife, stippling, drying, cleaning brushes, and correcting mistakes. Tonya was amazed at how many different materials that paint could be applied to.

The most important lesson of all, however, was that artistry is so individual that it can hardly be graded. The teacher reminded the budding artists that one generation of masters might be appalled at what the next considered great works of art.

She summed it up for them. "If you like your work, then what else matters? Keep learning new things, and have fun."

When the weekend rolled around, Mrs. T offered to help Tonya with another concern. At an office supply store, they browsed through a selection of used typewriters. Tonya decided on a gently used electric model, and she assured Mrs. T. that she had enough money to pay for it. She did not see the woman wink at the salesperson.

As the man placed it in the trunk, he told Tonya it was a gem, and he had a feeling that it would serve her well. He added that the manager had told him to give it away to the first person who showed interest in it. When

Miss Bizzy Belle

they went back inside, Mrs. T was closing her purse with a *Tone-yuh* kind of look on her face.

Kermit was MIA. Mrs. T informed Tonya, regretfully, that he had a steady girlfriend. The news stung at first and she briefly considered getting in touch with Connie. Ultimately, she decided that boys were not a priority that summer.

After art camp was over, Mrs. T still had not mentioned anything about a flight back to Asheville. Tonya was caught completely off guard when the woman asked if she thought Michelle would let her have the older Volvo.

"You mean . . .? Drive it home . . .? And it's mine . . .?"

"You can use the road atlas that we took with us last summer. I know you can read one. I've been watching you. You can handle a car, too." The driving lessons that Brad had given her, and the navigation skills that Mrs. T had taught her, were ready for a test drive.

"Oh, Mrs. T! How could I ever survive without you?"

Michelle was not too keen on the idea of her daughter driving that far by herself. Mrs. T offered to go with her and fly back, but Tonya convinced her mother that she could manage. Michelle then put another fly in the ointment. She said that maybe she should take over Mrs. T's car, and give Tonya Black Bart.

Tonya shouted into the phone. "No way, Jose! Mrs. T's giving this car to me."

Tonya could not remember the first few trips from Washington to North Carolina. She had good memories of the last couple, though, especially moving in the Me-Haul. Mrs. T told her to take her time and stop all along. She gave her money for a motel about halfway.

Tonya loved the serenity and solitude of the open road. Mrs. T had come through for her one more time. Miss Bizzy Belle had her own wheels and they could take her anywhere. For the first time, she was not really excited about the start of school.

Giving her the Dickens

KSHS had a new English teacher in the fall of 1985. Miss Edwards taught both junior and senior classes. Tonya liked her immediately because her specialty was writing. The woman did have one little mannerism that the student found annoying. The intonation of Miss Edward's voice rose at the end of each sentence, making it sound like she was unsure of herself.

For the first semester final, the students were given the assignment of writing a short story. Tonya already had several that she could draw from. All she had to do was retrieve one from her files and type it.

With a little extra time on her hands, she decided to do an extracurricular activity and submit an anonymous one as well. Tonya wanted to make sure it could not be traced back to her, though, and decided not to use her typewriter for that project. She tried to figure out how to access one at school but could not come up with a plan that would not draw suspicion.

The innovative student made her way to the hospital one day as the clerical staff was signing out. With an excuse about her own being out of ribbon, the receptionist sat her up at a desk in one of the offices. From her handwritten copy, she had it done in no time.

The English students were asked to leave their papers on the teacher's desk at the end of the period. Tonya used a little sleight of hand to slip the anonymous submission well below hers in the stack, and she walked out of the school for the semester break.

Miss Edwards went to the principal's office the next morning. He could tell by the grin on her face that something was up. She handed him a paper that was turned in by a member of her junior class. It was entitled, "David Cop-a-Feel and O-Feel-Ya – The Untold Story," by Charlene Dickens.

The principal got so tickled reading it that tears came to his eyes. "Do you have any idea who submitted this?"

"All the students turned in papers, so I guess that one came in as a bonus. What a shame, too, because this very clever student won't get any credit. As you can see, it's brilliant satire, and only vulgar if you have a dirty mind."

Then she went on. "I can think of only one student with that kind of imagination and writing ability. She's also smart enough to make sure there's no way to trace it back to her. I've already compared the type, and that one was not done on her typewriter. I think I'll shake the bushes, nonetheless, and see what falls out."

"You do that, and keep me informed."

As the new semester began, Miss Edwards made an adjustment to her lesson plans and fast forwarded to the works of Dickens. As she described the author and discussed some of his more notable books, her eyes panned the room. She spied not one pair of guilty eyes. Most of the students were bored, and she knew it.

She then put out the bait. "How do you think Dickens came up with a name like Copperfield? Is there any possibility that he might have had a

Miss Bizzy Belle

hidden agenda?"

There were shrugs all around.

Tonya's hand went up. "I have a theory. A copper is a coin like a penny. Do you think Dickens was saying something like 'a penny for your thoughts'?"

Tonya kept her expressionless eyes glued on the teacher's.

Miss Edwards then asked if they had ever heard of Queen Victoria. Most acknowledged that they had. The teacher went on to explain that Dickens wrote during the height of Victorianism in England.

"His works were highly entertaining. But anything of a sexual nature was censored out. Do you think we still live under that blanket, or have we swung the pendulum too far in the other direction?"

A lively discussion ensued. Some class members described how "uptight" their parents were. The subject then turned to pornography. Tonya's hand went up again.

"What's the difference between normal curiosity and lust?"

Heads nodded in agreement with the validity of the question.

Miss Edwards suggested something for them to think about. "Is the answer to be found in the distinction between the sacred and the profane?"

Contemplative minds were complemented by various facial expressions. Tonya's had a look of smug satisfaction. Her mission was accomplished.

That afternoon, the teacher reported to the principal. "Yep . . . Tonya Bell's the one, but there's no way to prove it. It's going to take a lot more than a penny to probe her thoughts, too."

Miss Edwards was not comfortable talking with the man about the discussion of the Victorian Era. The single woman, who came from a conservative background and had never been in a serious relationship, did not want to admit it, but she was just too "uptight."

Tonya wondered how she ever got along without her own mode of transportation. Mrs. T's generosity once again came through at the just right time. That did not mean she drove everywhere she went. Unlike other students who swelled the parking lot with their vehicles, the junior still walked to school.

The old Volvo gave her a feeling of independence. Mrs. T was surprised that Tonya already knew how to drive a straight shift. The mountain roads were perfect for shifting the gears up and down. When she wanted to go out and set up an easel somewhere, she had her own wheels.

At first, Tonya thought about calling her light blue vehicle "Carolina," but being a transplant, she had not gotten into all that state loyalty stuff. She decided instead to name her car "Agnes" after Granny Addie's cat.

Michelle was also glad to have this new member of the family. The Dart was about worn out, and it was nice having a reliable vehicle for when they needed to go out of town. Tonya would be driving anyway.

The first road trip that they all made together was to Pa Bell's for Thanksgiving. The old man was still having trouble convincing Mama Myra that the world did not end when their eldest son died. Tonya delighted in taking her great-grandfather for a spin in Agnes, demonstrating how she could work the manual four-speed. She thanked him again for her first driving lessons.

With a serious look on his face, Pa Bell gave her some advice. "You take good care of it, and this vehicle will take you far." Neither had any idea just how far that might be.

On the way home from Bellville, Tonya mentioned something to her mother. "I heard the bookstore is looking for some help during the holidays. I think I'll go by and apply."

Michelle froze and did not immediately respond. Pondering it, she realized that some work experience would be good for Tonya. The girl could certainly use the extra money. But what if she discovered Walt's book? Might she be as drawn to it as she was the old sweatshirt? Would everything start unraveling? There was one thing that she could count on. If her daughter's mind was made up, she would not be able to dissuade her.

She was finally able to respond. "I think working at the bookstore is a wonderful idea."

Before Tonya filled out the application, Hap told her that he was very selective. "This job requires more skills than it takes to flip burgers." Something about the girl was familiar to him. Then, he remembered. "You're Miss Bizzy Belle, aren't you?"

Tonya started working at Hap's Books and Gifts in the afternoons and on Saturdays. When school let out for the holidays, she went full time. The employee was a quick study learning the inventory. She was also gaining people skills that only working in retail afforded.

That her mother showed more than a passing interest in her job surprised Tonya. She gladly shared tidbits from her work.

Michelle went to the store one day and introduced herself. She thanked Hap for hiring her daughter. She said she was glad that Tonya could work in such a wholesome environment. While inside, she looked around. Since it had been out for a while, Walt's book was not openly

Miss Bizzy Belle

displayed, but one copy was in the local authors' section. It would not be there for long.

When Mrs. Webster, the high school counselor, brought the copy of *I. D. – The Identity Dilemma* to the counter, Tonya commented. "That's an interesting title. And I see it's autographed."

"I've been wanting to read it since it came out. I kept putting it on my wish list, but I guess I'll just go ahead and buy myself a Christmas present."

"Let me know if it's any good." Tonya then added with a devious smile. "Since it's a gift, would you like it wrapped?"

"No . . . I think I'll take it home and start reading it tonight, but that was sweet of you to offer." She missed the humor.

Tonya mentioned to Hap that she had just sold the last copy of a book and asked if it needed to be put on the reorder list. He shook his head and said the book's popularity had waned, and that he was glad to see it go out the door.

Tonya had no idea where she might go to college, and her junior year was half over. The school counselor insisted that she start looking at the possibilities. One thing seemed certain. It was unlikely that she would be able to go to a university and live on campus. The girl's so-called college fund had grown by virtue of compounding interest, but little had been added to the principal. Michelle never seemed to have anything left over, and Tonya could only make modest deposits from her earnings.

After the Christmas rush, she took a morning off from work and drove into Ephesus. She went to the state university to pick up a college catalog. A forty-five-minute commute from Knoxo Springs might be her only option. The counselor in the admissions office asked if she wanted to take a little tour of the campus. A work-study student was given the assignment of showing the visitor around.

As they strolled, Tonya mentioned that if she enrolled, she would be a third generation to attend. She was not aware that she would also be a second generation on the other side of her family.

The prospective student wanted to go to the university bookstore to look into part-time job prospects. A man and woman were exiting as they entered, and he held the door for them. Something about him looked familiar. He smiled at her, and she smiled back.

Then, it hit her. That was the same man who blew her a kiss at the movie opening, and the same person she saw at the grocery store later. She asked the tour guide if she knew who he was. The escort said that she was

241

just a freshman and did not know many people, but she thought he might be a professor or something.

Walt Williamson and his wife Ginny had flown in from Alaska to spend Christmas at their other home in Ephesus. Tonya did not associate the man with a copy of his book on display at the desk. His picture was on the inside of the book jacket.

Across the pond

When Tonya called Mrs. T to wish her a Merry Christmas, they discussed possible summer plans. Mrs. T said that they could go to Alaska as they had talked about earlier, or they might go somewhere in Europe.

"London? Mrs. T? Can we go to London? I've always wanted to go to London."

"I don't see why not. Let me work on it."

The exuberant teenager clarified that she still wanted to go to Alaska, but it could wait.

Mrs. T considered the possibility of the two of them flying in and doing things on their own. Something about that seemed a bit overwhelming, so she looked into tour options. The pressure would be off exchanging currency, making hotel arrangements, figuring out how to get around, and deciding on an itinerary. She mailed Tonya several brochures, and they agreed on the one that went to more of the places they wanted to visit. Mrs. T reminded Tonya to go ahead and apply for a passport.

Michelle was bitterly opposed to the trip. Mrs. Thornhill just continued to show her up as a mother. Sometimes she wished that she had never taken her baby to Mrs. T's. In the end, she relented. She was relieved again that her daughter would not be spending the summer in the same state where her father now lived.

For her seventeenth birthday, Michelle gave Tonya a camera. She told her that she picked out the Instamatic because it would easily fit in her purse. She did not mention that it was also one of the least expensive options.

Tonya tried to be appreciative, but it was nothing like what she wanted. With no zoom, the camera was only suitable for close-ups. Mrs. T told her not to fret. She could use her 35-millimeter anytime that she wished.

The last few days of school dragged on and on. It was still another

Miss Bizzy Belle

month before she would fly to Washington and then on to London with Mrs. T. With her mind elsewhere, it was hard to stay focused on anything.

Tonya managed to extract a little cash from her mother to buy a few travel clothes. Sammie accompanied her on her shopping trip to Asheville and then let her borrow a suitcase. Mrs. Flo gave her several film cartridges.

Finally, the big day arrived. Mrs. T met Tonya at the gate, and the two unlikely traveling companions found their way to the international terminal where they joined other members of their tour group. The aircraft took off to a brilliant sunset and landed the next morning at Heathrow to a sunrise muted by overcast skies. Another world was about to open up to the girl with no father in her life and a mother that she had to work around.

The group was made up of mostly retired people. Three other teenage girls were along, all with their grandmothers. Everybody presumed Tonya and Mrs. T shared the same relationship, and they told them nothing any different. Both Tonya and Mrs. T soon found out what jet lag was all about.

The first day's schedule was relatively light. After checking in and having a chance to shower and change, the bus headed to the famous Kew Gardens. Neither Tonya nor Mrs. T had ever seen so many beautiful flowers in one place. Tonya took many pictures wishing that she could paint them all.

The bus took them to Harrods for lunch, and of course, some shopping afterward. They stopped by Trafalgar Square on the way back to the hotel. Neither had to be rocked to sleep that night.

The next morning was reserved for the British Museum. Tonya was fascinated with the relics and artifacts from so many ancient civilizations. She especially enjoyed the Egyptian section.

Back on the bus and stuck in traffic, the tour guide wanted to know what the guests thought. After numerous glowing appraisals, Tonya made some observations and had a question or two. She acknowledged a misconception about the museum. Since it was called the British Museum, she had presumed that it was about British history. She wanted to know where the British floors were. Did they miss them? Were the local folks so concerned about preserving everybody else's stuff that they forgot to include their own?

The English guide had heard that question before. He said that Great Britain's accomplishments had been recorded by historians and were best preserved in libraries. He added that the greatness of the empire could not be reduced to collections. He went on to say that the tiny island had taken the Roman notions of civilization and spread them throughout the world.

When they got back to the hotel room, Tonya told Mrs. T that she did not buy that bunch of bunk. "If you ask me, they don't have much of a history to brag about, and not a lot to show for it. They might call it civilization, but what about spreading slavery? My history teacher said that the way the Brits divided and conquered, and then divided people again, is the reason there's so much conflict in the world today. They also gave us the English language, but just look how difficult and irregular it is. I do love the British accent, though."

Mrs. T cautioned Tonya that they were guests in the country and that she might want to keep some of her opinions to herself. She also reminded the girl that Londoners thought the Yanks were the ones with accents.

The third day focused on places more familiar to foreigners. Westminster Abbey was first up. Already the home to many royal weddings, the place was spiffing up for another later that month. Prince Andrew was about to take a bride named Fergie.

Tonya had seen pictures of Big Ben many times, but hearing it striking twelve noon gave her a whole new perspective. The afternoon included a stop at Buckingham Palace. The tourists were murmuring about the rumors that Charles was seeing Camilla again.

Back in the room, Tonya told Mrs. T that she just did not understand royalty. "Do subjects actually think that blue bloods are better than the rest of us?"

"I don't believe that's the case at all. I think it gives the people something to look up to."

"I guess you can say something for that. In our country, it's more about who you look down at."

Mrs. T conceded that the British do that quite well, too.

Day four was a tour of St. Paul's Cathedral and a cruise down the River Thames. The tourists were reminded that the historic church was where Charles and Diana were married. Tonya had never thought about famous people being buried inside a church, but she saw numerous tombs. She learned how St. Paul's was a great symbol of survival and resiliency for the English people.

Her favorite part of the tour was when she stayed behind for a few moments, standing before the famous Holman Hunt painting of Jesus knocking at the door.

She told Mrs. T later. "Now that was an artist. But I don't think Jesus would care for the halo."

The boat ride went beside the Tower of London, beneath the Tower Bridge, under several other famous spans, and docked at Greenwich. Back on the boat, Tonya whispered to Mrs. T. "Because they keep time for the rest of the world, is that why Brits think they're the center of the universe?"

"Hush . . . Tonya."

The tour took them out of London for the last three days. Tonya sent

Brad a postcard from Stonehenge. The group went to Oxford the second day, and from there, to Cambridge. Mrs. T especially enjoyed seeing the English countryside.

Once seated on the plane, Tonya looked over at Mrs. T and told her that was the most wonderful trip imaginable. "Why do you care so much about me?"

"Now, Tonya . . . Do you think I'm doing all of this just for you? Heavens no. I only bring you along to carry my bags."

"Why, Mrs. T. You know I don't believe a word of that."

Dilemmas

Tonya continued to work at the bookstore during her senior year, but she had to cut back on her hours. Hap was delighted to have her full time when the holidays arrived.

Reluctantly, she agreed to be the yearbook editor. She and Miss Edwards, the faculty advisor, developed a profound respect for each other. They did not always see eye to eye, but they ultimately managed to stay focused on the same objectives.

The inflection speech anomaly was ever distracting, but Tonya started noticing others from her teacher's age group doing the same thing. She kept thinking that Miss Edwards might ask her about the anonymous short story, but she never did.

The senior was busy with other activities as well. She served as president of the Beta Club and was also the school's first female captain of the debate team. They finished a disappointing second in the state, and Tonya thought that was only because she intimidated the top judge who happened to be a man.

When she went to the counselor's office to pick up a couple of college applications, *I. D. – The Identity Dilemma* was on the desk. "This is the book I sold you, isn't it?"

Mrs. Webster weighed in. "Yes. And it's one of the best books I've ever read. Tonya . . . I kept thinking of you. I want you to know that I've been a big fan of yours since the movie. You seemed so unaffected by it all. Nothing went to your head."

Tonya shrugged. "It was no big deal. I just had some fun."

"Nothing is a big deal to you. That's one of the things that I admire most about you. Now, back to the book. I suggest that you read it. It was almost as though you were playing in the author's head the whole time he was writing it."

Mrs. Webster asked about college plans, and Tonya told her that they were still very much up in the air. Getting accepted was not the problem. There was just never enough financial aid to fill in the gaps.

All of that changed on a dime one day soon after Christmas. Totally elated, Tonya entered the Villa waving the contents of an envelope ripped wide open. She had been awarded a full debate scholarship at Brixton University, about an hour north of Atlanta. The school had one of the top debate teams in the country.

Tonya had applied to the school only because of the encouragement of Mrs. Webster. "You never know what they're looking for, and what opportunities they might make available if they really want you. I know this for a fact. The university is striving for diversity. They take pride in finding a little diamond in the rough and polishing it into a bright gem."

Brixton was a private university, and without the grant, it was well beyond Tonya's means. She also knew that the scholarship would not cover all of her incidental expenses.

Sammic also had some exciting news. She had a big date for the senior prom, and she was certain that she was the first girl he asked. Who would turn down the captain of the football team? The couple was a cinch to be named king and queen.

Tonya was just not that into the promenade. She brushed off a couple of invitations and thought about just sitting it out. Twerp and Twit said they were going "stag."

Miss Edwards wanted to know about her plans, although she already knew and had something in mind. Eric, the assistant yearbook editor, wanted Tonya to go with him but was afraid to ask. She advised Tonya not to miss her senior prom.

The editor acknowledged that the assistant really was a nice guy, and she eventually gave in. "Since it's not a lifetime commitment, I guess I wouldn't mind."

The go between went back and gave Eric the go ahead. Mrs. Flo took Sammie and Tonya to Asheville to pick out their dresses.

Michelle came in from a doctor's appointment in Ephesus just as Tonya was getting home. Since her daughter was tall and thin, the prom dress needed a few adjustments. While Michelle was pinning some tucks, Tonya asked her something.

"Mother . . .? Don't you think it's about time you got me an appointment with your gynecologist?"

"Why? Are you having some problems?"

Miss Bizzy Belle

"Not really. But my daddy's not a doctor. At least you said he wasn't. How else am I going to get my birth control pills?"

"Tonya? Are you . . .?"

"You don't want me to make the same mistake you did, do you?"

"Tonya! I never said that you were a mistake. Please don't do this to me."

"I think it needs taking up a little bit more right here and we're done. I'll stitch it now. Thank you, Mother, for your help."

Graduation was a major event in Knoxo Springs. For more than half the class, it was the only diploma that they might well ever receive. Tonya knew that she would be an honor graduate and was hoping that might be her only distinction. Class rankings were irrelevant to her. She did not see how comparing performances based on flawed methods of testing proved anything. Nevertheless, just like in eighth grade, Sammie was declared the class valedictorian and she was named the salutatorian.

Tonya tried her best to talk the teachers out of the traditional speeches. She reasoned that few in attendance would have any interest in what the top two graduates had to say, least of all their fellow classmates.

She suggested to Mrs. Webster that they bring in an interesting speaker like colleges do. "Invite the author of the book that you like so much. He might say something that could really make a difference in the lives of these mountain kids."

"I think that's an excellent idea, but he lives in Alaska. We don't have the kind of funding that it would take to pay his travel expenses."

It was a lost cause. Like it or not, Tonya, and then Sammie would address the audience assembled in the auditorium moments before the Knoxo Springs High School Class of 1987 turned their tassels.

Sammie was really uptight about making her speech. One of her greatest fears was following Tonya. She pleaded with her best friend not to do anything to upstage her.

That put Tonya in a pickle. Part of her wanted to give the folks in that town a graduation that they would never forget. At the same time, she was sensitive to Sammie. Together, they poured over material Miss Edwards gave them, and gradually hammered out something that Sammie could go with. The top student typed it and rehearsed it several times a day. She wanted everything to be perfect.

That still left Tonya. She was brainstorming in the counselor's office when Mrs. Webster handed her some copied material. "This is from the book about identity. I know you never had a chance to read it, but see if there's something in there that you might use."

The crowd was lively, and the principal had trouble keeping order. Sammie was sweating profusely. She asked Tonya how she could be as cool as a cucumber. After getting a number of preliminaries out of the way, the principal moved on.

"I give you Knoxo Springs' own Miss Bizzy Belle." The audience cheered with many remembering the movie that helped put their town on the map.

After the customary salutations and greetings, Tonya moved right into her speech.

"In his book, *I. D. – The Identity Dilemma*, author Walter O. Williamson cites five keys to our survival as a civilization. I can hardly improve on them."

Michelle, already nervous, got very light-headed. Her daughter was about to push her just about over the edge.

"I suggested that we invite Mr. Williamson to be our guest speaker tonight, but I was told that the school could not afford to pay his expenses from Alaska. So you will just have to settle for a cloned version."

Michelle let out a gasp. The woman next to her reached for her hand.

Tonya elaborated on the five essentials.

> *Honesty: The key to knowing who we are*
> *Integrity: The virtue of who we are*
> *Dignity: The pride of who we are*
> *Morality: The conscience and character of who we are*
> *Civility: The arena within which we rediscover who we are*

Applause was more than just polite, but Tonya wondered if any in the crowd actually understood what she had said. Miss Edwards did. She stood to her feet, and everyone else followed.

Sammie reached for her, and they hugged. Tonya whispered in her ear. "I've got 'em warmed up for you. Break a leg, mate."

Sammie read her speech without missing a word. The principal concluded by saying that these were two of the finest students ever to graduate from KSHS, and that both were going to college on academic scholarships. Applause broke out again.

One unexpected person came to the graduation. When Tonya first entered the stage, she looked for her mother. Mrs. T was sitting beside her beaming. The woman had flown into Asheville for a stopover and rented a car. The next day, she was going on to Dallas for Brad's college graduation.

Tonya was not sure if her Grandmother Connie would make it, but she

Miss Bizzy Belle

did. She gave the graduate some much needed and greatly appreciated luggage.

Miss Edwards was waiting for Tonya after the recessional. "Good job ... 'Ophelia'."

"You knew the whole time, didn't you?" They both burst into laughter.

Two classmates graduated in absentia. Twerp and Twit both joined the U.S. Navy and had already left for assignment. Scuttlebutt had it that their haste to get out of town was related to what they were caught doing in the bathroom, and it was not smoking. Tonya was sincerely regretful for the way that she had denigrated the boys when she realized the struggles they had been facing all their lives.

Tonya did not know what to make of her mother. It was as if she was in a state of shock. She went to her before moving on to a graduation party at the Ringers' cabin. "Are you okay?"

Michelle nodded but said nothing.

Tonya said with a downcast expression. "I wish my daddy could have been here."

"Oh, he was." Michelle thought to herself. She steadied herself to keep from stumbling.

Mrs. T was observant but did not comment. Michelle politely invited Mrs. Thornhill to go home with her, but she declined. She said that she had a room near the airport and was flying out early the next morning.

Michelle was astounded that Tonya had quoted from her own daddy's book. His daughter had not only put his first and last names together in a sentence, but she also knew the state where he lived. Still, she did not seem to make any connection, or she would not have said so innocently that she wished he had been at the graduation. Then again, there was no reason why she should connect any dots. Michelle kept trying to calm herself down for overreacting.

With justification, she was concerned about how Mrs. T had interpreted her actions. The astute woman had warned her several years earlier that she would not lie to Tonya. Did she pick up on anything? For a change, Tonya was not the one taking everything in.

Something about Alaska was still calling Tonya, but it would have to wait yet again. Mrs. T was disappointed, but she understood that the future college student needed to work during the summer. The bookstore welcomed Tonya back. Hap said he felt confident enough with her in charge that he could take some much needed time off.

The high school graduate was once again in the familiar place of hanging between two worlds. Her secondary education was behind her, and her formal education was still ahead. Tonya could have never imagined how little of the latter would take place in an actual classroom. She got a few graduation gifts, but nobody gave her a crystal ball.

Mrs. Thornhill did indeed wonder if Michelle had tipped her hand in some way. She decided to research the man whose reference caused Tonya's mother to be visibly shaken. When she returned home, she went to the library and checked out a copy of Walt's book but did not get very far in her investigation of the author. The information on the jacket was sketchy.

The only possible connection she could make that might tie Walter Williamson to Michelle was that the book was published at the same university where she got her nursing degree. Maybe she misread Michelle that night. Perhaps, the mother was just emotionally overwrought because her daughter was on the stage giving a graduation speech before a large crowd.

Mrs. Thornhill counted herself among God's most blessed for being given a front row seat to watch Tonya grow up. And now her surrogate granddaughter was soon on her way to college.

Maybe showing up unannounced for Tonya's graduation was not the right thing to do, but she could not bear the thought of not being there. Tonya offered to go spend the night with her in Asheville, but Mrs. T insisted that her place was with her friends.

As they parted, the woman slipped her a present. Tonya could not have been more delighted. "Oh, Cornfield. A *real* camera. I love it! And I love you. Thank you so much!"

Mrs. T knew that she would also get a note in the mail. Sadness enveloped her, though, when she realized that she would not be with Tonya when she had the first roll of film developed. The woman, trying to manage her roller coaster emotions, wondered if they had made their last trip together. Michelle was not the only one facing an empty nest.

Tonya loved her job. She was energized being around good books and customers who appreciated them. She especially liked the children's corner. It stirred so many fond memories of Cornfield reading to her.

The sales assistant took delight in making recommendations to grandmothers. With a wily expression, she quipped to her boss one day. "The future around here is very bright. Every grandparent who comes in the store has grandchildren reading well above their grade level." Hap smiled. He assured Tonya that if she wished, Christmas and summer jobs were awaiting her throughout college.

Miss Bizzy Belle

As the summer was coming to a close, Michelle felt numb. Unlike most parents who feared offspring might not be ready for college, she had no such qualms about her daughter. Unlike her mother, Tonya embraced change.

Michelle's apprehensions were more about herself. She felt like she had squandered any chance that the two of them ever had of being close. Once her daughter drove away, she would be gone. Michelle just knew it. The Villa would be without its Belle.

The woman was also grappling with what to do with the rest of her life. Possibly, she had chosen her career for the wrong reason. Nursing had long ago ceased to be fulfilling. She had hastily picked out a place to live while in a crisis mode. Nothing about Knoxo Springs felt like it was home.

The same old misgivings were nagging her. What if she had moved on with Walt? Suppose they had gotten married? She might be living in Alaska right now. Of far more significance, she would have never fallen into disfavor with her father. Her family would not have been torn apart.

There was no way to run the clock back. Two of the people that she cared about the most were in their graves. Sometimes, she wished that she were in hers, too.

Michelle did not ask any questions regarding Tonya's departure date. She wanted to know, yet, she didn't. She also yearned to know what her daughter really thought about her, but at the same time, she was fearful of finding that out as well.

Tonya was aware of her mother's struggles, but she refused to get bogged down in them. With her own life ahead of her, she was eager to move to the next phase. That Michelle did not seem to share her exuberance was consistent with the mother that she had always known.

Sammie was also getting ready for college. Her big brother was at Duke in Durham, and she was about to be his neighbor at UNC in Chapel Hill. The girls giggled a lot while getting their things ready. They also renewed their promise always to be best friends, no matter what, but they were still no closer to figuring out what "what" was.

The first two things that Tonya packed were Watt and her secret file. Agnes was about loaded when Michelle got in from work two days before freshman orientation. Tonya hoped her mother might want to do something special their last night together, but she never mentioned it.

Michelle looked around the house when she got home. Her daughter had left the old sled, a few outgrown clothes in the closet, and some of her juvenile books, but nothing much else. The despondent mother took a bath and went to bed.

Bright and early on a warm mid-August morning in 1987, Tonya was ready to get going. Michelle had no last minute advice, but Tonya did. "Don't forget to feed the birds." The mother hugged her daughter, and then she hurried off to work before either had a chance to get emotional. With Watt in the seat beside her, Tonya said aloud as she shifted into fourth gear.

"Thank you, Mrs. T! C'mon, Agnes . . . Let's go see what's down the road."

Part III: The Metamorphosis

Brandi

Brixton University was a small liberal arts school with an emphasis on the performing arts. With an enrollment of about three-thousand, it was a suitable alternative for the well-to-do whose offspring were not accepted at more prestigious institutions. It also had appeal for those who wanted to keep their sons and daughters on a shorter leash.

Tonya did not have a chance to visit the campus before enrolling, but she trusted her high school counselor's assurance that she had been granted the opportunity of a lifetime. The college freshman was excited about beginning a new chapter in her life, and she approached it with a fierce determination to make the most of it.

After driving through the campus to get a good look at her new home, the enrolling freshman went by the housing office to check in. After Tonya identified herself, the assistant disappeared for a minute. The director came out, introduced himself, welcomed the new student to BU, and invited her to come into his office. Something about his demeanor indicated that this was not just a social visit.

"Can I get you anything? Water? Coffee? A soft drink?" Tonya thanked him but said she was fine. He sat back in his chair.

"Miss Bell . . . We have a situation on our hands, and we're hoping that you can help us with it." He paused, smiled, and went on. "In the interest of full disclosure, I took the liberty of contacting Mrs. Webster. We were graduate school classmates. She assured me that you have the temperament and other special qualities that we're looking for. If you are agreeable, you'll be doing this institution a great service, and we would like to make it worth your while, as well."

Tonya felt a little uneasy and did not know how to respond. The man seemed to be waiting for her to say something. "Can you tell me more?"

He leaned forward. "An incoming freshman was injured in an automobile accident. She has recovered from the initial trauma but will never walk again. She uses a motorized wheelchair to get around. Her parents are well off and can afford a private room, but our counseling staff does not think that's best for her. That's where you come in. This young woman needs a unique kind of roommate, someone who can be a stabilizing influence in her life. We're not asking you to be her caretaker, or anything like that, just a role model."

He gave Tonya a moment and then went on. "We're working to make our campus more accessible for disabled students. In fact, the brand-new dorm we're opening this semester has modifications to accommodate a variety of special needs. As compensation for your peer support, we want to upgrade your housing to this new modern dorm. And, we want to offer you an unrestricted cash stipend of $500 per semester."

Tonya sat very still. When she did not immediately reply, the director continued. "We are aware of your precarious financial situation, and we believe this could be beneficial all the way around."

Tonya was also well aware that her "financial situation" set her apart from the vast majority of the students who typically attended such an exclusive university. Something did not feel right about this. She wanted to know if she could meet the girl before deciding.

"Of course you can. I was about to suggest that. She has already checked in. Come with me."

Brandi Golden dispensed with the preliminaries and said rather indignantly. "So you're the one they're trying to stick with me. Maybe you need to have your head examined, too."

Tonya asked the director if she and Brandi could have a few minutes alone. He nodded and went back to his office.

Cheerfully, she extended her hand. "Hi. I'm Tonya. You're pretty perceptive. Nobody's ever accused me of being normal. If a shrink tried to get in my head, I suspect he'd wind up a couch potato in his own psychiatrist's office. So far, you're the only student I've met, and I was kind of hoping we might be friends."

"You better hope not. I murdered my last friend. Or, didn't they tell you?"

"I just got here. Why don't you fill me in?"

"Want a beer? There's some in the fridge."

Brandi began to loosen up. She told Tonya about the accident. Her parents had given her a BMW convertible for her sixteenth birthday. Just before her senior year, she was coming home from a party late one night. Driving too fast for the conditions, her right wheels slipped off the pavement. She overcorrected, lost control, and took down a power pole. Her best friend was killed instantly. Brandi barely survived, and every day since regaining consciousness, she said that she had wondered why.

After their conversation, Tonya slowly made her way back to the housing office. One of the university counselors was waiting for her along with the director.

After introducing herself, the counselor conjectured. "By the look on your face, I'm guessing that Brandi used her shock treatment on you. She's riddled with guilt and doesn't think that she deserves to live or have any friends. So far, she's been successful at scaring people away before they have a chance to reject her."

Tonya just nodded, still trying to get a handle on all of it. After a moment, the housing director spoke. "Brandi's parents don't know what to do with her. The one thing they're sure of is that she needs to get out of the house. Fortunately, her head injuries didn't cause permanent brain damage, and she's fully capable of doing college level work. Our staff will be monitoring the situation. For now, we think Brandi needs, perhaps more than anything, someone to accept her as she is and to make her laugh. Will you join our team?"

Tonya knew that getting a part-time job would not be easy, and that she might not even have time for one with her studies. She was also aware that the scholarship did not cover everything. The stipend was enticing since her mother had not said anything about offering any support.

As she was still mulling it over, the director explained further. "You'll only be committing to a semester at a time. If it doesn't work out, that's only sixteen weeks. How hard could it be? Really?"

Tonya had no idea "how hard it could be," but she agreed. Since she was receiving so much from the university, this afforded her an opportunity to give something back. The tipping point was that she was not afraid of a challenge. At least for the time being, the "Golden" girl and Miss Bizzy Belle were stuck with each other.

Over the next few days, Tonya learned that Brandi's seemingly charmed life was anything but "golden." The affluent parents from suburban Atlanta were just doing what everyone expected of them when they gave their only child exactly what she wanted. Brandi said her folks fought a lot and that their marriage was on the skids even before the accident.

Tonya learned more about the several surgeries that Brandi had undergone. Through both physical and occupational therapy, she was taught how to take care of her basic needs. She told her roommate she really did not want to go to college, but that her parents were tired of looking at her. She said that she could not blame them.

"There was never a doubt about which university I would go to, either. My great-grandfather helped found Brixton. My family has also endowed several scholarships."

Brandi was not sure that Tonya was impressed. "Brixton's mascot is the Golden Gophers. Did you catch that? The *Golden* Gophers. Those from really uppity schools call us 'The Golden Gofers' like we're beneath them."

The next day when Brandi barked a command, Tonya set her straight. "I'm not your Golden Gofer. I'm your roommate. There's still a chance that we could end up being friends, but not if you're going to order me around. I'm willing to pretend that never happened in case you'd like to try again. It's up to you."

The girl was momentarily stunned. She then hung her head and mumbled an apology. Tonya was not sure that anyone had ever talked to her like that. Maybe it was about time. The assignment of making Brandi laugh did not exactly get off to a rip-roaring start.

Tonya registered for classes and set up a meeting with the debate coach. When she introduced herself to Dr. Lester, he said that he had watched several of her high school debates on video and felt as if he already knew her.

He went on to say that they did not typically offer a scholarship without an on-campus interview. In her case, they were afraid that she might commit elsewhere. They pulled strings and made the "unprecedented" move of walking her file through the admissions process.

He reminded Tonya that she was the first female ever to receive a full debate scholarship. She was beginning to wonder if that was a blessing or a curse.

The new girl on the block was informed rather unceremoniously that she would not be doing any actual debating for the heralded team during her first year. She surmised that her role was more like that of an under-appreciated legal assistant, doing research for the vaunted stars.

At the same time, Tonya's pictures, including one from the movie premier, were always in promotional material. She had not supplied them and presumed that others had also taken liberties without her knowledge.

Tonya's Resident Advisor was African-American. He quickly gained the reputation of giving preferential treatment to the limited number of black students in the dorm. Affirmative action, quotas, and gender preferences were new to the freshman. Her sheltered upbringing was becoming more and more apparent. She was learning rather quickly that residential college life was about far more than academics.

The professors seemed more detached than what she was accustomed to in high school. Tonya had expected higher education to be about learning, but it did not take her long to find out that it was mostly about partying and a little bit about GPAs. It took her until midterm to figure out what games she had to play to get satisfactory grades. The classes she enjoyed most were English and Art Appreciation.

Brandi went home every weekend, and Tonya relished the quiet time. Mr. and Mrs. Golden seemed nice. They always asked Tonya if she had everything she needed. Once, Brandi's father slipped her a fifty-dollar bill and told her to treat herself.

As the semester progressed, Brandi stopped being overtly belligerent

Miss Bizzy Belle

and became increasingly withdrawn. Tonya was particularly disturbed by the number of pain pills she took, and especially by the alcohol chasers that she washed them down with.

Tonya was aware that Brandi had weekly sessions with the counseling office. She was not sure how they were assessing her roommate's condition, but she supposed that no one had any idea what was really going on. About two weeks before semester finals, she decided to confront her roomie about her increasing reliance on drugs and alcohol.

Brandi barked at her. "Miss Bitchy Belle. Mind your own biz and butt out." Tonya was beginning to think that might be the best plan.

Michelle had gotten in the habit of switching the television on when she came in the door. The background noise kept the house from being so quiet. In mid-November, she learned that Tonya was not coming home for Thanksgiving. The freshman had an English paper to write and needed extra study time to catch up in French. The nurse knew that it would not be a problem picking up a holiday shift. That might be better than spending Thanksgiving home alone.

She sat for a minute to go through her mail, and just as she got up to start the water for her bath, a news bulletin interrupted regular programming. A plane had crashed off the coast of Alaska, and from first reports, there were no survivors. Among the passengers was Nurse Virginia Sullivan, wife of author Walter O. Williamson.

Michelle sank back in her chair. Walt had married a nurse. How ironic was that?

The tension building up to finals week was unlike anything that Tonya had ever experienced. The pressure was exacting its toll. Her college experience had been considerably different from anything that she could have anticipated. Status seemed far more important than accomplishment. Standards had little to do with right and wrong. The superficiality of it all made her a little queasy, but something else was about to really sour her stomach.

The evening before her first final, Tonya attended a group study session at the library. She returned to her room just before midnight to find Brandi unresponsive and barely breathing. After calling 911, Tonya was reprimanded for not alerting university officials first.

All of that was more than she had bargained for. She was convinced now more than ever that she did not want to sign on for another semester as

Brandi's keeper. Tonya scheduled an appointment with the housing director so that she could go ahead and inform him before the holiday break.

She was surprised to see Brandi's parents in his office. They told Tonya how grateful they were that she was such a wonderful friend to their daughter. Mr. Golden indicated that the only way they would send Brandi back for the next semester was if she would stay on as her roommate. He asked if there was anything she needed that they could help her with. Her mother invited Tonya to come spend the weekend with them sometime.

The counseling staff picked up where the parents left off. They insisted that Brandi needed her presence now more than ever. It went against everything that felt right, but Tonya wanted to do what was best. She reluctantly agreed to continue with the arrangement through the spring term.

Despite the hellacious exam week, Tonya ended up with a B in each of her favorite classes and managed to pull a C in the other two. She was torn about what to do during the Christmas break. She could have benefitted from some therapy time with Mrs. T and hated to turn down the invitation to spend the holidays in D.C. At the same time, she was trying to process everything and wasn't sure that she was fit to be anyone's company.

If she was going to eat the next semester, she really needed to work. The little stipend check was helpful, but it did not cover all of her expenses. Tonya did not want to dip further into her savings if she could avoid it. She went home and spent most of her holiday working at the bookstore.

Michelle was morphing into a middle-aged woman. Tonya was surprised by how much weight she had gained. She also noticed for the first time that her mother's hair was more gray than red.

Tonya and Sammie reconnected. Sammie's big news was that she had a *serious* boyfriend. He was a prelaw student wanting to go into politics. If everything went according to plan, she would have her MRS whether she ever got a degree or not. The social butterfly was animated when describing how much fun the fraternity and sorority parties were.

Tonya told Sammie all about Brandi. She said that she resented being bullied into committing to another semester and admitted to having serious misgivings about it. Sammie told Tonya that it sounded like a really sweet deal for $500 and asked her what she thought about a Christmas wedding.

The reunion was awkward. Tonya was able to step back to where they left off, but Sammie had no idea that the best friends, no matter "what," were not even living in the same universe anymore.

During the winter break, Tonya decided—as her Pa Bell would say—to take the bull by the horns when she got back to campus. She realized that Brandi had no sense of grounding. She had nothing to believe in. Nothing—not her religion, not her friends, not her family—nothing had helped her get on with her life. Nobody had taken her hand and guided her toward any kind of hope.

The day before classes started, Tonya was able to get her roommate to open up a little. Brandi apologized for causing so much trouble and thanked her for being such a good friend. She acknowledged that she owed her life to her for getting help the time she overdosed.

"It's bad enough that I've been such a burden to my parents. The last thing I want to do is be a drain on you. None of this is your fault. All you've wanted to do is help me."

Finally, Tonya thought she had something to work with. Everybody seemed to be tiptoeing around the word forgiveness. The family of the girl who was killed had told Brandi that they had forgiven her, but she had a way of deflecting things. She said that she felt it was just a facade to make them appear noble, and that they really hated her guts.

She said that her own parents were unable to talk to her about her feelings and fears. For that matter, they didn't have the faintest idea how to deal with their own. Brandi did not think that they were sleeping in the same bed. She had no grandparents close by.

Tonya decided on a different approach. "Brandi. You could be such an inspiration to others trying to make their way through their own tragic struggles."

The paraplegic became very assertive at that point. "Let's get one thing straight. I'm not going to be a poster child for anything or anybody."

"Brandi. I wish you could see yourself the way I see you. You have so much to live for."

"How is it that you always manage to see the silver lining?"

"Oh, how can you not, Brandi? You don't have to be so miserable. Maybe it's time for you to take matters into your own hands and get beyond that cycle you're stuck in."

"Maybe, you're onto something. Let me think about it."

For the next few days, Brandi seemed less confrontational and more at peace with herself. When she was about to leave for the weekend, she thanked Tonya for helping her turn a corner. She also said that it felt good to finally have some clear direction.

Early the next Monday morning, Tonya was summoned to the counseling office. While at home for the weekend, Brandi had taken one of her father's guns and killed herself. Tonya just about lost it when she overheard the housing director say to the counselor. "I bet that was a mess. At least she didn't permanently taint our new dorm."

Already visibly shaken, Tonya had to brace herself yet again. The director directed his attention to her.

"Miss Bell . . . It's understandable that you might want to reach out to the Goldens right now, but that's not such a good idea."

Tonya's body language indicated bewilderment.

"We, at the university, appreciate all that you tried to do for her, but you're not among her family's favorite people right now. She left a note saying that you had helped her figure out what she needed to do."

"What . . .?"

"In a nutshell, Miss Bell . . . The Goldens blame you for their daughter's death."

"They blame me . . .?"

"There's something else that you need to know. They said that Brandi only took prescription medication until she met you. They believe you supplied her with illegal drugs and kept her stocked with booze."

"What . . .?"

"We know there's no truth to that, and we indicated that to the sheriff when he called."

"The sheriff . . .? Is there a warrant out for my arrest?"

"We've done our part, but we have no control over the folks down in Fulton County. The Goldens have friends in high places. Should they pursue this, please rest assured that our legal department will represent you."

The fugitive

Out of there—she had to get out of there. Tonya exited the administration building and took three deep breaths. She then went straight to the registrar's office and withdrew from her classes. Without saying goodbye to anyone, she packed her things. Agnes was soon headed up the road.

Just beyond the edge of town, Tonya looked at the speedometer. It was straight up on eighty. "Slow down, girl. The last thing you want to do right now is to attract the attention of the law."

Approaching a strip mall in the next town, Tonya said aloud. "Whoa! Agnes. Watt and I need to talk something over." The wheels had been spinning and all of a sudden they started getting some traction just as the vehicle came to a screeching halt.

"In the interest of full disclosure—Watt, what a crock." Tonya realized for the first time that her scholarship was a complete sham. Brandi even mentioned that her family had endowed some. Tonya's was no doubt one of them. Brandi's parents had been footing her bill from the onset.

Bit by bit, the pieces of the puzzle began to fall into place. She had been recruited just as surely as a top notch athlete. Why did Mrs. Webster encourage her to apply to Brixton, and why was the school counselor the only person not surprised when Tonya was awarded the unlikely scholarship?

"Watt . . . I'll bet she pocketed a tidy referral fee. And if I had not fallen for their ruse, they would have flunked me out at the end of the first semester. Diamond in the rough? How could I have been so gullible?"

The unthinkable also made sense to her for the first time. When Brandi's family no longer needed their daughter's roommate, they discarded her like a dirty old dishrag. With no shame, they were now trying to pin Brandi's death on her.

One part of Tonya wanted to return to the campus, go to the president's office and give him a piece of her mind. "You know what, Watt? I'd get about as far as a one-legged man in a butt-kicking contest."

Then, something else hit her. If the Goldens did come after her, she had been hung out to dry. "Rest assured that our legal department will represent *you*. Huh!"

Agnes fired back up. While Tonya had acted impulsively, there was no doubt in her mind that she had done the right thing in leaving school as she did. Her day had begun with another week of studies on her mind. Without warning, her life had been turned topsy-turvy. Righting herself, and landing on her feet would take a while.

Pa Bell's image popped into Tonya's mind. Two hours later, she was in Bellville.

Tonya's great-grandfather had the wisdom and presence of mind not to press her about anything. He knew something was troubling his Peanut, but he left it up to her to decide if she wanted to open up. She asked only if she could spend the night. He assured her that his door was always open to her.

After a restless night, Tonya took her Watt Not and WOWs with her to the creek. Brandi had a beautiful smile, but she just didn't wear it much. That was how Tonya saw her, it was the way she would remember her, and that was how she sketched her. She tried to put her feelings about the fragility of life into words. She wrote about the big hole in her own heart that nothing had been able to fill.

"Why did the world have to get so complicated?" That is what she asked the old man while they were sitting under the shade tree. "Why couldn't it have stayed just like it used to be right here?"

Sensing the gravity, Pa Bell carefully fashioned his answer. "Peanut. The world's made up of people. And people seem to complicate things. You know. I learned a long time ago that folks come in all shapes, sizes, and colors. If you try to change them, it will only drive you crazy. No two of us are alike. I cannot account for that, so I just have to trust the Good Lord Above to know what He's doing. He sure knew what He was doing when He created you."

Tonya got up and went and sat on her great-grandfather's lap. It had been a while since either had felt any genuine affection.

"Tonya . . . You just have to let folks be who they are. The main thing is that you be who you are. You're such a fine young lady."

"Pa Bell? Would you do something?"

"If I can."

"Will you whistle 'Amazing Grace' for me?"

Tonya nestled into the cradle of his arm.

"Pa Bell. I love you."

"I love you, too, Peanut."

The showdown

Bellville was but the first stop on Tonya's unplanned expedition. The next was Ferndale. She made her way to her other great-grandparents' now vacant and neglected house. The garden was all grown up, and the chicken coop empty, but embedded memories were still very much alive. How she missed her Great-Granny Addie.

The ferns at Ferndale were just beginning to arouse from their long winter's nap. Tonya felt a presence but could not fathom it.

Miss Bizzy Belle

She then made her way to the little Methodist church. The troubled young woman had a strange feeling standing at her Granny Addie's grave. A cool breath of air washed over her. Later she would wonder. "Might it have been the brush of an angel wing?"

The tears were cleansing but some pressing business lay just ahead. With her whole life already in turmoil, a moment of truth that Tonya had been sidestepping blocked her path.

Michelle was surprised to see her daughter's vehicle in the drive when she came in from work. Without any explanations, Tonya handed her mother a legal pad and a pen.

"Just write down his name." Tears were streaming. "I won't ask any other questions."

Michelle pushed the pad away.

"Mother . . . If you won't tell me who my daddy is, I'm going to walk out that door . . . And I will *never* come back."

"Tonya . . . Please don't do that."

With eyes steeled, she put it all on the table. "Mother . . . Your call."

Michelle turned away.

Tonya went out the door, collapsed into Agnes, pulled her seatbelt extra tight, and backed out of the drive. The vehicle was idling down the hill, but her emotions were in overdrive.

When her sobbing subsided, she realized that she needed to get off the road for a few days. She turned up the highway toward the Ringers' cabin. Likely, nobody would be there, but she knew where the hidden key was.

"Watt . . . Mother didn't even have a chance to mention it if the law had come by looking for us."

For the next three days and nights, not a soul knew where Tonya was. What Pa Bell had said kept playing in her mind. "You just have to let folks be who they are. The main thing is that you be who you are."

She could not change anyone else. Brandi was the proof of that. Not even the threat of walking out for good had any effect on her own mother. She was learning that letting others be who they are is a big step on the path to peace.

"Miss Bizzy Belle. It's time to pull up your big girl panties. Be who you are, and don't let anybody knock you off course." The perplexing part was that the nineteen-year-old had no idea what course she was on.

Buford Bell did not always sleep well. Even though his hearing was not what it used to be, he was sometimes unable to tune out Elmyra's snoring. He got up and slipped on his overalls. The new moon was shining brightly when he went outside. He made his way to an old split rail fence that he often stood before when nature called.

Pa Bell was worried about his Peanut. Lightning flashed in the not too far distance. Sand Mountain was in the midst of a dry spell and a thundershower would be a welcomed sight. The saintly old man went and sat in the chair under the shade tree, watched as the storm got closer, and started humming and whistling.

O Lord, my God, when I in awesome wonder
Consider all the worlds Thy Hands have made
I see the stars, I hear the rolling thunder
Thy power throughout the universe displayed
Then sings my soul, My Saviour God, to Thee
How great Thou art, how great Thou art

Some sprinkles from the heavens stung a bit as they commingled with the tears already streaming down his face.

A little guidance from a counselor

After the cabin interlude, Agnes was back on the road careening toward the nation's capital. A big detour was just ahead, but no sign along the highway gave any advanced warning.

As Tonya neared Asheville, it was Saturday already, and two things were on her mind. One was that she needed to find a pay phone to alert Mrs. T that she was on her way. The other was that she had not had a decent meal since leaving her great-grandparents' house. The mall seemed a likely place to accomplish both.

The food court was busy, but she found a vacant table on the fringe where she could be alone. About halfway through her meal, Tonya noticed a man in a motorized wheelchair exactly like Brandi's. He was accompanied by his wife, and they took the table beside her. They discussed what they wanted to eat, and the woman went to place their orders.

The sight of the wheelchair was unsettling. Tonya started to get up and move but was concerned that the man might take offense. She was almost finished anyway.

While waiting in line, the woman glanced back at Tonya and noted that she seemed troubled about something. When she returned to her table, she asked her if she would like to join them. Nothing like that was on Tonya's mind when she stopped at the mall. The only person she wanted to talk to was Mrs. T.

Without waiting for a response, the woman with beautiful blond hair and gentle blue eyes made a place for her. Tonya did not want to be rude, so she braced herself. She would make an excuse soon and be gone.

Hannah Parker introduced herself, and then her husband, Phillip. Tonya initially offered very little information in return. The woman shared that she was a junior high school counselor, and that her husband, who had been wounded in Vietnam, was the manager of an auto parts store.

This was weird. The woman was a counselor. Imagine that. Her husband was a paraplegic just like Brandi. And they beckoned her!

Hannah asked Tonya if she lived around there. How could she answer that? At the moment, she did not live anywhere. "Actually. I'm kind of in a state of transition right now."

With a little guidance from the counselor, Tonya opened up about Brandi. She also acknowledged how uncomfortable she had been when they came up.

Hannah suggested that it must have been impossible for her roommate to adjust after her underpinnings were knocked out. "It's difficult enough under so-called normal circumstances."

With a little prompting, Tonya described the encounter with her mother. That led to a discussion about being raised with an absentee father. Hannah saw the pain in the girl's eyes. She told Tonya about being adopted, and how she eventually came to understand that it mattered little who supplied the sperm and who contributed the egg.

She advised gently. "What's important is that we take whatever complement of genes and chromosomes we come with, and then become the person we want to be. But that's never a one and done process." Gesturing toward her husband, she continued. "We have to adjust to whatever life throws at us. This is my hero." Unmistakable admiration was in her body language.

"Tonya . . . As a professional counselor, the vast majority of behavioral issues I deal with are family related. And believe me, they run the gamut from overbearing parents emotionally crippling their children, to overprotective ones who smother, to kids freaking out because they are unable to live up to the expectations dumped on them, and all the way to some who are stifled because of abandonment issues."

She reached for Tonya's hand. "Now, here's where it gets personal. Tonya? Why would you surrender your power to a man who doesn't even know that you exist? If you so choose, you can use not having a father in your life as a perpetual hiding place. It's a ready-made excuse to explain away just about anything. The alternative is to thank him unendingly for the genes he gave you. From what you say, they are vastly different from the ones you got from the other side of your family."

"But what about you?" Tonya asked. "Do you expect me to believe that you never think about your birth parents?"

"Of course, I do. But I made the decision when I was just about your age that I was not going to let what was or what might have been govern my life. Tonya . . . We are never free until we let go."

Phillip then spoke up. "Would you like to come and stay with us for a few days?" Tonya said she was appreciative of the offer but insisted that she needed some time alone to get her head on straight.

As they were leaving the mall, Hannah remembered the time, two decades earlier, when she and Walt had a deep discussion about some of those very same things. "I think it was at that same table, too." She regretted not having a copy of Walt's book with her to give to the young woman.

Tonya had never thought much about chance meetings, and coincidences, and things like that. Meanwhile, her mind was grappling with something bigger than she was. Maybe it was no accident that the three of them were at the same place at the same time.

Finding a pay phone was no longer important. Tonya decided not to burden Mrs. T. with her issues. She knew that she had to work through them herself. Something was stirring in her soul, unlike anything that she had ever experienced. The serendipitous encounter was just the impetus that she needed to "let go." As Hannah had counseled, though, spreading her wings was not a one and done process.

Seeing a mall branch of her bank, she withdrew several hundred dollars. She, Agnes, and Watt were about to get very tight. The vehicle was already carrying just about everything that the driver owned. Tonya did not have the tiniest inkling of what was down the road, much less what road it might be down. She was a little scared, but she also had a strange kind of peace.

Mrs. Hattie

Agnes left Asheville going northwest. Knoxville was ahead, but nothing in Big Orange Country was calling her. Tonya breezed right through and continued toward Nashville. On another day and in a different time, she might have tried to get a ticket to the Grand Ole Opry. This time, she was not a vacationer, and nothing in Music City was drawing her.

Miss Bizzy Belle was homeless.

Conscious of her limited funds, Tonya drove well past the city and checked into an old motel. For the first time in years, she slept with Watt. She woke up early the next morning and took a stroll through the quiet little town while most folks were still asleep. Something about the city cemetery beckoned her. With no agenda, she wandered among the graves, stopping and calculating the years between birth and death dates.

Unconsciously, Tonya started whistling her favorite old hymn.

> *Great is Thy faithfulness, O God my Father;*
> *There is no shadow of turning with Thee . . .*

The second stanza was especially meaningful to her and she sang it aloud.

> *Summer and winter and springtime and harvest,*
> *Sun, moon and stars in their courses above*
> *Join with all nature in manifold witness*
> *To thy great faithfulness, mercy and love.*

In the older section of the cemetery, a number of infants did not survive birth, and numerous youngsters died before they were grown. Tonya's thoughts went to Brandi.

Marriages had been cut short by the premature death of a mate. Few of the residents, now in their final resting places, reached their eighties. Most never got far beyond their sixties. Tonya wondered what, if anything, about their lives, mattered.

She was fascinated with some epitaphs. Were the tombstones the only testaments that these individuals ever lived? She thought about what might be said about her and wondered if anyone other than a random stranger would ever visit her grave. She started humming again.

> *Morning by morning new mercies I see.*
> *All I have needed Thy hand hath provided;*
> *Great is Thy faithfulness,*
> *Lord unto me!*

With the sun behind her, Agnes continued westward, avoiding main highways. The road atlas was packed away. Without a destination, there was no need to look at a map.

Late morning, Tonya came upon a white clapboard church down a country road where folks were gathering. She looked at her watch and it was almost twelve. Then, she realized that she had crossed a time zone. Taking no notice of the name or denomination, she pulled in and parked under a shade tree.

No ushers were at the door. Tonya went about halfway to the front and took the only aisle seat left so that she could easily slip out. She could feel eyes. Shortly after she was seated, a matronly woman appeared beside her.

"Would you mind moving down? This is where I normally sit."

Tonya smiled and obliged. Her early exit just got blocked.

She was not familiar with the hymn book or some of the old songs, but that did not stop her from singing along. When the minister asked if there were any visitors, she kept still. The woman next to her did not.

"This young lady beside me is a guest today, but I didn't get here in time to find out her name."

The pastor gestured for Tonya to stand. She complied, stated her name, and said that she was just passing through. Folks all around tried to make her feel welcome.

The humble preacher with no formal education took his text from the Old Testament Book of I Kings. He described how Elijah was on the run. Nothing in the prophet's life had turned out like he planned. He felt like a failure and just wanted to die.

The preacher was not a great orator, but Tonya could almost feel the mighty wind as he described it about to blow the holy man of old off the mountainside.

The speaker stomped his feet, simulating the ground shaking from a powerful earthquake. Tonya could feel the pulsating of the sagging foundation beneath the worn planks.

She imagined the searing heat from a raging wildfire that roared in front of Elijah.

The minister toned it down. He concluded that God sometimes speaks through storms. He might have to move mountains to get a few folk's attentions. Some even get tried by fire before learning their lessons. Even so, God had nothing to say to Elijah in any of these manifestations.

Everything got very quiet. "Instead. He spoke to the prophet in the form of a still small voice."

"What doest thou here, Elijah?"

Tonya bowed her head.

After the benediction, she wanted to leave quickly and quietly, but all avenues were jammed. Mrs. Hattie, her seatmate, took her by the arm.

"You look like you could use a good home-cooked meal. I bet you didn't have any breakfast this morning. Yesterday, when I killed a chicken and dressed it, I knew I was going to be cooking for somebody. I just had no idea who it was. I figured it must be you when I came in the church and found you trying to take my seat away from me. Is that your car over there? Follow me home."

"Miss Bizzy Belle? What have you gotten yourself into now?"

Mrs. Hattie took her in the back door like she was family and told her to make herself at home. Putting on her apron, the woman reached into a drawer, pulled out another, and handed it to Tonya. "Now, make yourself useful and not just ornamental." Granny Addie used to say that.

"The veggies are already cooked, but there's nothing quite like hot biscuits and warm gravy. Let me get the oven fired up. The bread can bake while we fry the chicken."

Tonya was trying to make sense of it all. Something about the woman looked familiar, but she had never been in those parts before.

"You're awfully quiet." Mrs. Hattie commented around the dinner table.

Rather meekly, Tonya responded. "May I ask you something?"

"Of course, you can. Anything."

"How did you know that you were going to have company today?"

"Why, girl. Weren't you paying attention at church this morning? You have to listen to your inner voice. Now mind you. I'm not a pushover like old Elijah was. Had you not plopped down in my seat, I might have missed you."

Tonya began to relax a little, but this was all so weird.

Mrs. Hattie went on. "Young Lady? Have you ever given any thought to your inner voice? I call the still small voice 'inner-connectedness.' Do you have any idea how many people never connect with their innards? How in the world do they think they can bond with somebody else when they don't even listen to what their being is saying to them?"

The woman waited for that to sink in. Looking over her granny glasses, she then went on. "Tonya . . . You certainly have an inner voice. You followed it this morning when you decided to visit our little church. I think probably Somebody else had a hand in directing you to my seat, though."

Tonya could not take her eyes off the woman as she continued. "Inner-connected persons don't always have it easy. But they're the only ones who can see how things are so inter-connected. And they're the only folks who find contentment within themselves."

As they were clearing the table, Tonya shared something. "You're the third best cook in the world. Only my two great-grandmothers were better, and you give both of them a run for their money."

She had no idea what to expect next when the sweet old woman reached out and took both of her hands. "Tonya . . . You're free to stay as long as you wish, but I don't want to hinder you from the finding of whatever it is that you're looking for. Don't forget your way back. My doors are never locked."

Tonya gave Mrs. Hattie a hug, but she had trouble finding just the right words to thank her. The fascinating old lady walked her to her car, told her goodbye, and said that she was headed for a nap. Tonya was in no hurry and did not leave immediately.

After nodding for almost an hour, the saintly woman came back into the kitchen. On the table, was a sketch of her at the stove with her apron flying and her granny glasses dangling from her nose. It was signed, "Miss Bizzy Belle."

She uttered, prayerfully. "Thank you, Lord."

Mrs. Hattie picked up her daily devotional. The reading of the day was from Hebrews 13:2.

> *Be not forgetful to entertain strangers: for thereby some have entertained angels unawares.*

She lay back in her chair, smiled, and closed her eyes, yet again.

Tonya was deep in thought as she drove aimlessly, not even sure if she was still in Tennessee. The mind-boggling occurrences of the past few days kept replaying in her head.

Her thoughts kept coming back to something that Mrs. Hattie said. "Inner-connected people do not always have it easy, but they're the only ones who can see how things are inter-connected."

Her eyes were on the road, but her mind was trying to make sense of things. The wise old woman seemed unlike the other members of the congregation. "What did she mean by not always having it easy?" Tonya wondered if she'd had a hard life.

Even though the days were getting longer, it was already only a couple of hours until sundown. Tonya's awareness then jumped to something else that Mrs. Hattie mentioned. "She said I was looking for something, and that she did not want to hinder me from finding it. Watt, what am I looking for?"

The woman also told her not to forget the way back, and that her doors were never locked. Tonya's inner voice straightway told Agnes to do an about face.

She had not paid much attention to where she was going. After three or four wrong turns, she was finally certain that she was back on the right road. Some landmarks were familiar as the sun was just above the horizon.

Soon, the little country church came into view. Apparently, they did not have Sunday Evening services because no cars were in the yard. As she glanced back at the unpretentious house of worship, it did not look quite like she remembered it, but she had only been there once.

Tonya made her way down the road to Mrs. Hattie's with anticipation building. What she wanted more than anything was to sit at that woman's feet for however long she would allow.

The sun was methodically performing the last duties of its day job. Approaching the shadowy residence, Tonya let out a vocal sigh as she turned in the drive. She glanced over at the swing where she had sat sketching Mrs. Hattie, and it was falling apart. The dwelling did not look like it had been lived in for years. The front porch was dilapidated, and a "Keep Out" sign was nailed to a column. Bats startled her leaving the loft for their nighttime hunts.

She was sure that she was at the right place. Mrs. Hattie's car was parked under the detached shelter.

Tonya was utterly mystified. Was she in the middle of some kind of stupendous dream?

Cautiously, she got out of her car and made her way through the weeds to the back door. The rotting steps creaked but did not buckle. As Mrs. Hattie promised, the door was unlocked.

The kitchen was dark, but what she could see of it looked the same. A heavy musty smell hung in the air, and a thick layer of dust covered everything. That is, except for one stark item.

Tonya measured her steps as the rickety old floor beneath her feet groaned in protest. Her heart was pounding. She reached for the drawing on the kitchen table. Even in the faint light, she could see plainly what she held in her hand. The sketch was a perfect likeness of Granny Addie.

Time neither raced nor stood still. For an amazing moment, everything just was.

Clutching the drawing as though it were a Rembrandt, Tonya crept to her car. Darkness was spreading all around, but a new light had come on inside her being. The young woman was on holy ground.

She took her seat in the Volvo but was in no hurry to go anywhere. There was nowhere else that she wanted to be. Ready or not, however, something was about to get her moving.

Tonya did not notice the headlights coming down the road at first. Neither did the driver spot her immediately. He drove past and then backed up. As the vehicle pulled in behind her, the bright lights in the mirrors blinded her. She could not see a bar of lights atop the cruiser.

Somebody was getting out. She locked her doors. Like a smack in the face, her senses went on highest alert when a sheriff's deputy was looking at her through the window. Had the law caught up with her?

Tonya breathed a big sigh of relief when she found out that the lawman was just on routine patrol. After making sure that nothing was wrong, he asked her to move along. She was on private property.

Agnes's lights came on, and Tonya shifted into reverse. Nothing compelled her to go back the way she came. The deputy's tail lights were in that direction and were not moving on until he was sure that she had. The inadvertent nomad had no idea where the road went in the opposite direction from the church. Pilgrimages rarely come with a clear set of instructions.

Initially in no hurry, Agnes was abruptly compelled to pick up the pace. What if the officer called in her tag number? Speeding along while constantly glancing in the rearview mirror, Tonya tried to stay between the ditches of the worn out country road. She came to an intersection, ran the stop sign, hung a right, and after about two miles, breathed another sigh of relief.

After about five miles, Tonya hit the brakes. Agnes almost went into a skid on the loose gravel. She just remembered something. After lunch, Mrs. Hattie walked her to the car. As the old woman turned to go back to the house, Tonya had taken her picture. If tomorrow came, she must find a drug store with one-hour service and get the film developed.

First, she had to get through the night. The roads were like an endless maze. Rural farmland interspersed with forests seemed to go on forever. Tonya eventually decided that she would have to wait for daylight to find a town. She pulled into what appeared to be an old logging road and took a bathroom break.

"Mrs. T . . . Thanks to you, I've never been out of tissues."

The air was pleasant, and the moon had taken over the night watch responsibilities. In the distance, she could hear a whip-poor-will. Everything else was quiet.

Tonya locked her doors and reclined the seat. The moonlight bathed her through the windshield. Sleep did not come straightaway. Too many things were still swirling in her mind with no interpreter. She loosened the belt of her jeans and wiggled to get more comfortable. She reached for Watt and wrapped her arms around the old sweatshirt.

Something popped into her mind. Was the law enforcement officer's intrusion a parable? Was it a metaphor about finding a way to coexist in the natural world without trespassing?

Tonya's thoughts then transported her to when she stood at her granny's grave a few days earlier and felt the breath of the eternal. Was that pedagogical? Was some destiny guiding her?

Tonya's next awareness was that of a man in a dark blue denim work shirt and a straw hat tapping on her window. The sun had already resumed its day duties.

"Miss? Are you all right?"

Tonya rolled down the window and tried to explain. "I got so tired and sleepy that I pulled in to take a nap. I'm sorry if I've caused you any problems."

"Are you lost?" He wanted to know.

"No . . . I'm not lost . . . but I don't know where I am."

The old farmer scratched his head under his hat.

"Where you from, and where you headed? I see you have a North Carolina tag on your car."

She tried to be polite. "I'm taking a little time off from school. A lot has happened, and I just needed to get away from everything. Where's the nearest town? I have some film I want to get developed."

Finally, the farmer had something to work with. He told her how to get back to the main highway.

"You ain't bothering nothing. I just wanted to make sure you wuz okay. You know . . . There's so much meanness going on in this old world. I just didn't want you to run into no trouble."

Tonya thanked him for his kindness and headed toward town. She was especially grateful that he did not call the law.

Twenty minutes later, she pulled into a convenience store, got some gas, and went to the restroom to straighten herself up. Her tank was running on empty, too. Still trying to sort things out, she dropped the film off and went to find some breakfast.

An hour did not always mean an hour as advertised. It was more like two before the prints were ready. The film had been in Tonya's camera for some time. Earlier, she had taken some candid shots of the university campus. There were also a couple of Brandi, perhaps the last ever taken.

Quickly, she thumbed through them. At the end, she found the one that she was looking for. Tonya held in her hand a photograph of the run down old house. No one was in the picture.

"I'll never be able to tell anyone about this. Nobody would ever believe me."

The Manila Villa

Miss Bizzy Bell was a vagabond. Tonya had entered college as a naïve freshman. She withdrew before the end of her first year, but her education was far from complete. In a series of crash courses that she did not sign up for, she was learning life lessons not taught in the classroom. School was still very much in session, but her education had been moved off campus.

Tonya had always admired kids who could take a gap year between their studies. She had read about young people touring Europe on a few bucks a day. She knew of others who stayed in the U.S., roaming around on somebody else's dime or earning their keep by picking up odd jobs along the way. She hardly realized that something like that might be thrust upon her.

The nineteen-year-old was in some kind of inexpressible interlude. Trying to find just the right way to put it in perspective, she scribbled.

> *How can I be true to myself, and at the same time, traverse in this universe without trespassing?*

Her college fund had almost doubled since the royalties from her brief acting career were deposited. Interest rates had been good, and she had added to it from her bookstore earns. She had a few hundred dollars in her pocket but knew that would not sustain her for very long.

Driving aimlessly, Tonya hit upon an idea. She decided to find a sporting goods store and purchase a tent along with a few camping supplies. At a rest stop, she did an Agnes inventory. Everything in the trunk could be shifted to the backseat. Watt might have to share some space in the front. There should be room enough for a cooler, too.

The gear was more expensive than she had imagined, but still no more than motel and restaurant bills for a couple of days. The man at the store

Miss Bizzy Belle

gave her a lesson in how to pop the tent. He warned her that it might be awkward at first, but that it wouldn't take long for her to get the hang of it.

She scrambled through her books and found the old road atlas. According to the map, a state park was not far ahead. With other folks nearby, a campground might be a good place to begin the experience. A stop for food supplies was next.

True to the salesman's prediction, Tonya struggled with the tent. A couple came over to assist. They were cooking over an open fire and invited her to join them. Tonya was welcomed into their don't-give-a-damn world. They asked no questions, and she had no need to offer any explanations.

Tonya decided to call her tent the "Manila Villa." It was about the color of a large mailing envelope and had a corresponding flap.

The couple moved on the next morning, but Tonya decided to stay. She took out her journal and attempted to explicate the inexplicable, but the right words kept eluding her.

The vagabond discovered hiking trails in the park. She ventured off the path and salvaged a dead limb for a makeshift stick. It would have to do until she could do better.

A newly discovered sensation of wanderlust eventually kicked in. Folding the tent was cumbersome, but she finally got everything stashed. Agnes seemed determined to keep going westward, and Tonya gave her free rein. Campgrounds were not hard to find. For the next two weeks, she followed a pattern of checking in, staying for two or three days, and then moving on. The little cook stove that she picked up at a pawn shop was working well. The nomad made sure to restock her writing and art supplies but had little desire to consult a calendar.

Tonya saw the famous arch in St. Louis as she approached the Mississippi River. Learning to listen to her intuition, she was not compelled to stop. Pilgrimages aren't necessarily about the destination. Sometimes they are about taking the road less traveled and getting off the beaten path.

After ambling through Missouri and Kansas, the Rocky Mountain National Park summoned her. Binoculars purchased at a yard sale had now been added to Tonya's treasures. At an observation point, she watched a herd of elk foraging in the valley far below. Plans for camping at the summit came to a screeching halt. Agnes got to play in a late snowstorm. Hitherto, the camper had no need for a sleeping bag and had to retreat to a warmer clime.

Michelle presumed that Tonya returned to school when she stalked off after her little snit. Her daughter said nothing about why she was home during the middle of a term and must have been on spring break. The mother understood how strong-willed Tonya was, and she saw her actions as still another ploy to wear her down. It never occurred to her that the girl really meant what she said and would not be back at the end of the semester.

Should she go ahead and tell her? What did she have to lose? Tonya was already slipping away. After their daughter turned eighteen, Walt was relieved of the burden of supporting her. It hardly mattered anymore what he might think of the mother of his child. Not much of anything mattered.

Mother's Day and Tonya's nineteenth birthday came and went, and Michelle heard nothing. She knew the spring semester would be over soon, but she did not know exactly when to expect her daughter home. What she found in the mailbox on the way in from work one evening, sent a chill through her. A birthday card to Tonya from Mrs. Thornhill and the freshman's grades had been forwarded from the university post office. Tonya had received a "withdrawal passing" in each subject.

What did that mean? She looked at the date when her daughter withdrew from school, and it was about the same time of their unfortunate clash. Where had she been since then? Where was she now?

Michelle started trying to figure out what to do. Should she call Mrs. Thornhill? That was most likely where Tonya would go. Should she check with the Ringers to see if they had heard anything from her?

The first stop was the bookstore. If Tonya had been in touch with Hap and was going to work during the summer, he might mention it. He asked if Tonya was planning to work.

Michelle could not sit idly by. She placed the call to Mrs. T who had heard nothing since Easter. The girl's mother made a simple request. "Please let me know if Tonya contacts you." She did not mention the last conversation that she had with her daughter.

Mrs. Flo told Michelle that Tonya had stayed at their cabin for a few days back in April and had left a sweet note. They had not heard from her since, and neither had Sammie.

Michelle's daughter was a missing person. Should she go to the police?

One more possibility haunted her. Tonya might be with her daddy. Had she possibly seen the same news flash about her stepmother's death? She never mentioned it during Christmas if she did. Was she finally able to connect the dots? Did she find her father in Alaska? In his grief, did Walt find her?

Tonya was okay. She just had to be okay. But where was she?

Michelle hated herself for letting her daughter walk out the door after

Miss Bizzy Belle

what appeared to be a veiled threat. She knew Tonya was headstrong, but she was only just beginning to realize how badly she had underestimated the girl's tenacity.

Perhaps, she had handled it wrong all along. Maybe she should have never kept that information from Tonya.

Perhaps . . . Maybe . . . All of that was driving Michelle crazy.

Tonya kept driving west, and the Grand Canyon was calling for a revisit. With Memorial Day weekend approaching, the campgrounds were filling up by the time she got to the park. Her stick, such as it was, came in handy during a strenuous hike to the Colorado River at the floor of the massive gorge.

On her subsequent visit, Tonya had oils and was totally immersed in the blending process. The novice artist made every effort to match the colors she saw in an attempt to replicate the unparalleled grandeur. With the camera Mrs. T gave her, she captured scenes to sketch later. Sunset was her favorite time of the day. The wanderer was there during the latter stages of the new moon and got to witness the canyon bathed in its magical light.

Tonya was also understandably awed by how much had changed since her prior visit. The first time around, her mind had been far more on Brad's attention than on what was going on all about her.

In WOWs, she tried to depict how the Grand Canyon setting was in syncopation with her own spirit. She was becoming more aware of something. Both what was before her and inside her transcended the ordinary and the commonplace.

Some evenings, the camper cooked and ate alone. On others, she joined the revelry of her neighbors. There was a sense of urgency amongst most of them. They were trying to absorb as much as they could, as fast as they could, and then get back to their daily grinds. Tonya was in no hurry to get anywhere. She had no notion of next.

Tonya did not think that she had left anything to the imagination with her mother regarding her intentions. Thus, she felt no need to get in touch with her. The payphone at the bathhouse, on the other hand, reminded her that she should check in with Mrs. Thornhill.

Her mentor and dear friend just listened as she told her about Brandi's death and how that precipitated leaving school. Mrs. T told Tonya to have fun, but to be careful, and to please call her now and then. The woman did not mention Michelle's call, and Tonya said nothing about her last conversation with her mother.

Mrs. Thornhill was torn. Her little Bizzy Belle was out on her own. A big part of her was celebrating the girl's excitement and adventure. The other portion naturally feared for her surrogate granddaughter's safety and well-being. She was certain that there was far more to the story. The only thing that Mrs. T knew to do was pray.

As promised, Mrs. Thornhill gave a report to Michelle who was polite and thanked her. Tonya's mother felt a sense of relief flow through her that her daughter was alive and well. This news also unleashed a torrent of despair. Had her own flesh and blood really walked away for good? At least, the girl was not with her father.

Bashville

The not always so reverent throngs descending upon the Grand Canyon began to weigh on Tonya's spirits. She folded the Manila Villa again and continued moving westward. As the summer heat unfolded, she found that the desert southwest was not the best place for sleeping in the great outdoors. When she got to Lake Tahoe, snow was still visible in the higher elevations.

Tonya was unfamiliar with the immensity of the far west. She wanted to cross the Golden Gate Bridge and to explore the renowned Napa Valley. She also knew about the giant redwoods from her geography studies. The wayfarer took her atlas and plotted a route that would take her up the Pacific Coast Highway.

Never bashful, she talked with locals all along the way. Tonya learned that people came to the California coastal region for categorically different purposes. Some were drawn to it because of its infinite beauty. Others were trying to become enormously wealthy.

Standing in a cemetery right in the shadows of giant Sequoias, she unearthed an astute perspective. Living things were standing tall, some of which had been around since near the time of Christ. In their shadows, the entombed had a combined average lifespan of barely half a century.

Tonya found the Pacific Ocean considerably different from the Atlantic. She loved the outcrops and hanging cliffs. Sunsets were peaceful, and she painted several. The Manila Villa was set up some nights on the shore where she could listen to the surf.

From her tent about halfway up the Oregon coast, Tonya could see smoke from a wildfire but was not aware of the danger it posed. The handsome young ranger who came into the campground to help evacuate it

Miss Bizzy Belle

knew otherwise. She was the only one who had not already packed up and left. He helped gather her belongings, and she thought he might be flirting with her.

While loading the gear, the forester philosophically explained how fire is such a harbinger of death for those in its path. Yet, he described how at the same time, the redwoods could not survive without it. He said fire is a naturally occurring phenomenon, and that in his opinion, old Smokey the Bear had done too good of a job. Tonya thanked him for his help.

"Where are you headed next?" The ranger wanted to know.

"Why? Will you come rescue me again if I'm in harm's way?" Tonya teased and he seemed pleased. She took his picture when he was not looking and later that night, did a pencil sketch.

By the time Tonya arrived at the mouth of the Columbia River near Astoria, the summer was almost gone. She thought about driving on to Alaska, but the timing was not right. She might find a place to live for the winter and then reevaluate in the spring.

Following the road along the river, Tonya stopped to take in several majestic waterfalls. She toured a couple of the dams and learned about some unintended consequences resulting from the production of renewable energy. It was supposedly environmentally friendly, but the salmon and the displaced Native Americans were among those with differing opinions.

Camped at a state park, she went into a nearby town one morning to see about making a withdrawal from her account. The name of the place caught her attention. There had to be a story behind Bashville, Washington.

The bank would not give her cash until her draft cleared, and that might take a couple of days. Tonya decided to look around while she was waiting. She went in a bookstore and asked about the possibility of getting a job. The owner was impressed that she had experience, but he had no opening. He said that he and his wife were barely making ends meet managing the store by themselves.

On an impulse, she went into the office of the local newspaper. The little weekly had just gone to press. The owner, editor, and publisher, Fred Ellis, had his feet propped up on his desk reading a big city paper. He politely put both down and asked Tonya how he could help her. She said that she was looking for employment and wondered if he needed any help.

Mr. Ellis asked if she had a résumé, and she told him that her decision to come inside was spur of the moment. She mentioned her bookstore experience, and that she had been the editor of her high school yearbook.

He quipped rather curtly. "Can you write?"

Tonya reported that she wrote short stories and had done many pages of journaling. Just for fun, she told him about her brief acting career and her stage name. The man liked her appearance, but he did not have much to go on. He asked if she could drop some samples of her work by for him to see.

Tonya returned to the Manila Villa and started selecting some items to put into a little portfolio. Instinctively, she included the anonymous short story that she wrote for the English class. She dropped the folder off the next morning on her way to the bank. The teller told her that her funds would be ready the following morning if everything was in order.

Before noon the next day, Tonya had her money, and she got the job. When she returned to the newspaper office, Mr. Ellis was still laughing. "That Cop-A-Feel story is the funniest thing I've read in years. Things are slow around here, but you might be just the one to liven them up."

There was not much to the job interview process. "Do you do drugs?"

Tonya assured Mr. Ellis that she did not.

"Ever?"

"No."

"Have you ever been arrested?"

Tonya shook her head, but she failed to mention that a warrant might be out at that very moment.

When she got her money, she tried to open an account but could not do so without an address. She drove around looking for a place to live.

When she showed up for work the next morning, the first thing Tonya wanted to know was how Bashville got its name. Mr. Ellis explained that the first settlers were Bashams, but calling the burg Bashamville, did not catch on. Before long, people just started saying Bashville.

"And by the way . . . This newspaper has been known to enhance the town's image and reputation. We're not bashful. We don't pull no punches."

The second part of the conversation involved Tonya's housing situation. She told Mr. Ellis that all she needed was something small. The editor had an idea. One of the town's matriarchs took in boarders. He picked up the phone and gave her a call.

Mrs. Westin lived in a large old two-story house that stood out. Her late husband had come to the area as a forester. He built his own residence like those he was familiar with back in south Louisiana. On the way, Mr. Ellis pointed out things about the town.

Two bedrooms were already occupied, but a smaller one was available. It was Tonya's if she wanted it. Wow! A real bed—she would get to sleep in a real bed again. Breakfast and dinner came with the package, but not much else. Bashville's newest resident took the rest of the day to get settled in.

Stretched out on a mattress for the first time in weeks, Tonya decided to call her new place, "the A.C." She began her life in the Washington on the other side of the country also known as D.C. The name also seemed appropriate since her mother once kidded her about being a live wire switching back and forth from A.C. to D.C.

Mrs. Westin mentioned that the other boarders were both men. They occupied the two upstairs bedrooms. Tonya's was a converted studio on the ground floor. She had her own small bathroom with a shower. The renters provided their linens and all had access to a washer and dryer. Both meals were served promptly at seven. Mrs. Westin liked to keep things simple.

If Mr. Ellis had ever heard the expression "job description," he never mentioned it. Tonya learned that she would do whatever she was told. Her boss qualified that by saying unless he asked her to do something either illegal or immoral. Tonya loved the man's candor.

Once she got her new checks in the mail with her address on them, she made a beeline to the tag office. Having Washington plates on her vehicle, put her mind a little more at ease.

The newspaper had one other employee who did most of the general reporting. The editor indicated that Tonya would be primarily responsible for human interest stories. She was thrilled with the prospects of that. Her first assignment was to interview the new high school principal.

Mr. Ellis gave his new employee a brief orientation. "People don't like to be misquoted. While it's nice to have your name in the paper, it's also sort of like seeing yourself in a photograph. Is that what I really look like?"

He continued with her impromptu preparation. "Keep your opinions to yourself. Your job is to reflect those of the ones you are interviewing. Our editorial page, not the front page, is for opinions." With a twinkle, he added. "And we do have them." Tonya liked his wryness.

The new reporter also learned that a face to face meeting often got better results than a phone call, so she went to the school office to schedule an appointment. The secretary was not very positive about Mr. Ballew granting an interview since school was about to start, and her boss was still trying to get settled in.

The principal saw it differently. This was just the opportunity that the new administrator was looking for to help connect with the community. He agreed to see her the next morning at seven before anyone else arrived. Tonya would miss breakfast. Newspaper work was not a nine-to-five job.

Mr. Ballew was in his late forties. He handed Tonya a folder full of material as he ushered her into his office. She thumbed through it and said that she could glean from it. For the first time *not* being a student, she faced a school principal sitting across the desk as the person gathering information.

"I suspect the material you handed me is about what you've done. I'd rather like to talk about who you really are."

"Who I really am? How interesting? About all I've heard since I first applied for this job has been, 'What can you *do* for us?' I came prepared this morning to discuss my plans for making this a better school and community."

The school official had no idea that Tonya had never done anything like this before. She just followed her intuitions.

"I'd like to get to know you. Not just your pedigree, but who in your life has mattered. What hardships have you overcome? What were the turning points when you could have gone one way or the other? What do you treasure, and what gets you all riled up? Mr. Ballew? What makes you tick?"

The principal had only penciled in thirty-minutes. An hour later, Tonya apologized for taking up so much of his time. He said that it had been the most enjoyable hour he could remember in a while, and he looked forward to seeing the article.

As she rose from her chair, the reporter reached for her camera. "One more thing. I've got to shoot you with my Canon."

Tonya was provided a desk and typewriter at work, but she preferred writing this first article in the A.C. She dropped the film off and went to work.

The next morning, she put the article and photos on Mr. Ellis' desk and went for a stroll around town. Bashville was about the same size as Knoxo Springs, but the lay of the land was completely different. Her new residence had only a few scrubby trees. The terrain was flat, but the Cascade Mountains were little more than an hour away. She looked forward to exploring them.

When Tonya came back to the office, Mr. Ellis was waiting for her. "The most apparent thing about your story is that you obviously do not have a degree in journalism." She braced herself.

"And I like that. I don't have one either. The last couple of upstarts who found their way to my doorstep thought they had all the answers. They came in here and tried to tell me how to run my newspaper. All they were really interested in was getting some experience. They could then brag about helping save a broken down old paper. I won't have to worry about that with you, will I?"

Tonya just shrugged.

Miss Bizzy Belle

"Now, back to your article about Mr. Ballew. I'll clean up a few technical issues. That's my job. But basically, it's very good. You did not just write things about him. You captured the man. I feel like I know him so much better now."

Picking up the pictures, he went on. "I also see that you know how to use a camera. I was going to find a file photo, but your shots are much better. I especially like the one with the principal kneeling and talking to the boy in the wheelchair. That puts a human face on both of them."

When the 1988 Labor Day weekend issue of the *Bashville Clarion* hit the streets, Miss Willa Bell was a published writer.

About a week into her new job, Tonya decided to give Mrs. T a call. The woman was relieved to know that her little butterfly had lit somewhere. Nothing was said about Michelle. Mrs. Thornhill decided to let mother and daughter handle their own issues.

Tonya learned little about the other boarders. Both men had jobs somewhere, and they kept mostly to themselves. Mrs. Westin read a lot and enjoyed working with her flowers, but the growing season was about over.

The landlady welcomed Tonya's assistance putting the meals on the table, and especially with clearing up afterward. The woman seemed lonely and isolated. Tonya wondered why she did not return to her southern roots after her husband died. Then again, some people have no roots to go back to.

A new task was soon added to Tonya's work routine. Advertising, for the most part, funded the newspaper. Mr. Ellis began sending her to businesses to pick up ad copy. She became familiar with proprietors and learned how the system worked.

The neophyte correspondent had a suggestion for her next story. She wanted to find out more about the crippled boy whose photo had already been in the paper. Mr. Ellis concurred. He knew the family and called to set up an appointment.

When the lad's parents met her at the door, they thanked her for including their son's picture with the feature about the principal. She learned that the boy was diagnosed with cerebral palsy soon after birth. They intimated how unprepared they had been, and how limited the resources were.

At the same time, Tonya sensed how diligent these dedicated parents were in providing the best life they could for their son. She quoted the boy several times in the article and took more photos. He liked getting shot by the Canon.

Mr. Ellis did not just sit and wait for news to come to him. He went out and got about to feel the pulse of the public. After Tonya's first two articles, his cronies were talking about her at Mabel's Kitchen. One of them chided him. "It's about time your old rag started putting a positive spin on some things."

"The girl's got good instincts. If I sent her to interview Daniel in the lion's den, she would come back with a story from both Daniel's and the lions' points of view."

When a group of anti-government malcontents bought a place not far out of town, folks were a little nervous. With a twinkle in his eyes, Mr. Ellis asked Tonya if she wanted to go out and interview the alpha male.

Tonya did not bat an eye. "That's probably not a good idea. I would only force him to get in touch with his softer side, and that would really make him angry. Anyway . . . The government's not his enemy. He's his own worst enemy."

Mr. Ellis smiled, and then she made a counter proposal. "I'll go with you, though. While you talk to the macho man, I'll visit with the women and children."

The editor was growing more appreciative of his young employee. That visit to the compound was not going to happen, at least not just yet. Even the *Bashville Clarion* did not always go where angels feared to tread.

Mr. Ellis shared another news bulletin with his coffee drinking buddies at Mabel's. "It's amazing the kind of people, places, and things that fresh eyes see when they look around. Miss Willa Bell's pieces are becoming very popular. Advertising and subscriptions are also up. If she hangs around, I might not retire for another year or so."

One friend hassled him. "Oh, no. You'll die sitting at your desk pecking away at your old typewriter with two fingers."

Anonymity was one thing Tonya really valued in her new locale. Nobody cared that she was raised in a single-parent home, or that she didn't even know who her father was. She was accepted without having to explain anything and did not have to worry about people whispering behind her back. Using her middle name as her pen name boosted that feeling of freedom. It also made it more difficult for the law to catch up with her just in case.

Ranger Rick

When Tonya stopped by the volunteer fire department's booth during

Miss Bizzy Belle

the fall festival, she saw a familiar face. It was not behind the table, though. It was on the table. As a fundraiser, the department was selling "1989—It's Gonna Be a Hot One" calendars. A different firefighter was featured each month. Mr. January was her summer rescuer. Tonya purchased one with the intention of getting it personally autographed.

On Monday, she asked her boss if she had any travel expense money.

"Why? What did you have in mind?"

"I'm just learning about the threat of fires in the west. What do you think about a story from a forest ranger's point of view?"

Holding up the calendar, she went on. "This forester helped me escape a fire when I was camping earlier in the summer. He said something about Smokey the Bear perhaps doing his job all too well. It's only about fifty miles to the headquarters where he's stationed. I'd like to find out more about his thinking."

While Mr. Ellis might tip his hand with his not so subtle wariness, Tonya knew how to play it straight. Her boss took the bait.

"I think you might have a story there. Let me see if I can tickle the till."

Tonya now had a name to go with the face. She called the station and set up an appointment with Ranger Rick. She did not tell him that they had already met.

Agnes was well-rested and ready to get going again. Ranger Rick's instructions about how to get to the headquarters were clear, and Tonya arrived about fifteen minutes early. The workstation had few amenities, but the female forester at the desk offered coffee. The interviewee was due back any minute.

When he came through the door, she rose from her chair, extended her hand, and introduced herself as Miss Willa Bell from the Bashville paper.

"I've seen you somewhere before. Oh, yes. You were that damsel in distress who hardly knew how to take down a tent when a fire was approaching."

He remembered her.

"You're the one in distress now, Ranger Rick. I've come to pick your brain."

Tonya felt a twinge of guilt that she was getting paid for the story. Sometimes, you just have to take the perks. If Mr. Ellis did not bother with a job description, then why should she worry about a conflict of interest?

The reporter learned much about the positive benefits of fire. The ranger also expressed concern for the growing number of housing developments being built in fire zones. "It's not a matter of if, but merely when fires will threaten them and destroy some."

After taking notes that she could cipher later, she surprised him. It was just a harbinger of things to come. Tonya pulled out the calendar, along with something else she was lugging around. The interviewee looked on curiously.

Tonya had only a few posters left from the movie. "I'll trade autographs with you. Now that we're both celebrities, I think that would be a fair trade, although a movie star's signature might be worth far more than a cheesy calendar model's."

Ranger Rick was amused. After the signing ritual, and answering some questions about her acting career, the reporter got back to business. "Now, I get to take my own pictures." The forest ranger posed with various pieces of equipment. At the photographer's request, he put on his firefighting gear and helmet. She took some action shots and several stills.

Tonya flirted with him. "Too bad, I don't have any of the stuff that football players rub under their eyes. I could smear it all over your face, and make it look like you were just coming in from a fire all hot and sweaty."

As he was walking Tonya to her car, she caught him off guard again. "Invite me to your next fire, and we can roast hot dogs on some coals."

He was finally getting the hang of it and bantered back. "The fire season's about over, but it only takes an ember to cause a lotta heat."

"No kidding." Tonya felt the burn rise in her face.

Since the paper was paying for the film and the developing, Tonya did not want to disappoint her editor by giving him too few pictures from which to choose. She went ahead and had the film developed and cropped the stack before handing over the remainder.

A copy of the paper with the forester on the front page was put in the mail before the ink was hardly dry. Miss Willa Bell had her own business cards, and one was attached. Two days later, the ranger in the feature story called to say thanks. He was wondering if he might express his gratitude in a more tangible way.

He surprised her. "We could always go camping and roast wieners."

"Are you serious?" Tonya asked.

"Serious as a heart attack. We both have tents, and I can start a fire as well as put one out."

She sealed the deal. "I'll bring the food. You bring whatever you like to drink."

Sparks were already flying.

"We're sitting on a powder keg." Sheriff Langford told the group gathered in his office. "The ring leader of the anti-government dissidents

Miss Bizzy Belle

has warrants out for his arrest in both Oklahoma and Texas. We're getting reports of polygamy and underage girls having babies. What makes it personal for us, is that they refuse to pay their local taxes. They say the government has no authority over them."

"What's going to happen next?" The press wanted to know.

"None of us wants any violence, but this thing might not come to a peaceful end. It's far bigger than any one law enforcement agency. The state and the feds are planning some kind of raid, and they've promised to let us in on it when they're ready."

Editor Ellis could ignore this story no longer. The citizens had a right to know what was going on in their own backyard.

"How can you determine if somebody has an outstanding warrant?" Tonya wanted to know when they got back to the office. Her boss explained that it was not an exact science and that many wanted folks fell through the cracks. He added that with new technology using computers, it was getting much easier for various agencies to share information. Tonya still did not know if she was a fugitive, but she did not ask Mr. Ellis to do any investigating.

The development also put a damper on the recreational plans of the ranger and the reporter. Federal land backed right up to the anarchists' compound. The clan was using it illegally for grazing, hunting, and harvesting firewood. The Forestry Service was put on alert.

Sheriff Langford told Mr. Ellis that the press would not be notified about the secretive operation. Since Bashville was where it was going down, he promised the *Clarion* an exclusive.

The raid took place during the wee hours on a Monday. The element of surprise was mostly successful. No women and children were hurt, and the menfolk were all taken into custody after only minor scuffles. No law enforcement officers suffered any injuries.

Mr. Ellis discovered that his paper was by no means the only news outlet given a heads-up. He told the boys at Mabel's that more reporters showed up than officials.

"Too bad all the vultures survived. I do hope they move the trials somewhere else."

Tonya had gone out on a limb with the forester. Things were going almost too well when his work got in the way. If the ranger had any real interest in her, the next move was his.

Since the paper did not have a receptionist, she often kept the office open and answered the phone. About mid-afternoon one day, she looked out to see Ranger Rick coming across the street.

After she greeted him, he explained that he was in town on business. "I had to come and do a personal inspection of the encroached upon federal land. I was wondering if I might catch you. I know of no regulation that prohibits me from taking the press. Want to come along?"

Tonya left a note on the desk saying that she had gone to do a follow up on the story. Unlike her boss, Miss Willa Bell did have this exclusive.

As they were returning to town, Rick asked Tonya if she had been to Mount St. Helens. She told him that she hadn't. Furthermore, she had seen little of the Pacific Northwest.

"If you do a good job on this story, I might consider letting you come along with me on other assessments. The devastated area that was in the path of the mighty eruption has just begun to recover. I go every month or so to see for myself, and also to write some reports. I'm going on Saturday. You're welcome to join me if you'd like."

Tonya just had to point out a little technicality. "But I will not have today's article ready for your inspection before then."

"Guess I'll just have to trust you. What do you say?"

Rick was indeed both a forester and a ranger. He had a degree in forestry, and he was a ranger with extensive training working for the Forestry Service. Tonya was impressed by the scope of his knowledge. Yet, no aura of arrogance jaded him.

She was also cognizant of his immense appreciation for nature. The forester took the time to show her small details that others miss. The ranger explained the larger picture, illustrating in various ways, the interrelatedness of creatures and their habitat. Mount St. Helens blew her away.

Tonya was not sure of Rick's intentions. She was only nineteen, and he was at least in his mid-twenties. This was his first job out of college, and he said that his goal was to work for the National Park Service. The ranger was fun, and she was learning so much just being around him. Was she acting like a silly teenager while he was all business? Would every month of the year be January?

Tonya was thrilled when he called and rescheduled the camping trip. They hiked during the afternoon and then sat around the fire and talked for hours. She was a bit miffed when he made no effort to move closer to her. When she said that she was getting a little cool, he stoked the fire. The only time he held her hand was assisting when crossing a creek or when footing was a little treacherous. She was disappointed when he did not kiss her goodnight before they crawled into their separate tents.

Christmas was coming, and Tonya did not know whether to buy Rick a present or not. She thought about framing the sketch she did of him after they first met, but she did not want to part with it. Perhaps, she should do one of the two of them around a campfire. No. That might be too forward if he had no romantic interests in her.

Tonya got her oils out and started working on a painting of Mount St. Helens with its snow cap and blown-out crater. With each brush stroke, she glanced at snapshots of the mountain. "Thank you, Mrs. T, for my camera."

The proposal

Rick did not know what to make of Tonya. She was a girl without a past, and she had no definable speech accent. He was not even sure how old she was. She once made a reference to something a professor said, so she must have had some college.

The young man had always detested the extra burden that his good looks placed on him. A guy does not necessarily have everything figured out just because he is handsome. With females, he was shy and reserved, and he knew it.

Ranger Rick was reluctant to do the calendar spread. He could not help it that others thought that he had a nice physique. He relented eventually because the proceeds were going to a worthy cause. He had taken a good bit of ribbing, but Tonya was the only person who had asked him to sign his picture.

The first time they met, he thought that she was just like all the rest. The young woman was making no move to get out of the campground with a fire approaching. Was she just waiting to be rescued, or was she so new to the area that she did not understand the danger? He even made reference to her being a damsel in distress the day she came to interview him. The young reporter turned the phrase back on him.

Tonya seemed genuinely interested in him but did not gush all over him. She got in his face but respected his space. She was not stunningly beautiful, but he liked it when she walked ahead of him. The girl was graceful like a deer, sly as a fox, and as sure-footed as a mountain goat.

The holidays were looming, and he did not know whether to get her something or not. They had gone exploring together several times, and he liked the touch of her hand in his when he offered it. Maybe he could get a better feel for the situation if he upped the ante—as in taking the relationship to a higher level—literally. The first snow of the season had fallen in the mountains and the ski slopes were open.

Rick was nervous when he gave Tonya a call. "Want to have dinner with me? I have a proposal I'd like to make." They had not actually been on a date out in public.

"Are you going to ask me to marry you?"

She did not make it easy. Why did he make such a poor word choice? Rick stumbled with a comeback.

"I might before we get back, but that's not what I had in mind."

Tonya pressed him. "Can you give me a hint?"

"No . . . You'll have to go out with me first."

"Okay . . . When and where?"

They agreed to meet about halfway in a town with a restaurant well known for seafood. Rick arrived early and was waiting for her in the rocking chairs on the porch. It was a bit cool, but they decided to sit and chat before going inside.

Tonya's curiosity spilled over. "Are you going to make your proposal now? Just know that I'm not ready to grow old together in rocking chairs."

"No . . . You're going to have to wait. Maybe I'll get up my nerve after a couple glasses of wine."

In the few months that Tonya had been on the left coast, she had developed quite a taste for northern Pacific fish. She liked Pollock, found salmon irresistible, but had never sampled halibut. Her date suggested the beer battered. It was love at first bite.

Rick started second guessing himself about a ski trip. He was in too deep, though, and he did not have a backup plan. Tonya stopped needling him, and that made him even more apprehensive. When the waiter brought the check, the time had come.

Without any buildup, he just blurted out. "Want to go skiing? The snowpack is deep enough on the slopes now. I've only been a time or two, and so far, I've managed not to break any bones. Is that something you'd like to try?"

Tonya had imagined all kinds of "proposals," but that one caught her by surprise.

"Sounds like fun, but I don't have clothes for anything like that. Anyway . . . I think you're just trying to find out what a klutz I am."

It was not Tonya's intention to knock Rick off balance. It just seemed to come naturally for her. He went from a tailspin into a free fall, and then he retracted. "Maybe that was not such a good idea."

Tonya steadied him. "Oh, I love it. When do you want to go?"

She thought about driving into Longview, or even to Seattle to do her shopping. The one time that she went to the seaport city, she really liked it. However, the newspaper was promoting a seasonal shop-at-home campaign, so she decided to trust the recommendations of Bashville's lone department store. If about to make a fool of herself, the choice of attire would not be her downfall.

Rick assured her that they would have plenty of company on the beginners' slopes. He asked if she was okay with a two-day package, which included an overnight stay. She reminded him that neither had a tent lock the weekend they went camping. She added that he could just shut his eyes if he didn't want to see her parading around in her jammies.

The forester trusted his four-wheel drive rig in the mountain snow. Tonya felt safe with her escort. Both were just trying to relax and have fun.

A group was gathered around a roaring fire in the lobby of the lodge when the two novices checked in. Tonya was feeling a different kind of heat. If she was blushing, maybe Rick would just think that her red cheeks were from the bright sun and cold wind.

Rick took charge of making the slope arrangements, but he felt little control over anything else. The ice was broken when he wiped out on his trial run. On her maiden voyage, Tonya fell on her face, and he helped her back on her skis. It was all downhill from there.

Laughter can signal a variety of things. Sometimes hilarity is nothing more than an outpouring of pure delight. Giggling might well mask uncertainty and uneasiness. Snickering is sometimes a spontaneous reaction to idiocy. An outburst could well be aimed fiendishly toward the folly of another. Tonya and Rick did not have to pick and choose. They laughed incessantly for two days.

Tonya's phone card still had several minutes on it. When no one answered immediately, she was about to hang up.

"Merry Christmas, Mrs. T. I thought you might be in Dallas."

"No . . . I'm home. And even better, Dallas is here with me. Would you like to wish Brad a Merry Christmas, too?"

"Sure . . . Put the boy on the phone."

"Miss Bizzy Belle . . . What in the world have you been up to? And where in the world are you?"

"Merry Christmas, to you, too, Brad. If I told you the truth, you wouldn't believe me."

"Why should I start now?"

"In that case, give the phone back to Mrs. T."

"Not so fast. Give me a try. I could always tell when you were lying, anyway."

"Well, actually. I'm living in a little town called Bashville."

"You're lying. There's no such place as that."

"Is, too. And I write for the local newspaper."

"Did they rename the town after you got there?"

"Did they rename the base where you're stationed Fort Bratville?"

"I don't know how I've managed to get along without you around to pester."

"My sentiments exactly. Just give the phone back to the other person there—the one with a civil tongue."

The ranger station shut down during Christmas Week, and Rick went home. He thought about asking Tonya to go with him, but he did not want to give his family the wrong impression. He was not even sure what the right impression was.

Both of the other boarders left for the holidays. Mrs. Westin invited Tonya to have Christmas dinner with her. Christmas had never been a time of big celebration growing up, and her favorite memories were the times that she spent with Mrs. T. Now, another sweet old lady included her. The girl with no home to go to appreciated that.

Not much was going on at the paper so Tonya had some free time on her hands. She got caught up on personal writing projects while waiting for the paint to dry on Rick's present. This landscape was her first time to use a canvas-stretched frame.

Meanwhile, she had something to look forward to. Ranger Rick said that he would be back in time for the year-end fireworks. Unlike what happened one Fourth of July in Philadelphia when she got kissed, this time, Tonya's date fizzled. He held her hand but did not put his arm around her.

Tonya's work responsibilities continued to increase. Mr. Ellis assigned several regular advertising accounts to her. He also sent her to cover events needing little more than a photo and cutline. She usually came back with more. His neophyte young reporter had an eye for the story behind the story.

It was Tonya's opinion pieces that kept getting her noticed. She resisted a mug shot, but the editor prevailed. Strangers now walked up to her and asked if she was Miss Willa Bell. They might then comment on something she had written that was especially insightful or meaningful.

Tonya saw what others missed. She made folks stop and think. Nature stories were her favorites. She wrote about the birds. She wrote about the bees. But not the birds and the bees.

Except for customary editing, Mr. Ellis gave Tonya lots of leeways. The only notable exception was that she could not say anything that might offend advertisers. Even the free press had to pay its bills.

The reporter's worthy efforts were rewarded with a nice little raise starting the first of the year. She had been able to save some money and thought about looking around for an apartment. Rick had been to the boarding house to pick her up, but he had never been to her room. Her current living arrangement afforded no privacy. She had not been invited to his place.

Tonya and Rick were different in many ways. At the same time, they had much in common. For one thing, neither had ever been in love.

Uncertainty was something else that they shared. The ranger understood that his was a steppingstone job. The assignment at the remote station was just to get some necessary professional experience. Nobody retired there. If he caught on with the National Park Service, he might wind up anywhere in the country.

Tonya landed in Bashville on a lark. Nothing had prepared her for working at a newspaper. Then again, perchance everything had.

What the young woman was more sure of than anything, though, was how she was transformed after the happenstance encounter with Mrs. Hattie. Only three things hung on her wall—the sketch of the old woman that turned out to be the effigy of Granny Addie, the picture of the rundown old house, and a 1989 calendar.

"Did you ever get a sleeping bag?" They were doing a replay at the seafood place.

"Why do you ask?" Tonya wanted to know.

"I was thinking about going camping again, and it gets cold at night. I have an old one you can borrow if you don't want to get one of your own."

She responded with no show of emotion. "We could always just share yours." Why did she enjoy making him blush?

He was learning how to deal with her. "Okay . . . Fine with me. But if it won't zip up all the way, it will be your butt hanging out."

Tonya got her own sleeping bag, but they only took one tent along. Rick's was large enough for two people.

As they were unpacking, he held up something. "Here . . . I made this for you. I think it's about time you had a real hiking stick." Tonya was still lugging around the improvised limb that she picked up when she first pitched the Manila Villa.

The ranger once more exhibited his expertise around a campfire. He knew how to build one and the way to cook over the open coals. His venison chili was the best that Tonya had ever tasted. Nevertheless, the forester was much less proficient when it came to fanning the flames of romance. When Tonya lay back on the quilt looking up at the stars, he went and gathered more wood.

As he came back, she sat up. "Look. The moon is just coming up. I can barely see it through the trees."

"Where? I don't see it."

"Come here. I'll show you."

Standing behind her, he squinted. "Are you sure? I still don't see anything."

Tonya reached for his hand and pulled him down on the quilt. She got a fix on the tip of the moon just visible and then placed Rick's head against hers.

"Wow!" he exclaimed when he finally saw the light.

Then, she kissed him.

After dousing the fire, Rick started preparing for lights out. "Since you've never owned a sleeping bag, I guess I'd better give you some instruction. It might not make sense when you first think about it, but you're much warmer sleeping in the buff. It's going below freezing tonight, and you'll get cold before morning if you don't."

"I don't believe you. You're just trying to get back at me for embarrassing you. Nice try, mister, but I don't buy that."

"It's the naked truth. Check it out."

"Rick . . . You can sleep the way you want, but I'll keep my sweats on—thank you very much."

He stayed outside until she was zipped up and the flashlight went off. It was dark in the tent when he undressed. Tonya had trouble going to sleep wondering. Before daybreak, she woke up chilly. The next night, Rick wondered.

Tonya still had not presented the painting to Rick. He had given her the hiking stick, but it was not actually for Christmas. She decided to wait for just the right occasion.

Occasions were not coming with any more frequency. Both had jobs, and they lived an hour apart. Time off did not always coincide. Rick finally got the hint about one thing, though. Tonya liked to be kissed. He took the initiative the next time they were together. He wanted every kiss to be special. Tonya was so very special, and he knew it.

Her doctor "friend"

As Christmas was approaching, so was the first anniversary of the last night that Tonya spent at the Villa Bell. Michelle's only child was of legal age, and she was somewhere out there, but her mother knew not where that *somewhere* was.

Sensing the woman's vulnerability, one of the married doctors started coming on to her. She knew having anything going with him was a dead end street, but why should that bother her now? She had been on the road to nowhere for some time.

The nurse thought about asking off for Christmas so she could go to Bellville. Then again, what if Tonya tried to call while she was gone?

Michelle had not taken much time off since her father's death, and she had managed to accrue quite a bit of leave. Supervisor Jobson told Nurse Bell that if she did not use it before the end of the year, she would lose it.

"You've worked too hard to forfeit your reward. You should treat yourself to some time away."

The last thing that Michelle wanted was to stay home alone, and her hopes that Tonya might call were fading. Her doctor "friend" would certainly have no time for her during the holidays. Perhaps, she should go to Bellville after all. Maybe her mother would take her in for a few days.

Hiding her bad habits might not be easy. Michelle let her mind drift back to a Christmas two decades earlier when she was trying to hide what was growing inside her. That sent her scurrying to see if she still had any of those gosh-awful Christmas sweaters. She suspected that they were still in vogue in Bellville.

Black Bart had died back during the summer, and Uncle Charles let Michelle have Granny Addie's old car. It was older than dirt, but mileage-wise, it was just approaching middle-age. Whatever happened to the little redheaded nurse who once drove a red sports car?

"Nurse Bell . . . The phone's for you." Michelle was coming back from a patient's room. The only two words she spoke were "Hello," and "Okay." She then made her way to the nursing supervisor's office. Barbara told Michelle to come in and close the door.

"Girl . . . Looks like you've been called in on the carpet. Hold your tongue, and don't let that old self-righteous hypocrite get to you."

The chief nurse paused to get her composure. Then she began.

"You're probably aware that I'm finally retiring. I wanted to awhile back, but Mr. Griffin insisted that I stay on. It's no secret that when he hired you, he started grooming you to take my place. Regretfully, he has asked me to deal with you as my last official act."

Michelle asked without emotion. "Does that mean I'm fired?"

"No. This is the 80s, almost the 90s. We can't do things like we used to. Mr. Griffin has asked me to suggest to you that you seek employment elsewhere."

Then the supervisor turned to the nurse and addressed her in a professional manner. "Nurse Bell. We try to stay out of our employees' personal lives. That's impossible, though, when it affects their work. You've lost pride in your appearance, you're making far too many mistakes, and you don't get along well with your associates. Morale is always low on the shift you work. The administrator is committed to maintaining the high standards set by Dr. Lane, the founder of this hospital."

It was not easy, but Michelle held her tongue. The supervisor paused and then went on. "When I advised you to use your vacation days before the end of last year, I did so at Mr. Griffin's request. We both hoped that some time away might give you a chance to get your life back on course. We cannot do anything about your doctor 'friend.' He's in private practice. But we need to put a stop to the undercurrent that's distracting our other staff."

"So I am fired?" Michelle asked again.

"No. We do not want to go through the hassle of doing that. If, however, you stay here, you'll be demoted with cause. Your performance reviews will go into your personnel file. They will be there should anyone else ask for a reference."

Michelle got up and walked out.

The supervisor reported back to the administrator that she had done her job. "But I don't like it. It's just not fair. The nurse gets punished, but there's no penalty for the doctor when he gets caught with his hand in the nookie jar."

No further mention was made of the conversation for the next two weeks. Michelle put her best foot forward and went to the retirement party. Her doctor "friend" ignored her, with his dutiful little wife hanging onto his arm as if that would fool everybody. Mr. Griffin was nice and cordial like nothing was going on behind the scenes. Barbara did not mention Nurse Bell's name when she thanked the many others who had made her job so enjoyable.

Michelle did not know what she was going to do next. If the hospital administrator wanted to talk with her, he would have to summons her.

Mr. Griffin began avoiding her. The incoming nursing supervisor

Miss Bizzy Belle

remained distant. No doubt, she had been apprised of the situation.

Michelle felt certain that none of the local doctors would offer her a job in their offices. Their wives wouldn't let them work with a scarlet woman. She could move, but that was the house where Tonya grew up.

Michelle detested her job anyway. She loathed her profession and everybody associated with it and dreaded getting up every morning. A thought that she had entertained a time or two before resurfaced. No one loved her. Nobody cared about her. No one would even miss her if she was gone, not even her own daughter.

If she did it, it would have to look like an accident. No alcohol or pharmaceuticals would be in her system to be blamed.

A phone call from Michelle's mother rattled her cage. Pa Bell was in the hospital for the first time in his eighty-nine years. He was asking for both Michelle and Tonya.

The drive was pure torture. Not only was the woman fearful of what she might find when she arrived, but she was also tormented about how to cover for not even knowing where her daughter was.

Much to her relief, the old man was sitting up in his hospital bed sporting with the nurses. After a horrible bout with the flu, he had contracted pneumonia. The antibiotics were working, and he was about to go home.

He addressed his granddaughter, apologetically. "I'm sorry you had to come all the way here for nothing, but it's sure good to see you." He added with the familiar sparkle returning to his eyes. "I haven't seen you in a coon's age, but now I know what it takes to get you here."

"It was worth the drive just to see you feeling so much better. Mother was really concerned about you when she called."

"As for my little Peanut, I sure hope you've headed her off. She came by to see me a while ago. She'll be back when she gets a chance."

Michelle breathed another big sigh of relief.

Pa Bell went on. "Do you have any idea what a wonderful daughter you have? She might be about grown, but she still comes and sits in my lap. Do you know what that means to this old codger?"

The giant of a man smiled and laid his white head back on the pillow.

On the way back through Ephesus, Michelle decided to stop by the hospital and check on job prospects. With a continuous pool of graduates from the university's nursing school, it might well be fully staffed. The director remembered her from when she was in the program.

Michelle was informed that they probably could find a spot for her, especially with her experience, but that it might take a few weeks. If she was looking for an immediate opening, a crusty old physician was having trouble keeping a staff nurse. He had made it plain that he was not interested in any hippie under forty.

"Nurse Bell . . . You just might be the one to keep that old fart in line. Would you like for me to give him a call and see if he wants to meet with you?"

Michelle agreed, and so did Dr. Baskin.

"I don't care if you chew, dip, smoke, drink, or cuss." He began the interview. "In fact, cussing might be a stipulation. I don't care who you sleep with so long as you don't do it on my examining table. I don't want a nurse who misses work to mollycoddle her snotty-nosed kids. Are your urchins raised, or do you still have brats at home?"

Michelle assured Dr. Baskin that was not a problem.

He moved on to the most important qualification. "Can you follow orders? I might not know everything, but by God, I'm the doctor."

"If you want to run my references, I don't think you'll find any mention of insubordination."

"Good . . . How much will I have to pay you?"

Michelle thought to herself. "Every damn penny I can extort from you, you old cheapskate."

Then, she modified it a bit. "There's no way that you can pay me what I'm worth, but I'll settle for 10 percent more than I make now."

She could play that old geezer's game. By God, it might be fun. She did not worry about Dr. Baskin nosing around in her past, either. He operated from his gut.

Michelle had left the Villa Bell with the world on her shoulders. She returned home with a new lease on life. Her next order of business was getting a lease on an apartment. She was weary of grass to cut and leaves to rake, especially since Tonya was no longer around to help. She just wanted a place where she could crash and not have to worry about upkeep.

Other matters needed tending first. When she went to Mr. Griffin's office to submit her resignation, she was hoping that he might release her immediately. Instead, he asked if she would stay on until he could find a replacement. They settled on the customary two weeks. Dr. Baskin would have to make do with his rent-a-nurse a little while longer. Michelle did not get any kind of going away recognition.

She went to the same agency that helped her purchase the house on Lane Lane. The realtor told her that it would be easier to market if it were lived in. Since Michelle could not afford both a house payment and rent, she would have to commute until the house sold.

The forty-five-minute drive in each direction was manageable for the time being. On the plus side, it was a beautiful ride. If snow became a problem, she could always get a room in town for a night or two.

The homeowner was beginning to think that her house was never going to sell. After two months on the market, an engaged couple showed interest in it as a starter home. She had to concede that it was not the Taj Mahal, but "starter home" sounded a tad condescending. She dropped the price twice and ended up agreeing to take only a little more than what she had originally paid.

The next day, she signed a lease for an apartment on the south side of Ephesus. Michelle had stopped worrying about having a new address and phone number. Tonya could always get in touch with her relatives in Bellville. The woman knew that she should pay down her credit cards, and put the rest of the modest equity from the sale of her house in savings. Instead, she bought a new VW.

The Englishwoman

Mr. Ellis had a suggestion for a feature article. "Tonya . . . There's someone I want you to visit. I'm not sure if she'll open up to you or not, but I think she has a hell of a story to tell if you can get it out of her."

After dinner that evening, Tonya asked Mrs. Weston to tell her about Margaret Stratton. The landlady shared what she knew.

"She was a war bride. Her late husband met her in England, and he brought her home with him after the Second World War. He died a couple of years ago. So far as I know, they had a good life. They never had children . . . Perhaps, because of his war injuries. Why do you ask?"

"Mr. Ellis wants me to interview her. He seems to think there's more to her story than what's on the surface."

"Tonya . . . There always is."

Miss Willa Bell called Mrs. Stratton and asked if they could meet for tea. She told her she had heard so much about her that she wanted to meet her.

"Aren't you the girl who writes for the paper? I know that I am an anomaly around here, but I really do not want to be treated like some exotic animal."

"Okay . . . Off the record . . . Can we just chat?"

"Only if you promise that nothing will appear in print without my permission."

"So promised."

"In that case, I would like to invite you to come to my home. Maybe I can make a Brit out of you with afternoon tea and a biscuit."

"Oh, I've been to Great Britain. And I would love to have tea with you. Do you have any Lady Grey?"

The white frame house sat a couple hundred yards off the road. The driveway crossed a small tree-lined creek and the meadows were lush. Tonya knew immediately why the couple had settled there. She could close her eyes, and except for some missing rock walls, imagine that she was in the English countryside.

Tonya clarified her name situation and asked her hostess to call her by her first name. The woman tendered in kind. "Please call me Margaret."

The newspaper correspondent felt at ease, immediately. "I know this is improper. But I just love your British accent. I know. I know. The rest of us English-speaking folks are the ones with our dialects."

The hostess also felt comfortable with her guest. "When I go back home, my few remaining friends and family tell me that I speak more like an American. I appreciate that you don't make fun of the way I talk. I have certainly had to deal with that some during the forty years I have been here."

Margaret then proceeded as though she were the person conducting the interview. "Tell me about yourself. I can't tell where you are from, but it is not from around here."

"There's not much to tell. I began my life in a Washington on the other coast, and now I live in the one on this side of the country. In between, I grew up in the North Carolina Mountains. But I'm not here to talk about me. I want to learn all about you."

"All in good time." "All in good time."

Tonya sensed something about the woman that went beyond ethnicity. She felt an affinity, a connection of some kind, but she was not sure what it was.

"Would you like for me to show you around my house?" Margaret asked. "I have a few pieces that you might appreciate since you have been to the mother country."

"That would be lovely."

The nights were still cool, but the days were getting warmer. Mrs. Stratton suggested that they try the front porch facing the afternoon sun for their tea time. "I see you wore a sweater."

Seated in white rocking chairs with a little table between them, Tonya commented on the peacefulness. After the teacups were almost empty,

Margaret turned to her.

"You said the purpose of the visit was so that you could get to know me. I'll go along with that for now. But I sense that it might be more like the other way around. Tonya. I believe you have been guided to my doorsteps because there is something you want to share with me that you've never told another living soul."

"What do you mean?" Tonya asked sheepishly.

"I think you know exactly what I mean."

Tonya was cautious before the conversation went any further. "Are you a clairvoyant?"

"Let's not worry about labels. Let's just say that you and I have been privy to things outside the realm of other people's perceptions. I felt it when you walked through the door."

Tonya had to take a step back. She had presumed that she would never have anyone to share her experiences with. The opportunity before her was thrilling, but it was also a little unsettling. Was Mrs. Stratton genuine, or might she be coming from a dark side?

Margaret sensed her hesitation. "Okay. Let me go first."

"Tonya . . . Something happened to me when I was a child that I could not talk about for years. I couldn't even tell my parents. I was certain that nobody would believe me. Even though I still do not have the adequate words to describe it, never once, in all the years since, have I doubted what I experienced."

Tonya was spellbound.

Mrs. Stratton spoke with a blending of humility and tranquility. "I left my body, and I saw the other side."

"Wow! What was that like?"

"I was deathly ill with a high fever. My parents said I was delusional, and the village doctor did not know what to do. Don't forget. That was the late 1920s, and medicine has come a long way since then. I remember floating above my bed and looking down at those below. I could hear their panicky voices. My mother was wailing and said I was dead. I knew I was not dead, but I had no way of telling her."

The woman took the last sip of tea in her cup and then continued. "Then, I saw a glorious, magnificent, pure light. I was drawn toward it. I had crossed into eternity. I cannot begin to tell you how peaceful and serene it was. This could not be death because I was alive more than ever."

"What happened next? Why did you come back? How did you come back?"

"To this day, I still do not have the answers to those questions. At some point, I regained consciousness back in my body. Mother screamed and then fainted. I thought I had killed her."

"Wow!" Tonya said again.

"As I mentioned earlier, I could not tell anybody about this. I feared that I might be ridiculed in the same manner as if I claimed that I had been kidnaped by space aliens."

"Who was the first person you told?"

"My Anglican priest kept pressuring me when I was a teen. He said he believed that I needed to confess something. I thought he was prying for details of promiscuity, and I kept putting him off."

Margaret paused with a little glint in her eyes. "He might have been right about that, but it was none of his business. When he persisted, my near death experience was the only other thing I could think of that he might be talking about. Just as soon as I started talking about it, I wished I hadn't."

"Why? What was his reaction?"

"When I tried to explain it to him, he said I had unresolved issues with my mother and suggested that I see a psychiatrist. I learned that even the church is afraid of things that do not fit into its neat little doctrines."

Margaret looked over at Tonya's teacup and then continued. "After that, like you, I did not think anybody could, or would, understand. Then, I met my husband. When he was wounded and left for dead, he, too, saw the other side. When we shared our stories, we sat and held each other for hours."

Without saying another word, Margaret got up and took the pot to the kitchen to add more tea. When she returned, she refilled the cups.

"Okay, Miss Willa Bell . . . Have I established my credentials? Do you trust me now?"

Tonya was not alone.

Beginning with her college roommate's suicide, she detailed each development leading up to the Mrs. Hattie encounter. It was so freeing to actually say the words aloud in the presence of another human being who believed her unreservedly.

As Tonya was about to leave, Margaret put in a request. "I want to see that drawing and the photograph of the old house. Will you bring them next time?"

"Next time." There will be a next time.

The potlatch

"Do you believe in ghosts?" Tonya asked Rick.

"I'm not sure what you mean by that. Are you talking about haunted houses and that sort of thing?"

"That too. But I'm mainly referring to the spirits of dead people. Do you think they ever come back where we recognize them?"

Rick had never told Tonya much about his background. "Did you know that my grandmother is Native American?"

"No. You never mentioned it, but I've wondered. You have a connection with the living world that's different from anybody I've ever been around. Is she still alive? Could I meet her?"

"She's an old woman now, but still very much alive. I would love for you to meet her. Going to her house was always special when I was growing up. She saw no distinct separation between the physical world and the spiritual, as westerners do. I guess I carry a little of that in my genes, and maybe some of her ways rubbed off on me, too."

Rick's demeanor changed as he faced Tonya. "Do you have any Indian blood in you? You're a little like that yourself. That's the main reason I think I'm drawn to you."

"Well . . . That certainly explains a lot." She said with a twinkle in her eyes. "I'd already decided it wasn't my body."

Rick blushed. "Oh, Tonya. That's another thing I love about you. You keep me on my toes. I didn't mean that I don't find you attractive. You turn me on like no other girl ever has. But you see. It's not just a physical attraction. I see you as the embodiment of both the physical and the spiritual. I cannot separate the two. I pray that I never do anything that might be disrespectful of either."

"Oh, Rick. That's one of the nicest things that anyone has ever said to me." She reached for him, and they shared a passionate embrace. It was followed by their first kiss that was not just lips briefly brushing each other.

Tonya had deftly sidestepped her heritage situation. The fact was that she had no idea where half of her blood came from. Regardless from whence, she had sprung, all of her was turned on to him.

Tonya reported back to Mr. Ellis that Mrs. Stratton did not wish to be interviewed again as a war bride. The reporter thanked him, nonetheless, for mentioning the woman to her. She added that there might be another story, but she was not sure about that yet.

She then asked her editor about the Native American influence in the area. He said that except for some adopted nomenclature, nothing much else had been retained. She sensed that he was not very sympathetic to their plight. He did not seem overly enthused when he mentioned that the country had given them some federal land, and that they were more or less self-governing when on it. "They drink and gamble a lot."

Tonya took Rick up on his offer to go with him to visit his Grandmother Crow. On the way, she asked him to explain totems to her. He suggested that they wait and let his grandmother have that honor. The old Indian woman and her grandson's girl felt immediately at ease with one another as she explained that important aspect of her culture.

Tonya found in Mrs. Crow a gentle spirit. She was a descendant of one of the Chinook Tribes. On the one hand, the woman was Americanized. Except for a few relics, her home did not look that much different from others in the region. On the other, she had certainly not forsaken her heritage.

Mrs. Crow invited both of them to come back on May 11 for a potlatch. Tonya did not want to show her ignorance so she waited for Rick to tutor her once they were back on the road. He said that the word means roughly, "my good friend."

Rick then shared his impressions of a potlatch. "It refers to the gathering of a tribe to celebrate a significant event like a wedding, the naming of a baby, a family moving away, or the death of a tribesman. If I remember correctly, some potlatches are gatherings just to hallow the seasons."

Tonya acknowledged her excitement about being invited to one.

Rick continued describing this part of his culture. "It's customary to share resources with the family to assist them during these transitional times. We have showers and benefits that are similar."

He also mentioned that the celebration incorporates festivities of song and dance where the rituals and traditions of the tribe are reenacted and renewed. He said he had only been a couple of times, and he was thrilled that Tonya was going with him.

On the way to the potlatch, Mrs. Crow promised some great food. "I hear the elders are doing a salmon bake." The old Indian squaw delivered on that prediction. Rick stayed by Tonya's side as her interpreter and guide. When she had questions that he could not answer, he sought out his grandmother.

Tonya said to Rick on the way back. "I'm so fortunate. I not only get to enjoy myself so much when I am out and about with you, but I also get paid to write about it."

"Now, wait a minute. I do hope you know that some stuff we do is off the record."

"Oh, Rick. You're so cute."

When he gave her a passionate goodnight kiss, she reassured him. "Don't worry. You'll not read about this in the paper." Tonya did not mention that it was her twentieth birthday.

When Mrs. Stratton invited Tonya for Sunday brunch, she reminded her not to forget to bring the pictures. "I think it will be warm enough for us to eat outside."

Spring had sprung and the days were getting longer. It was only a month until the summer solstice. Tonya was still getting used to an hour of more darkness in winter, and then an hour of more daylight in summer than back in Carolina.

Two topics were on the discussion agenda. Tonya was not sure which one she wanted to address first. She had to tell Margaret about the potlatch, and she wanted to talk more about Mrs. Hattie.

As Tonya was finding a place for her purse, Mrs. Stratton said she hoped that she liked what Americans call a continental breakfast. "Of course, I do. Let me help you bring everything out. I'm a little famished."

Margaret made an inquiry while they were eating. "Tell me about this guy, Rick. You have mentioned him a couple of times. Is he the forester that you wrote the article about?"

"Yes, he is. Since then, we have become very good friends. One thing I wanted to talk to you about is his Native American roots and the potlatch he took me to."

After Tonya described the experience, Margaret shared an observation. "Isn't it amazing how indigenous people all over the world have their own similar rituals? While the festivals may vary in how they're carried out, they are all expressions of cultural identity, unity, and spirituality."

Tonya shared another observation. "Another thing they often have in common is ridicule by those who do not understand their customs. And sometimes even fear."

"You are so right. Most of the merciless things that people have done to their fellow human beings throughout history involve desecrating what others hold sacred and trying to annihilate those who are different."

"Why can't individuals just be who they are and accept others for whom they are?" Tonya asked pensively.

"You have just asked the $64 question, although I doubt you know what that means."

"I've heard my Pa Bell say that. I presume it means a question with no simple answer."

"Right you are, again. It has always mystified me how religion after religion preaches peace and charitableness. Yet, fanatics always seem to hijack the faith and then go about ethnically cleansing those who do not see eye to eye with them."

After they put the leftovers in the refrigerator and reconvened at the garden patio for tea, Margaret reminded Tonya that she did not really say much about Rick. "Are you getting serious?"

"Now, you've asked the $64,000 question. I really like him, and I think he likes me, but neither of us has had much experience with the opposite sex. We're just feeling each other out as we go along."

Margaret laughed. "Thanks for the visual. And you thought Brits didn't have a sense of humor. Now let me see the pictures you brought."

Holding out the photo of the old house so she could see it without her reading glasses, the Englishwoman was in awe. "Oh, Tonya. This is beyond amazing. Now, show me the sketch you did of the woman."

After Margaret perused it, Tonya opened her wallet and showed her a picture of Granny Addie.

"I'm speechless."

Tonya looked to the woman for some direction. "What really happened?"

"Why is that so important? Tonya . . . Humans are beset with this notion that they have to understand everything. We presume that if we cannot see or understand something, it does not exist. We only have to look all around us to see how ridiculous that is. Animals in their kingdoms grasp things that are way beyond our perceptions. We do not have to know everything."

Margaret then redirected the conversation. "Let me ask you something. Have you always felt that you understood people better than they understood you?"

"It's always been that way. I could see right through my mother, but she never had a clue who I was." That got Tonya to thinking. "I could get her to do things and make her think it was her own idea."

"I suspect she's not the only one."

Tonya grinned and the woman went on.

"Tonya . . . You have a powerful gift and you must use it wisely. Mrs. Hattie talked to you about inner-connectedness. You have strong intuitions and you must follow them. This also allows you to dabble with inter-connectedness. You have the rare ability to peer into the souls of others and see what they do not even see themselves."

Margaret gave Tonya a moment to let that sink in. "Let me ask you something else. How many people have actually known you?"

She did not even have to stop and think. "I thought my best friend, Sammie, did, but the older we got, the more I realized that she could see only through her own eyes. I was elated when I thought Rick was getting to know me, but there seems to be some kind of hurdle that he's having trouble getting over. My daycare owner who became my mentor knew me pretty well. The two other people who got a glimpse were Pa Bell, and of course, Granny Addie. That's about it."

"It's persistently going to be that way. Life is not easy for those who know but are not always known. It really gets thorny when people think they know you, but they don't. Often, they even try to turn you into the person that they need you to be."

"As an immigrant, I'll bet you've faced that a lot."

"All the time. Tonya . . . We are all immigrants, but many people just do not understand that."

Holding patterns

While no one else celebrated with Tonya, she did not overlook the significance of her birthday. She was no longer a teenager. The date stamped on the 1989 calendar validated how she had felt for some time. As she began her third decade, there was nowhere else she wanted to be at the moment, but she also knew that Bashville would never be her home.

Rick feared that he was falling in love. He had steered clear of females while getting his education. He always knew that it would take a special kind of woman to survive in the isolation of the wilderness within which he thrived.

Seemingly out of nowhere, Tonya waltzed into his life. Ranger Rick knew there was something special about the young woman on the day that he helped her evacuate. He wanted so much to ask if he could contact her later, but in the haste to make sure that she was safe, he let the opportunity slip away.

Amazingly, Tonya reconnected with him. He tussled the day of the interview not to act like a teenager with a big crush. When she asked him to autograph his calendar photo, his hand was shaking, and he struggled not to mess up his signature.

There had not been one moment when they were together that he had felt uncomfortable. They had slept in the same room at the ski lodge and had even shared a tent without any unnerving awkwardness.

She was always just herself. The girl was neither trying to impress him, nor making demands of him. He had never known anyone like that.

Tonya was intriguingly mysterious. He still knew so little about her past, and she acted as though it did not matter. About all that she would say about herself, she framed in a way that he had never considered. "What you see is what you get." Ranger Rick liked what he saw.

One thing was beginning to really trouble him. The application for his dream job might be approved at any time. That would undoubtedly involve him relocating, perhaps a considerable distance away. Could he leave Tonya? Would she go with him? That seemed unlikely since they had never even been intimate. Would he wake up one morning and find out that she had moved on without him?

For now, Rick was just in a holding pattern. He was not the only one.

Since her husband's death, the most dismaying aspect of Margaret's golden years was that she had no one to confide in. A couple of old geezers tried to court her, but another cozy relationship was not her cup of tea.

When she accepted invitations to socialize with other matronly women, she found herself looking for ways to escape gracefully. Mrs. Stratton was just not that interested in a fare consisting of juicy gossip commingled with a plethora of complaints and ailments. The Englishwoman had lost much of her stiff upper lip, but she never felt comfortable with how much American women revealed about themselves.

Tonya blew in like a breath of fresh air. Margaret had to put herself on guard. The young woman had wandered into town on the way to God only knows where, and her pilgrimage was far from over. It was an effort, but the woman determined not to let her own neediness stand in Tonya's way.

Editor Ellis still had a hard time believing what good fortune had befallen him. His little weekly was just about a goner. The tired old printing press moaned and groaned in syncopation with his aging body.

Without officially advertising it, he had put out feelers a couple of years earlier to see if a larger conglomerate might gobble up his paper. The only ones that showed any interest wanted him to give it to them. He was certain that no individual in his right mind would buy the *Clarion*. The only reason he had not closed the doors was that he had nothing else to do.

A bright and cheery young woman strolled into his office one day. She acted as if she hadn't a care in the world. If he had an opening, she might consider it. If not, she was just passing through.

Miss Bizzy Belle

Tonya continued to puzzle him. He had been around business people, civic leaders, politicians, religious individuals, educators, and just ordinary folks all of his life. As a newspaper man, Mr. Ellis had a gift for sizing people up. Not so with Miss Willa Bell. A year later, she was just as enigmatic as ever.

There was no denying one thing, though. She had helped turn around his little rag. The newspaper man actually looked forward to coming to work again. It seemed that even the worn out old press was humming with some renewed vigor.

Editor Ellis did not know how much longer his string of luck would hold. Tonya never mentioned where she might have been headed when she just showed up. The only clue to her whereabouts was the North Carolina plates on her car. The observant man noticed that they were quickly replaced, indicating that she had no intention of returning anytime soon. He wondered if he would open the office one day and find a note on his desk saying that something else was calling her, and that she had gone to chase it down.

Tonya's birthday and another Mother's Day had come and gone with no word. Michelle no longer felt deserving of being honored anyway. She never wanted a baby, to begin with. More significantly, she had never forgiven herself for actually making the decision to "take care of it." Nothing would ever change the fact that what stopped her was how far along she was.

Michelle had a new life now. As far as she knew, her daughter had no idea where she worked or that she had moved. What the accidental mother enjoyed most about her empty nest was that no one was in her face trying to show her up, or needling her about the way she lived her life.

She also had privacy. Her "friend" from back in Knoxo Springs had patients to see in Ephesus. Sometimes, he stopped by and played doctor with her.

The nurse was enjoying apartment living, and she loved her sassy yellow Volkswagen Beetle. It got her noticed even if the usual comment had to do with the highway department having a paint sale.

Michelle also went about the smug satisfaction that she did not resign as a mother. Her daughter fired her.

Spending parts of the year in each residence, Walt Williamson made annual trips back and forth between Ephesus, North Carolina and Kenai,

Alaska. One day when he was having lunch with his chaplain friend, Eli, he heard a Nurse Bell being paged. He thought about Michelle. He wondered where she was, and how she was doing.

Walt still occasionally thought about the child that might have been, never doubting for a moment that she would have been a girl. He had sensed his daughter's spirit several times. For some inexplicable reason, he felt it the strongest during stops at Ferndale along No Bidness Creek.

Strangely, he did not detect anything about his baby's presence the time he was back in D.C. Now, something mystified him. Walt felt a vibration once when he was in Seattle visiting with Ginny's parents.

The man was very much aware that there were still missing parts in his life. He had no way of knowing that not one, but two pieces would soon fall into place.

Dancing close to the edge

"Rick, the phone's for you." The ranger was delighted to hear Tonya's voice when he picked up the receiver in his office.

After the obligatory, "I'm fine. How are you?" she said there was a new movie just out that she wanted to go see. "Do you realize that we've never been to a movie together?"

"Sounds like fun. Can we sit on the back row and make out? What's the name of it?"

"It's 'When Harry met Sally.' We'll have to go into Seattle to see it. It won't be in local theaters anytime soon. And by the way, you still haven't taken me to that famous fish market or to the Space Needle."

They blocked off a whole Saturday for the adventure. During the hour and a half drive, Rick asked if she had any idea what the movie was about.

Tonya slid to the middle of the bench seat as she answered. "Not much. I suppose the title itself gives us some hint."

She had only been to Seattle once. Not long after settling in Bashville, she needed new clothes more appropriate for her job and was also looking for some hiking boots. Still new to the Pacific Northwest, she found the city charming and had been looking for an excuse to go back.

The middle of the summer was the prime tourist season. Rick was finally able to find parking within walking distance of the places they wanted to visit. He brought along his cooler and "caught" a couple of flying fish at the Pike Place Market. After icing them down, he promised to

Miss Bizzy Belle

grill them for Tonya.

"You mean you're going to invite me to your place?"

"Maybe . . . Or we could cook them over coals on another camping trip."

While Tonya held their spot in line at the Space Needle, Rick found a restroom to try and wash the smell of fish off his hands. One of them then held hers during the elevator ride up. He put his arm around her as they circled the observation deck.

On that clear day, Mt. Rainier was majestic with the brilliant blue sky background framing its snowcap. Other mountains were visible in the distance and parts of Puget Sound stretched out as far as the eye could see. The vantage point also provided a fantastic view of downtown Seattle. Tonya pointed out Rick's truck far below.

After the smell at the fish market, neither could stomach seafood for dinner. They settled on Chinese instead. The movie was getting rave reviews, and by the time they got to the theater, the back row was already filled.

Tonya said with a smile as they sank into seats a few rows down. "I guess you'll just have to behave yourself." Rick let his hands do a little exploring in the darkness, and she made no attempt to stop him.

It was definitely a date movie, but the couple had no idea that the flick was going to hit so close to home. They walked in silence back to the truck.

Tonya slid over next to him. "Okay, Ranger Rick? What did you think about that?"

Before turning the key, he turned to her. "Do you want to get a room and spend the night?"

"Could we still be friends? Or, would sex just get in the way?"

Rick started up the Chevy and headed back toward Bashville.

Lost and found

"You still want to go to Alaska?" Tonya just blurted out when Mrs. T answered the phone.

"Be still my heart. Girl . . . It's so good to hear from you."

After some catching up, Tonya returned to the reason for the call. "Mr. Ellis is shutting down the newspaper for a couple of weeks. I was just wondering if you wanted to catch a flight to Seattle, and then hop on the ferry with me. Just like the cruise ships do, it goes all the way to Alaska through the Inside Passage. I'm going to take Agnes along for the ride so I'll have my own wheels when I get there."

"I don't know. Tonya? Are you sure you want an old woman tagging along?"

"Come on Cornfield. You know better than that. Let me sweeten the pot. This trip is celebrating my twenty-first birthday."

"When do we set sail?"

Tonya was caught off guard when she saw how much Mrs. Thornhill had changed during the past two years. The woman was stooping and walking with a cane. Nevertheless, the reunion renewed her spirits. After collecting the luggage, the two were off for another great adventure.

When Mrs. T she saw her old Volvo, it stopped her in her tracks. "Would you look at that? I never thought I would ever get to ride in that old car again. And it's a long way from home, too."

"Mrs. T . . . I cannot thank you enough. I'm still not sure where I am, or where I'm going. But I there's no way that I could have gotten this far without you."

On the way to the port at Bellingham, Mrs. Thornhill said she presumed Tonya had already paid for everything, and that she wanted to write a check to cover her part.

"No." "No." "No." "Mrs. T. This is my treat. You've done so much for me. Now, it's my turn."

When the woman found out that Tonya was going to drive back to Washington, she went ahead and purchased a plane ticket from Anchorage to D.C. Tonya took along her camping supplies so Agnes had little room to spare once Mrs. T and her things were aboard.

The ferry was a working vessel, but not without amenities. Food was served in the galley, and a ranger was aboard to explain things as they went along. Tonya imagined how much Rick would love that job. The British Columbia coastline was beautiful, but the marvels were reserved for the last leg of the four-day journey.

After Mrs. T agreed to go with her, Tonya called and reserved a cabin on the ferry. She had planned to just sleep on deck in her bag. The accommodations were small and the bunks uncomfortable, but the two old friends did no complaining.

The ship's captain alerted the passengers when whales and other wildlife were in the area. They got a good look at several pods of humpbacks through the binoculars. Eagles were in trees near Juneau, and glaciers were visible along the rest of the way. Tonya was in a new element, and she could feel some kind of indefinable momentum building.

Mrs. Thornhill sat with her on the deck for hours at a time. If it got a little breezy, they went back inside and found a window seat. While

Miss Bizzy Belle

Tonya's eyes were panning endlessly, she was not aware of how much Mrs. T's were on her.

Agnes was raring to go when the ferry docked in Skagway. Mrs. Thornhill was in no such hurry. Tonya had planned on driving to Whitehorse to spend the night, but the other passenger was ready for a real bed. The next morning, they took the scenic train that rode the narrow gauge rails laid during the Klondike Gold Rush. That delayed them even more.

Tonya reminded Mrs. T that they had to keep moving if she was going to make her connecting flight. They had allotted only three days, which allowed very little wiggle room.

Tonya's sharp eyes did not want to miss anything. An old brown bear boar sauntered across the road near the Canadian Border. Patches of his hair were gone. It turned and looked at them as she snapped a picture through the car window. Mrs. Thornhill told her to get going before the bear crawled in the car with them.

Not far into the Yukon Territory, Tonya said that she wanted to see swans in the wild. "That has been a dream of mine since you took us to see 'Swan Lake' in Dallas." Unlike her father, when his first trip to Alaska was built around that singular objective, she did not have to wait long. They spotted a pair in the headwaters of the Yukon River before they got to Whitehorse.

The man at the outpost wanted to know if they came up the Alaska Highway or had just gotten off the ferry. When Tonya told him that it was the latter, he reminded her not to let the gas tank get low. "You have miles and miles of wilderness ahead of you."

The farther north they went, the rougher the roads were. Black bears were feeding on the wildflowers along the side of the road. "Mrs. T . . . I loved those flowers in Kew Gardens, but they had some of the best horticulturalists in the world looking after them. Just look at what these wildflowers do all by themselves."

A moose and twin calves posed for a photo not far out of Tok where they spent their second night. The scenery was breathtaking in every direction, and senses were hovering near overload. When they did not think that it could get any better, the Wrangell-St. Elias Mountains came into view.

"Mrs. T . . . This is so awesome. Why did we wait so long?"

Tonya had not counted on frequent stops for road construction, and she was concerned about getting to Anchorage for Mrs. T's flight scheduled to leave just before midnight. Trying to make light of it, she told Mrs. Thornhill that she might have to stay and ride out with her.

"This old woman is tired. You'll be glad to get me on that plane so that I'm no longer holding you back. Let me assure you of something else, too. I'm not going to sleep in that tent with bears prowling around."

"Oh, Mrs. T."

Agnes rolled into Anchorage well before dark, and but with three hours to spare before check in time. Only a few days before the summer solstice, the sun was still above the horizon. Mrs. T insisted on getting a room for Tonya. She said that was the least she could do. The woman even had enough time to stretch out and take a little nap before dinner on the way to the airport.

Of the many times that Tonya and Mrs. T had parted, that was the most difficult. They lived on opposite sides of the country and had no idea when they might see each other again. Mrs. Thornhill reached in her purse. "Here's a new phone card. Please stay in touch until you get back home."

When the woman took her seat on the plane, it hit her. Something was left unspoken. Tonya did not say what she always had before. "I'm not going to say goodbye because I will see you again." A tear started making its way down her cheek.

As Tonya exited the airport parking lot headed back to her room, she was overwhelmed with a cognizance of being lost. Curiously, that awareness was counterbalanced with an equal measure of irrefutably feeling found.

She was excited about the next few days, but not exactly sure which way to turn. Turning in for the night was about all the tired driver could deal with at the moment. As she pulled down the covers, she found an envelope under her pillow. Mrs. T had left her an especially sweet note. Folded neatly inside were five crisp one hundred dollar bills.

Tonya sighed as she laid her head on the pillow. "That woman." The next thing she was aware of was the maid knocking on the door to clean her room. The clock said it was already ten.

Before leaving Bashville, Tonya went to the bookstore and purchased a "Milepost" travel guide. After studying the map on the ferry, her plans were to explore the Kenai Peninsula for a couple of days. On the way out of Alaska, she wanted to drive past Denali, go on through Fairbanks, and then down the Alaska Highway. After crossing the border, she anticipated about four days of driving to get across Canada and back to Washington. That should get her home about the time Mr. Ellis was returning from his vacation.

What the newcomer to America's Last Frontier seriously miscalculated was how impossible it would be to hurry along. Before she

Miss Bizzy Belle

left Anchorage, she broke one of those hundred dollar bills and bought a sack full of film. Her camera was ready to capture images to paint later. Her mind was busy recording memories that did not have to be developed and that nothing could ever erase.

After a walk downtown to pick up tourist materials at the welcome center, Agnes was pointed toward the Seward Highway. It was the only road going out of town besides the one she came in on. The vehicle's first stop was at an overlook called Beluga Point. Tonya saw others pointing toward something high up on the coastal mountain. With her binoculars, she spotted the white animals. Her travel guide identified them as Dall sheep.

Resisting the pressure to keep pressing along, Tonya crossed the railroad tracks between the road and the inlet and climbed atop an outcropping. The breezes were brisk, and she had to steady herself. The young woman's emotions were every bit as woozy, but Mrs. Hattie's words were never more sure.

Sitting on the rock ledge and letting the wind blow through her long black hair, she felt an energy, a presence. She looked at her feet and saw a piece of shale shaped like a heart. Tonya had found her first Alaska treasure.

The "Milepost" did not exaggerate when it identified the highway as one of the most scenic drives in the world. When Tonya stopped for something to eat in Girdwood, it was already early in the evening. A person would only know that by looking at a clock.

Not far down the road, Agnes took a left toward Whittier. The stunning glaciers positioned in the passes of the snow-covered mountains were unbelievably mesmerizing as the sun filtered through. Icebergs were bobbing in the huge lake. Tonya had never witnessed such unspeakable magnificence and splendor. "Wow!" she kept saying.

A campground beckoned, and she set up the Manila Villa. When she tried to do a little scribbling in WOWs, words were woefully inadequate. She also remembered what Mrs. T said about bears on the prowl and was careful not to leave any food out.

One thing was very apparent by the next morning. Tonya would not see much of the peninsula in a mere two days. She had still not fully grasped that in the Land of the Midnight sun, time resisted being governed by a timepiece.

The next day, Tonya took the left fork at Tern Junction. If anything, the drive to Seward was even more amazing. After strolling about the town, she set off to discover Exit Glacier. Walking right up to and touching the mammoth river of ice generated yet another magical rush.

When she took a path alongside the glacier, she was awestruck by the bluish color of the dense ice. Spotting a park bench, she sat for a moment to catch her breath. The glacier might be the main attraction, but when she panned the area, her senses struggled to process it all. As she rose to keep walking, her eyes spied another heart-shaped rock. She now had two tangible treasures to go along with an infinite number of perceptual ones.

Where did the time go? On the drive in from the main highway, Tonya saw others camping along the river created by the melting glacier. She joined them.

Around a campfire, she missed Rick. When she gave him the Mount St. Helen's painting the night he grilled the fish, the uncertainties both were feeling put a damper on what would have otherwise been a cause for celebration. Each seemed to realize they had danced on the edge of a precipice that night in Seattle, but neither was ready to take the plunge.

Tonya had a decision to make the next day. If she had a prayer of a chance to stay on any semblance of a schedule, she needed to go straight back through Anchorage and keep on moving. Yet, she had to contend with something. The end of the other road on the Kenai Peninsula was calling her. Margaret's instructions about following her intuitions popped into her mind. What could Mr. Ellis do if she were a couple of days late? Fire her? Bashville, Washington seemed like it was on another planet.

Nearing Cooper Landing, Tonya saw a black bear fishing in one of the streams. It did not seem to mind when she stood on the bridge and snapped some pictures. She wondered if it realized how comical it was bouncing and pouncing and coming up empty. Finally, the giant paws hit pay dirt, and the happy bear scampered toward the brush. For the first time, the onlooker saw shiny coal-black twin cubs waiting for mama to bring them a feast.

Up ahead, Tonya saw a truck waiting to pull into the highway from an unpaved road and wondered where it went. Even though the tracks were wide enough for only one vehicle, it was not a driveway. She saw no mailbox, and it had a stop sign. Something nudged her.

Not far up the rough road, Tonya feared that she had made a mistake. Ruts were so deep that Agnes dragged her undercarriage. She could not turn around so she inched forward up the steep climb.

Good. A clearing was ahead. When she brought the car to a halt and engaged the parking brake, Tonya looked to her left. The emerald Kenai Lake stretched out before her with mountains cradling it for the jewel that it was. She must take some photos to paint the scene later.

Why later? The artist dug out her paints and easel and got lost in the

Miss Bizzy Belle

immeasurable moments. After securing the wet painting for travel, Tonya paused to take in the view one more time. As she turned toward Agnes, her eyes were drawn to her feet. Another heart-shaped rock was in her path. Are heart rocks found only in Alaska?

The loop road continued forward and going down was easier than coming up. After passing through Cooper Landing, she saw hordes of humans fishing in the Kenai River. They did not seem to be having as much luck as the bear did.

Signs all along pointed to hiking trails. As tempting as they were, Tonya kept heading toward Homer. The place justifiably billed itself, "The End of the Road." She stopped in Soldotna for lunch and also picked up a few supplies. Spotting a payphone just outside of Safeway, she placed a call to Mrs. T.

The woman breathed a sigh of relief. "Child . . . It's so good to hear your voice again." Mrs. T told her that the flight was almost as long as the one from London, but she survived it. She also made Tonya promise to stay in touch. "I'm so proud of you and so thrilled that you're having such a wonderful time."

"Kalifornsky Beach Road? There's got to be a story behind that crazy name." Tonya turned down it, pulled over, and took out her map. It went to the town of Kenai and then looped back to the Sterling Highway. The travel guide said that a herd of caribou lived in the Kenai area.

As she approached the mouth of the Kenai River, she took the right fork toward the city center. Some cars were pulled over up ahead so she stopped. With her binoculars, she zoomed in on five caribou grazing in the river flats on one side of the road, and a moose and calf on the other. As she turned back toward Agnes, an eagle glided right in front of her.

At the welcome center, the wanderer learned of a spot where she could access the beach, and she saw pictures of an intriguing nearby church. As she walked along the rocky shore, the marvelous volcanic Mt. Redoubt across the Cook Inlet was peeking out of low-lying clouds. Tonya was soon lost in the grandeur and strolled for almost an hour. After taking several photos, her eyes were drawn to her feet. Another little heart-shaped rock was in her path.

The Russian Orthodox Church was unlike any that she had ever beheld. It was definitely art material. As she maneuvered to get a better angle for a snapshot, her eyes went to another heart rock.

Her collection was growing. Tonya saw a picnic table nearby, and she spread the rocks out. She held each one up and recalled the spot where it was found. Something was significant about each locale, but she was not sure what it was. She decided to mount the stones in a shadowbox when she got home.

Father Nicholas, the priest at the church, was Walt Williamson's friend. He had performed Walt and Ginny's unconventional progressive wedding where various parts of the ceremony were conducted at locations miles apart. Walt occasionally revisited those sacred places.

The widower had vowed to himself to keep Ginny's old 4x4 Ford truck up and running. Henry also came in handy for getting around during Alaska winters. The truck was a little low on fuel when he took it out for a spin one late June afternoon in 1989. He always filled up at the convenience store where he and Ginny met. As he came out after settling up, he hastened his step. A light blue Volvo was waiting to get to the pump. The driver's face was buried behind by a map.

Walt thought to himself when he saw the Washington plate in the front. "Tourist . . . You don't see that many Volvos in Alaska."

Homer-sapiens

According to the guides, Homer was a hub for those with all kinds of creative energies. Tonya wanted to mingle for a couple of hours with artists, writers, musicians, and other assorted artisans. Perhaps, she could find some inspiration for her own irresolute talents.

As publicized, young people migrated to the town each summer. Many camped on the fabled Homer Spit, a four-and-a-half-mile narrow finger of rocky land jutting out into Kachemak Bay. Tonya found a spot and set up the Manila Villa. It was already late in the day and many of the shops were closing. Her intention was to leave at least by lunchtime the next day and then try to make up for some lost time.

The newcomer straightway became a beachcomber. Tonya took a grocery sack with her as she collected rocks with quirks and oddities. One of the first she picked up was marked with white streaks in the shape of a T. Her thoughts went to Mrs. T.

When she returned to the campsite, a group had gathered around a fire singing folk songs. Simultaneously, several arms beckoned her. Tonya felt

Miss Bizzy Belle

a warm sense of camaraderie commensurate with the glow from the burning embers. She did not feel at all like a stranger in a strange land.

A chill was in the air when she entered her tent. Getting out of her clothes and quickly crawling in her sleeping bag in the buff, Tonya's mind went to Rick. She looked forward to telling him all about her Alaska adventures.

The best-laid plans were far more susceptible to getting waylaid in America's Last Frontier than in most places. Tonya was about to become the latest first-timer to find that out. The laid back locals were in no hurry to get going in the mornings. Her noon departure had to be reset.

In every gift store that she entered, shopkeepers were eager to converse. One theme was recurring. A number mentioned how they came to Alaska to visit and never left. Tonya was glad that she had not packed her tent. Savoring halibut and chips, she thought of Rick again. Where did the time go? She decided to stay one more night.

Tonya drove into town the next morning to find some breakfast. Quaint was not exactly the right word to describe Homer. The residents had certainly exhibited some originality in their constructions, often with makeshift resources. Picturesque was certainly fitting. How could anyone tire of looking across the bay at the snow-laden mountains and glaciers? She acknowledged again running out of adjectives when she wrote in her journal.

Two things caught Tonya's eye on the way to the café. One was a little newspaper office. The other was a bookstore. For a fleeting moment, she imagined herself working in one of them.

Over eggs, reindeer sausage, and hash browns, the vacationer did some recalculating. If she stopped just to sleep, she might be only a couple of days late getting back to Bashville. If Mr. Ellis fired her, she would turn around and head back up the road.

Before breaking camp, Tonya wanted to go back to one of the shops featuring local art. Trying to make her rounds the day before, she had not tarried. The sign said the store opened at ten, but it was almost fifteen minutes afterward before someone came to unlock the door. The woman greeted her and remembered her. No other customers were inside, so the proprietor gave her guest a little tour, sharing information about the artists. Based on their artwork, they were all individualists for sure. The woman asked Tonya if she painted.

She started shaking her head. "When I look at these works, I realize that I'm just a dabbler."

"We do take things on consignment if you would like to bring some samples by. My guess is that you're better than you think. Many tourists want an Alaska original, too. We sell a number of paintings."

About that time, Tonya spotted a "Help Wanted" sign behind the counter. It wouldn't hurt to ask about the position.

The woman who had identified herself only as Bekka indicated that the sign was not there the day before. She said that the girl working part-time had to return home because of a family emergency.

"You interested?" She asked Tonya.

"I'm really just passing through and have a job back in Washington."

Bekka then asserted confidently. "I'll probably fill it by lunchtime. Some of the summer squatters are still looking for a way to make some pocket money."

"Let me think about it."

Tonya thought about it. In fact, she could not stop thinking about it. "No way." She kept telling herself, and she started packing to break camp. Something would not allow her to pull that first stake.

As she reentered the little gallery, Bekka was busy. When the owner finished ringing up a sale, Tonya was waiting in line. "Is the position still open?"

"I knew you'd be back. I held it for you."

The young people making up the little tent city was an interesting lot. Several had hitchhiked to Homer. A goodly number had their own wheels. Agnes was one of the few vehicles not rusting out. A few of the summer transients had no visible means of support. Some worked in the fish canning plants. Others waited tables or clerked in the shops. Tonya was now one of the latter.

As she mixed and mingled, she sensed that with their sundry agendas, these young people were just seeking to be themselves. Devoid of pretentiousness in their trappings, live and let live was the persistent mantra of these carefree kids.

Tonya was only twenty-one, but she felt older than most. She was certain that some were sampling substances that did not interest her, but nobody tried to force anything on her. At the end of the summer, they would scatter. She presumed that she would, too.

Homer's newest vagabond wondered how many of the parents knew where their offspring were. Her mother certainly didn't, and her father did not even know that she existed.

Tonya used her phone card and called Mrs. Thornhill. Mrs. T gave her the affirming reassurance that she needed. "I am so envious. I never had opportunities like that when I was young." The woman asked if there was a number where she could be reached, and Tonya gave her the one at the art gallery.

Miss Bizzy Belle

The former newspaper correspondent waited until the day she was supposed to be back to use the card again. Mr. Ellis turned to his reporter. "I told you the day that girl left that she wouldn't be back."

The next call was to Mrs. Westin. The landlady said that she would store Tonya's things, and she looked forward to seeing her when she came to retrieve them.

"Gran-T . . . The phone is for you." Brad got to it first and handed her the receiver.

Since she had closed the daycare center, her phone almost never rang. "Is it Tonya?"

"No . . . If it was Tonya, I would have hung up on her."

Overhearing this, Michelle wondered if she had made a mistake and almost put her finger on the button.

"Mrs. Thornhill . . . This is Michelle. I do not wish to trouble you, but do you know where Tonya is?"

"Yes. I know where she is."

"Have you seen her lately? Is she okay?"

"Yes."

"Is she with her father?"

"No."

"Did she talk about her father?"

"No."

"Mrs. T . . .? Will you please tell me where my daughter is?"

"Michelle . . . I told you from the beginning that I did not approve of how you were handling that situation. My first inclination is to stay out of your business. I'm not going to tell you where Tonya is. That will be up to her if she wants you to know. I will, however, give you a phone number where she can be reached. I strongly encourage you to call your daughter and to make things right with her."

Michelle was fuming when she hung up. "How dare that woman infer that I'm the one who needs to make things right? Tonya is the one who stalked out and never came back."

Mrs. Thornhill had given her a clue, nonetheless. Michelle got out her phone book and scoured the continental area code map looking for 907. Unable to find the location, she wondered if in her annoyance, that she had written it down wrong. Since the woman had told her that Tonya was not with her father, it never occurred to her to think outside the box.

Bekka came to Homer much like Tonya did, only twenty years earlier. Several of her paintings were on display. She kept an easel set up outside and was always working on something. She encouraged Tonya to do the same.

"People like to see a work in progress. Often, they preorder it, and I ship it to them when it's finished."

No one had ever looked over Tonya's shoulder, and she was a bit nervous when tourists stood around and watched. She soon got used to it and talked to them, explaining what she was doing. It was a big thrill when she sold her first painting, a portrait of a resident eagle from among the many hanging out in Homer.

As the season wore on, Bekka was curious. "Are you going to keep staying over in tent city?"

Tonya told her that she really could not afford anything else. "I guess I'll just be here for the summer, anyway." Her job was part-time so she had opportunities to get out and look around. She was paid a meager salary that was just enough to get by on, and she got to keep the money whenever she sold a painting.

The gallery was one of the larger shops on the Spit, and it had a bathroom for employees. Tonya was thankful that she no longer had to use the public facilities, except when she needed to hose herself off.

From Rick's Native American grandmother, Tonya had learned the meaning of the expression "subsistence." In her own sort of way, she was doing just that. The Manila Villa was her subsist-tent.

She had dipped heavily into her savings to pay for the ferry. Tonya still had some of the cash that Mrs. T left for her. All she wanted to do was get by until the end of the summer. She did not know what she was going to do then, but she was not about to live in the Manila Villa throughout the winter.

Living under those circumstances, was not for the squeamish, and that kind of uncertainty was not for the fainthearted. Tonya was thriving and learning how to trust her instincts. In a lengthy entry into WOWs, she tallied all of the circumstances that had brought her to that place. The last piece of that puzzle was following her intuition to go back to the art gallery the day she was planning to leave.

The young woman kept pinching herself. "I'm really holing up in this incredible place." The blossoming "painter" was eventually able to meet most of the other artists. She was invited to some of their shindigs and enjoyed hobnobbing with them. Homer also had a lively community theater, and she volunteered to take up tickets for its summer production.

The bequest

"Phone call for you." Tonya was out front putting the finishing touches on her latest painting—sailboats in Kachemak Bay with the mountains in the background—when Bekka called out to her.

"Who could that be?"

The man on the line identified himself as Mrs. Thornhill's attorney. Tonya braced herself. He said that he regretted having to tell her that his client had passed away in her sleep.

Tonya let out a yelp.

He paused to let her gather herself and then went on. "Per her instructions, I've already booked a flight for you from Homer to D.C. The first leg of your journey begins this evening at nine. You can pick up your tickets at the counter. Brad will meet you at the airport in the morning when you arrive. Miss Bell. I look forward to meeting you, although I wish it were under different circumstances. Mrs. Thornhill has said so many wonderful things about you."

Tonya could not remember how the call ended. Not knowing how long she might be gone, she decided to pack all her things in the Volvo. Bekka said that it would be safe in the little airport's parking lot.

At another time and under different circumstances, Tonya would have delighted in the thirty-five-minute commuter flight over the Kenai Peninsula to Anchorage. She would have then been in awe of the scenery below as the much bigger bird winged its way over fjords and ice fields toward the panhandle. She might have gotten some good sleep during the overnight flight to the city of her birth. But not this time.

Brad told her that he had visited Gran-T a month earlier, and that she was never happier in her life than after returning home from Alaska. He said she had told him that was the last of her unfilled dreams, and that you made it possible. "Tonya . . . She died in peace."

On the way to Mrs. T's house, Brad filled her in. "I know you haven't had much rest, but we have a meeting this afternoon at the mortuary. Gran-T had her arrangements made, but they want to go over everything with us. You know where your bedroom is if you want to try to take a nap."

The kindly old funeral director extended his hand and ushered them into his office. "I feel like I already know both of you. Mrs. Thornhill outlived the rest of her folks, so you are the only family she had."

He handed each a folded obituary note. "The funeral will be at her church. The minister will be in charge."

Tonya and Brad said in unison. "I'd like to say a few words."

The mortician said he saw no reason why that would be a problem. "I

323

think Mrs. Thornhill would be honored."

"You first." They both said at the same time pointing toward each other.

Brad yielded. "Ladies first."

"No. Age before beauty." Tonya prevailed.

Mrs. Thornhill was somewhere smiling.

"Has the blanket for the casket been ordered yet?" Tonya asked.

"No. That's the family's responsibility."

"I would like to take care of that. If you have no objection . . . Sir."

When they got back to the house, Tonya took Mrs. T's car and went to a florist. She then had some shopping to do. Looking for something suitable to wear to the memorial service, she recalled the many times that Mrs. T had bought clothes for her.

As a steady stream of mourners passed by to pay their respects that evening, many looked at the card pinned to the casket arrangement. It read. "To Cornfield, from Miss Bizzy Belle." Tonya had presented her loving grandmother figure with a bed of long-stemmed red roses.

Brad stood straight and he stood tall in his U.S. Air Force Second Lieutenant's uniform. The words he spoke over the casket would have made both Grand-T and his father very proud.

Tonya braced herself because she was up next. She had scribbled some notes but put them aside. After her impromptu tribute, she turned to take her seat. Tears were running down Brad's face. He rose from his chair and reached for her.

The minister stood and addressed the mourners. "What those two just embraced is emblematic of everything that Mrs. Thornhill strived to exemplify during her allotted time on this earth. There's not much I can say to improve on that."

At the conclusion of the service, the decedent's attorney introduced himself to Tonya. He and Brad had already met. He asked them to come to his office the next day. Neither had any inkling of what to expect.

First off, the lawyer told Tonya that he had only purchased a one-way ticket because he was not sure how long she might be staying. He then assured her that provisions were already made for her return flight.

Next, he informed Brad and Tonya that they were the heirs of Mrs. Thornhill's estate, to share and to share alike. Then he added. "I guess she didn't like lawyers much because she left very little for us to do."

"Miss Bell. She put your name on all of her liquid assets except her checking account."

Miss Bizzy Belle

"Mr. Thornhill. As you already know, she added your signature to that when you were here last. I also told you that your grandmother had a little insurance policy that should take care of her funeral expenses with you named as the beneficiary."

"Miss Bell. The accounts are already in your name with full rights of survivorship. After the various instruments receive death certificate verification, your signature, and your social security number, Mrs. Thornhill's name will be removed. The funds are yours without stipulation."

"Mr. Thornhill. Your grandmother added your name to the deed to her house and the title of her car. She knew that the value of the real property was greater than what Miss Bell has already received. She has left you to dispose of her house and all personal belongings, and then to settle with Miss Bell for half of the proceeds that exceed the bequest already signed over to her. None of that is subject to probate. Our firm will be honored to assist you if you need us. Are there any questions?"

Neither knew what to say.

The attorney then handed a copy of Mrs. Thornhill's financial holdings to each. "In the interest of full disclosure, Mr. Thornhill, you need to know the portion of the estate that is already Miss Bell's."

Tonya took her copy but could not bring herself to look at it.

The lawyer went on. "As you can see, Miss Bell has already inherited just less than $125,000. The house has been appraised at around $200,000. Mr. Thornhill. Once you convey title to the new owner, your grandmother has entrusted you with making a final settlement with Miss Bell. As I have already mentioned, you will not have to make a report to anyone. Do both of you understand?"

They both nodded.

On the way back to the house, neither spoke at first. Tonya eventually broke the silence. "I had no idea she had that much money in savings. I thought she barely scraped by."

Brad looked over at her and smiled. "She did not spend much of anything unless it was on you. The only reason she bought a new car was so she could give you her old one."

"Brad . . . I certainly did not expect her to leave any of it to me. I will give it all to you if you think I had anything to do with that, or if you think you have been slighted in any way whatsoever."

"Miss Bizzy Belle . . . I went in there today fully expecting to learn that Gran-T had left everything to you. I could not be more pleased with the way she divided things. You were her favorite, though. You just walk away, but she left all the dirty work for me."

On the way to the airport, Tonya asked Brad to take her back by the cemetery. As they stood at Mrs. Thornhill's grave, she reached into her purse and took out the rock with the T naturally engraved in it. She knelt and placed it at the head of Mrs. T's grave.

"You know, Brad. I really do appreciate Mrs. T remembering me so generously. I can certainly use that money. But her bequest to me is far more valuable than those stocks and bonds."

"I know . . . Tonya . . . I know. I feel the same way."

Tonya arranged for a stopover in Seattle on the way back to Alaska. She rented a car and went to Bashville. Mr. Ellis was chomping on his cigar and at the bit to hear about her exploits. He told her that her old job was still open if she wanted it back, but he already knew what her answer would be.

True to her word, Mrs. Westin had stored Tonya's belongings. She filled her empty suitcase with a few clothes that she still wanted, some old journals, a stack of paintings, and various other items small enough to be stuffed in without popping the zipper. She really missed her typewriter but decided that it was not worth the cost of freight.

Tonya was especially grateful that her landlady had taken down the items hanging on the wall. The calendar still on January, the sketch of Rick, and the picture of Mrs. Hattie's house went in her carry-on.

She then retrieved one other important item. Tonya went through her secret file and decided nothing was worth keeping except for one little scrap of paper. She took the note on which she had scribbled the name Wyatt Williamson and a phone number when she was a child and folded it neatly. She then placed it in her wallet behind her driver's license.

Tonya thanked Mrs. Westin and told her that she really enjoyed staying with her. She also mentioned how she missed the kindly old woman's cooking. They sealed their friendship with a hug, and Tonya bid adieu to the A.C. She said nothing about where she had just been.

Tonya tried to call Rick but found out that he had been transferred. The ranger who answered the phone said it was his first day on the job, and that he was not sure where his predecessor had been reassigned.

She had one more stop to make. Mrs. Stratton was surprised when Tonya was standing at her door. The visit was brief because of the connecting flight. She gave her trusted friend the abridged version of what had happened since she left and invited the woman to come visit her.

"Does that mean you are going to settle there?"

Tonya responded with a confident smile. "I am until something else calls me."

Only as she buckled up for the flight to Anchorage did her emotions begin catching up with her. Tonya's heart was heavy, but she felt a greater sadness for those who never have a Cornfield in their lives. Once the aircraft was at a cruising altitude, she started entertaining some thoughts about what she might do next. She could take her inheritance and use it to go back to college. She might buy a modest little shack and call it home. Tonya closed her eyes. All she could imagine at the moment was getting her feet back on the ground, crawling in her sleeping bag, and curling up inside the Manila Villa.

The eagle has landed

Homer really was at the end of the road. The only way to go farther north, south, or west was by boat or plane. Nevertheless, the residents displayed no consciousness of feeling hemmed in. The community was vibrant, swarming with tourists during the summer, and a great place to interact with like-minded creative types the rest of the year. Paradoxically, many who came to that dead end discovered a new beginning.

Mrs. T had put her investments in interest and dividend bearing securities. The proceeds went into a money market account to supplement her income. Almost $10,000 had accumulated. Tonya made no changes, and she mentioned her inheritance to no one.

Bekka called out to Tonya as she came through the door to hang a painting to dry. "Package for you." She approached it curiously and then let out a sigh of relief when she saw Mrs. T's return address. In the note, Brad said he thought that she might want what he had discovered. In the box, were several albums with photos of her from the time she was a baby. Prints from each of their trips were also preserved. Tonya went to the bathroom to blow her nose and give her eyelids a chance to return to their natural color. Her shift was almost over, and she was already looking forward to turning the pages.

Brad also mentioned that the real estate agent had a good lead on selling the house. It was in a very desirable location for development and might bring a premium.

Soon after getting back, she started looking around for a place to live.

The summer was coming to an end. One by one, she said goodbye to her camping neighbors as they dispersed.

With the mass exodus of the summer crowd, finding an apartment was the easy part. Tonya sent Brad a note thanking him for the parcel and informing him of her new mailing address.

Cruising yard sales, she soon furnished her new space and picked up a typewriter for next to nothing. She did not want her apartment to look like an art gallery, but about the only things she had to put on the walls, were some of her paintings and drawings. The shadowbox with the heart rocks provided a nice touch.

Finding a way to supplement her income was Tonya's next concern. She dropped by the newspaper office, but they did not need any help. When the editor learned of Tonya's experience, he encouraged her to submit guest articles but said that he could not pay her for them.

The news was about the same when she popped in the bookstore. The owner said that she did not need any additional help until the Christmas season.

From Bekka, Tonya learned that the winter weather in Homer was mild according to Alaska standards. They could expect some snow, but the coastal area rarely got colder than the low teens. The artist friend also reminded her helper that she would soon close the gallery for the season.

Looking across some rooftops from her second floor apartment, Tonya could see the mountains across the bay. She started calling her new residence The Nest. The eagle had landed. The butterfly was still fluttering.

Walt Williamson was soon on his way back to Ephesus. During winters, he helped staff the counseling office with his partner, Lynda.

The little town of Homer had a special place in his heart, and he wanted to visit it again before he left. It was at the end of that road that he came to a major turning point in his life. On his first journey to Alaska, while on a quest to see swans in the wild, he decided to drive on to Homer after finally realizing his dream.

Struggling with the letdown that the search was over, and with only one way to get back home, he wondered if he had reached some midpoint in his life where everything was then downhill. The next day, he met the love of his life. He and Ginny spent their first Christmas in Homer.

Walt faced a steady stream of traffic as tourists and transients were scattering. He could always count on getting some good halibut in Homer. When he went out on the Spit, he parked beside a baby blue Volvo.

"Hmm." He mused. "That looks like the same vehicle I saw at the

Miss Bizzy Belle

pump in Kenai, and it now has Alaska plates. Another one of those who came and got captured. The Cheechako has to be a female with a car that color." Cheechako was slang for a newcomer to Alaska unfamiliar with the culture, wildlife, weather, and especially lacking in necessary winter driving skills.

Walt got lost for an hour or so ambling on the rocky beach and taking photos of eagles. Most of the shops were closed by the time he circled back. The parking space beside his vehicle was vacant.

Back in Kenai, he poured his rocks out on the back steps. He remembered picking up some flat gray stones with white streaks in them. Sorting through the pile, he came upon one engraved with the letter B. Another formed a distinct T, and a third was definitely a W. He rearranged them to form TWB.

"I'm the war baby." Hannah had suggested that for the title of his memoirs whenever he got around to writing them.

"Tonya Willa Bell . . . What would Samantha Ringer think about you right now? You've been homeless and now you're shiftless. You just spent the summer living in a tent. You've moved into a scant apartment sparsely furnished with things that you picked up at garage sales. You don't have a telephone or a TV. You don't have a job. You don't have a family. You don't have a college degree. You don't even have a boyfriend. But you know what, girlfriend? I wouldn't trade places with you for anything in the world."

After her little soliloquy, Tonya tried to imagine Sammie as a university student. "I surely do hope that she has her head on straight."

Tonya had sold a total of three paintings by the time the art gallery closed its doors to customers for the winter. Most of the other artists came by to gather up their remnants. Tonya was delighted to find out that the facility would be open two nights a week for the locals to congregate and paint together. She also learned of a creative writer's group that met once a week.

As they were painting one evening, Bekka asked Tonya if she wanted to become involved with the community theater. Her painting partner told her lightheartedly about her brief acting career.

Bekka called out to the others. "Hey, folks. We have a hidden talent in our midst. And her stage name is Miss Bizzy Belle." Tonya was soon the newest cast member for the winter production just about to begin rehearsals.

Tonya did not know what to expect the first time that she went to the writer's meeting. She already knew some of the members. One of her artist friends told her that they had cross-addictions.

The facilitator was nearing the end of a series of workshops devoted to short stories. Tonya picked up handouts from the previous sessions. Several published authors were in the group, and others were interested in getting their collections in print.

When asked to introduce herself, no one seemed impressed that she had written for a newspaper. Interest picked up, though, when she told them about the kinds of stories that she had written. She was encouraged to bring some samples to the next meeting. Since the emphasis was on creative writing, Tonya shared the "Cop-a-Feel" spoof.

After the laughter died down, Bekka put her in the spotlight. "So . . . We already knew that you were an artist. We're finding out that you can act. And now we learn that you're also a comedian. What else are you holding out on us?"

Tonya was now fully initiated into the group. The interaction was fun, but she felt woefully inadequate when she stacked her abilities alongside the works of artists with such raw talent. Then again, she remembered the words of the only art instructor she ever had. "If you like your work, then what else matters? Keep learning new things, and have fun."

Homer's newest sapien was learning new things, and she was having loads of fun.

With time on her hands, she sorted her photographs and identified a select few that she wanted to paint. It was beginning to look like she would not live long enough to do everything that she had already imagined. The apprentice artist mixed and smeared the oils as the canvas called her, and the novice journalist tickled the keys of her typewriter when she found inspiration.

Homer got its first dusting of snow just before Thanksgiving. Tonya was worried about getting around without studded tires. She soon found that she could put on her hiking boots and walk just about anywhere she needed to go.

When the Cheechako took ribbing about her old un-Alaskan Volvo, she fired back. "My Pa Bell used to say, 'Don't look a gift horse in the mouth'."

Four nights a week, Tonya hung out with her growing number of new friends. Her day often started with coffee at one of the two or three gathering places. One morning, the congenial crowd was in no hurry to disperse. She finally got to The Nest just as the postman was making his rounds.

"Is this your box? I think this is the first mail I've ever delivered to you."

Miss Bizzy Belle

Tonya saw Brad's return address on the envelope. Inside was a check for a little more than $50,000. He said that it was her remaining portion from an estate sale, the vehicle, and the sale of the house.

Tonya never doubted that Brad would be honorable, but she was surprised at the additional amount she received. With that padding her account, the wolf need not come prowling around her door anytime soon.

The new resident did not mind the winter cold at all. The humidity was so low that it felt nothing like winters back east. No snowfall even resembled a blizzard, and when it did come down, the plows cleared the roads quickly. Tonya had a little trouble adjusting to the short days and long nights and learned the meaning of sunlight deprivation.

In late March, Bekka invited Tonya to go with her to Anchorage to do some shopping. She said some supplies were just not available in Homer, and that she could save enough money on other things to pay for the trip.

On the way up the road, she turned to Tonya. "It sounds like I need to justify myself. Sometimes it's hard to get away from your raising."

With that setup, she went on. "Speaking of raising, you've never said much about yourself." Tonya gave her the skinny but it did not seem to satisfy her.

"I don't mean to pry, but are you doing okay with your finances?"

"Oh! Did I forget to mention? I'm turning tricks down at the Salty Dawg."

Tonya just loved it when she could divert somebody's attention without tipping her hand. She learned that little trick years ago dealing with her mother.

It was the first time that Tonya had been back up the highway since she had driven in. The four-and-a-half-hour trip was even more spectacular with snow covering the mountains. They saw two moose before Soldotna, and a lynx ran across the road just beyond Sterling.

Bekka had planned to get her shopping done and do a turnaround. Tonya suggested that they stay the night.

"My treat."

"Are you sure?"

"Positive."

"We didn't bring any make-up, or clothes, or anything."

"This is Alaska."

"Okay."

Tonya directed Bekka to the same motel where she spent the night on the last day that she saw Mrs. T alive.

Larry G. Johnson

By the time the art gallery reopened for the next season, Tonya had several paintings to display. The summer of 1991 seemed to fly by. She wondered why anybody would want to live anywhere else.

One disadvantage of living in Homer was that it was so remote. Alaska was immense and so much of it was still out there. Agnes was well-rested, and her driver had cabin fever even before the first snowflakes began to fly.

Tonya packed a couple changes of clothes, a cooler, the little cook stove, her boots and binoculars, the Milepost, her hiking stick, her sleeping bag, and the Manila Villa. The tourists were long gone and traffic was light. She was hoping that the bears were already in hibernation.

The first thing the explorer figured out was that she could not stop at every park and hike every trail. It was hard to discriminate from the descriptions. Not far beyond Sterling, she took a road that looped back to the highway near Cooper Landing. Now that was the wilderness. The unpaved road was a continuous Alaska grade washboard. Agnes grumbled.

Side roads led off to parks and landings on huge lakes. Trails often went along the shoreline. How could someone not love the sounds of silence punctuated only by the occasional crackling of a raven? Why would anybody object to sleeping with rain gently falling on a tent?

On one trail that went all the way to the Kenai River, Tonya saw some fresh bear scat. Not a good sign. That hike was cut short. After four days and nights of wilderness solitude, she returned to The Nest. Both driver and vehicle came back with their batteries recharged.

Christmas lights

"Tonya . . . The phone's for you." It was a couple of days before Christmas, and several artists had gathered at the gallery to gab and dab when Bekka called out to her.

She thought to herself before answering. "I wonder what this is about."

"Tonya . . . This is Brad."

"Brad? Where are you?"

"Believe it or not, I'm in Anchorage. I'm on a temporary assignment at Elmendorf Air Force Base. Want to come up and spend a couple of evenings with me?"

"Are you serious?"

"As a train wreck." Tonya wished he had not used that analogy as she strapped herself in the seat of the twin-engine propeller plane. She started to drive, but Agnes did not have studded tires.

Brad was waiting at the gate in his spiffy uniform. He waved to her and then formally greeted her. Tonya was briefly transported back to her puppy love feelings. The age difference was too much for him to be interested in her then.

Times had changed, and they had, too. Sporting with him had been so much fun, but their love-hate relationship was mostly immaterial when they were in Washington for Mrs. T's funeral.

"I've booked you a room, but since I know you're not destitute, I'll expect you to pay for it."

Here we go again.

"Let's get you checked in and then find some chow. What do you folks in Alaska eat, anyway?"

"Our meats are mostly road-kill. Moose . . . Bear . . . Caribou . . . Whatever is hauled to the markets."

"Okay . . . Enough of that. How about some Alaska salmon? Do you know any place around her where we can find some?"

"Let's go to the restaurant where I had my last meal with your grandmother."

"Sounds perfect."

The bantering back and forth just seemed to fizzle. As they feasted, Brad had an insatiable appetite for more information about Tonya's fascinating life. She invited him to Homer. He was intrigued but said that his schedule would just not allow for it.

When he took her back to her room, he walked her to the door. Tonya invited him in, but he said that he had to get back to the base and prepare for an early morning meeting. He turned and looked at her, and for a moment, Tonya thought he was going to kiss her. She was not sure what her reaction might have been.

She then walked him to his service-provided car. Brad said he would be tied up all the next day, but that he would pick her up around five. She said not to worry, that she was in walking distance of downtown, and that she knew how to entertain herself.

He drove away nodding. "I don't doubt that for one minute."

Tonya had trouble going to sleep. Unable to joust with him, she bantered with herself.

"Maybe, it's just my money. Perhaps, that's all he's interested in. He's the only person who knows I have a little. He just wants to get his grubby hands on what he thought was his, to begin with." With a smile on her face, knowing not a word of that was true, she turned over to go to sleep. "But what were his intentions? Why did he look at her the way he did?"

Tonya was excited when she woke the next morning to see that it was snowing. She had not had a white Christmas since childhood. After breakfast, she bundled up and walked toward the city center as the flakes were swirling. The tiny little stings on her face were, oh, so stimulating. The holiday lighting was perfect in the semi-darkness.

Stores were just beginning to open. The seasonal theme was apparent, but Tonya did not sense any overdoing it. She had a dilemma and was not sure what to do. When packing hastily, she picked out a painting to give Brad for Christmas. Might he consider that vanity on her part, or put him on the spot if he had not gotten her anything?

While out and about, she saw a neat little restaurant, went inside, and made a reservation. Brad arrived in civilian clothes and looked stunningly handsome. He seemed more serious but was just as courteous. Tonya liked it when he opened doors for her. Rick was not into that sort of thing.

The conversation had been mostly about her the night before. Tonya turned the tables. After briefly describing his life in the military, he turned it back again.

"Miss Bizzy Belle? How do you do it?"

"How do I do what?"

"I do know a little about your background. Did Gran-T tell you that your mom called when I was at her house not long before she died? In fact, I answered the phone. I could not help but overhear the conversation. Did you hear from your mother after that?"

"No and no."

"Gran-T gave her the number where you could be reached but did not tell her where you were. She begged your mom to reach out and make things right with you."

"I'm not holding my breath."

"I'm also aware that you have no idea who your father is. Gran-T suspected that was the reason for your falling out with your mother."

Tonya sighed and shook her head. "I never could get anything past that woman."

"Now back to my question. How do you do it? How are you so free to live your own life without worrying about what others think about you?"

"Brad . . . I just have to be me."

"Okay . . . Here's the thing. I barely remember my father. Even so, every day since he was killed, I've wanted to make him proud of me. I know it was rough on my mother, and I was a handful. I also realize that she meant well. But do you have any idea how many times she said to me when I was going out, 'Now son . . . Don't do anything that would not make your daddy proud'?"

"Oh, Brad."

"No matter what I did or where I went, those words were hanging over me. It was not always a bad thing. I'm sure feeling that my daddy was looking over my shoulder kept me out of some serious trouble."

After reflecting a moment, he went on. "And I wanted *so much* to make him proud. As you might remember, I tried to become a Navy SEAL. I was sure that would do it. When I was turned down, I thought I had failed him so I went to college instead. He was in school when he was drafted and never got to finish. I was looking at the military for a career the whole time. With my education, I leapfrogged to becoming an officer when I joined the Air Force. All I could think of was my father during the commissioning ceremony."

"Brad . . . He would be so proud of you."

"But Tonya . . . You don't understand. I hate the military. It's as though I'm living somebody else's life and not my own."

He began to sob. Tonya wanted to comfort him but was not sure how. Then, she took his hands and began to speak.

"The night I graduated from high school, I asked my mother if she thought my father would be proud of me. I remember so well what she said."

She made sure they had eye contact before she went on. "'Tonya . . . The thing that would make your daddy the proudest is for you to be proud of yourself.' At least that one time, the woman got it right."

Brad let go of her hands, but he was not pulling away. He was withdrawing into himself. He had come to Alaska in the dead of winter darkness, and a little light had just come on.

After they said their goodbyes, she crawled into bed. "Talk. The whole time, all the boy wanted was just to talk." When she checked out the next morning, her bill had already been taken care of.

The Kenai Peninsula was all decked out in white for the Christmas Eve flight. Tonya grabbed a window seat and could not take her eyes off the wonderland below. Homer was not spared, either, and it was still coming down. Agnes moaned and groaned on some unplowed streets but eventually delivered her back to The Nest.

About midnight when Old Santa was out making his rounds, Tonya was awakened by shadows dancing across the walls. When she went to the window, her spirits leaped for joy. The skies had cleared, and the Aurora Borealis was putting on a spectacular show. She put on a coat, grabbed her camera, and went outside to get a better look at the Northern Lights.

Tonya was making more memories, and she had something new to paint. Brad got a Christmas present, after all, but it was just a bit late. A little heart rock accompanied the painting that she entitled, "Christmas Lights."

She revisited the conversation with Brad several times. He was trying to escape his cocoon. Could he ever make the metamorphosis? He had seen the light, but would he let go and follow it to the freedom of just being himself?

Tonya took the newspaper editor up on his offer, and one day she dropped off an article for consideration. It appeared in the next edition of the weekly. She used her own name in the byline this time. Members of both the writer's group and the loose confederation of artists commented on it and encouraged her to submit more.

In some ways, expressing herself on paper was easier than on canvas. Tonya began dabbling with poetry but was reluctant to let anyone see her silly compositions.

When she dared to share samples of her writings with the group, she encountered criticism different from that of teachers, and even from Mr. Ellis. While the untrained writer was not anticipating rave reviews, she was surprised that the more accomplished authors rarely found anything of a redeeming nature. Rather, they seemed to think it their job to highlight some minor foible and then run it into the ground.

If that floated their boats, then it was fine with Tonya. She missed a meeting or two and decided to drop out altogether. Only one member of the group mentioned her absence afterward.

As the snow began to melt, Tonya laced up her hiking boots and reached for the stick that Rick had given her. Reflexively, she turned in at the bookstore, and instinctively, she went to the children's section. It looked about the same as it did the last time she was in, except the display was in disarray. Impulsively, she began straightening it up.

The perplexed owner approached her curiously. "May I help you?" And then she sighed. "Oh . . . It's you."

Tonya began to apologize. "I'm sorry. I guess I just couldn't help myself. A bookstore gets in your blood."

"Looks like you are doing a good job. I had never thought of arranging them like that."

The woman then surprised Tonya. "I remember you from the first day you came in. You asked about a job. I had a good feeling about you then, but I also knew that you had only recently come to town. We business owners have grown weary of training newbies only to have them run off

Miss Bizzy Belle

chasing another wild hair. Are you still interested in working here? It would only be a part-time job. I mainly need someone to keep the doors open so that I can get out and get some fresh air. I haven't been salmon or halibut fishing in almost three years."

Tonya smiled. "Does that mean I can finish what I've started here?"

"You go right ahead."

When she dropped another article off at the paper, the editor motioned for her to join him in his office.

"I like what you submitted last time. I hope this is just as good. I was inclined to hire you when you wandered in the first time. I really liked what you told me about doing human interest stories. Lord knows. We have some characters around here with interesting tales that have never been told."

Tonya waited for him to continue. "The last two reporters I hired left without even saying goodbye. From what I hear, I think you're going to be around for a while. The pay's not much, but if you want to come aboard, I think we can work together."

Tonya chuckled under her breath as she went out the door. "It's a good thing they didn't check references." She now had not one, not two, but three part-time jobs. More important than the money, she could just be who she was in each of them.

"There's a phone call for you." Dr. Baskin's receptionist paged Michelle. The nurse presumed that it was her doctor "friend" disguising his voice as he always did.

"Ms. Bell . . . This is Sammie. I'm getting married and I need to get in touch with Tonya. I want her to be my maid of honor, and I need her phone number."

Michelle froze. For one thing, she did not have the number Mrs. Thornhill had given her with her. She had initially put it on her refrigerator as a reminder, but then she got tired of being reminded. It was gem clipped to the inside of the back cover of the phone book.

"Sammie . . . I'm with a patient right now. Can you call me back in fifteen minutes?"

Michelle told the receptionist that she was going on a break. She had to have a smoke while trying to figure out what to do. It would be very embarrassing to admit that she had lost contact with her daughter. Still, she could not bear the thought of Tonya coming home for the wedding and ignoring her as though she were not even on the face of the earth. Michelle had feared something like this might happen.

Then, her countenance changed. "It's brilliant. I'll tell Sammie that I don't have the number with me and for her to call Mrs. Thornhill. Let that old hag deal with it. She's got Tonya's number."

Thirty minutes after Sammie called back, she called again.

"Ms. Bell . . . Mrs. T's phone has been disconnected. I was finally able to track down Kermit. He said that Mrs. Thornhill's dead."

Michelle hung up and Sammie's line went dead.

The Cornfield Legacy

Tonya decided to treat herself for her twenty-third birthday. Agnes was in need of several repairs, and the closest Volvo dealership was in Anchorage. The service manager said that the older model would cost more to fix than it was worth, and they tried to sell her a new one.

She thanked them, went across the street, and purchased a new Subaru. With three jobs, her financial holdings were not only holding their own but growing a little. In honor of Mrs. T's last vehicle, Tonya drove off the lot in a 1992 maroon Legacy Wagon.

Why not? The woman would be thrilled.

"Well, 'Cornfield.' Let's get you out of the patch."

The art gallery had not yet opened for the summer season, and Tonya was caught up in her other work for a couple of days. She turned Cornfield toward Wasilla, and then on up the Parks Highway toward Denali. She spent the night in Talkeetna from whence she got her first glimpse of the lofty peak peeking out of the clouds.

Tonya interviewed a bush pilot during breakfast the next morning without him even realizing that he was talking to a newspaper reporter. She then drove farther north to get a closer look at North America's tallest mountain.

Cornfield was turned around a little after noon and headed toward her new home at the end of the road. Eight hours later, the vehicle was limbered up, and Tonya was glad to be back in The Nest. She had a fresh story to write and inspirations for several new paintings. When would she ever get them all done? With her new wheels, the Alaska resident was no longer a Cheechako.

When tents started popping up along the Spit, Tonya stopped by. It was a mostly new motley crew, and they made her feel old. She would never forget the days and nights she had spent in that campground nestled

Miss Bizzy Belle

in the Manila Villa, but she had no desire to do it again.

Tonya thought often about her Grandmother Connie and especially Pa Bell. She was glad that her mother had the gallery phone number. True to the end, Mrs. T always seemed to know the right thing to do. Surely, her mom would use it if anything happened, or share it if anybody was trying to get in touch with her.

Maybe the next summer she would go "outside," Alaskan for temporarily leaving the state. After a Bellville visit, she must reconnect with Sammie. They had a lot of catching up to do.

"Phone call for you." Tonya was painting outside and had drawn a little crowd when Bekka beckoned her. "Give me just a minute, and I'll be right back."

"Tonya . . . This is Margaret. Margaret Stratton. I've had you on my mind for days and decided to see if this number works."

Tonya's excitement was unmistakable. "It's *so* good to hear your voice. Are you coming up to see me?"

"You don't dilly dally, do you? I was going to test the waters to see if you were serious when you invited me. I presume you were."

"Of course, I was. Book your flight to Anchorage, and I'll meet you there. You absolutely must experience the drive from there to Homer. I'll get us a room in Anchor Town so that we can start fresh the next morning."

By the time Tonya got back to her painting, the tourists had moved on. It didn't matter. Her mind was on another visitor about to make her first voyage to Alaska.

A big perk about living in Homer was that nothing was set in stone. In each of her part-time jobs, Tonya's work was always flexible. Arranging some free time to show a guest around just fit right into the spirit of things.

Each time Tonya went to Anchorage, she saw things that she had missed. There was no way to ever see it all. She was thrilled about Margaret's visit, and especially with getting to see Alaska through the woman's eyes.

As they set out on their adventure, Mrs. Stratton asked a question in her lovely British intonation. "Will I have any trouble finding a place to stay near where you live?"

Tonya's mind started hatching up a little plan. "That will be no problem at all. I have some connections."

Margaret sat up straight. True to her cultural heritage, she took it all in but did not over exude. As they approached Homer, Tonya explained the Spit, and how it was formed by the wave actions of the bay lapping on one side and the ocean on the other. She then pulled alongside the camping area overflowing with the summer transients.

"Margaret. All the rooms were booked since this is the height of the tourist season. But not to worry. I will go get my tent and set it up for you here. I think you will really enjoy interacting with these young people. I do want you to have a genuine Alaskan experience."

When the woman looked at her in disbelief, Tonya could keep a straight face no longer. "Just checking to see if you still had your Brit sense of humor." Mrs. Stratton relaxed as she breathed a big sigh of relief.

After Tonya lugged the luggage up the stairs to The Nest, she ushered her guest into her bedroom. Margaret protested, but Tonya assured her that she had slept in her sleeping bag many nights. She told her that she had not even tried to get a room because she wanted them to spend all of their time together.

Tonya took Margaret to her favorite gathering spot the next morning. Mrs. Stratton ordered tea and was surprised that she had so many varieties to choose from. Afterward, the tour guide took her to all three of her places of employment. Margaret assured Tonya that she did not wish to interfere with her work.

She added that she wanted to come down and watch her paint. "And I also want to purchase one of your pieces while I am here."

Not long after getting back from lunch of the best soup and sandwich either had ever tasted, Margaret lay down to rest. Tonya tweaked an article that she was working on. When the woman arose, it was tea time and the hostess was prepared. She had purchased some scones from her favorite bakery and a teapot with matching cups at a moving sale.

On her last day, Margaret shared an observation. "I don't see many people wearing watches except for the tourists, and I'm not sure I've seen a clock since I have been here."

Tonya chimed in. "Alaskans have a different concept of time."

She then turned to Mrs. Stratton as her demeanor changed. "Why don't you move up here with me?"

"Of all the places I have visited, this is the only one I think that I might enjoy relocating to. But I'm just too old to start over somewhere else."

"Margaret . . . You're the only person I've ever told about Mrs. Hattie. That experience is just as vivid in my mind as ever."

The woman nodded her head but said nothing. Tonya continued.

"I just don't want to cast this precious pearl before impervious swine. A number of my friends here are tuned into the cosmos, or at least they think they are, but I'm still not sure any of them could grasp it."

The Englishwoman faced her squarely and reassured her confidently.

"You will know it when the right person comes along."

When Tonya saw Margaret off at the Homer Airport, the woman was carrying a parcel under her arm. Her prized possessions included a pencil sketch of the two having tea, and a painting of the Russian Church at Ninilchik, the favorite stop for both on the drive down. Tonya also slipped a little heart-shaped rock into her hand.

When the calendar rolled over to 1993, Tonya could not imagine where the time had gone. She had been in Alaska for some two and a half years, and she had made herself right at home in Homer. In that span, she had seen some old friends go and had welcomed a few new ones.

Something was always going on, and she had been tapped for committee service several times. She was now on a first name basis with the movers and shakers, although it seemed like more shaking was always going on than moving.

Bekka was getting restless and had approached her about purchasing the gallery. Then again, everything was for sale in Alaska for the right price. A "For Sale" notice had been in the window of her favorite mom and pop grocery store since she first arrived. Real estate signs had also been in some of the same yards the entire time.

Tonya was not sure that she wanted the added responsibility. For the time being, she was content just to be.

The Bell tolls again

"Tonya . . . The phone is for you." It was a dreary, early May day in 1994. Bekka and Tonya were at the gallery spiffing things up and getting ready to reopen for the summer.

"Hello."

"Is this Tonya Bell?"

"Yes."

"Is your mother's name, Michelle?"

"Yes, it is. Who's calling?"

The voice sounded familiar. Whatever this was about, it was not good.

"Tonya . . . This is your Uncle Charles. I wanted to make sure that I had the right number."

"What's wrong, Uncle Charles? Why are you calling me?"

"There's no easy way to say this. Your mother was killed in an automobile accident . . . Are you still there?"

"Yes . . . I'm here. It just took me a moment."

"Your mom had led her family to believe that she did not know where you were or how to get in touch with you. Your grandmother and I had about given up on finding you. Then, Connie remembered where she kept little notes and looked just to see. Sure enough, she found this number clipped to the back of the telephone directory."

Tonya was having trouble following what he was saying. "That doesn't seem very important right now, does it?"

"How soon can you get here? Connie has taken the body back to Bellville where Michelle will be buried in the family lot. We were waiting to schedule a graveside service until we could get in touch with you."

"I'll see if I can get on a redeye this evening. I'll rent a car and should be there sometime after lunch tomorrow."

"I can meet you at the airport."

"No. I will need my own wheels."

"Unless we hear otherwise in the next hour or so, we'll go ahead and plan the memorial service for the day after tomorrow. Tonya . . . I'm so sorry."

"Thank you, Uncle Charles. Tell Grandmother that I'll be there as soon as I can."

The airport was near the Spit, so Tonya decided that it would be easier just to go to the terminal and let an agent help figure out the best schedule. Since flights to Birmingham or Chattanooga went through Atlanta, she decided to get off there. She told Bekka that she did not know when she would be back and asked her to get word to the others.

Once buckled in, she asked herself. "How many ways can you say 'numb'?"

An hour later while waiting for the next boarding call, she thought about something else. "This is my second flight out of Anchorage. And both times I was on the way to a funeral."

Much like the captain did when he got the plane to a cruising altitude, Tonya put herself on autopilot. She was facing so many unknowns and would just have to deal with them in due time. Sleep did not come easily, but she caught a couple of catnaps.

When Tonya got to Bellville, she would not remember much of anything about the exhausting flights or the two-and-a-half-hour drive. There was, nonetheless, one very important exception. While having a cup of coffee in Salt Lake City during a layover, something punched her right in the gut. Her mother was now gone, and so was Tonya's only chance of finding out who her father was. Her mother had taken the secret to her grave.

A tragic death in the family is never easy, and that one was more difficult than most. Tonya's grandmother asked questions but reserved judgments. She could not resist the temptation, though, to stick in a justifiable barb about her granddaughter not keeping in touch with her.

Tonya and Uncle Charles huddled in the kitchen. He told her what he knew about the accident. No one was sure exactly where Michelle had been. About twenty miles out of Ephesus, she ran off a mountain road in a sharp curve with no guardrail and plowed right into a large oak. She was killed instantly.

Tonya asked about toxicology reports.

"They have not come back yet, but the coroner said he saw nothing to indicate that she had been drinking. Apparently, she was just driving too fast for the conditions and lost control of her Volkswagen."

"Her Volkswagen?"

"Yes. She bought a yellow Beetle when she sold the house and moved to Ephesus."

"Sold the house? Moved to Ephesus?"

"She was living in an apartment on the south side of town and working for a local doctor."

Tonya's great-uncle paused to let things settle in.

"Your grandmother is so proud that you're here to help dispose of things and settle up the estate. I hope you're not planning to retire on your inheritance. From what Connie has found out so far, your mother took out an insurance policy about a month ago and named you as the beneficiary. It is only for $20,000. Not much, if anything, will be left after paying off her credit cards and her funeral expenses."

Tonya mumbled that her mother was never very good at managing her money.

A small contingent came to the graveside service from Ephesus, but no one showed up from Knoxo Springs. Tonya sat under the funeral tent between her grandmother and Pa Bell. The old man was taking it hard.

Tonya remembered the minister from the hospital and her grandfather's funeral. She saw him check his zipper while the family was being seated. For once, the long-winded preacher didn't have much to say.

About two hours after the folks had dispersed, Tonya returned to the Bell cemetery lot. After struggling for fifty years, half of them before her daughter was born, and the other half afterward, Michelle's body was laid to rest beside her little brother's whose battle only lasted a few days. Her head was just a yard or so below the feet of her father. At the bottom of the fresh mound of dirt, Tonya placed a smooth gray stone with the letter "M" naturally engraved with a white vein. At the head, she put another flat stone. That one was in the shape of a heart.

I'm what?

"What the F&#*@%$!?" Walt Williamson bellowed when the phone rang. About out the door, he added with a little disgust. "Not now, Gus." Walt was not prone to profanity, but when Ma Bell rudely interrupted his solitude, he knew that nine times out of ten, the person on the other end was either a telemarketer or the bearer of bad news. When he moved to Ephesus, he started calling his phone "Gus" after the big brown trout that his Grandfather Williamson rightly predicted would make him cuss when it always got away.

Not wanting to get in a time bind, he almost just let it ring. Five minutes later and he would not have been around to answer it, anyway. He was on his way to his other home in Alaska for some much-needed R & R. Eli Pierce was now the senior chaplain in a big Asheville hospital. Walt left his vehicle at his friend's house when he was gone for extended periods.

He had just gotten home the day before in time to cut the grass before leaving again. Walt had taken his mother's frail lifeless body back to Mason, Georgia to be laid to rest beside her husband. The graves of his Grandpa King, the woman who raised him, and the biological father that he never knew were in the same cemetery. He then went to his old college town of Adamsonville and stayed a few days with Earl and Mary Beth, his uncle and aunt.

When he called to let his friend know when to expect him, Eli asked if he knew the Ephesus woman who had been killed in a car wreck while he was gone. Walt said he had not heard about it, and that he had stopped his papers before he left. The chaplain indicated that she was a nurse, but he did not recall ever meeting her.

Since it might be Eli trying to reach him, he decided to take the call. Trying to mask his impatience but not too hard, he answered rather curtly. "Yes . . ."

"Is this Walter Williamson?"

"May I ask who's calling?"

The person on the other end asked another question without identifying herself. "Did you write *I. D. - The Identity Dilemma*?"

With a softer tone in his voice, the author was pleased to say that he

Miss Bizzy Belle

did. It had been a while since anyone had asked about the book that he had written a decade earlier.

"Mr. Williamson . . . I have a copy of your book, and I was wondering if you would autograph it for me."

Of all the things that Walt could have anticipated, it would have never occurred to him that he might hear those words when he yielded to Gus's incursion. Just as he was about to explain his travel plans, the woman on the other end interrupted his thoughts.

"I'm in Ephesus on business, and I could meet you somewhere. How about the library? Would that be convenient for you?"

Walt looked at his watch and figured that he had just enough time. His bags were packed and the library was right on his way. Why would he not run by and honor this request? He had not signed a copy of his book in some time.

"I would be delighted to sign it for you." He asked the woman if she could meet him in ten minutes. She agreed.

As he hung up, the man in a hurry realized that he had not gotten the caller's name. Not that many people would be in the reading room with a copy of his book. As he went by the front desk, he saw a young woman sitting alone in the periodical section. She was neatly dressed, had a slender build, long dark hair, and looked to be in her mid-twenties. She rose from her chair as he approached, and he saw that she was holding a copy of his book.

She greeted him with a pleasant smile. "You must be Walter Williamson."

Extending his hand, he acknowledged that he was. "My friends call me Walt. My mother was just about the only person who called me Walter."

He was so preoccupied that it did not even occur to him to ask her how she came about having a copy of his book. As he took a seat at a table, he reached for his pen with his right hand and for the book with his left.

He had signed so many books that he just automatically went back into the familiar mode. "Is there anything in particular that you would like for me to inscribe?" Without even a moment's hesitation, the young woman responded.

"You could say, 'To my daughter, Tonya'."

Walt dropped his pen. He looked up at her, and their eyes locked.

"Before you do, though. There's something I need to ask you." She was poised and very composed. "Were you ever involved with a woman named Michelle Bell, and did you take her to see the movie, *Dr. Zhivago*, on your first date?"

Walt missed his flight.

You what?

Walt was mute, and at least for the moment, immobilized. Conversely, the person standing before him was calm and collected. Dumbstruck, he just gazed at the beautiful young woman. A surfeit of emotions was surging, all simultaneously vying for top billing.

The young woman's words punctuated the undulating shockwaves. "Would you like to move this conversation to your house?"

Without answering, Walt stood and they started toward the door. He finally found his voice. "Follow me. I'll try not to go off and lose you."

For the next of countless more times soon to follow, she surprised him. "Oh . . . I know the way. I saw you cutting your grass late yesterday afternoon."

"You what?"

As Walt drove back up the street that he had just come down, dots were jumping around all over the place beseeching to be connected. Was this an imposter? If so, what did she want? If she was a phony, she had certainly done some homework.

Glancing at her in the rearview mirror, he allowed his mind to venture. "Could she really be . . .? Othell, what the hell is going on here?"

Walt sensed nothing in her demeanor to indicate that she might create any kind of security risk. Should they just talk in the yard where he could gather more information? As he turned up the drive, he decided to go ahead and invite her in.

As they went in the back door, Walt tried to make his unexpected guest feel comfortable. "Welcome to my humble abode. We can sit at the kitchen table, in the living room, or in the swing on the front porch." What Tonya saw when she went in the kitchen, confirmed what she suspected when the man entered the library.

She suggested the porch. As they took their seats, Tonya sensed his trepidation and tried to put him at ease.

"I talked to you on the phone one time. I was eight. It rang one evening while Mother was out. You said that you once worked with her, and you were trying to get in touch with her. I wrote down your name and phone number and gave it to her as you requested. Only, we had a bad connection, and I got your first name wrong."

Tonya reached for her purse. "Here it is." She pointed to the weathered scrap of paper that she held up for him to see. "That is the number I called a few minutes ago."

Walt was finally able to speak again, but his speech was still a bit shaky. "Why do you think I am your father?"

There was no indecisiveness in Tonya's voice. "I only knew for sure when you did not deny that you knew my mom, and that you saw *Dr. Zhivago* the first time you went out together. When I was a kid, I naturally asked her all kinds of questions about my dad. I could get almost nothing out of her. She had a real fascination with that movie, and one day in a moment of weakness, she admitted that the man who took her to see it was my father."

Walt took a deep breath. "Is this really my . . .?"

His mind was having a hard time knowing which way to turn. Just as the next words escaped his lips, he realized how dumb they sounded. "Did she tell you anything else?"

"When I was old enough to understand, Mother told me that I was not planned. She said that she made an appointment to have an abortion, but for some reason, she couldn't go through with it. She was emphatic that you knew nothing about me. I could get her to say little else other than that you were a very nice person. I really didn't know if that was true, or if she was just trying to placate me."

Tonya was going with the flow. Walt was paddling upstream.

A what?

Not many things caught Walt Williamson flatfooted, but this bolt of lightning right out of the clear blue Carolina sky certainly did. While he was struggling to get some traction, Tonya's clutch was fully engaged, and her hand was on the throttle. She looked at him with a devious smile.

"When I was a teenager, that fiery redhead reminded me several times that the only reason I was here was because she got cold feet. A time or two she got so frustrated with me that she said it was not too late to change her mind."

Walt managed a nervous little laugh. What she had been saying all started settling in. From the night of the phone call when Michelle said that she "took care of it," he had always felt a strong connection with the daughter he thought he never had. He had not said anything about Michelle being a redhead, either. He nodded for her to go on.

"I always knew I would eventually find you." Tonya then broke into a big smile. "Mr. Williamson. I hate to inform you, but you weren't the first candidate, either. At one time, I thought her old boyfriend who died in Vietnam might be my dad. I suspected that she juggled the dates about his deployment to confuse me. Then, I tricked her into taking me to his grave and the dates on his marker matched her story."

Relishing every moment, Tonya continued. "Other names kept coming up. Mother never married, but she did have some social life. I became a regular little Nancy Drew checking out the possibilities. One by one, they, too, fell by the wayside."

She kept watching his expressions as they changed. "One possibility was a D.C. cop, but Mother convinced me that she met him after I was born. She bragged about racing with him in the streets of Washington in the AMX."

Before Walt had a chance to respond, she put more evidence on the table. "Mom told me that a friend at work talked her into buying the X. I'm guessing that was you."

Walt nodded. "Whatever happened to that car?"

"I loved it, but Mother wrecked it. I think that's when she met the cop. And then she didn't take care of it. We got a dull old Dodge Dart when she couldn't afford to get it fixed."

Tonya then picked back up. "Anyway . . . When the well went dry, I had about decided that she must have had a one-night stand. I told my friend Sammie once that I wondered if my mother might have just had a quickie."

Walt couldn't stop laughing. "Then, I suppose she didn't tell you that we did use birth control. She had an IUD."

"A what?"

"It was a little contraption that was supposed to prevent an embryo from implanting in the uterine wall. I guess it failed or you wouldn't be here."

"I'm so sorry Mother didn't tell you about me so that we could have been a family."

"Baby . . . Me, too."

Tonya's demeanor shifted dramatically. She now had one foot on the brakes and the other on the accelerator.

"What should I call you?"

"Mr. Williamson?"

"Walt?"

"Dad?"

"Father?"

The counselor in Walt kicked in. "What do you want to call me?"

With that, Tonya rose slowly to her feet. She walked to the end of the porch with her back to him for what seemed far too long. Walt eventually got up and went to her. For several moments, she did not acknowledge his presence standing behind her. She then turned and faced him. Tears were streaming down her cheeks. Her arms reached for him. Nobody had to tell Walt what to do.

As his daughter wrapped her arms around him tightly, she whispered in his ear. "Can I call you Daddy?"

Before Walt had a chance to say anything, she released her grip and backed up a step or two. Her eyes went exploring. Walt wondered how he was measuring up.

Tonya's expression changed yet again. With some sparkle in her eyes, she spoke from her heart. "You don't know how many times I've dreamed of this moment. I will savor it forever."

Unable to speak, Walt beheld his daughter in pure and unadulterated amazement.

With their heads in the clouds and feet searching for a place to touch down, Walt asked Tonya if she would like a cup of coffee.

"I'd love one."

While it was brewing, he placed a call to Eli. He told his friend that he was not going to make his flight, and he would fill him in later. He also said that he might need a chaplain before it was all over.

He then called the airline to cancel his reservation. The agent said that he could use his ticket anytime within a year. In just a few days, he would be rebooked.

When Tonya came out of the bathroom, she overheard part of the conversation and asked him if he was going somewhere.

"Just to Alaska."

Concern was written all over her face. "Oh, no. I hope I haven't caused you to miss your flight."

Walt now had a moment that he could relish. "Girl . . . First, I got grounded by my mother when I finally found out who she was. And now my own daughter has just found me and grounded me once again." That put a big smile on her face.

Reaching for a couple of mugs, he asked what she took in her coffee. She replied that she used a little cream and sugar.

He responded playfully. "I like a little cream, but somewhere back there, I wish I'd marked it on the calendar, I was sweet enough."

As they sat at the kitchen table, Walt was ready to keep going, and nothing was holding Tonya back.

"Now where were we? I think you were still explaining how you found me."

Tonya reached over, took Walt's hand, and squeezed it firmly.

"Daddy—I'm still trying to get used to saying that—I've got to tell you some things that are not going to be easy." He sensed his daughter tensing up.

"Your book was the missing piece of the puzzle." She paused. "I told you this was going to be difficult."

Walt did not rush her. He let his daughter proceed at her own pace. For the moment, she was stuck. He braced himself.

After a few sips of coffee, she went on. "You have not asked, but I know you want to know about Mother. She was killed in a car wreck a few days ago."

Walt was stunned. Tonya's floodgates opened. Instantly on his feet, he stood behind her chair with his arms draped around her. He watched his own tears dropping onto Tonya's beautiful dark tresses.

Right in the midst of the immense joys of finding his daughter, he had to make room in his heart to grieve the loss of her mother, while still in deep mourning from losing his own. She said that it was not going to be easy. That was nothing new for the father that Tonya was just getting to know.

He eventually broke the embrace and went to get a box of tissues. When he came back in the kitchen, he placed it in front of her. Tonya looked up at him lovingly as she plucked first one, and then another. Her eyes stayed on him as she blotted the salty tears making their way to the corners of her mouth.

Tonya was finally able to mumble. "Mom lost control of her car in a curve."

Through his own sobbing, he managed to say. "Oh, baby. I'm so sorry."

She wanted to know if they could pick back up later.

"Of course, sweetheart."

Tonya went out into the yard and disappeared into the woods. Walt let her be.

When he woke up that morning, his whole agenda was about a long flight with two layovers before finally arriving in Kenai, Alaska. He not only missed his flight, but the axis of his world had also wobbled. So had that of his daughter.

With that hard part now behind her, Tonya knew what she must do next when she rejoined her daddy on the porch. His right arm was resting on the swing, cradling her right shoulder. She reached for his other hand. They both shifted their bodies a bit to face each other.

Tonya looked up into the man's eyes. Tenderly, she spoke. "I'm not the only one who just recently lost a mother."

For several moments, additional words were unnecessary. Walt finally managed to say what was in his heart. "How I wish that she could have lived to know about her wonderful granddaughter."

Then, he thought of something. "How did you know about her death?"

"Have you so soon forgotten? I told you that I was a sleuth."

With the tension resolving, they were ready to move on. "What other evidence have you dug up?" She just smiled at him.

Say what?

As they got up to stretch their legs and take a few deep breaths, Tonya chided her father about something. "You never did autograph my book."

"And I probably won't anytime soon. I just keep discovering adjectives that I want to insert between the words 'my' and 'daughter'." The way he looked at her sent a tickle all the way to her toes.

As they sat back down, he mentioned something. "And by the way . . . You never did tell me how my book was the key that unlocked this amazing door."

Tonya started piecing it together for him. "Mother's death was devastating to me in so many ways. While we certainly had our share of mother/daughter issues, she was the only parent I had. Losing her, under those circumstances, was hard enough. It was also crushing that whatever connection I might have had with my father was apparently severed as well. I presumed that the secret died with her. Knowing how adamant she was about protecting your identity, I did not expect to find any clues that she had left behind."

She took a deep breath. "When I was going through her things, I found a manila envelope sealed with several layers of tape. It was buried deep among some of her stored away clothes. Naturally, I was curious to see what was inside. When I finally got the tape cut off, it was a book. I knew immediately that there was something highly significant about it. We always had books around when I was growing up. Why was this one hidden away? I was already familiar with that particular book and she knew it. So why did she not want me to know that she had a copy?"

"Am I to presume you are talking about my book, and that you already knew about it? How so?"

Tonya looked at him and beamed. "Would you believe that I quoted you in my high school graduation speech?"

"You did what?"

"After I finally got the wrapping off, something about the author's name rang a bell, pun intended. Could this be the name of the same man I talked to on the phone years earlier? I remembered well what happened the night I gave her the note. She looked at it and pretended that she didn't recognize the name. She said that the caller must have her confused with someone else. The next day I found the note in shreds in the trash can."

"But . . .?"

Tonya looked at Walt with a glint of amusement. "Ah, come on, now, Williamson. Do you think any daughter of yours wouldn't be crafty enough to make her own copy?"

Tonya had turned over the tickle box.

After the laughter died down, she continued explaining.

"Holding the book in my hand, I went and got my wallet. I'd been carrying that note around with me for years. Walter O. Williamson and Wyatt Williamson was a near match. My heart fluttered, chills ran up and down my spine, and I broke out in a cold sweat all at the same time. The prospects were good that I had stumbled upon the father lode."

Walt just shook his head again in astonishment. She surely did have a way of putting things.

"Now mind you. I said I quoted from your book, but I did not actually read it. My high school counselor copied what you said about honesty, integrity, and that sort of stuff. That's what I used in my speech." She looked into his eyes. "Two nights ago, I started it from the beginning."

Tonya paused as though trying to frame what she was about to say next.

"Dad. I'm sure that you understand this, but let me try to explain something that happened to me. You know how there are some people that you simply feel no connection with whatsoever. Of course, you do."

She grinned at him confidently and continued. "But then again, there are those that you think you have known forever. When I started reading what you said about identity, you kept using my words. I often knew what you were going to say before you said it. You were already in my head. I knew I had to find you."

This aroused Walt's curiosity. "How long did it take? How far did you have to come to get here?"

"You don't have a clue, do you?"

"I guess not."

Tonya made him wait for several seconds.

"Mother lived right here in Ephesus when she died. She got her nursing degree from the same university that awarded you your master's and then published your book. I grew up in Knoxo Springs. And that's just for starters."

Say what?

It's what?

Walter Othell Williamson had once again landed in the world of awe. Since Gus went on a rant about mid-morning, it had been one WOW moment after another. Walt asked Tonya if she could spend the night. She agreed and went back to her mother's apartment to grab a few things. He ran to the grocery store.

As she was gathering up her stuff, she looked over at Watt. "You might as well go along, too. This is the first night of the rest of my life." She had already put everything else in a bag, and it was full so she carried the old sweatshirt under her arm.

Walt was putting groceries in the refrigerator when she came in the back door. "Just a minute. I'll go with you. We'll have to put sheets on the bed."

She placed the bag in a chair and put Watt on the dresser. When Walt opened a drawer to get sheets, he saw the shirt. Tonya looked on curiously when he picked it up.

"Where did you get this?"

Tonya was so young when she adopted Watt that she could not remember *not* having him. It was going to be awkward trying to explain lugging along an old sweatshirt all of her life. Would her father think that she was just a silly girl? He was waiting, so she tried to explain.

"Dad. This is Watt. I know this might sound strange to you, but he has been with me like for . . . forever. I could always talk to Watt about anything. When I was a kid, I dragged him with me everywhere I went. I slept with him. Even now, I fold him and put him on the pillow."

Walt said nothing. He was in the driver's seat for a change.

Tonya reached for the shirt and wrapped herself in it. "Okay counselor. You can write a chapter in your next book about how your own daughter took 'security blanket' to a ridiculous level."

"You really don't know anything about the origin of this shirt, do you?"

"All I know is that Mother kept trying to take it away from me and I wouldn't let her."

Walt reached for the shirt and held it out. She did not know if he was going to make fun of her or what.

"Tonya . . . This is my shirt."

"It's what?"

"I wore this sweatshirt the last night I was with your mother. I forgot to pack it the next morning and always wondered what happened to it. I assumed Michelle just tossed it."

Watt found himself in the middle of a three-way hug.

Neither really wanted to go to bed, but both were exhausted. Each was brimming with anticipation, but both wished to slow down and enjoy every moment. Watt got a good night's sleep.

Walt was up early the next morning. He tiptoed around the kitchen making coffee and planning breakfast. Just down the hall in his little bungalow bequest, his daughter was sleeping behind the closed door. He knew that he had not dreamed the events of the day before, but he was eagerly awaiting reaffirmation.

Tonya was chipper as she came bouncing into the kitchen. "You're bright-eyed and bushy-tailed this morning." Walt smiled to confirm her observation. Only twenty-four hours earlier, Walt had heard her speak only once, and that was years ago over the phone with a bad connection. His daughter's voice now seemed like it belonged in the house, as though it had been there all along.

"I like my eggs soft-scrambled." With a little glint, she watched for his reaction.

He was not going to be outdone by his own daughter. "If you don't like my cooking, then you'll just have to take over K-P."

Ignoring what he had said, she continued placing her order. "And I want my toast light with no butter." Walt feigned a huff.

With that, she went scrambling to find the plates and silverware. "Are any of these mugs off limits?"

"Only the one with the Vaughn coat of arms on it. That was Mother's special cup, and I don't want it accidentally broken."

As they were eating breakfast, the daughter, and her newly found father made small talk like there was nothing unusual about it. Walt was aware that he did not even know where his daughter lived, or if she had a career. He looked forward to another day of exciting discovery, and oh boy, was he in for some big surprises. Tonya interrupted his thoughts while they were still sitting at the table.

"I know I'm going to have zillions of questions, but there's one I want to ask right now. You really did go see *Dr. Zhivago* on your first date. I know that, but here's what I'm dying to find out. What did you do when

Miss Bizzy Belle

Mother called the wine, Sin Infidel?"

"You mean she actually admitted that? She didn't think it was so funny then. Do you know that's what I call a good glass of wine to this day? To tell you the truth, I was not sure what she said at the time. Only after I got home and poured myself a glass of zinfandel did I put it together."

Tonya teased. "It might have been new to her back when, but she sure 'Sinned' a lot trying to get your daughter raised."

After savoring that moment, Walt speculated about something. "I think I know what you're going to tell me next. Your mother named you Tonya, after the orphan girl in the movie who was not mired in her past, but only forward-looking."

"Now I'm in your head." Tonya then continued explaining it to him.

"I'll never forget the day she told me how I got my name. She said *Dr. Zhivago* was the most powerful movie that she had ever seen. She went on to say how excited she was about actually going out on a date. She had not been out with anyone since her fiancé was killed. Mother told me how nervous she was, and that she just about talked your ears off. She said she was afraid that you lost interest in her when she became so engrossed in the movie."

Just oozing mischievousness, she went on. "I remember her telling me that you seemed in a hurry to get home when you dropped her off. She dreaded seeing you at work. She didn't think that you would ever want to do anything with her again."

Tonya made sure she had eye contact before delivering the punchline. "But apparently, you did. At least once."

The tickle box got turned over again.

"Aren't you glad I was a girl? Otherwise, you might be talking to your son, Yuri, right now."

Walt was not about to disrupt the momentum, and he gestured for her to go on. "I remember telling Mother one time. 'Some of my friends think that they might have been conceived in the backseat of a car at a drive-in. I'm the only kid I know who can trace her roots back to a movie theater where her parents didn't even make out'."

He could not stop snickering. "Do you have any idea how funny you are?"

Up to this point, Walt had not equivocated with any kind of ambiguity about the girl's paternity. After the last exchange or two, how could there be any doubt that Tonya Willa Bell was the daughter of Walter Othell Williamson?

About mid-morning, Tonya made a suggestion. "Let's go get some ice cream."

Walt was all for it. "There's nothing more Alaskan than that. Did you know that Alaskans consume more ice cream per capita than any other state?"

"Would it surprise you if I did know that?" She really was loving this.

"I don't think anything would surprise me right now." His daughter knew that he was wrong.

It was not far into town, and Walt was thrilled to walk with Tonya by his side. They held hands, and then she skipped ahead of him like she was a little girl back in her childhood. While they were giggling and licking, trying to stay ahead of the melting, Walt started doing some math.

"When's your birthday?"

Tonya turned and gave him a look that he had not seen. Her expression mystified him. He was rather good at reading faces, but what he saw gazing at him had so many mixed messages that he could not make heads or tails out of it.

Without taking her eyes off him, she did not answer his question. "Why would you ask me that, and why right now?"

Walt saw no reason to withhold his thoughts. "About nine months after I left D.C., I had the strangest feeling on Mother's Day. I had trouble sorting everything out. Then it hit me. That would have been just about the time my daughter would have been born."

Tonya was staring at him in astonishment. Slowly and deliberately, she began to speak. "I was born on Mother's Day in 1969."

The pieces were falling into place, but Walt had still not gotten the full picture. "And what day of the month was it that year?"

She hesitated yet again. Walt could not take his eyes off her.

She said in a whisper as her eyes welled up. "May 11."

Walt looked at his watch that kept both time and the date.

Coming up out of his seat, he almost dropped his ice cream cone. "That's today!"

In words so softly that they were barely audible, she whispered. "I know. I'm sitting here having an ice cream cone with my daddy on my twenty-fifth birthday."

All the years that they had been apart were melting away.

As Walt and Tonya came up the sidewalk to the house, they just automatically took a seat in the swing. They soon returned to the subject of Michelle. "So, your mother never married?"

Miss Bizzy Belle

"No, she didn't. As I got older, I actually encouraged her to have a man in her life." With a magical quality in her voice, that was now becoming all so familiar to Walt, she went on. "Of course, I knew that it would take a special kind of man to put up with her. No offense. Sir. But I'm not sure even you would have been up to the task."

"What about you?" Walt asked. "Why has some smart bright fellow not swept a sweet thing like you off your feet?"

"You make me blush."

"You really are blushing."

"Now that I've found my daughter, is there any chance that I might be a grandpa someday?"

"Don't put all that off on me. That could depend on who else might come knocking on your door. Now, I'm making you blush."

Walt could not get Tonya's mother off his mind. While he had thoughts about her occasionally, Michelle spent her days with a living, breathing part of his being under her feet.

As they were still sitting at the kitchen table after lunching on sandwiches, he turned to Tonya. "By any chance, do you have a picture of your mom with you?"

She went to her purse and pulled out a newspaper clipping about the accident. A photo of Michelle accompanied the article. Walt was trying to imagine how she might have changed during the two and a half decades since he saw her last.

He muttered as he looked carefully at the photographic image of the mother of his child. "She was beautiful."

Walt said to Tonya, later that afternoon. "Since this is my daughter's birthday, I would like to take her to dinner at the best restaurant in town."

"Oh, thank you. But I was thinking of something else. Do you have any Alaska salmon in the freezer?"

He answered with a bit of a swagger. "I just happen to have a couple of filets left of the forty-pound king I snagged last summer. You know a cooler is the second piece of checked luggage for Alaskans when they fly out."

Tonya put in her order. "What I want for my big birthday bash is grilled salmon and a glass of Sin Infidel. Anyway . . . I didn't bring any festive clothes for a night out on the town, but I think my jeans will be proper attire for this feast."

"Then, let's get it thawing."

Tonya said that she wanted to go stretch out for a few minutes. Both of them needed an emotional break. She was amazed by her daddy's restraint. He was letting her go at her own pace. She thought to herself. "I'll bet he's a good counselor."

When Walt lit the grill, she put on some wild rice and tossed a salad. It had been a while since anyone had helped him in the kitchen.

As she took her first bite of the Chinook, she said coolly. "Hmm. This is delicious. It's almost as good as if it had just come right out of the Kenai River."

"And what would you know about the Kenai River?"

Tonya just shrugged with that look in her eyes again. Ignoring his question, she asked if he would take her salmon fishing.

He responded playfully. "I don't know. Let me think about it. I thought about it. Yes . . . But you have to promise not to out fish me."

"No such promise."

Lifting her wine glass high, Tonya got serious. "I think we were about to forget something."

Walt reciprocated with his glass.

Neither of them knew exactly how to propose the toast.

Their eyes locked.

He proposed. "Looking forward . . ."

She accepted. "Looking forward . . ."

What?

After both were stuffed and the dishes put away, Tonya could wait no longer. "Do you really want to know where my playground is?" When he nodded, she added. "I think you'd better pour yourself another glass of Sin, take a seat, and prop your feet up."

Walt was intrigued but trying hard not to let his exuberance overflow. Tonya had given him a couple of clues, but she knew they went right over his head.

As they were getting comfortable in the living room, Tonya said that she just thought of something. "I met your Grandpa King once when I was about nine or ten. He came to visit my great-grandfather, Pa Bell."

Walt never saw that coming, either. He could tell by looking at her that she was just dying to say more.

"You'll never believe what your grandpa told me. He said that he tried to fix you up with my mother, but that you were all awkward and backward

Miss Bizzy Belle

and such, and that you would not even send her a letter. Pa Bell said it was a shame that they never got the two of you together. I told Mother about it and asked her if she thought it was too late. Now I understand why she about fainted."

The tickle box just could not remain upright.

"Now, where was I? Oh yes. I was going to tell you where I hang out." Tonya tantalized him further. "Well . . . Let me think. Do I start from the present and work backward, or from the beginning and go forward? Okay. Let me just cut to the chase. Daddy. Not only were you and Mother neighbors here in Ephesus, but you and I are sort of like neighbors, too."

"What are you talking about?"

"I live down the road not too terribly far from you . . . At the end of that road, actually."

"How far is that from here?"

"I'm not talking about Ephesus."

"Do you still live in Knoxo Springs?"

"No . . . Daddy. I don't live around here any longer."

"I still don't get it."

"Take another sip of Sin. Are you ready for this?"

"I'm not going anywhere."

"I'm a Homer Sapien."

Walt was bewildered.

"You still don't get it, do you? Dad. I live in Homer, Alaska."

"What?"

As the shadows were growing long, Tonya went to sit in the swing again. Walt came out just in time to see his daughter's right arm extending. It was beckoning a beautiful blue butterfly. He stood by and watched reverently as it lit on her hand. She slowly moved it toward her face and gazed into its eyes.

It was just like the butterfly that once landed on his knee in that very swing. Only Tonya's did not have a broken wing. She stretched her arm again and the butterfly fluttered away.

He took a seat beside her. Neither spoke at first.

Tonya finally broke the silence. "Just think. I searched and searched for you and thought I would never find you. You were so close the entire time. I had your number and didn't even know it."

"Oh! You've got my number all right."

Walt's daughter moved closer to him. "I wonder how many times our paths crossed and we were oblivious."

"Tonya . . . So often what we want, what we are striving for, even yearning for, is right at our fingertips, right in front of our noses."

Both retreated into their thoughts. The spell was punctuated only by the rhythmic squeaking of the swing. Then, Tonya sprang back to life.

"By the way . . . I've thought of one way that you could sign my book."

"And what might that be?"

"To Miss Bizzy Belle, From Othell."

"Was that you? I still have that movie poster."

"I know. That was the first thing I spotted when I came into the kitchen."

"Wow!" they both said at the same time. How many times had they said that in the past two days?

Snuggling against him again, she said softly. "Walt Williamson . . . I'm so proud that you're my father."

"And, Miss Bizzy Belle . . . I'm so honored to have you for a daughter."

"Dad?"

"Yes? My daughter?"

"How do you feel about inner-connectedness and inter-connectedness?"

"I'll be glad to share my impressions, but I'm more interested in what you think."

"Daddy. Let me tell you what happened to me . . ."

Walt waved to his daughter as she drove out of the yard. He felt a sense of fullness and emptiness at the same time. She had to get back to her mother's apartment and finish cleaning it out. Apart for Gus interrupting him, they would have missed each other one more time.

Tonya could not get her mind off the butterfly. She had felt such a presence when she looked into its eyes. She tried to imagine the struggles, squirming and writhing to get out of its womb.

When she crawled into the same bed that she had slept in many times, but at another location, she kept pinching herself to make sure that she was not dreaming. She had finally found her father, and he had been so close all the time.

Missing from the picture was her mother. Coming to terms with her sudden and tragic death had been difficult. Settling the estate was the easy job. The unfinished business between them was the problematic part. So much was left unsaid, and so many issues went unresolved.

Miss Bizzy Belle

Tonya sat in amazement as she watched Walt's reaction and response when he viewed her mom's photograph. In his kindness and graciousness, he said that she was beautiful. In truth, there was nothing attractive about her.

The woman overmedicated herself, did not eat properly, smoked, and consumed copious amounts of Sin Infidel. As the years passed, she took less pride in her appearance. By the time of her death, she was grossly overweight, diabetic, and suffered from heart disease. Tonya realized that like many health care professionals, her mom did not heed the same advice that she dished out.

As she was coming of age, Tonya remembered sensing that she was just another burden for her mother, something else for her to take care of. More than anything, she always felt as though her mom blamed her for all the things that she had to give up. The teasing hit close to home about it not being too late to change her mind about having her.

Tonya lay in bed wondering why she never got any satisfactory answers for why her mother kept her from her father. There was nothing scandalous to hide. Maybe she did not want the man in her life, but what right did she have to deny that to the other parties with such a vested interest?

As Tonya's grief for her mother mounted, she felt a particular sadness for her. As a young woman, she never moved on after the death of her first love. She never got beyond her unexpected pregnancy, nor dealt with the consequences of slamming the door on the possibility for a traditional family. Furthermore, her mother never assumed her own responsibilities for the family rift that never healed.

It troubled Tonya that she never had a chance to tell her mother that she had forgiven her. She also suspected that her mom had never forgiven herself.

The timing of and the amount of the insurance policy cast doubt on whether or not the death was really an accident. In lieu of any overt message left behind, Tonya wondered if clipping her daughter's contact number, in a place where her own mother was certain to find it, had a hidden agenda. Did Michelle think that Tonya might read between the lines, feel guilty for causing the estrangement, and blame herself for her mother's death? There was no way to ever know for sure.

Piecing it all together, Tonya tried to put some things in perspective. Under the pretext of selflessly taking care of others, she wondered if her mom was ever true to her own self. Hiding behind the ubiquitous shield of always being a disappointment to those whose approval she so desperately needed, had her mother missed her own life?

Somewhere back there, Walt started calling himself a "Meanderthal." He was feeling more and more like a relic in the new age of technology and political correctness. As he watched individuals trying to manage their circumstances, he noticed a consistent pattern. Most folks busied themselves, surrounded themselves, and anesthetized themselves precisely in such a manner that they did not have to think about the nature of their beings or deal with the scope of their destinies.

Walt went meandering when he was contemplative. Just after sunup the next morning, he put on his boots and grabbed his hiking stick. The vast undeveloped wooded area above his house connected to a national forest. He had established several miles of private trails starting at the edge of his yard.

It was during treks like this that Walt embraced synchronicity. It did no good to try to structure his thoughts.

On that particular wondrous late spring morning, birds were singing all along the way. The converted naturalist came to realize years ago that many animals crave the attention of humans. They want to be acknowledged and appreciated. That was especially true of birds.

About a mile into the woods, the hiker and the birdies were carrying on some serious banter. In the distance, a woodpecker added to the drama as he noisily announced his location with his drilling. Walt said aloud. "Othell. I think he's proud of his little pecker."

The fifty-year-old-man was still getting used to the idea that he really did have a daughter. His instincts had been right all along. Should he have made more of an effort to find Michelle? He had a direct link to her through his Grandpa King and her Pa Bell. Yet . . . Nothing had compelled him to do so.

He reminded himself that some things cannot be orchestrated, that they cannot be rushed, and that they happen when they are ready to happen.

Alongside Tonya's aura, his mother's face slipped into his consciousness. The last few months had not been easy watching the mother who took so long to claim him start leaving him. Heart disease had so clogged her arteries that everything started gradually shutting down. With advanced arthritis, she lost complete use of her hands. As the blood flow became more and more restricted, the woman's mind retreated into the dark shadows.

As her health deteriorated, she was usually able to acknowledge her son's presence with a peaceful little smile. When she drifted away for the last time, Walt was holding her gnarled hand.

As he walked farther and farther into the forest, Walt went deeper and deeper into his existential being. Amidst the joys of the daughter that he knew only intuitively finally finding him, the immense grief after losing his mother still overshadowed him.

Walt was overwhelmed with an abiding sadness for her. She spent the bulk of her adult years mired in the mess that she had made as a young woman. Under the guise of living the good life, she was haunted relentlessly by the secret that she could not even share with her own husband.

Walt was not sure that the woman ever forgave herself. Neither was he certain that she believed him when he told her that he had long ago forgiven her.

As he started meandering back toward the house, something kept niggling at him. Did the mother, who gave him life before giving him away, then miss her own?

Walt made his flight

Walt left in plenty of time to drop off his car at Eli's. The chaplain did not even have to give him a lift to the airport. He caught a ride with somebody else also going his way. The passenger's itinerary indicated that he was flying coach, and that he had a couple of layovers on his way back to Alaska.

Never-the-less, he had a first class seatmate all the way home.

Looking forward . . .

In Appreciation

The author would like to thank the numerous individuals who rendered sincere and straightforward support. The many of you who kept asking when the sequel to *The War Baby* was coming out provided inspiration that kept me looking forward............

Special appreciation goes to Martha Sanders who volunteered to read and react as each section of the book was reduced to writing. *Miss Bizzy Belle* would not be what it is without both her superb editing skills and her shrewd observations.

About the Author

Larry G. Johnson's nondescript business card identifies him as a self-unemployed wanderer, writer, winemaker, and woodworker. A case could be made that he has established some impressive credentials in each of these areas.

When individuals talk about what they would like to do, many say own an independent bookstore. The author has done that. He owned one of the oldest bookstores in the United Sates.

When people talk about where they would like to go, a number say Alaska. The author has not just been, but he also migrates back and forth on a regular basis.

Other folks wish they could write a book. *The War Baby* was Johnson's first highly entertaining and poignant work of fiction. *Miss Bizzy Belle* is the equally engaging and thought-provoking sequel.

missbizzybelle@mindspring.com

Larry G. Johnson

Made in the USA
San Bernardino, CA
27 February 2017